Ready To Burn

Due South Book 3

Tracey Alvarez

Icon Publishing
New Zealand

Tracey Alvarez/Icon Publishing
Box 45
Ahipara, New Zealand
www.traceyalvarez.com

Book Layout ©2013 BookDesignTemplates.com
Cover Art by Kellie Dennis at Book Cover by Design
www.bookcoverbydesign.co.uk

Ready To Burn/ Tracey Alvarez. -- 1st ed.
ISBN 978-0-473-30079-1

For my dad, who so faithfully cooked for my mum all those many years, and demonstrated to me how love can be shown in the simplest of ways.

Cooking is like love, it should be entered into with abandon or not at all.

– Harriet Van Horne

Chapter 1.

So...his life had come to this.

Del Westlake, sous chef at *Cosset*, one of the up-and-coming, hottest restaurants in LA, applying for a job flipping cartoon-shaped pancakes.

Make that *Cosset's* "ex" sous chef.

His mom always warned that the bigger a person's ego, the bigger the crash when he hit rock bottom. And Del had hit rock bottom. No job, a messed-up reputation, rent overdue on his Venice Beach apartment, and about to grovel for a position as line cook from a man who'd probably grill him to charred ashes.

Del snorted. Seated on the hotel foyer's armchair, he scanned the entrance to the character dining restaurant then checked his watch. His knee bounced uncontrollably. Fifteen minutes until the interview—an interview he'd only gotten because one of Cosset's servers, Larry, was a drinking buddy of the restaurant manager. When a month had gone by and no other reputable LA restaurant would touch Del, Larry called in a favor.

Shrill giggles stabbed Del's ears from across the foyer. Some guy in a giant dog costume hammed it up with kindergarten-aged twin girls. Del winced, but at least it wasn't from the mother of all hangovers.

This morning the pounding head and sweaty palms were only due to the depressing thought of how righteously he'd screwed up.

The phone in his dress pants pocket vibrated. He fished it out and glanced at the screen. *Mom...speak of the devil.*

Could he ignore her? Nah, she'd keep trying until she reached him. Better to deal with her now.

He jabbed the *talk* button. "You're up early, Mom—too much nasty fresh air down there?"

"Hello to you too, son. I assume you're still on your morning break?"

Del's knee jiggled again. He'd be on his morning break if he still had a *job.* Admitting his current unemployment status to Claire Gatlin would be the equivalent of waving an upside down crucifix at the Pope. And his mother had enough stress without knowing her youngest son's career was in the toilet.

"Yeah. We're pretty slammed, so—"

"I won't keep you long, and I'll get straight to the point. It's your father."

Del's stomach plummeted like a freight elevator with its cables freshly cut. Mom had flown halfway around the world to New Zealand to look after her ex-husband after she'd found out his kidneys had packed up.

Was the old bastard dead?

Del surged to his feet and strode to a potted fern, tucking the phone closer to his ear. "What about him?"

"He's getting worse."

"Oh."

What the hell else could he say? That he was glad the SOB who'd forced Del as a kid to go to LA with his mother still stubbornly clung to life?

"Shaye's struggling with the workload now that Bill can barely put in any hours."

Shaye's name sent a ripple through his mind. Three years his junior, she'd been part of the gang of kids he hung out with in his hometown of Oban. But more than just being part of the gang, Shaye and her older siblings had accepted him and his brother, West, as part of the Harland family when theirs had broken down.

He stared at his shoes. Shaye had only been eleven when he'd left. A studious kid with stars in her eyes and a killer bowling arm when they'd played cricket on the island's many beaches. She'd be nearly twenty-five now. Twenty-five was too inexperienced to run Due South's restaurant solo.

Not his problem. He had more pressing matters to worry about. "You've advertised for another chef though?"

A sharp inhale from seven thousand miles away.

"Ahh..." He guessed the problem immediately. "Nobody wants to work at the ass end of New Zealand?"

"Delmar!"

"Sorry. I'm sure lots of people are dying to work in such a wild and beautiful jewel of the Pacific, yadda-yadda-yadda." Del rolled his eyes over at the twins, who clung to the dog so fiercely it was a wonder the poor sucker beneath the fake fur could breathe. "Mom, why are you calling?"

"Always so impatient. Can't you hold a conversation without rushing?"

He had a scummy, beneath-him job to grovel for. "Now's not a good time."

"It never is." She huffed out a sigh. "I want to ask you a favor. You-know-I've-never-asked-anything-of-you-before."

Oh, shit. The Mom-Guilt favor. Nothing good ever came from those words.

"Bill refuses to let a stranger into his kitchen. Your brother posted an ad for a chef, but Bill pulled it. I heard him mutter something like, 'Del should be here; it's his bloody legacy.'"

Her meaning tumbled past his worries of how he'd get his career back on track, and knocked him on his ass. "Are you asking *me* to take over for Bill?"

"Well...yes. Yes, I am. Just until you can train Shaye up to speed or we can find a replacement. Ryan's a wonderful manager; I'm sure you'll both figure out what's best for Due South."

Ryan, who only answered to "West," had taken over the running of Oban's one and only hotel/pub/restaurant four years ago. West coped pretty well working alongside their father without cracking the old bastard over the head with a skillet. Del, however, would rather sauté his own nuts before stepping through Due South's door again. He hadn't been back to Stewart Island since he left thirteen years ago, and as far as he knew, hell hadn't frozen over yet.

"Mom, I—"

"You've always wanted to run your own restaurant."

He tipped his head back and it *thunked* on the wall behind him. "Yeah. But in LA, not down there in the bowels of the earth."

"Head chef is head chef. Your father's right—Due South is your legacy."

"He's lying. Bill would rather gnaw off his own arm than let me touch his precious restaurant."

Del angled his face toward the hotel windows. His reflection, dressed in a white shirt, his dried-mud brown hair perfectly combed and his usually scruffy jaw freshly shaven, glared back. On a good day he'd get a pretty girl's number with minimal effort. Not today. Today, he felt like three-day-old leftovers that some first year culinary student tried to pass off as cuisine.

"That's no longer the case, Del. He needs you." Oceans of emotions surged through his mom's voice, but he didn't care to dip his toe in those waters.

"Does Bill know you're ringing me? Does West?"

"West knows."

He imagined Bill would have something to say on the subject of his youngest son taking over his kitchen, kidney disease or no kidney disease. Not that it mattered. Del wasn't that desperate.

Turning away from the window, he caught sight of the big dog posing for an obligatory photo. While the woman repositioned her camera for another shot, the dog pretended to nibble on one twin's head. Her sister shrieked with mirth. Del shuddered.

"I have a job here—a good job." He hunched a shoulder, waiting for God to smite him for lying to his mother.

"I know. I wouldn't ask if there were any other way. You must have a bit of paid leave due—or couldn't you take a vacation?"

A vacation? Who had time for a vacation when they were trying to get ahead in one of the most competitive, diabolically insane careers? Take a vacation and you may as well take off your fucking apron—permanently.

He flexed his fingers a few times and squeezed his eyes shut. Soft breaths puffed down the phone line, but his mom damn well knew silence worked best. Just as she knew there was very little Del wouldn't do for her.

His eyes blinked open. A short ferret of a man with designer eyewear and dressed in an expensive suit, hurried across the tiled foyer toward him.

"I've got to go."

"Just think about it. Due South needs you. I need you. West needs you." A brief pause, then she added, "And Bill needs you most of all."

Didn't need me thirteen years ago. Del clenched his teeth until his molars ached. "I'll think about it. Bye, Mom."

He disconnected the call and shoved the phone back in his pocket.

Channeling his older brother's infamous charm, Del stuck out his hand, donned a confident smile and prepared to eat a double helping of humble pie.

***

No one would ever guess the contents hidden inside the gold-stamped *Flirt* shopping bag. No one would believe what good-girl Shaye Harland had purchased from Invercargill's exclusive lingerie boutique.

She hurried toward the Stewart Island ferry before it left on its last voyage for the day, grinning like a crazy woman. Picturing the shock on Piper's face when she opened her hen night gift soothed Shaye's twitchy stomach as she boarded. Her big sister would die—just fall out of her size nine combat boots after unwrapping Shaye's carefully chosen selections.

After a quick thumbs up to one of the ferry's pursers, Shaye scanned the backs of her fellow passengers at the boat's rail. Three women and a tall, broad-shouldered man in a black wool pea-coat were on deck, facing the white-capped waves of Foveaux Strait. The often treacherous stretch of ocean separated the tiny town of Bluff on the mainland from Stewart Island. A cloud-covered haze hung in the distance. In a few weeks' time, come the high season later in October, tourists would outnumber the handful of locals who normally used the ferry. Today, a Monday afternoon, the ferry would make the one-hour crossing at only a quarter capacity.

Shaye slipped inside the enclosed passenger lounge and patted the shoulder of Mr. Peterson, who'd opened the door for her.

"Wanted to thank you for the meal you dropped around last week, Miss Shaye," he said. "That veggie casserole sure worked a treat. Better than the time Ben unblocked my kitchen drain."

Not the kind of image a woman wanted in her head while holding a bag of sexy-fun-time lingerie. If Mr. Peterson caught a glimpse of her goodies the scandal would clean him out quicker than her big brother's plumbing heroics. She hugged the bag tighter against her chest.

"I'm glad you enjoyed it. I'd better grab a seat while there's still one free."

"Shouldn't be a rough crossing today. Nothing too bad to scare off the loopies, eh?" He nodded to a young couple seated by the ferry's salt-spray stained windows, a matching set of hikers' backpacks at their feet.

The loopies—or non-locals—glanced up at Mr. Peterson's bugling voice. As usual, the man had forgotten to put in his hearing aid. Shaye patted his arm again and smiled apologetically at the young couple while she found an empty spot in the last row of plastic seats.

The ferry's engine powered up, and the craft pulled away from the wharf. An hour on the boat was do-able. Easily do-able. She'd made the same trip hundreds of times, and unlike Piper, she didn't suffer from seasickness. But after thirty minutes of Mr. Peterson loudly detailing his health issues to the hikers who'd had the misfortune of choosing the seats next to him, Shaye needed fresh air and alone time.

Tucking her shopping bag close to her body—like heck would she leave it on her seat for some sticky beak to peer inside—she pushed open the outside door. A stiff breeze wrapped her cute 1960s kick-pleat skirt around her legs as she closed the door. Spray stung her calves as she turned toward the deserted stern deck—

A rogue splash of sea water hit her directly in the face.

Blerk!

Air and salt droplets sucked down into her windpipe, both lungs contracting into fists for two endless seconds before the first brain-hemorrhaging coughs exploded from her chest. Nothing like a coughing fit to ruin a girl's poise and—dammit, not alone after all. The wool pea-coat guy spun away from the deck railing and strode over.

"Are you okay?"

Her vision blurred as the effort of hacking salt water from her lungs made her eyes tear up. She fumbled with her handbag clasp and extracted a crumpled tissue to press to her eyes. Like trying to stop a river in flood with a bucket and spade. *Hah.*

A hand touched her shoulder. "Can you breathe?"

Her skin heated, and she didn't dare look up as she nodded. What a spectacle she was making, hunched over and spluttering.

An unopened water bottle appeared in front of her. "Here, sip this."

A lull in the sound of the boat's engines took the man's voice from generic male tone to a voice that melted along her frazzled nerves. Boy, a woman could fry eggs on a voice that hot.

Shaye blinked and reached for the water. Paper handles slipped off her fingers and the bag plummeted to the deck. A set of fur-lined handcuffs, hot-pink crotch-less panties, and a pair of nude briefs guaranteed to hold her wobbly bits in place under a bridesmaid dress spilled out of the bag.

Oh, crapola!

"Let me get that—"

Cheeks igniting like a gas hob, Shaye dropped to her knees. Ouch...rough decking on bare skin—and double ouch...her forehead collided with a rock-solid object.

"Fuck!" said the rock-solid object bent over opposite.

Shaye clamped a palm over her throbbing forehead and moaned. Blinking back tears, she focused on two black and white man-sized Converse sneakers. Then lifted her gaze to denim-covered calves leading to muscular denim-covered thighs, and, since the pea-coat had parted, the bulge of a denim-covered—

She covered her eyes, the pretty colored flashes dancing on the backs of her lids almost blotting out the memory of that bulge. Almost. It'd been a looong time since she'd been up close and personal with that part of a man's anatomy. Shaye groaned again. Wasn't this mortifying enough without ogling the poor guy she'd head-butted?

"Are you okay?"

The second time he'd asked and the answer remained the same. She cracked open an eye and peeped between her fingers. Grazed kneecaps? Check. Empty *Flirt* bag? Check. And oh, fudge! Handcuffs? Crotch-less panties? Ugly support knickers? Check, check, check.

So not okay...

But in his concern for her wellbeing, her Good Samaritan might've missed the items from her shopping bag. Maybe she could scoop everything back into said bag before she suffered any further humiliation.

"I'm fine." She peeled the hand from her face and inched her fingertips across the deck.

A gust of wind caught the Flirt bag and scooped it into the air before dumping it into the ocean. The gust also flicked up the scrap of lace and ribbon masquerading as panties, which she'd paid nearly thirty bucks for, and blew them in the same direction. The Good Samaritan pounced like a giant cat, darting past her to snag the panties before they disappeared into the Foveaux Strait.

Meanwhile, the handcuffs hadn't teleported into her purse. And neither had her new panties, which evidently were constructed of industrial-strength fabric capable of holding out against wobbly bits and errant wind gusts. Both items sat in plain sight, just out of reach. No way in hell the man now standing behind her hadn't seen them.

Shaye's chin sagged toward her chest. *Suck it up, Buttercup.* At least once the ferry disembarked she'd never see him again.

A warm grip on her elbow. "Need a hand?"

"Thank you," she muttered, her throat sill raw from coughing. She let him help her to her feet.

Shaye staggered two steps across the deck, snatched up the handcuffs and panties, and stuffed them into her purse. If the man had any sort of decency, he'd return the pink ones in silence and allow her to slink away.

She turned back to him, pasting on a *let's just ignore this embarrassing situation* smile. Pale blue eyes stared straight at her—eyes belonging to a nearly six foot tall, brown-haired, unsettlingly familiar male.

It couldn't be.

Shaye's heart ping-ponged around her chest. Could it be...?

Her Good Samaritan grinned, exposing straight white teeth—except for one slightly turned out front tooth missing a tiny chip. A chip she'd created bowling a cricket ball at him fifteen years ago.

It could be. It totally could.

He chuckled, a low and dirty laugh that made her scalp prickle. "Well, well. If it isn't little Shaye Harland, all grown up."

Shaye glanced down at the scrap of pink lace peeping out of his fist.

Fudge. What a perfect way to be reintroduced to Del Westlake, her future brother-in-law.

She gawked at him. The skinny fourteen-year-old boy she'd known had transformed into a too-good-looking-for-his-own-good man. Good looking, but not drool-worthy—like, say, Due South's bartender, Kip, or a shirtless Joe Manganiello. Not her type at all. So why couldn't she drag her gaze away?

Shaye smoothed down her skirt while she wrangled her tongue into action. "Hello, Del. What brings you back to the bowels of Middle Earth?"

He folded his arms, the panties vanishing under his coat. "Lord of the Rings, right? Still can't keep your nose out of a book?"

"Probably no more than you can keep your hands out of a cookie jar."

*Or out of a woman's panties...*Oh yeah, a certain type of woman would be drawn to Del Westlake like an ant to sugar.

"Been a while since I've raided a cookie jar." A dimple appeared in the crease of his cheek.

A woman susceptible to the Westlake's charm might've gotten a little tingle down in her happy-place. But not Shaye. She'd worked with Ryan "West" Westlake for too many years.

She sniffed and tossed her ponytail over her shoulder. Limping slightly, she crossed to sit on one of the benches beneath the hand rail. She brushed grit off her knees, and Del eased down a few feet away. His assessing gaze roamed over her like laser beams, and her shoulders knotted into little rocky beads. Judging from Stewart Island's green hills in the distance, she had at least another twenty minutes to suffer in his company.

Company she wouldn't have suffered in at all, if the man hadn't captured her panties. *Piper's hen-party panties*, she silently amended. Shaye'd wear underwear like that the day she started baking muffins from a box mix.

Granny knickers and handcuffs and crotch-less panties...oh myyy. Why, why, did it have to be Del? *Play it cool, Shaye. Just play it cool.*

She leaned back and tugged her handbag closer to her side.

"So. Stewart Island's a long way from Hollywood."

Well, duh. So much for playing it cool.

"Thank God for it."

Her hands bunched into fists around the hem of her skirt, stopping it from flapping up in the wind. No loyalty left from his New Zealand childhood, obviously. She brushed away a twinge of irritation. It made no difference to her. She expected West's only brother to attend the wedding—Piper told Shaye that West had already asked Del to be best man. But given that Del worked as some hot-shot chef in LA, what was he doing here a month before the big day?

"You're a little early for the wedding."

"I am." He shoved his hands into his coat pockets, tipping his head to stare at the sky. "Change of plans."

What plans? Oh, of course—Bill.

Her stomach lurched sideways. "Your mum rang to tell you about your dad?"

"Yeah."

Del jerked up from his slouched position and hunkered forward, his hands dangling between his thighs—hands empty of the lacy panties. Damn. They must still be in his pocket. Shaye wriggled on the hard bench, her gaze drawn from his coat to the tanned skin on his wrists and hands. A couple of fine white scars criss-crossed his fingers, and across his knuckles was an ancient burn mark, probably caused by a brush with an oven element—she should know; she had one like it on her pinkie finger. A chef's badge of honor.

"Is he working at all?" he asked after a long pause.

"Three mornings a week on light prep, the rest of the time he's bugging suppliers on the phone and doing paperwork."

Del grunted—not quite a laugh, not quite a sneer. "Bet that doesn't go down well."

"No." And it hurt to see her mentor struggle to keep up the pretense of coping with kitchen duties while still making the weekly trip to Invercargill hospital for dialysis.

If Del had come to see his father after thirteen years of silence...then Bill must be worse than she knew. Maybe Del had arrived early to go through the necessary medical rigmarole to see if kidney donation was a possibility. Her throat felt scratched raw, as if she'd swallowed an unpeeled kiwifruit.

"He'll be glad to see you."

Del twisted his head toward her. His eyes, so pale a blue they were almost steel grey, pinned her still.

"I doubt it." The flat tone of his voice masked any emotion.

Well. That was odd...

Del must feel something about seeing his father again after so many years. But being a guy, he'd think confessing to emotions other than the acceptably masculine happy, bored, or horny meant turning in his man-card.

But did she want to pry further into the mine-laden fields of this man's ego? No, she did not. She had a bit of a reputation as an eternal peace-maker, but not today, ladies and gentleman. She wouldn't get in the middle of the Westlake family reunion if someone threatened her with one of her knives.

Del shifted positions again, arching his neck to glance past her at the rolling hills of Stewart Island. Then he checked his watch—because her company was just that stimulating—and shoved his fists into his pockets again. Which reminded her...

She stuck out a hand. "Can I have them back now? Please."

Del's brow creased over his baby blues. "What?"

The man really did have pretty eyes, but seriously? Making her ask?

"The underwear. For Piper's hen party." *Don't-blush-don't-blush.* She dropped her gaze from his eyes to his mouth...perfect lips circled with a trace of stubble. Just as pretty as his eyes.

Ah, not helping the anti-blushing efforts, Shaye-Shaye.

"Oh? They're not for you?" He tugged the panties out of his pocket and held them up. There wasn't much to hold, and the breeze caught the scrap of lace and wrapped it around his fingers.

"They're a gift."

"Like the handcuffs?"

"Yes. I thought they'd be funny, considering Piper's previous job."

Funny at the time...not so funny now that panties and handcuffs were subjects of discussion.

"That's right, she's an ex-cop. West mentioned it."

Shaye launched into a defense of Piper's credentials as the first female member of the New Zealand Police National Dive Squad.

"And the ugly brown panties?" Del interrupted. "Another gift?"

"None of your damn business." She wriggled her fingers. "Now, hand them over."

He tilted his chin, highlighting a small cleft. For a moment, she thought he'd dangle them out of reach. Instead, he leaned over and dropped them into her palm.

"Too practical for pink lace? You always were the sensible one."

Yep. That was her. The youngest Harland sister—practical, sensible, dutiful, and in the minds of men like Del, b-o-r-i-n-g. Not that it mattered if the man thought she was dullness personified—he sure wouldn't appear on her Mr. Perfect checklist either. Men like him weren't perfect for women like her.

And she needed perfect.

With as much dignity as she could scoop up from the toes of her boots, Shaye shoved the panties into her handbag and stood. "Nice to see you again, Del. Enjoy your visit."

She turned and walked toward the passenger lounge door. Give her Mr. Peterson's bowel problems any day.

"Shaye—" The wind caught the rest of his words and tossed them into the whitecaps.

They'd be docking soon, and she'd be able to avoid the pain in the rear behind her.

At least until her sister's wedding.

Chapter 2.

Atta-boy, Del.

Shaye yanked the passenger lounge door open so hard it missed clipping her nose by a fraction of an inch. Whatever passed for the health department in this God-forsaken country would have a field day with him—"Quick, isolate the guy with a raging case of foot-in-mouth-itus." Wouldn't working in his father's backwater restaurant be fun when his new sous chef—who didn't seem to realize she'd soon be his sous chef—found out why he was here?

Assuming his mother hadn't jumped the gun since their conversation a week ago and filled the head chef position with some moron who didn't know an *allumette* cut vegetable from his asshole. The ultimate irony, considering he'd given up his apartment, put all his stuff into storage, and had been in transit for the last twenty-something-hours.

Del scraped a hand along his prickly jaw, tempted to check his breath, though he'd brushed his teeth in Auckland airport before boarding the flying tin-can to the old-school South Island city of Invercargill. He stretched out his legs again and rested against the ferry's side with a groan. Guess bad breath wasn't the reason Shaye looked at him as if he were a fat roach scurrying out from underneath the refrigerator. It didn't matter.

Lately, he looked at himself in the mirror the same way.

But Shaye...his lips tugged upward. She still had long, nutmeg-colored hair strangled in a prissy ponytail, and big hazel eyes that gave away every damn emotion churning in her brain. There, the similarity to his childhood memories ended.

He rolled his head, and through the spray-splashed windows he glimpsed her three-quarter profile. The bony, bookish little thing had grown into a woman with knock-you-on-your-ass curves, a lush mouth begging a man to nibble on it, and she smelled so damn good you could plate her and serve her at an A-list restaurant.

Add those pink panties to the mix? Holy hell.

He was a guy, after all—and imagining her naked except for those knickers went with the territory. He closed his eyes, the rise and fall of the ocean as they chugged along almost soothing. Del couldn't help wondering what she wore under her chef whites...

"Mate? Wake up, we're here."

He cracked an eye open and sat up, rubbing a hand down his aching neck, while the uniformed purser who'd shaken Del's shoulder strode away to help an old guy onto the wharf.

Jesus, he'd been out cold.

He glanced at the remaining passengers. No brunette hottie in sight. Just as well. If he accepted the position of head chef—and let's face it, he didn't have a choice, because even a theme-park restaurant refused to fucking employ him—he couldn't allow fantasies about the youngest Harland sister to stop him achieving his goals.

Del retrieved the sports bag he'd earlier kicked under the bench seat, collected his suitcase, and strode onto the wharf. The sun blasted through the straggly clouds, beating a fierce tattoo on his head. The heat probably sped up the evaporation process or something, because the stench of brine choked the air. Brine and diesel fumes from the ferry behind him. And damn good coffee.

He paused at the squat building with wide-open doors, drawn by the hiss of an espresso machine. A short line of people queued at the counter, some scanning a menu folder, others pointing at the display cabinet of baked goods.

"The Great Flat White café." He read off the script above the door. At each end of the sign was a logo of a Great White shark, one of Stewart Island's tourist attractions. "Cute."

He continued along the wharf, dragging his suitcase and feeling like the biggest loopie ever. Yeah, he remembered how he and his buddies used to snicker about the tourists and their fancy luggage and fancier clothes. Now he was one of them.

Damn straight.

Del's teeth clicked together as he stepped onto Oban's main street. To the right, the road wound off through a ton of trees and a scattering of houses—West lived somewhere up there. To the left, the tiny settlement of Oban itself, pretty much unchanged since he was a kid. A couple of small, quirky shops, Russell's grocery store, a garage still ran by one of his old buddies' dad, the playing fields and little school, and the historic Due South hotel. He walked toward it, the sun his childhood orbited around growing bigger with each step.

The two story building was a sour cream color with contrasting yellow trim and a blue roof. Part of him expected to find it with paint peeling, weeds sprouting out of the concrete patio where diners could sit outside, a crooked sign, and hell, maybe even vampire bats nesting under the verandah eaves. But his big brother wouldn't allow Due South to deteriorate; he loved the damn place.

Go figure.

A familiar face strode out the front doors and jogged down the steps to the road. Speak of the devil. West ran toward him—so much for his brother's innate coolness, which went with being two years older—and wrapped Del in a bear hug.

"Little bro!" West thumped his back, pulled away, and planted a smacking kiss on both cheeks.

Del barked out a strangled laugh and jerked his head away. "The hell is wrong with you?"

West grinned, apparently not offended, and slugged Del in the biceps, a much more acceptable gesture. Affection in his family was plain weird.

"I've almost got an Italian sister-in-law, kinda rubs off. Shaye told me you were here. Good to see your ugly face on something other than a screen."

Del bet his left nut Shaye hadn't told West about their little run-in on the ferry, though. Remembering her face flushed with embarrassment caused his mouth-spasm to turn into a smile.

"You're the one who insists on using video chat. Like I want to see you spill cookie crumbs all over your laptop when you're meant to be working."

"Hey, normal people aren't psychotically obsessive about work and take regular breaks to like, I dunno, talk to their family from time to time." West crooked an eyebrow. "And besides, jealous, much? Shaye makes frickin' amazing cookies."

"Cookies? You're such a pussy." Del shoved his sports bag into West's chest, knocking him back half a step, and grabbed the handle of his suitcase. "Can we get out of the middle of the road now?"

People still walked on the road here, though it drove the locals nuts. But with limited vehicles in Oban, sidewalks were largely ignored. Across from the hotel, a couple of kids played in a tiny playground, the grass surrounding the swing set and slide sloping down to the beach. An elderly couple strolled along the smooth sand. Shallow waves bubbling past their bare feet toward the dinghies lined up near the jumble of stout boulders separating beach and grass.

Del followed West across the road.

"We'll leave your bags here, and I'll get them dropped up to my place later—you'll bunk with us, of course," West said.

Crash the lovebirds little feathered nest? Thanks, but no. "It'd be easier if I stay at the hotel."

West paused, a frown dancing across his lips before he shrugged. "Up to you. I'll check to see what we've got."

Through the bar's open window came good-natured laughter and the rumble of conversation. Happy hour started soon, and both locals and loopies would gather to circle around battered wooden tables to chase away the day's worries with a cold one.

God, could he use a beer. Or two. Or a dozen.

Jerking his chin away, Del clenched his fist tighter on the suitcase handle and surreptitiously stared at West. While they'd never be mistaken as twins, and his big brother still had an inch or so of height over him, they both had the same non-receding-and-thank-God-for-it mess of brown hair and a similar lean, athletic build. West probably outweighed Del by a few pounds, most of it muscle since the cookies and home-cooked meals didn't appear to have gone straight to his gut.

Being this close to West felt weird. The last time they'd seen each other face to face was five years ago when West had a two-night stopover in LA on the way to a free-diving course in the Caribbean. They'd hung out a bit, gone to a ball game because West wanted to experience the Giants getting their asses handed to them by the Dodgers, but then Del's boss called. Brother bonding time over. Yeah, West was Del's brother, but West had remained relegated to Del's past life, disconnected from the here and now.

"By the way—" Del said as they climbed the hotel steps to the front entrance. "I'm not psychotically obsessive. Just...driven. You used to be too."

Hell if he knew why he needed to defend himself. He was doing West and his father a favor.

Chuckling, West jabbed him in the stomach. "Guilty. But I got my priorities straight."

"You mean you got laid."

"Yeah, that too. Piper's amazing."

Del cut him a sharp glance. The man really was a smitten kitten. "I thought Shaye's cookies were amazing. You comparing your woman to cookies?"

"Oh. She's better than cookies."

A dreamy light slid into his brother's eyes, and Del knew West's brain was conjuring up images of sex. Hot, sweaty, bang-her-up-against-the-wall sex. The kind of sex Del hadn't had in far too long. The kind of sex perfect for taking his mind off a cold beer. He conjured up an image of his own. Shaye's bare legs clamped around him, her pouty lips crushed against his.

Fuck. That image alone was better than cookies.

He blinked rapidly and glanced at West, who continued to talk, though Del had no idea what about. "Say again? Sorry, I was tuning out all your girlish gushing."

West rolled his eyes. "I said, 'I'm lucky Shaye's brilliant in the kitchen and provides leftovers. Piper can't cook worth shit.'"

"Gotcha."

Shaye again. Why had his dick chosen to fantasize about the one woman on Oban he couldn't do, even if she stripped naked, bar those pink panties, and covered her tits in whipped cream? Getting tangled up with his soon-to-be sister-in-law in any shape or form meant trouble. He had enough trouble of his own to cope with.

So settle down dick, no booty call with Ms. Harland for you.

West led Del through the front door and down the hallway to the reception area tucked beside the wide flight of stairs leading to the upstairs rooms. Other than a new coat of paint and a small explosion of potted plants, everything was the same as he remembered. Wood paneling below lemon yellow walls and faded blue carpet on the stairs. Even the receptionist—a late-middle-aged brunette poured into a turquoise Due South-logoed shirt and tapping on her smartphone—hadn't changed since this hotel was his second home.

An instant remedy for any stray sexy thoughts.

"Forty-eight points for axle—take that, Betsy Taylor, you Word-With-Friends ho." With one final triumphant tap of the screen, she set down the phone and peered at him over her glasses.

"Look what the tide washed up."

"Mrs. Komeke. Always a pleasure."

"Full of charm and twice as good looking as your brother, aren't you?" Her sharp brown gaze skipped over him. "About time you came home."

A muscle tic twitched in his jaw. Stewart Island was hell, not home. But Denise Komeke, mother of his two childhood best mates, Ford and Harley, would drill him like an oil rig if she caught a whiff of animosity toward her beloved Oban.

"Yes, I guess it is. It's good to be back." In the sense that having regular rectal examinations to prevent prostate cancer was good.

She huffed, leaned across the desk, grabbed him by the lapels of his coat and planted a kiss on his cheek. What was it today with people kissing him?

"Still fast on your feet?" She rubbed a thumb over the spot she'd kissed—removing her cherry-red lipstick, most likely—and sat down in her office chair again.

"Not as fast as when you chased me and the boys out of your house for putting a baby weta in the coffee jar."

West snickered beside him—but softly enough not to warrant a clip on the ear from Denise, who, if she hadn't changed, still treated Ford and Harley's old mates as her own sons. He and West, Harley and Ford, and Ben—the five of them had been like brothers. They'd grown up with the freedom of six-hundred-and-fifty square miles of wilderness to explore and more than enough locals to play practical jokes on. He'd never had friendships so intense again. Nor had he the time or inclination to bother with the whole bromance bonding crap.

Denise barked out a laugh. "For a white boy, you sure could move."

"I'm sure he gets lots of practice chasing after the lay-dies." West laid a heavy hand on Del's shoulder and squeezed. "One day he might catch one and not know what the hell to do with her."

Del shrugged so his brother's hand slipped off. "Screw you." Though West was right.

West chuckled and reached over the desk to tilt the small computer monitor. "What have we got free in the way of rooms, Denise?"

Denise slapped his hand away. "Nothing. Shaye's in the last double room, and we're booked out with a group doing the Rakiura track for a team-building exercise." She said the last words with a twist of her red lips and an eye roll, which indicated air quotes should be used.

West turned to him. "Could've phoned to tell us you were coming, dickweed."

"Hadn't decided up until a few days ago, shit-for-brains. I had stuff to work out."

"Guess you will be bunking in my downstairs guestroom." West shoulder checked him. "I'll find you some ear-plugs so you can sleep. Piper and I get a little...enthusiastic."

Wow. Sounded like fun.

"TMI, young man." Denise tutted and stood up. "Leave those bags here for now. You'll have things to discuss with your father."

They dropped off the suitcase and sports bag in the storage area behind reception. Del turned, and West laid a hand on his arm.

"Does your return mean you're taking over for Dad?"

Every muscle in Del's body went rigid. "Maybe. Probably. Guess it all depends on...Bill." He couldn't bring himself to say "Dad."

West grunted, a world of worry in the low sound. "He's not doing great. I don't know how much longer he'll even be able to cope with a slow night like tonight without exhausting himself."

"He won't like stepping down."

West sent him a crooked grin and a shrug. "Hell, no. How long can you be away from *Cosset*?"

Considering Wayne Tanner would flash-fry his nuts if he walked onto *Cosset's* premises, a long time. "Until you can get a decent replacement."

"Shaye's solid and a fast learner."

"You haven't told her about the possibility of me working here?"

"Nah. She's not keen about anyone new being in her kitchen, but she knows she can't do it alone for much longer. She'll be glad to have someone with your experience running the show."

Considering their little interaction on the ferry, Del didn't think Shaye would be thrilled to see him again under any circumstances.

West cast Del a level glance. "Claire and I never really believed you'd come, little bro. Not even for the wedding."

Fair enough. Del couldn't believe he'd come either. Except, thanks to good old Larry, whose cousin knew someone who knew someone at CBS about to shoot a reality TV series, Del had a chance to start over. The chance centered solely on him being a head chef in a restaurant needing a makeover from Ethan Ward, celebrity chef and entrepreneur. Due South fitted the bill perfectly.

But if the audition video he intended to shoot and submit within the next two weeks failed to make it through the first round of *Ward On Fire*, Del was gone. Wedding or not.

"Let's go talk to the old man."

Shaye planned to stay in her room, break into her emergency supply of Russian fudge, and finish her book club novel. If she'd still been living with her friend Kezia, she would've cooked up a storm. But since Kez and her brother moved in together, and Ben decided to rent his house out over the upcoming tourist season, Shaye opted to live in Due South until the tiny flat she planned to rent off one of the locals had been refurbished.

But man, she missed having her own kitchen space when she needed to burn off some tension. And the muscles along her shoulders were as hard as a line of jawbreakers.

Tense or otherwise, she'd done her duty as future sister-in-law by flying into Due South to tell West his brother was on the ferry. Neglecting to mention, of course, that she'd rather dig out her eyeballs with a melon baller than ever see Del Westlake again.

But once the burst of brain-clearing sugar finished exploding through her system, she realized she needed to tell the most important person of all.

Bill.

Time for a cunning plan—whip down to the kitchen, talk to Bill, and run back upstairs before the fireworks started. That'd work.

She hustled along the first floor hallway and glanced over the thick wooden banister. Their receptionist's head was bent over her phone as she tapped away on the screen. With her ears straining for West or Del's voice, Shaye crept down the stairs, darting past the front desk while Denise was engrossed with her word-battles. So far, so good.

Humming the guitar riff from the James Bond theme song, she pushed through the swinging doors into the familiar steamy smells of garlic, seared beef, and caramelized onions. The rapid chop of knives on boards and the clatter of pans soothed her tense muscles. Due South's kitchen was home.

First cook, Vince, who'd worked with Bill since God was a boy—or so the grizzled veteran claimed—winked at her from behind the pass.

"Evenin', Chef."

At the multi-burner simmering the afternoon's sauces, Bill turned, a testing spoon halfway to his lips. "What're you doing here?"

"Maybe I couldn't keep away from your wonderful self."

Bill grunted.

"Where's Robbie?" Her gaze zipped around the kitchen for their other line cook and expeditor when the dinner rush slammed them into the weeds.

"Told her to go play bridge with her cronies; no use her working tonight. We're only quarter booked again. The Rakiura crowd are off eating tofu or something, according to Denise." Bill slipped the spoon into his mouth, grimaced, then pointed it in her direction. "Thought you'd gone shopping in the city?"

Annnd, perfect example of the community grapevine in action. No one did anything, went anywhere, or talked to anyone without everyone getting in on the gossip. Luckily, they didn't know what she'd been shopping for. Give it time though—someone on the ferry would've noticed her Flirt bag.

"I did, and now I'm back. There's nothing else to do on a boring Monday night but hang out with you. Not as if I have a social life." She edged farther into the kitchen and snatched up a julienned carrot from a prepared bowl of salad ingredients.

"'Cause you're too damn picky. Vince and I don't need you hovering here. Go and giggle over bloody flower arrangements or something with your sister."

"They're sorted." Shaye cast Bill a glance from beneath her lashes as she nibbled on the carrot.

Judging by Bill's normal testiness, he hadn't a clue who'd accompanied her on the ferry. But the shock of his youngest son arriving unexpectedly early? He needed her at his back, whether he admitted it or not.

Bill returned to his sauce. "Whatever. Just keep out of my way."

She scanned the neat rows of bowls lined up along their workspace, habitually checking all ingredients were *mise en place*. Sometimes, she'd make pretty garnishes to trick a fussy child customer into eating their broccoli or baby carrots. Other times, no amounts of creativity could disguise a plate of vegetables. As the messenger, she'd likely bear the brunt of Bill's shocked temper. Swallowing Del's arrival would be a lot worse than choking down a serving of veggies. But she'd known Bill her whole life and had worked for him in one capacity or another for almost ten years. He'd taken a skinny ugly duckling under his wing and trained her to be a swan.

Staying silent wasn't an option.

She had a fifteen minute head start on Del, since he'd still been crashed out on the ferry bench when she'd disembarked, but any second now, two Westlake men would blast through those doors...

Shaye walked to Bill's side and laid a hand on his forearm. "Chef. There's something I need to tell you."

Bill ran a tight but casual kitchen as Due South's head chef. With an army background of cooking for men who'd eat anything not nailed down, Bill considered himself a *salt of the earth* cook. Which was one reason why his staff addressed him by his first name and saved the affectionately teasing but respectful title of Chef for her. When Shaye called him Chef, Bill knew she meant business.

He stilled, giving her his best crabby-old-man glare. A glare without any animosity backing it up. "Service is starting soon, so this better not be about wearing a damn suit for the wedding."

"It's not the suit." Which he would wear if his ex-wife and Shaye's mother had anything to say on the matter. And they had plenty to say. "It's Del."

"What about him?"

A tone in Bill's voice prickled over her scalp. In all the years she'd worked for him, they'd never discussed West's little brother. None of Bill's funny stories featured Del and he never mentioned his son's accomplishments, as if his youngest boy had chosen some obscure field of neurobiological research instead of a career which mirrored Bill's own. Yet with all those years of radio silence, why the lack of surprise at the sudden mention of Del's name?

"He was on the ferry this afternoon," she said. "He's back on the island."

The rapid chop-chop-chop of Vince's knife stilled. First cook had radar ears, and the weight of his stare prickled her spine. The ropy forearm muscles under her fingertips tightened into knots. Bill shook off her hand and continued to stir the *Bordelaise*.

"You're dreaming, girlie. Del's a sous in some upmarket Hollywood place."

"I just spoke to him, Bill. He's here, he's—"

The swinging doors blew open, and West strode in. Del followed him, tension etched in the clench of his jaw and his braced-for-trouble shoulders.

Dammit. Out of time.

Bill swung around at the soft whoosh of the doors. His weathered face remained bland, as if West had shown up for another nag-fest about him working too hard. Nothing indicated he'd clapped eyes on a son he hadn't seen in over a decade. Nothing out of the ordinary.

Nothing, unless you noticed Bill's knuckles turning white around the wooden spoon and the reddish-brown *Bordelaise* drip-drip-dripping onto the kitchen floor.

"Uh, Dad? Del's here." West hesitated at the pass, sending her a wary but apologetic glance.

Del and Bill faced each other across the gleaming expanse of the stainless steel counters. Del with arms crossed like dueling pistols, Bill with lips thinning to a bloodless line. Both Westlakes showed as much emotion as the quietly humming refrigerator. A silent, *my balls are bigger than your balls* stand-off.

Men—such children.

Bill tossed the dripping spoon into the sink. "My eyes are in working order, son."

Del's lip curled in response. "That's all you got to say?"

"You want me to go kill one of Lou Gibson's pet sheep for a homecoming feast in your honor?"

Del tilted his head, looking down his nose at his father. "Mutton's the best you can offer? Figures."

Guess neither man was ready to mend those burned bridges. Shaye's stomach flip-flopped, and she clamped her lips shut before her peace-keeping tendencies flooded to the surface. She should sneak out, but movement would attract the three Westlakes' attention like a gazelle twerking in front of a lion pride.

"So, you came, after all," said Bill.

Wait—what? Her gaze leaped from Vince to Bill to West, skipped past Del, and returned to Bill.

"You *knew* Del was coming today?"

"Course not. I didn't think he'd show up for the wedding, let alone listen to Claire's crazy idea—" Bill's lips clamped shut and his eyes widened a fraction in an, *oh crap I've said too much* way.

What sort of crazy idea had his ex-wife come up with?

Shaye had missed a pretty damn big piece of the jigsaw puzzle so far as Del's appearance was concerned. She frowned, and West, who'd developed the same expression as her newly discovered niece Jade when caught stealing a still-warm cookie, provided another puzzle piece.

West knew why Del had come home.

Her warm cheeks grew hotter. Yes, Bill called her girlie sometimes, and maybe she had the occasional ditzy moment in her personal life. But as far as work went?

She was focused, solid, unshakeable.

With a keen nose that could pick individual ingredients out of a dish at ten paces, what she smelled now was a rat. A whole bunch of things combining into something her potty-mouthed sister would describe as a *sewer rat sucked up in shit-tornado.*

"Could you please explain this crazy idea?" She directed her terse question to Bill and West, since she had no intention of engaging Del in conversation.

"Well, now." Bill scratched the front of his chef's jacket then smoothed his fingers over the line of snaps. "Claire rang Del in LA a week or so ago—I didn't hear this 'til afterward, mind." Bill twitched his bushy eyebrows at West in an obvious *you tell her the rest* gesture.

West held up his palms. "It's not a crazy idea. Now that Dad can't do as many hours, it's too much pressure on you. I told you that earlier in the year. You know we put an ad out for a chef—"

"And Bill pulled it. Because we don't *need* anyone else."

"In hindsight, I may've been a bit premature pulling the ad," said Bill.

"So, Claire rang Del to ask if he'd consider taking over for Bill—temporarily," West added.

If West had just slugged her in the stomach, it couldn't have hurt less. All the years she'd put in at Due South, before and after her chef training in Invercargill. The hours of menial work and late nights. Even waitressing in what little spare time she had to help out. A few times, Bill mentioned that when he'd had a gutsful and wanted to hop on a cruise ship bound for the islands, Due South would be Shaye's to run. All of that, and they were shoving her aside for a man who wouldn't know loyalty if it jumped up and bit him on the butt?

West blathered on. Phrases including *Del's experience will benefit us all*, *just until after the wedding*, and *Del will train you up* blistered her brain, churned and steamed inside her belly. So Shaye had never dared voice out loud that Bill making her Due South's head chef one day was her life-long dream, but still. She could do it now—she totally could!

She tuned out West's explanations of why he'd sold her out and addressed Bill.

"Why didn't you ask me to take over for you? I don't understand—we've talked about this." Pressing her lips tightly together, she glanced at West's slack-jawed amazement.

"You want to be head chef?" said West in an *oops-oh-shit* tone of voice. "You never told me you wanted..."

Shaye expected fire-bolts to shoot out of her eye sockets and fry her future brother-in-law.

West scratched his jaw helplessly. "And mum and I thought you'd be happy to have someone with his...ah."

Bill held up a placating palm. "One day, you will take full responsibility for Due South. But Shaye, I'm sorry. I just don't think you're ready to go it alone. West's right—maybe it's a good thing Del's here for a bit. He's worked in restaurants a lot bigger than our little place; he can teach you stuff I can't."

Like hell. Like *hell* would she let some know-it-all walk all over her and her plans for Due South. Every muscle in Shaye's neck ratcheted tighter than piano wire as she swiveled to glare at Del. He still stood arms folded, but his gaze—soft and sympathetic—scanned her face.

Well, bugger him too. Mr. Fancy Hollywood chef could take his "pardon me while I screw you sideways" fake sympathy and shove it.

"Why are you even here?" She stalked over to him. "Why would you want to work in a tiny hotel in the middle of nowhere?"

"I have my reasons, and I haven't agreed yet." His guarded reply poured gasoline on her temper.

"Oh. So you've not decided whether you'll lower your standards to work here? *Nice.*"

A muscle in Del's jaw ticked.

Touched a sore spot, had she? Hah! This was her job, her career, her pride on the line. People considered her a pushover because she strove to be nice, strove to keep harmony between those she loved.

But those people were wrong.

Her blood boiled so hot she could've served it as chili sauce. "Couldn't you hack the LA pace anymore?" she asked. "Or maybe they fired your ass?"

Del's eyes narrowed to slits, and he stepped so close she could've stomped on one of his black and white Converse sneakers. "Are you always this unprofessional when your employers make decisions regarding the future of *their* business?"

Her heart slammed into her throat, choking off her air supply. Her fingernails dug sharp crescents into her palms. At nine years old, she'd slapped Ben for deliberately breaking the head off her favorite Barbie, but since then she'd never hit another person in anger. Right this second, though, Del's face resembled a big-ass neon target. His choice of words stung her pride even worse—she bloody well *knew* she was acting unprofessionally—but she just couldn't get control of the hurt rampaging through her system.

"Shaye, c'mon now. Pull your head in." Bill's voice sliced through the red haze, the resignation in his tone draining a fraction of her temper away.

Bill was a proud man—letting anyone take over his kitchen was tantamount to admitting he was beat. A bitter pill for both of them to swallow.

She gave Del her back and appealed to her mentor one last time. "You don't need him; the two of us are doing fine. He doesn't know Due South the way we do."

"So *you'll* teach *him*. Working together, the pair of you are gonna keep this place alive until I'm well enough to kick both your miserable butts into shape." Bill chuckled, but the sound rattled in his throat like gravel crushed in a blender.

Her inner temperature gauge dropped out of the red-zone. "I won't work under him."

Vince's muffled snicker dropped into the sudden silence, and she froze.

Shoot. That came out wrong. Had the men noticed? Of-freaking-course they had.

Men—*such* children.

"I'm sure working under me won't be a problem," Del said. "Unless you make it one."

"Oh, go to hell, Hollywood."

The man had the audacity to flash a grin at her, showing off the cute crooked tooth and all. Jerk.

Lani, one of their servers, pushed through the kitchen doors. "Table three wants his steak cremated and a—" Glancing up from the order pad, she skipped her gaze around the room, her brown eyes widening as they settled on Del.

At nineteen, Lani probably wouldn't remember Del from when she was a kid, but the resemblance between all three of the Westlake men was unmistakable. Del switched on his mega-watt smile and aimed it at the young Maori woman. Incredibly, their often sullen but hard-working server returned the expression.

He'd won another ally. Super.

"Enough chit-chat." Bill flicked his fingers at Lani. "We've got customers waiting. We'll sort this shit, and you"—He paused to glower at Del—"out tomorrow. Staff meeting at eight."

"Shaye, let's go to my place and talk this through," said West.

A group roasting by the two brothers and her big sister, all of them insisting Shaye's objections were unreasonable? *Hah.* Thanks, but no thanks. She tossed her ponytail over her shoulder, hoping it'd flick Del in the eye.

"Let's not. Let's see if your brother can even handle a few days on Stewart Island without going stir crazy."

And with the shreds of her dignity intact—she plain refused to let that man provoke her temper again—Shaye swept out of Due South.

Chapter 3.

Well, that went about as smoothly as his first conversation with the feisty brunette. Which was to say, he'd come off like a complete douche—muscling in on Shaye's territory and stomping all over her dainty feet. Letting her needle him into losing his cool.

Again—*attaboy, Del.*

He yanked his gaze from the back door and met his father's speculative stare, the old man's caterpillar eyebrows almost touching his hairline.

"Eight sharp, not a minute late." Bill clipped an order to the rack. "Now get out and go see your mother, since this whole damn thing was her crazy idea."

Crazy idea being the understatement of the century.

With another quick glance around the kitchen, which would almost fit into one of *Cosset's* restrooms, Del shrugged. He could point out that at twenty-seven he was too old to be ordered about, least of all by a man who was his father in name only. But frankly, he wanted to get the hell out of this kitchen.

West clapped Del on the shoulder, and he jumped.

"Let's go. A quick fuss-over by Claire and we'll head to my place."

"Aren't you going after Shaye?" Del asked.

"It'd do more harm than good at this point." West shook his head. "She needs to work off that head of steam—she'll be on her way to trash-talk about us to one of her friends. I'll speak to her in the morning."

"Great start to our working relationship. What a total fuck up."

"You'll feel better after a beer and a good sleep after your long flight."

Del sighed. His brother had no idea. "I'm whipped, but yeah, I'd better say hi to Mom." He jerked his chin toward the back door. "She in the cottage?"

"Last I saw." West grinned. "Nothing much has changed here, Delly. You'll fit right into the groove again."

"Don't call me Delly, butthead." He managed a returning smile.

Although he'd rather catch the next ferry to the mainland and pretend this whole trip was a hallucinatory episode brought on by determined sobriety, he wouldn't. He was stuck at Due South, in the shitty position of ousting Shaye as head chef. He could fool West, he could fool Bill and his mother—he could even fool Shaye by pretending he had options. But he couldn't fool himself.

Claire was mixing cookie dough when he and West walked into their old house, but Del didn't have the heart to tell her he no longer had a sweet tooth.

West had been right. His mom fussed a little, scolded him for not letting them know his arrival plans, and made up a container of cookies for him. Painless in comparison with his brief interaction with Bill.

He hadn't always gotten on so well with his mom. He'd been a right shit to her for the first year in LA, convinced if he made her miserable enough, she'd return him to his father and brother. Didn't happen.

Claire had moved in with Lionel soon after Del had turned fifteen, and he'd decided to hate his new stepfather and thirteen-year-old stepsister. Fortunately, Lionel, a former Air Force officer, believed in crack-of-dawn, five-mile runs and brutal—but not physical—

disciplinary actions. He also took Del and Carly on camping weekends in nearby state parks and showed up at every high school baseball game and parent-teacher conference. Hard to keep a hate campaign going when pitted against genuine tough love, especially as his stepsister turned out to be his greatest ally.

Then last year, Lionel died after a nightmarish battle with malignant Glioblastoma, a nasty type of brain tumor. The big, *don't take crap from anyone, let alone a punk kid,* fly-boy had been decimated, turning into a transparent ghost of the man Del loved. Yeah, he'd loved him. Took him until his stepfather lay on his deathbed before Del called Lionel "Dad", but Del had meant it when he'd said it.

"Don't be too hard on Bill." His mom passed over the container of cookies. "Just give yourselves some time to adjust to each other."

"Sure. Don't worry."

Like he intended to take a swing, verbal or actual, at the old man. Bill Westlake warranted only a small part of Del's energy, no more than the energy it'd taken to have him shipped off so many years ago.

Del stepped outside and crossed the gravel parking lot separating the hotel buildings from his parents' cottage. West had already left five minutes ago to organize a ride to his place. A white van with Due South sign-writing on the panel parked with its engine running, a dread-locked dude in coveralls hoisting Del's luggage inside.

"Hey, buddy!"

He didn't believe the man would bail with his suitcase—because where could you escape to on Stewart Island, which was eighty percent frickin' wilderness? He just didn't want the little camera and laptop in his sports bag damaged.

The man spun around, aiming dark sunglasses, and a slight scowl in Del's direction.

Del squinted, and as he strode closer his eyes popped wide. "Ford?"

Scowl transforming into a lazy-cat smile, Ford Komeke shoved his shades up into his dreads. "Heard you were here."

"From your mom?"

Ford snorted. "Mom? Listen to you. Yep, my *mum* came over to the shop and said you'd rolled into town."

"Still working for your dad? Thought you'd be outta here like Harley years ago."

"Nah. This is my turf; I'm not going anywhere. And somebody's gotta stay and maintain people's shit with Dad, otherwise it all falls apart."

"Mr. Fix-it man and his pet grease monkey."

Ford shot him a wide, teeth-bared grin. "Wanna walk up to West's lugging your own suitcase?"

From behind him a hand ruffled Del's hair and knocked his head forward. "Stirring up the locals already, brother?"

West sauntered over and opened the van's passenger door. "I'm calling shotgun. Del—you ride in back. Piper's making you up a bed downstairs." He climbed in and glanced over his shoulder. "And she's cooking dinner. We'll stop for a pie at Russell's on the way. Hope you can wolf it down then act like you're starving."

Del hopped onto the first row of seats, and Ford slammed the sliding door. Del jumped, pent up nervous energy sparking up and down his spine. After the day he'd had, he needed to let loose in a kitchen. He needed the concentrated focus of being in the weeds during a busy dinner service. Backlogged orders and utter chaos kept his mind on a singular track with no room for anything else. Working a crazy shift, sex, or a long run were his go-to methods of burning off the fidgets. As sex wasn't on tonight's menu, he'd go for a run later—he sure didn't want to listen to West banging his fiancée upstairs.

They drove the short distance to Russell's grocery store, and West disappeared inside, returning a few moments later with three brown paper bags, small spots of oil already soaking through in places.

Del took the offered bag and bit into the steaming pastry. "Fuck!" he spluttered, fanning his open mouth and burned top pallet.

Laughter erupted from the front seat.

West passed him a water bottle. "Blow on it first, idiot. The Russells keep their pies thermo-nuclear, remember?"

No, he did not fucking remember. The last time he'd eaten the Kiwi tradition of a hot, savory meat pie, he'd been a different person. He'd been a kid whose greatest worry was if he'd ever be good enough to play for Southland's Under 16's rugby team. Or whether the pretty, blonde Bree Findlow smiled at him, or if he and West would end up sleeping at the Harland's yet again, since their parents were fighting.

He wasn't a naive kid anymore. He was a professional chef who shouldn't be soiling his taste buds with ground beef, gravy and golden pastry. Like everything on Stewart Island, it looked good on the surface, but underneath lurked things which burned.

Del unscrewed the bottle cap and gulped water. "How can you put this kind of shit in your body?"

"That shit you're eating cost me four bucks. If you don't want it, Ford'll eat it."

"Hell, yeah." Ford finished blowing on his pie and took an enormous bite.

They ate in silence for a few minutes.

West grinned at Del over the seat. "Maybe you should save room for dinner."

Ford gave a low snicker. "I'd pay to be a bug on the wall after your bro insults Piper's cooking."

"I'm not going to insult her damn cooking." Del ate the last chunk of pie, refusing to lick the buttery crumbs of pastry off his fingers, because that would make it look as if he'd actually enjoyed it.

"You haven't tried it yet," Ford muttered and started the van.

They drove along the waterfront and wound up a steep hill, turning into the driveway of a two story house overlooking Horseshoe Bay.

West crumpled his paper bag and stuffed it into the coffee holder. Del and West hopped out of the car and unloaded the bags.

Sliding the van door shut, West banged on the panel. "Poker tomorrow night."

"Better save my cash for the stripper we're hiring for your stag do," Ford yelled out his window. "Shit. Uh—hi, Piper! Just kidding."

With a quick wave, Ford revved the engine and took off.

Del turned to the woman leaning against the open door frame. Taller than her sister, Piper still had the Harland family brown hair, hazel eyes and athletic build. Shaye's eyes were more green than hazel, and although still a tall woman, she had softer curves.

Dressed in khaki shorts and an *It's not that time of the month, I just hate you* tee, Piper picked her way in bare feet over the driveway.

"You're not going to hug me, are you, Stubby?" Her old nickname popped into his head and slipped off his tongue.

That gave her pause. She slapped a hand on her hip and studied him. "Nope."

Piper moved closer—way closer—grabbed either side of his face with both hands, and planted a solid, smacking kiss on his lips. She pulled back and smiled a Cheshire-cat grin, hazel eyes sparking. "A hello-my-hawt-brother-in-law kiss, instead."

"Don't you know never to tell a woman not to do something?" West dragged Piper close for a kiss a lot friendlier than a hello one.

Before Del could suggest they take it upstairs, Piper stepped out of West's arms and jabbed a finger at his stomach. "Have you been eating a pie?"

West held up his hands. "Blame your new brother-in-law. He insisted on having a Russell's pie on the way home. I tried to tell him—"

"Yeah, right. What am I, stupid?" She slapped West on the ass, and they grinned goofily at each other.

Del shifted his sports bag from hand to hand, cleared his throat and glanced at the house. "Nice place you got here."

"Not fancy, like your bachelor pad in LA, I bet," Piper said. "But we've got a killer view."

His old Venice apartment looked out over an alley dumpster, that often doubled as a sex-club for stray cats.

"Can't argue," he said mildly.

Not gonna mention he'd give up this postcard sunset and endless green in an instant for his old life in LA before everything turned to garbage.

He tagged along into the house, West lugging his suitcase and Piper his sports bag, since they both seemed determined to play happy hosts.

West directed Del through a door inside the ground floor's hallway. A contrast wall painted a deep purple dominated the big bedroom/living area, with contrasting feminine touches of a frilly comforter and some of those little pillows women seemed to love cluttering up the beds. On the opposite side of the room, an open door revealed a white tile floor and the corner of a shower cubicle—thank God he wouldn't have to go upstairs to the main house when he wanted the bathroom.

Piper placed his sports bag on a two-seater couch angled toward sliding glass doors and the view beyond. "Hope it's not too girly. We had it repainted after Ben moved back to his place. He broke his ankle earlier in the year and stayed with West awhile—and oh, I'm babbling." She touched her fingers to her lips.

"It's kind of you to offer me your spare room on such short notice." Look at him, being all affable and polite.

She tilted her head, small wrinkles appearing on her brow. "You're family. Of course you're staying with us—long as you want."

"Or for as long as he can stomach your cooking." West hauled his suitcase over to a large chest of drawers.

"He's such a funny guy." Piper rolled her eyes at Del. "I'm going to go check on dinner—homemade pizza. I was gonna throw on a frozen pizza, but I didn't want you to go all Gordon Ramsey on me."

"Oven on one-eighty, babe?" said West.

Piper strode out the door, saying, "Leave Del to try out the shower. Dinner's in twenty."

Del pretended to continue his examination of the bathroom as Piper's footsteps faded along the hallway. Hoped West would get the hint and follow.

His brother huffed out a sigh. Nope. West never was great at picking up signals.

"You okay? With being back here, Dad, Shaye, and all of it?"

Like Del could admit the truth to anyone. He hadn't been okay in a long time. "I don't require hand-holding and a group hug, if that's what you're asking."

Anything less than sarcasm and West would suspect.

West folded his arms and leaned against the door frame. "Always were a proud little bugger—too damn stubborn to ask for help when you needed it."

"I don't need help."

"Maybe not. But there's stuff you're not telling me about why you took a leave of absence to come work here."

Del leveled a stare at his brother. He'd need to work more on his poker face because West wasn't buying it. Maybe a partial truth would convince him rather than an outright lie.

"I didn't take a leave of absence. Me, the owner, and the head chef had different ideas on where *Cosset* should be heading, so I walked."

"You quit? You told me you fought like a bloody lunatic to get a job there." West's surprise changed to a frown and a speculative eye narrowing. "When I told you I was getting hitched, you mentioned a woman you were seeing—Jacy? Julia? The owner's daughter. Is she the reason?"

"Jessica—and no, she's not the reason." Okay, forget partial truth. This time he needed to employ a bald-faced lie. "Things didn't work out, but we parted friends."

Although maintaining a friendship with his brain-injured ex-girlfriend now residing in an expensive, long-term care facility bordered on impossible.

"You got another job lined up?" West walked to the sliding doors and tugged the drapes closed. "Back in LA?"

"I've got a couple offers to think about." His nose would shoot out five inches any second.

"I'm assuming you're going to stay after the evening's drama?"

"Drama doesn't worry me, and Shaye had good reason to be offended. She'll come around; it's not as if I'll be permanently stepping on her toes."

"She'll come around?" West gave him a grim smile. "Have you forgotten what the Harland women are like?" He shook his head and stared out the window. "Man, I still can't believe you're here."

"I still can't believe you eat frozen pizza." Del kept his tone light. "Now piss off, so I can have a shower."

West laughed. "You'll believe it after you taste Piper's home-made version." He swaggered out of the room, pulling the door shut behind him.

Del stared after his brother a moment longer, his accumulated travel grime making him feel less dirty than the half-truths he'd told. He wasn't being completely honest about his motivations in helping out with the family business, but he'd still work his ass off training up Ms. Harland and getting Due South on track.

For the short term.

***

Holly, Shaye's bestie since forever, flung open the door to her second floor apartment. "What did he do, and how much are we gonna hurt him?"

Shaye, still in her shopping clothes, which looked worse for wear with sweat stains soaked through the fine cotton fabric of her shirt, stood on Holly's doorstep. She'd taken off like a competitive speed walker after leaving Due South, heading non-stop to Holly's place.

"You've heard about him already?"

"Him who? Spill." Holly fisted a hand on her bare waist. Above her tight skinny jeans, the wink of her belly button ring sparkled in the last rays of sunlight. "Because I know it's a guy. You've got that *I'm gonna set fire to someone's balls* look on your face."

"I have?" Shaye blinked.

Oh, right. She'd little ability to mask her emotions, like, say, Piper, who often cleaned up on the poker nights they gate-crashed with the guys.

"Damn. I guess I have. Well, Del Westlake is who I'm talking about. The jerk."

"*Del* Westlake?" Holly parroted but stepped back. "You'd better come in. I'm assuming you want chocolate."

"Yes to the power of hell, yeah." Shaye toed off her shoes and followed her friend inside, wrinkling her nose at the chemicals drifting out of the tiny spare bedroom Holly used to cut hair. "Am I interrupting?"

Holly crossed the floor of her family room/kitchen-dining area and perched on the arm of an over-stuffed orange and yellow floral couch. She patted the hideous sunflower-patterned cushion in a sit-down gesture. "Nah, Mrs. Taylor just left after her rinse and set. It's definitely wine and chocolate o'clock."

"Hold the wine, break open the emergency chocolate." Shaye curled up on the couch, tucking her feet under her and smoothing her skirt.

Holly's gaze zipped to Shaye's bare legs. "What happened to your knees? Is that why you're pissed at Westlake junior? And what on earth is he doing back in Oban a month before West's wedding?"

Shaye held up a palm. "Whoa, Hol. One question at a time."

"Fine." Holly got up and went into her tiny kitchen. She flung open the door of her fridge. "White, milk, or dark—what's your poison?"

"Definitely a night for all three."

"That bad?" Holly dragged out a plastic container with a cross taped to the lid. "But not bad enough for a glass of Hol's remedy for big dumb males?" She fished out a wine bottle and waved it encouragingly. "Take the edge off?"

Shaye arched an eyebrow and said nothing. Holly flashed an unrepentant grin and put the wine back into the fridge, grabbing two Dr. Pepper's, instead. "I've been saving these. This Del Westlake story better be worth it."

"Oh. It's worth it, Hol. The arrogant, insufferable jerk."

"Ouch." Holly pried off the container lid. "While I'm fixing our emergency rations, start at the beginning."

Reaching up to adjust her ponytail, which had somehow gone feral on the march to her friend's, Shaye gave a quick recount of the evening.

Holly carried over a plate loaded with broken chunks of chocolate and the two cans of soda.

"Let me get this straight," Holly said after Shaye lunged for the soda and cracked open the tab. "Del, whom no one in Oban except his bro has seen for thirteen years, has rocked back into town."

"Yep."

"And he's going to be head chef at Due South for the next few weeks."

"Over my dead body." Shaye gulped, and the soda fizzed up her nose making her cough.

Which reminded her of the humiliating ferry debacle.

God. Maybe Hol would mistake the heat glowing in her cheeks as being righteously indignant. Which Shaye totally was.

How could Bill and West think Del could do a better job as head chef? She jammed a chunk of dark chocolate into her mouth and sucked greedily. It'd go straight to her butt, but what the hell. Being thwarted by that man warranted something other than her usual cup of diet hot chocolate.

"Sweets, weren't you complaining the other day how overworked and understaffed you guys are with Bill sick?"

Shaye had a mouthful of chocolate, so she could only glare and stab a finger at Holly's slightly smug expression.

"Yes, I know that's not the point, and he's a horrible, despicable bastard who should be fed to the Great Whites." Holly leaned over from the other end of the couch and selected a chunk of white chocolate.

"You knew Due South needed another chef, and fast."

Shaye swiped the tip of her tongue around her mouth and gusted out a sigh. "Yessss—but I thought *I'd* help choose a chef. That *I'd* be in charge."

"Ah. The in-charge, everything has to be perfect thing."

What was wrong with aiming for perfection—or close to it? "Del thinks because he's worked sous in LA, he knows how to run this kitchen. Dammit, Due South's mine—" She squeezed her fingers around the can. "Well, technically it's Bill and West's, and you know how territorial Bill is, but..."

"But you hoped someday it'd be yours?"

"Yeah. Look, none of us ever expected Del to come back. Bill never talks about him—he's practically disowned the man—and any time he mentioned the future of Due South he talked about *me* taking over, not *Del*."

"Well, maybe Due South still will be yours, sweets. Just not today," her friend said gently. "Like it or not, if Bill's decided Del's going to be head chef for a while, you bitching about it won't change his mind. Bill's a Taurus, stubborn as they come. Besides, if Del's been working in Hollywood, he can't be a totally incompetent ass."

Actually, she imagined Del was very good at his job. Being a bigger person and all, she wished him to drown in success and accolades for his work—just not in her kitchen!

"I can't work with that man."

Holly cocked her head, twisting a hank of dyed hair around her finger—this week's color choice, apple green.

"I don't think I've ever seen you take such an instant dislike to someone. What aren't you telling me?"

Shaye drooped farther into the couch. "I'm so embarrassed."

"Just the kind of story I love."

Without moving from her supine position, Shaye wriggled her fingers in the direction of the chocolate. "More sustenance first. This ranks up there with the whole Derek-gate disaster last year."

Holly passed her a piece of milk chocolate. "Oh dear God, what did you do?"

By the time Shaye told her about the panties and handcuff incident, Holly had fallen off the couch and lay on the rug clutching her stomach and drumming her heels, tears spilling down her face.

From the floorboards came three sharp bangs. "Quiet down, girls, I can't hear myself think."

"Sorry, Mrs. Dixon," Holly bellowed to the rug and the elderly widow who lived in the downstairs apartment.

Mrs. Dixon and the broom-handle-tattoo were a familiar sound when visiting Holly, but Hol wouldn't move, claiming Mrs. Dixon, who owned the house, couldn't live alone if not for Holly upstairs.

Shaye jabbed Holly's leg with her big toe. "One more 'bwahahaha' out of you and I'll kick your ass. It wasn't funny, it was mortifying—and don't you dare tell my sister!"

Holly swiped at her wet cheeks and sat up. "Oh, she won't hear it from me. But don't you think Del might let something slip?"

Shaye groaned. "Guys don't talk about that sort of stuff, do they?"

"Not unless they're close."

"Pretty sure West and Del aren't close. Not like West and Ben."

"Or Ford and Harley."

Shaye cocked her head. Something about the way Holly said Ford's name. A little gasp-ish, as if she'd forgotten to breathe.

"Del's birthday is at the end of March, isn't it? Or maybe April?" asked Holly.

Shaye slid away from her previous train of thought into *oh no, star signs. Here we go again...*

"His birthday? Not sure—beginning of April, I think."

"He's an Aries. That's why there's friction. You being a Cancer almost guarantees you'll clash—professionally and personally."

Aries her butt. "I'm pretty sure it's because he's a gigantic, fat jerk."

"Del's gotten fat?" Holly wrapped her arms around her knees, leaning forward with her gleeful gossip face on.

"No, not literally fat—he's not fat at all. About the same build as his brother. Y'know, athletic—with a few muscles."

"Buff."

"Guess he's quite buff."

"And kinda hot."

"Yeah, he's kinda—wait." Shaye poked Holly with her toe again. "I see what you're doing."

Holly shuffled backward, out of reach of Shaye's toes. "Ooh, the ram and the crab, burning it up in Due South's kitchen. Pity Aries and Cancer are like oil and water."

A pair of ice blue eyes and a slightly crooked yet sexy smile floated to the surface of Shaye's mind. Ignoring the tingle skittering down her spine, she placed her soda can on the coffee table. "I'm thinking of quitting."

Holly rolled her eyes. "You are not. Where would you go? Manning the grill or making cappuccino's at Erin's?"

Damn. Holly knew her too well. "It's a possibility."

"You'd hate it. Plus, you and Erin would kill each other within a week."

"Hey, we're friends."

"You wouldn't be for long if you worked together." Holly sighed and snatched up another chocolate piece. "Last one, I swear." She nibbled and then paused, her expression concerned. "There's nowhere else you could work as a chef but off Island. You wouldn't leave Oban, would you?"

Shaye thought of the responsibilities of being the youngest daughter, a loving crutch to buoy her mother's spirits since her father had drowned nine years ago.

"You're the glue, Shaye," her family often told her. "You're the one who keeps this family together."

Most of the time, she loved being the glue, but some days...alone in her room with *Masterchef*, or on those occasions when she got a selfie from a friend blowing her a kiss with the Eiffel Tower in the background...

Some days, she wanted to cut those sticky strands free.

Then she thought of all her friends, her family, her pet projects and her position at Due South.

Sous today, head tomorrow. She could endure the man's jerk-tastic-ness for a few weeks. She'd pretend she was a contestant on *Survivor—Outwit, Outplay, Outlast.* And she'd win, too. Holly was right. Harlands never quit.

She smiled. "Of course not, Hol."

It was Del Westlake who'd be running back to Hollywood. The other thing Harlands were good at was being a pain in the ass until they got their own way.

Later, alone in her bed at Due South, Shaye blinked rapidly, the words on her e-reader blurring after hours of determined distraction. She just couldn't seem to fall asleep. She flipped back the covers and padded over to the window. Parting the drapes, she leaned a hip on the sill and stared out into the night.

The position of her room at the side of the hotel gave her a partial view of low waves curling around the wharf's pylons and surging ashore on an empty stretch of beach. Midnight fell quietly in Oban, especially on a Monday night when the pub closed early and locals kept to their own homes for entertainment in the wee hours. Sea breezes stirred the trees, the odd cry of a small owl hunting split the heavy silence, and the tides scouring the land hissed endlessly. She was home, even if the peace she wanted was out of reach.

A glowing pool moved on the sidewalk above the beach and a rangy form appeared, running along the deserted road. The man stopped opposite Russell's grocery store, the building dark since Murray and Caroline had shut up shop hours ago.

The cool glow of Oban's few streetlights cast the shadows from the man's face, and her heart rate skittered into a fast trot. It was Del.

Leaning against the wooden handrail that spanned part of the beachfront, he switched off his head torch and tugged up his white tee to swipe his brow. He let the shirt drop and braced his hands on his thighs.

Shaye moved closer to the window, straining to catch a glimpse of his expression. Why on earth was he jogging after midnight?

He paused, going still, like a nocturnal creature that'd suddenly heard footsteps nearby. His spine straightened, and his head turned toward Due South. Shaye sucked in a breath and held it. He couldn't see her—no way he'd know she was watching. Yet, across the distance she sensed a connection, felt a tiny part of the darkness in him.

Del Westlake was alone.

He must've chosen to run solo because West would've insisted on going for a jog too, if he'd known his little brother was heading out.

Del was alone, and he looked so damn lonely.

Shaye scrubbed the heel of her palm between her breasts, rubbing away the dull ache of empathy. She didn't dare return to her bed for fear he'd spot her movement, so she stayed, in breathless tension, until the little head torch came on again and bobbed down the road out of sight.

Chapter 4.

Early the next morning Shaye took her frustrations out on a batch of cinnamon rolls in Due South's kitchen.

"You know." West blasted through the swinging doors, addressing her as if they were already in the middle of a conversation. "It would've frickin' helped if I'd known you wanted to be head chef."

Shaye continued to knead the dough on a floured board without glancing around. "Would it've made any difference?"

"It would've made me feel less of a jackass for not giving you a heads up first." He crossed to stand beside her at the counter and leaned his jean-covered butt against the edge.

One raised brow was all it took to make him move two steps away.

She dug her fingers into the dough again. "Because it's all about you not feeling like a jackass."

He grinned, the patented West charm switching on full power. "You love me even when I am being a jackass."

"No. That's my sister." She stabbed a finger at him. "Next time, a little warning would be nice."

"Well. I really *am* sorry for the way it went down." West gave her his best *poor-bad-doggy* grimace. "But Del is—"

Shaye held up a flour-covered hand. "If one more person tells me how great your brother is and how I can learn so bloody much from him, I will personally ram this dough down their throat until it squishes out their belly button."

West retreated another step and showed her his palms. "Gotcha, my favorite soon-to-be-sister-in-law."

"You don't have to baby me. Bill's made a decision, and I've dealt with it."

Outwit, outplay, outlast, she reminded herself. Until she had the pleasure of snuffing out his torch and sending him off her damn island. She pounded the dough some more.

"So, we're good?" West said after a long pause punctuated by her frequent thumps. "You'll put up with Del being here for a couple of months?"

Shaye's shoulders prickled with cold fire. Did West really think his brother would stick that long?

"Sure, but when it comes time to hire someone else, I'd like a say in it."

West darted in and kissed her cheek, then moved out of her orbit again just as quickly. "Of course."

"No kissing, it's unhygienic and unprofessional." Her mouth curled into a small smile.

Staying mad at West was impossible, especially since their relationship had always been more like sister-brother than traditional employer-employee.

"Dad and I will make it up to you, Shaye-Shaye."

"Whatever." She lifted the dough into a prepared bowl, and covered it with a clean dishtowel. "Putting aside my feelings for the moment, how do you feel about Del being back?"

"I'm rapt that's he's home."

"I don't think he considers Stewart Island home anymore."

West's forehead crinkled. "Noticed that, eh? You picked up on the bad mojo between him and Dad too?"

"Kinda hard to miss." She crossed to the sink with the floured board. "I've always wondered why Bill never made more of an effort to stay in touch with Del—though it's none of my business, I guess."

"Dad did make an effort, at least, for the first year or so. He got up at three a.m. every Sunday to catch Del on Saturday morning, LA time. I'd hear Dad trying to get him to talk on the phone, but you know—" West shrugged. "Teenage boy. Angry and hurt teenage boy. Not much conversation went on from Del's end that wasn't in monosyllables."

Shaye's chest tightened. "Must've been hard on you too, your mum and brother moving so far away."

"It sucked." West's tone was flat, but she didn't need a counseling degree to sense the old pain shimmering beneath the surface. "And it took years before Del and I were easy with each other again."

"You've missed him."

Another shrug, aiming for a casual gesture but failing miserably since the faint lines around his mouth deepened. "Every. Single. Fucking. Day. He's my baby brother."

West shoved a hand through his hair, eyes cutting away as if he were embarrassed at his admission. "I'd better head to the pool, get some laps in before the meeting."

"Okay."

"Spot you later." West headed to the back door, and Donny barked once in greeting from his basket outside.

She ran the tap and scrubbed down the board, trying to deflect the dull ache forming a stranglehold around her heart.

Shaye-Shaye, the big softie who wanted everyone to get along with their families—even Due South's ego-swollen new head chef—though more for West and Bill's benefit.

Shaye-Shaye, who suspected the Westlake men coming to any sort of truce would be an epic battle worthy of the stubborn settlers from which they were descended.

***

Del left for the eight o'clock meeting alone, since West had headed out early to the local pool to swim laps at the crack of dawn. The walk would help clear Del's mind, because with little sleep over the last forty-eight hours, a posse of tiny men tunneled through his frontal lobe with miniature jackhammers.

He waved goodbye to his future sister-in-law, narrowly avoiding having to ingest her version of scrambled eggs.

West hadn't been kidding about Piper's skills in the kitchen. After choking down two pizza slices the night before—doughy center and a singed crust—Del escaped downstairs with the convenient excuse of jetlag and the need for eight hours solid. He'd nursed a single beer over dinner and refused the offer of a second, keeping his gaze averted from the bottles in the pantry. Done and dusted with that poisonous shit. He kept the solo beer at the end of the night as a vice because it proved that one was enough. One beer needn't lead to two, or half a dozen, or a shot of amber amnesia that lurked in those glass bottles.

Del walked down the hill until the narrow road connected with the main thoroughfare. Two fat grey-feathered birds waddled along a fence. One screeched in greeting, ruffling the shorter more colorful plumage around its neck. Kaka, his brain supplied after a moment. The raucous hooligans of the parrot family. Not something you encountered on the I10 into LA.

Goddamn, he'd forgotten how cold it got on this island—even on a spring morning. Del shoved his fists into the pockets of his coat. His boots kicking up tiny chunks of gravel, he dodged a few potholes filled with murky water. It'd started to spit by the time he'd returned from his run last night. The rain splattering the windows of his downstairs room kept him awake for another hour. While the exercise had done the job of exhausting him physically, mentally he'd been wired.

He forced a pleasant *it's great to be back* expression on his face as he raised a hand to the few locals who called him by name—but kept his chin down and power-walked until he stomped up Due South's front steps.

Bill waited for him in the restaurant, seated stiffly at a table for four, looking like a man out of place in his own environment. Why bother with fancy tablecloths and flax flowers in vases when they served swill night after night? And yeah, he'd commandeered a copy of the menu to study.

"You're ten minutes early," the old man grumbled to Del as he crossed the dining room.

Swallowing snark, Del merely grunted. He removed his coat and draped it over a chair. Someone had lit the open fire on the other side of the restaurant, and the wood popped and hissed. He sat opposite his father, pretending to examine the turquoise-themed water colors on the wall. Hoping West would hurry the hell up and arrive.

"Had breakfast?"

"No." Silence ticked. Del's knee bounced a few times until he laid a steadying fist on his thigh. He could do the painful small talk thing until West arrived. Surely.

He cleared his throat. "Piper wanted to make me eggs this morning."

"No wonder you're early." Bill snorted out a laugh, which transformed into an embarrassed cough, just as West pulled out the chair beside Del.

"You two criticizing my woman's eggs?" West slouched down with a grin, his hair still wet from the pool. "Watch it or I'll tell her you were hinting for a Sunday brunch invitation."

"You'll laugh out the other side of your face once you've had to put up with her cooking for a few years, my boy."

A wolfish grin from West, who tipped back his chair on two legs. "I do half the cooking, and besides, I don't keep Pipe around for her kitchen skills."

Shaye walked out of the short hallway connecting the dining room to the kitchen, carrying a platter. Today, she dressed for work—black pants, black kitchen Crocs, and a white chef's jacket. Prim and proper, she wore her long brown hair tightly braided. If her plait was pulled any tighter across her scalp, her pretty hazel eyes would start to drag up at the corners. No doubt the whole super-chef outfit was a subtle reminder of her professionalism and a less-than-subtle reminder of his lack of it. He'd rolled out of bed, dragging on the first tee shirt and jeans he found in his suitcase. Clothes he wouldn't have worn to work in LA if he'd wanted to keep his job.

"That's my sister you're talking about." Shaye placed the platter on their table.

Immediately, the delicious aroma of spices and sugar rising from the still-warm cinnamon rolls made his taste buds sit up and beg.

"Yes, and I love her. But, Shaye, you"—West snatched up a scroll and waved it under his nose—"you, I adore."

Shaye cocked her hip, the hand on her waist emphasizing her curvy shape under the boxy jacket. "Yet you never bring me flowers."

"Because your big sister's the possessive sort, and I fear her wrath." West bit into the scroll, and a blissful expression flittered across his face.

Shaye turned to Bill. "You can have *one*."

His father's face crinkled. "I'd rather have bacon and eggs."

"No bacon," she said. "Too much sodium, remember?"

"Claire's still making me eat this God-awful cereal with antibiotic yoghurt stuff." He said the words as if he'd just delivered a dressed-up description of dog turd.

Shaye placed a scroll on a plate and passed it to Bill. "It's probiotic yogurt, you poor lamb."

The whip of her hazel gaze flicked over to Del. "Help yourself."

His mouth continued to water, but Del didn't move. Food other than fuel hadn't tempted him for a while—but hell if he'd give her the satisfaction by eating something she'd made.

"You're the baker?"

"I woke up early." She shrugged. "And West and Bill love my rolls."

"Oh, yeah," West said around a mouthful.

"Don't eat them all—I'm going to save one for tomorrow." Bill broke off a chunk of scroll and popped it into his mouth.

"I don't have a sweet tooth, so I'll pass," Del said. "I'll grab a protein shake later."

"A protein shake?" Offense grated through Shaye's words.

West nudged him with his elbow. "You need more than a shake."

"I'm good." Del shot a glance at Shaye.

Her outraged expression faded, replaced by narrowed eyes aimed at him.

"You've lost a bit of weight." All teasing stripped from his tone, West scanned Del with frank appraisal. "I didn't notice with that bulky sweatshirt you wore yesterday, but I can see it now."

Okay, he'd been forced to move up a notch on his belt, but he ate. When he needed to.

"It's only a few pounds. I've been working hard and for long hours. I could still take you."

"Our nineteen-year-old bean-pole of a dish-hand could knock you on your ass," growled his brother. "Hell, even Shaye could."

"Happy to prove him right." Shaye looked at Del with what he labeled as reluctant pity.

Her softening gaze made his skin crawl.

"Drop it, West." Del kept his hands loose on the table, even though tension crawled over his shoulders and he nearly jerked his arms defensively across his chest.

"Eat something and he will," Bill said.

Refuse to eat now and he'd appear as a candidate for an eating disorder.

Screw it.

Del picked up a scroll and bit down. Buttery, cinnamon, orgasmic warmth exploded onto his taste buds. *Sweet merciful fuck.* Did his eyes just roll up into his head? Pride—the only thing keeping him from stuffing the rest in his mouth.

He took another nonchalant bite while Shaye sat at the table.

"So, you're here to work." Bill licked his thumb and glared at Del from under bushy eyebrows.

"If the terms are right."

Sugar and cinnamon coated his fingertips, too. Hell would freeze over before he licked them.

"Terms, huh? What sort of terms?"

"—*Dad*. Just hear him out, willya?"

West. Doing the big brother thing of running interference, because everyone knew he was Bill's favorite son. First born, first priority.

"So, these terms..." Bill said.

On the flights here, Del had thought a lot about how he could work at Due South and not lose his mind. B and C-grade restaurants weren't beneath him—he'd worked in them before, and due to screwing up his life, he'd be doing it again for the foreseeable future. But running a kitchen with Bill criticizing his every move? Not. Gonna. Happen.

"Two terms, non-negotiable."

Bill folded his arms across a chest much skinnier than the one in Del's memory. He'd bet a hundred bucks the old man had bitten his tongue in order to prevent himself from telling Del to piss off.

"One..." He met Bill's cool stare without blinking. "When I'm on shift, you stay out of the kitchen. I won't work with you breathing down my neck."

Bill harrumphed but didn't comment.

"Two. If there's any disagreement amongst the staff with how I run my shifts, I'll discuss those issues with West and the staff in question."

His glance slid once again to Shaye. She stared at him, lip curling slightly as if she'd sniffed Bill's probiotic yogurt and found it had gone sour.

"I'm not working for you as your son. In fact, consider me a contractor, not an employee."

"A contractor?" Bill said. "Well, bugger me. I still don't know why you're here."

Even though Del was a total screw up in other areas, he wouldn't be dissed on his cooking. "Because I'm damn good at what I do."

"And because we need him," West said quickly. "I don't give a shit about why he's here if it means you'll stop working yourself half to death."

Silence dripped around the table as they all stared at each other. Trying to ignore the fact that Bill Westlake already looked half worked to death.

Del shifted on his chair so he faced Shaye. "I know you're pissed about me being here, but it doesn't have to be a competition. Instead of working *under* me, how about you work *with* me?"

Shaye scratched the bridge of her nose with her middle finger, rolling her pretty eyes.

Del squished a grin. Yep, under that sugary-sweet exterior, a little wolverine bared her cutely sharp teeth. He kinda had to admit he'd enjoy baiting it out of her.

Bill caught sight of Shaye's gesture and gave a gravelly chuckle. "I'll stay out of the kitchen while you two battle it out. I haven't the energy to avoid the fireworks." His lips tugged down. "I've worked my bum off in that kitchen making Due South what it is. I'll agree to your damn terms, but just don't screw it up, ya hear?"

"I'll try not to let you down." Would Bill even understand the irony coating his voice? Doubtful.

West said, "I'll go grab the paperwork."

Shaye stood, her face a study in composure. "Are we done? I've got prep to do."

West and Bill's gaze sliced to him, sizing him up. Head chefs in big restaurants didn't bother with the menial tasks like food prep or making the daily stocks and sauces for service. But this wasn't a big restaurant. This was Due South, where even as a boy, when he'd first been old enough to take an interest in cooking, he'd been expected to chip in and help.

"I'll come back with you in a minute. We'll go through the details, and I'll give you a hand."

"Super," she said.

Against his will, Del's gaze zeroed in on the twitch of her perky ass as she stalked away from the table and disappeared into the kitchen. *Ring that bell, Pavlov.*

Working with the little wolverine would be a whole barrel of laughs.

***

Calm before the storm.

The words spun through Del's head as he and Shaye worked the last tickets of the dinner service.

Both shifts had gone too smoothly, with Shaye being the epitome of a polite and accommodating employee. Putting up with his presence, basically.

After a quick tour of the kitchen that morning—he could see little had changed—and a discussion of the weekly specials and staff scheduling, they'd worked like a well-oiled machine. And once everyone had left for their afternoon break, Del had no problems positioning a tiny camera unit on a little-used kitchen shelf. He kept the remote in his pocket, ready to hit record when dinner service started. With twenty hours recording time on the camera card, he'd use the footage taken over the next few days to compile an audition tape.

But the evening's dinner service had been a breeze. With the front of the house a quarter full the servers were on cruise mode, and nobody complained about the boring crap they served. Nothing even potentially interesting happened that could be used in his audition. Not even a dropped plate.

After plating the last meal and closing the kitchen for the night, Del sat at one end of a stainless steel counter, hunched over Bill's ancient laptop, viewing an out-dated spread sheet program.

A glass jar half filled with gold coins rattled beside his face, and he glanced up.

"First service is a freebie," Shaye said. "Tomorrow, shit, fuck, and any of the other dozen or so foul words I heard you use will cost a buck each. Proceeds go to charity."

Del put down his pen. "You're shitting me."

"'Fraid she's not." Fraser, their dish-hand, hoisted his crate of dirty plates onto the counter beside the dishwasher.

"Shaye never kids about the swear jar." Vince had already stripped off his cap and apron and now slipped on his battered sheepskin jacket. "And I'm off. See you in the morning."

After saying goodbye to Vince, Shaye raised an eyebrow and rattled the jar. "I'm asking you to adhere to my little rule."

"In God's name, why?" This was Stewart Island, not the Queen's frickin' throne room.

She paused, tucking a wispy strand of hair behind her ear, which had slipped out from under her cap.

The sudden glimpse of vulnerability dampened his initial indignation. "This is important to you?"

Angling her chin, she said, "A pleasant workplace is good for morale. Nobody likes being shouted and sworn at. It's disrespectful."

Flickers in the back of his mind. A memory of hanging out at the Harlands' as a kid. Of Michael, Ben's father, dressing down Ben after an accidental "fucking bastard" slip in front of his mother and younger sisters. A firm reminder that part of respecting women meant watching your damn mouth.

Del suspected there was an element of Bill allowing Shaye a sense of control in a male-dominated workspace. Wisdom suggested he keep his opinions to himself.

"I'll try."

Shaye nodded and replaced the jar on the shelf directly below his camera. He'd have to watch his language if he didn't want her pulling the jar down every five minutes.

"You don't mind me cussing around you out of the kitchen?" he asked.

She yanked off her checked chef's cap. "I doubt we'll spend any time together outside of work hours."

For some reason, his male ego smarted. Yeah, she'd made it clear he'd been lumped into the asshole category, but a sneaky part of him wanted to observe her beyond Due South. To peel back her prickly layers and see if the little zap of awareness between them was hostility or attraction. *Mutual* attraction.

Though maybe she was right. With working his ass off here for at least the next two weeks, he wouldn't have time for socializing—with her or anyone else. Better that way. Better to avoid interactions with his old crowd and just do his job.

Fraser disappeared through the swinging doors with his plastic crate ready for the final batch of dishes.

Shaye swiped a dishcloth over the already spotless countertop where he worked. "But there's the wedding, I guess."

"I'll show up on the day, don't worry."

"You can't just do that!" She gaped at him, her hand stilling on the countertop. "You're meant to organize suit fittings and the toasts—I assume you've gotten your speech prepared?"

"Ben can do a speech—he's West's best buddy."

"But West is *your* brother."

"Ben's known him longer. Besides—" Del shrugged, opening a second spread sheet on the screen. He wasn't prepared to discuss his complicated feelings for his older brother with her. "I've got plenty of time to write it."

"Typical guy. Leave everything to the last moment then improvise."

Shaye pursed her lips in a scowl and threw the dishcloth at the plastic-lined hamper by the far end of the counter—goddamn, she nailed it, too!

"Yeah, yeah." He tried to concentrate, but the numbers kept dancing across the page. The woman had thrown him off his game.

Huffing out a sigh, he slapped the laptop screen shut. If she wanted to talk about the wedding, they'd talk about the damn wedding.

"So Ms. Harland. Got a date for the big day?"

"Yes." She rolled down the sleeves of her chef's jacket and avoided his gaze.

Liar. Either that or her choice of date embarrassed her.

"Anyone I know?"

And no, he wasn't checking out the competition—just mildly curious. How many single men could this town have? Granted, any straight, single male would have to be a moron not to try to score an evening with Shaye in a pretty party dress with bountiful free booze on offer.

"No." She flicked him a glance from under her lashes. "Have *you* got a date?"

The prospect of finding a date for West's wedding made his gut curdle. "Nope. I'll be going solo."

She snorted softly—a buckshot-loaded sound. Which meant what? Where to find a female translation manual when you needed it?

Fraser returned, his crate loaded with dishes, and set to rinsing and stacking. The silence following Shaye's little snort grated along his nerves.

"You know, we used to hang out. As kids," he said.

"No. You hung out with my brother and sister. I was a boring bookworm who sometimes tagged along."

Ah. So she remembered the flippant comment he'd made back when he'd thought snapping a girl's training bra was the ultimate form of flirtation. Before he could figure out whether he should apologize for being a little snot, West strode into the kitchen.

"Poker game starts in an hour," he said by way of greeting. "Shaye's boyfriend is closing up tonight."

Del's fingers clamped around the pen and it flexed dangerously. Holy shit—she *hadn't* lied? "Her boyfriend?"

"Our bartender," replied West. "The reason why so many local women come for Happy Hour. Drooling over Kip makes them very happy. Right, Shaye?"

Shaye whipped off her apron and hung it on the row of hooks. "Absolutely. The man is a stone-cold fox."

"You're dating the bartender?"

Her lips tightened into a wafer-thin line.

"She won a dinner with him at the charity bachelor auction earlier in the year," said West. "It didn't work out—no chemistry."

Shaye sent West a look that should've set his eyebrows on fire.

"What? Are you like my dating adviser now? We had a nice time." She addressed the statement to them both, baring her cute little teeth.

West snickered.

Big brother—completely oblivious to the undercurrents circling the room.

"You said it was like having dinner with Ben. Or me," West said. "Though I'm a lot more interesting than Kip or your verbally stunted brother."

"Chemistry isn't everything, and Kip's very sweet." Shaye stuck her nose in the air.

Definitely directed at him. Sweet was something he'd never be. Not unless it was part of tempting a woman into his bed, and he seemed to do well enough without resorting to *sweet*.

Del dropped the pen and leaned forward on the counter. "The guy's doomed to the friend zone forever."

"Poor bastard. So, you in tonight, Shaye-Shaye?" said West. "My bro here is easy pickings."

Del didn't miss the quick glance she shot at him before her gaze skipped to his brother. "Not tonight, sorry."

"Hot date with your Kindle?" Once again, oblivious to Shaye's murderous glare, West rambled on. "Aw, come on. You can't let Piper be the only woman there; it just encourages her to be mean. Real mean."

"Oh boo-hoo, Westy," she said.

"You know she'll come and drag you to the game—unless you're on your deathbed."

Shaye grimaced.

For some reason, Del wanted her at the game tonight. To see if there was an alternate Shaye—one who wasn't so uptight outside of work hours. But he wouldn't admit that outright.

He cleared his throat. "I think she wants to avoid spending any more time in my company."

West frowned at Shaye. "You're not holding a grudge about the whole head chef thing, are you? We talked that out this morning."

Another eyebrow-scorching glance from Shaye. The woman was a knockout when her temper kicked in.

"Of course not." She tossed her ponytail. "I'm not holding anything against him."

Del grinned. Couldn't damn help it. He'd started to hope she would hold something against him—preferably herself.

"So you'll come?" he said. "I'll play nice."

She sniffed and swept around the counter, giving him a wide berth. "Maybe for a little while. I hope you picked up some New Zealand currency, because I don't take US dollars. Or credit cards."

Shaye blew through the swinging doors and disappeared.

"Quite an accomplishment."

Del glanced over at West, who studied Del with a thoughtful expression.

"Accomplishment?"

"Having her make you public enemy number one." West's nose crinkled. "She has a soft spot for strays, but she sure has taken a dislike to you."

"I'm no stray."

"Own it, bro."

"Screw you." Del stood and gathered up the laptop. "And it doesn't matter one way or the other if she hates my guts, so long as we get the job done."

"Just don't get into a scuffle with her for the bouquet toss at my wedding."

Del shook his head and grinned. "How about we aim for coolly ignoring each other?"

"Won't work. She ignores you, you'll take it as a challenge. Trust me—it's a battle you'll lose."

"That's how you ended up pussy-whipped."

West laughed. "There're worse things than being pussy-whipped." He sobered. "You're not sniffing around her, are you?"

"Jesus, West. I've been here less than forty-eight hours, and you're already imagining me and your sister-in-law in the sack? First man-rule—don't shit where you sleep."

He'd screwed that rule up once or twice with cringe-worthy results, and had taken it to the level of epic disaster with Jessica. Not going there again.

"Yeah, okay. My bad." West wandered over and slapped Del's back. "Sorry. Just wondered if this animosity between you was a front for something else—Pipe and I fought like demons to start with."

"No front. I'm here to work, period."

"Well, good. See you at the house." West walked to the kitchen doors, paused and turned with a crooked grin. "Strays make the most loyal pets, you know. If they're given a bit of love and a chance."

"I'm not a dog, West. So fuck off with your lame analogies." Del softened the comment with a smile of his own.

Fortunately, his older brother didn't know what a royal screw-up he was.

Fortunately, West didn't have a clue that Del was not only a stray but a stray who'd bite the hands that fed him.

Chapter 5.

"How bad was it? On a scale of one to five?" Piper lowered her voice as she ripped open a bag of potato chips and dumped them into a bowl. "One being 'I can house train him in less than a week,' and five being, 'I need an extra set of hands to dig a shallow grave.'"

Shaye refused to look over her shoulder at Del, who was making small talk with Noah Daniels, Oban's police force of one. Both men sized up the other across West and Piper's circular card table, in the middle of the family room.

"Two-point-five," Shaye said.

Piper had enough pre-wedding stress without Shaye bitching about West's brother.

"Really, it was fine. He's not my favorite person, but we worked well together." By worked well, she meant they hadn't burned anything or each other.

Piper pulled a six-pack from the fridge. "West was worried. He didn't mean to step on your toes by hiring Del."

"I know. It's only short term." Shaye pasted on a smile. "And Del's talented. I'll learn a lot from him." Good grief, she sounded like a game show host reading off a tele-prompter.

Piper placed the beer on the kitchen counter and squeezed her arm. "I'm so glad you're being cool about it all."

"Who's cool? Other than me?" Ben tweaked her ponytail.

"Here—" Piper picked up the cans and shoved them into Ben's arms. "Make yourself useful and take these out."

Ben tucked the six-pack against his broad chest and made a gimme gesture at the bowl of chips. "Load me up, ladies."

Shaye grinned up at her brother and balanced the bowl on top of the cans. "Don't eat them all between here and the table."

"Now, how would I do that with no free hands?" He raised the chips closer to his face. "'Course, I could chow down this way."

"Doofus," she said.

Ford appeared and stole a chip over Ben's shoulder. "Five bucks says he couldn't eat every chip in the bowl without using his hands."

"Five bucks says if we recorded him trying, Kez would make him sleep on the couch tonight." Shaye held up a palm for Ford's high-five.

Ford gave her some skin. "Burned him, baby."

"Will you lot stop gas-bagging in the kitchen and hurry up," West yelled from the family room.

Shaye snickered and followed her brother to the table.

When she first arrived at West's, splattery shower sounds drifted out from under Del's door. She'd hurried past and kept busy with Piper in the kitchen, grateful not to be caught in the hallway exchanging awkward "Hi again" greetings with Del. By the time he wandered into the family room, Noah and Ford had arrived.

Now, sitting opposite him, squeezed between West and Ford, Shaye couldn't ignore him any longer. Dressed in a plain grey-marl sweater, Del fiddled with his stack of poker chips. With sleeves shoved casually up to his elbows, each movement of his hands emphasized the corded muscles of his forearms. The man had sexy forearms.

Shaye stacked her chips in four equal piles and breathed deeply, inhaling cedar wood with a hint of basil, and the same smell that wrapped around a woman when a man draped his leather jacket across her shoulders. She'd caught faint whiffs of it all day, every time Del walked past. If he'd been a department store sample strip, she would've rubbed him over her body to transfer the delicious smell onto her skin.

A thought she didn't need showing on her face.

She edged her chair closer to Ford. He smelled like pine soap with a touch of grease. A comfortable smell.

"Noah?" she said. "Finished gossiping with Hollywood? Decorate the table, willya?"

Noah cocked a finger at her. "Feeling lucky tonight, Shaye?"

"I bought a new skirt from last month's pot, so yeah, I'm feeling lucky."

"Let's go to Texas." Noah tossed two poker chips on the table.

Del followed with four of his, and West dealt.

Shaye picked up her cards and gave a mental fist pump. A marriage—king of clubs and queen of hearts. Game on.

Ten hands later, Shaye rethought her lucky feeling. It wasn't her night. She'd taken the pot twice, with a three of a kind and a full house. Piper and Ford had also won a game each. Noah—with his perfected blank cop face—had scored twice, but Del had won three hands. Not in a row but still, he'd cleaned up three times.

Del was no baby-beginner fish. In fact, she'd bet he was a shark pretending to be fish.

Down to the final hand of the night, only four players remained. The others threw in their cards—leaving her and Del, and Ford and West. Piper, the last round's dealer, burned a card and placed the final one of the game face up.

"And the black bitch joins the river, boys and girls."

Ohmygawd. The corner of Shaye's mouth twitched so she clamped her lips and tried to look as if she didn't have pocket queens to play with. Her lashes flicked up to find Del studying her—the heat in his gaze either meant he had killer cards or something else, entirely.

"Ford? You in?" asked Piper.

Ford ran a hand over his shoulder-length dreads and slapped his cards face down on the table. "Nah. I'm folding like a cheap car jack."

"Shaye?"

Shaye considered her remaining poker chips. Del would bet last, positioned as he was two places away from the dealer. He'd play big, guaranteed. Earlier, he'd nailed her as a conservative player, and she hadn't denied it. Being "tight" most of the time gave her a cover for the odd reckless move.

A move she considered now.

Though Del had won three games, he'd lost big in the other seven—because Del didn't like to fold. He gambled to win, but to win, he'd have to play big and risk everything.

Shaye slid her remaining chips forward. "All in."

Beside her, West whistled long and low, nudging her arm. "You go, girl. But too rich for me." He dropped his cards face down and grinned at Piper, who made clucking noises.

"Del?" Shaye raised a brow.

Del leaned back and crossed his arms, his two hold cards pressed against one nicely rounded biceps. "We could make this last bet interesting. Something more personal than just cash."

Noah and Ben, who'd both gotten up to raid the chip bowl, paused in their munching.

Ben returned to the table. "Better not be suggesting anything inappropriate to my sister."

"What's the guy rule about workplace relationships?" Del asked.

Ben gave Del a grim smile and made an "I'm watching you gesture" with two fingers.

Del turned to her, moved his pile of chips forward. "I win, you dump the swear jar for the time I'm here."

Shaye tossed back her ponytail. "Honestly? You can't go a month without saying fuck?"

Her sister sucked in a soft gasp, and Ford straightened from a slouch to full alert.

Shaye gave Piper an *oh puh-lease* eye roll. She kept her language clean—so what? It wasn't as if she couldn't cuss with the best of them. The odd time her temper reached volcanic levels, she could creatively out-swear both her siblings. But she was her father's little princess, and princesses who tragically lost their daddies always tried to keep their tiaras shining brightly.

In case Daddy was looking down from heaven.

Del stroked the edge of a playing card with one long finger. "I like that verb."

How on earth did he make that sound so...dirty?

Shaye shifted on her chair. "All right, agreed. But if I win..." She paused, knuckle pressed to her lip, racking her brain for something that would take Mr. *I Like that Verb* down a peg or two. "If I win, you help cater the kids' Halloween party."

Ben snorted out a laugh. His two girls—Jade, his daughter, and Zoe, his almost stepdaughter—were already planning their costumes for the big night.

The smirkish curve of Del's mouth straightened. "A Halloween party?"

"You know, kettle corn, cupcakes decorated to look like jack o' lanterns, lots of excited kids hyped up on sugar." She smiled winningly. "But if you're not a risk taker..."

He showed her a lot of teeth in return. "Oh, I'm a risk taker. Only both payoffs seem to be in your favor."

"What do you suggest?"

"If I lose, I'll run the damn Halloween party, but"—another flash of teeth and Shaye's heart rate kicked up a notch—"if I win, you give up the swear jar and be my plus one for West's wedding."

Laughter and catcalls erupted around the table. Ben's humor evaporated, and he glared at Del.

Before she could ask why, Del said, "Simmer down, boys. We're both going anyway."

Ah, got it. Good ol' equivalent-to-comfort-food Shaye was convenient and easy—so she'd do as his wedding date.

"I have plans, remember?" She fired vicious glances at Ben and Piper, hoping West would keep his damn mouth shut and not contradict her.

Del tapped his cards against his arm. "If I win, maybe you'll change your mind about those plans."

Dammit, the smug bastard knew she was bluffing.

Shaye straightened her spine. "Maybe I will. But first, let's see what you've got."

"Sure."

Del flipped his two cards face up. Two aces. Put that together with the ace of clubs, the three and seven of hearts, and the two queens on the turn and river, and it made a full house. A good hand. Actually, a great hand. Only not great enough.

Shaye batted her lashes at him—bad lashes and bad gloating smile—and flipped over her two lovely ladies.

Didn't. Say. A. Word. The cards spoke for themselves.

Ben whooped. "Four of a kind, *loser*."

"Bazinga!" Piper reached around Ford and shoved Shaye's shoulder. "You got him gooood."

"Ouch, bro," said Ford. "Those Halloween parties are wild."

The whole time heckles flew around the table, Del watched her with hooded eyes. A hot gaze that dropped to her mouth and up again but didn't leave her face. Her blood pumped faster and faster. She'd won. He'd lost. She'd keep her swear jar and he'd help with the Halloween party.

So why did she regret making those silly bets? Why did a blush creep over her cheeks as her heart galloped around her ribcage? Had she secretly wanted him to win so she'd have a date on Piper's big day? Her fingers locked together in her lap.

Of course not. What a silly idea.

Del stood, fished in his jeans front pocket and pulled out a roll of banknotes. Tossing two twenties across the table, he said, "Guess I'll get a double helping of humble pie, next time you make one."

Shaye swallowed the ball of nerves tingling in her throat and prayed her voice came out steady. "Guess you will. And I guess you'll have to find another date for the wedding. I hear Mrs. Taylor's free."

Mrs. Taylor, an octogenarian widow, was a dreadful flirt with wandering hands. A good-looking young man relaxed in her company at his own peril. Which was why, in reception-planning discussions, Piper elected to place the older woman safely between Denise Komeke and Caroline Russell.

Del raised an eyebrow. "That old cougar still alive?"

"That old cougar is alive and kicking, and she'd say yes to you in a heartbeat." Noah stood and slid his chair under the table. "Anyone want a lift back to town? Shaye?"

She shook her head. "No, I'll stay for the clean-up."

Ben and Ford also rose, collecting their winnings and jackets. After a quick round of goodbyes, they left.

Del and West collapsed the card table and manhandled it down to the garage, while Shaye and Piper tidied the family room and loaded the dishwasher.

Piper continued to slip sidelong glances in Shaye's direction as they worked in silence—a well-oiled team effort, polished through years of sibling practice. Piper collected dirty dishes, Shaye rinsed and stacked them. If Ben had stayed, he would've been all big brother, giving orders until either she or Piper squirted him with the sink spray hose. At last, they were a family again, and for that, she'd put up with Ryan Westlake and his irritating younger brother.

"I know what you're going to say," Shaye said after receiving yet another glance.

"Nope, I don't think you do."

Shaye slotted a glass into the dishwasher. "You're thinking I'm too hard on Del. That I should quit giving him hell and play nice."

Piper snickered and tossed another two beer bottles into the recycling bin. "You may've convinced half the town that sugar wouldn't melt in your mouth, but I know you. You've got a little mean streak once someone gets under your skin." Piper shut the laundry door on the recycling bin and leaned against a counter. "And for some reason, Del's gotten under your skin."

"He's in my kitchen, being a pain in the butt."

"Short term, as you pointed out earlier. Plus, you said you worked well together."

"I hate it when you remind me of stuff I said earlier."

"I know. But big sisters are good at that sort of thing." Piper pressed her lips shut and popped them open a couple of times. "Just be careful, okay? Don't burn any bridges."

Shaye huffed out a breath she hadn't known she'd been holding and unscrewed the lid on the dishwasher powder. "This coming from a woman who doesn't just burn bridges but annihilates them with nuclear bombs."

Piper grinned and wrapped her arm around Shaye's shoulder. "Yeah, but you're only a baby ass-kicker. I'm a pro."

"Well, this baby ass-kicker made forty bucks tonight and found a slave to do all the hard labor for the kids' Halloween party."

"Make that a big mean streak." Piper's laugh sobered quickly. "Del doesn't strike me as the kind of man who's into the whole family and kids scene."

"That's my impression, too."

Piper flicked a glance over her shoulder at the footsteps clomping back up the stairs. "I hope the anti-family thing is mostly an act. West and Claire are pinning their hopes on Del being a kidney donor."

Shaye's stomach plummeted to the toes of her boots. "I hope so, too."

But Del being a match was the least of the Westlakes' problems. Even if Del proved to be compatible, would he agree to such a huge step? Would the boy she'd seen hiding in the corner of their garden crying thirteen years ago turn around and give the father who sent him away a kidney?

She'd no idea, because she still didn't know what kind of man the boy had become.

***

Shaye turned down West's offer of a ride home. Clambering on the back of his motorbike for the short trip into town was fun—but tonight, she needed the solitude of walking under a quarter moon.

Del had disappeared downstairs ten minutes earlier with a curt, "Night."

Shaye hugged her sister at the door. "I can't wait until the dress-fitting in Invers."

Piper's nose crinkled. "You know, I'm having second thoughts—"

"You rock the dress."

"I do. I could rock a cute pantsuit, too."

Shaye laughed and stepped outside. "You're not getting married in a pantsuit."

"Fine." Piper huffed, crossing her arms. "But I get to pick the shoes."

"Yes. You may pick the shoes that go under the gorgeous dress we spent many, many insufferable hours finding."

"It's not too late to change the bridesmaids' dresses to candy-floss pink with ruffles, you know."

Shaye swatted her sister's arm. "Oh, go play hide the salami with your man, you vengeful cow."

"Love you, Shaye-Shaye," Piper called as she shut the door. She whipped it open again. "And don't forget you promised your special macaroons for my bridal shower. Sweet dreams."

Shaye continued to smile as she followed the thin beam of her little pocket flashlight down the driveway. Fresh, salty air with a hint of smoke from the many coal and wood fires ruffled her hair. Electricity was expensive on Stewart Island, since they relied on four diesel generators to provide for their needs. Without a honey to keep you warm on icy winter nights, coal or wood wouldn't bankrupt you like electric heaters would.

She buttoned up her vintage, Kelly-green wool coat and drew the collar higher around her neck.

Lights still glowed in a few homes nestled in the bush-covered hills above Oban. Some nights, her own company became too much, and she'd take her little flashlight and walk through the town. Sometimes, a shadow moved past a window in one of those homes as the drapes were tugged shut, the person snugly enclosed by the warmth of family inside.

One day, she'd tell herself. *One day a man who loves me will close the drapes against the world and take me to bed.*

Footsteps thudded on the road behind her. Shaye whirled, a beam of light blinding her. She threw up a hand to shield her eyes.

"Sorry," a male voice said.

Not West and probably not sorry in the slightest.

Del, dressed in long black shorts and a long-sleeve running shirt, flicked off his headlamp. She took half a step to the side, since he didn't move past her.

City people—they had no idea of personal boundaries.

"No problem." She waved a hand in the direction of the main road. "Ride like the wind, Bullseye."

"Huh?"

Not a *Toy Story* fan. She wasn't surprised. "Never mind. I'll get out of your way."

Moving a little farther to the side, because—damn her nose—he still smelled like something begging to be bitten, Shaye flicked her fingers and mimicked a southern accent. "Run Forrest, run."

In case he hadn't gotten the subtle context of run far, far from her.

"Are we playing guess the movie?"

"We're not playing anything. You're off for a run; I'm going home." Pointlessly rolling her eyes in the dark, Shaye walked down the hill.

Men. Always so obtuse when it suited them.

Del switched on his headlamp and followed. "Thought I'd walk with you. At least as far as Due South."

Her scalp prickled. "That's not necessary."

Ick. That sounded uber-bitchy. Especially since Del pitched his voice in a *can't we get along* tone.

Her mum raised her to have manners. "But thank you."

She walked faster, though because of his height advantage, he kept up, as if he were taking a midnight stroll.

"It's no problem. This'll be my warm up."

"Wouldn't want you to strain anything." Like his giant ego.

He chuckled, and she slanted a glance at him.

The giant ego was packed into a rangy yet muscled frame. The black top clung to his upper body, but with the lack of light, she couldn't see much except the breadth of his chest and the width of his shoulders. Not that she paid attention to the lean muscles flexing in his calves as they turned onto the main road. Not if she didn't want to trip over her boots and tumble head first onto the beach.

"You're not a runner?"

She snickered. "Only if there's someone chasing me with a knife."

"That happen much?"

"Not on my shifts."

Since Del appeared determined to ruin her quiet stroll, she kept a wide gap between them. It wasn't wide enough. Even through the layers of wool and satin lining, through her merino sweater and thermal top, she reacted to his nearness with goosebumps rising on her skin.

This was the first time she'd been alone with him. Alone and not in Due South's kitchen—as God knows, a speedo-wearing Joe Manganiello could arrange himself on her workspace during dinner service and she wouldn't stop for a lick.

"Maybe they do things differently in LA?" she asked.

"Can't say I've ever been chased by a knife-wielding maniac."

She didn't need light to see him smile.

"I did have a line cook threaten to cut my dick off and feed it to her pet snake once."

"Do you make a habit of pissing off your staff?" Or only his female staff?

Her shoulders hunched. *Be civil, Shaye-Shaye.* Pretend he's some summer guy here for a long weekend, making chit-chat in the pub while shouting over the dull roar of a dozen other conversations.

"Tempers flare in the weeds. All sorts of shit gets said. Doesn't mean anything."

Maybe she'd been a little sheltered working at Due South. Bill, sometimes crankier than a goat with a burr up his bum, treated her like a daughter. But as a substitute daughter, she didn't get an ounce of leniency that a simple employee got. If she screwed up, she heard about it. At volume. Then they'd work through the issue and make sure it didn't happen again. There were no personal insults or threats of dicks being cut off. They were family.

Still, on days when Bill patted her hand and rejected yet another of her suggestions, Shaye wondered about the dark side. Could she leave everything and everyone behind for an opportunity of a lifetime?

Like that would ever happen.

She sighed as they rounded a bend, their footsteps crunching on gravel. Oban's few streetlamps and the ferry wharf's outside lights to their left cast enough shadows aside to allow her to switch off her flashlight.

"So, what's it like, working at *Cosset*?"

"Hard—back-breaking hard. You're pushed to your limits each night, but it's an electrifying atmosphere to work in." Del switched off his headlamp and stuffed it into his pocket.

Their steps slowed to a stroll while their eyes adjusted to the sliver of moonlight and the spread of stars overhead. He definitely wasn't telling her everything.

"Sounds like the abridged version."

"It is."

"You're not going to tell me what it's really like?"

"Why? Thinking of moving to LA?"

Chef training in Invercargill had been challenge enough for the scared, twenty-one year old she'd been almost four years ago. "I don't think Hollywood's quite my scene."

"There's always New York, London, Paris. I've heard cruise ships are great if you've the urge to visit lots of different places."

Cruise ships? Nuh, uh. "Boats are not my thing."

She shrugged, glancing past him to the slow wash of white water surging over the sandy beach. In summer, she swam in the shallows close to shore, which didn't bother her too badly. And not using the ferry as a means of transport was silly—and costly. So what if she avoided most outings on Ben's boat, and she'd scuba-dive with her siblings when imps ice-skated in hell?

Farther along the road running alongside the arc of Halfmoon Bay, Due South's outside lights glowed like beacons in the velvet darkness. Nearly there. Just another five minutes of small talk.

"You think I could work in New York or London?" she asked.

"I haven't seen you pushed to your limits, so I'll reserve judgment."

"I work well under pressure."

"Due South is a fucking cakewalk compared to Cosset and kitchens like it. No offence."

If he predicted her reaction would be denying and defensive, he'd be disappointed.

"None taken," she said.

His footfalls slowed, and then stopped. He leaned his forearms on the foreshore railing and gazed out over the bay. She could've kept walking. Could've said a quick goodnight and scurried away to the safety of her room. But Del had some serious gravity, and he drew her to his side to lean where he leaned, to stare where he stared. Pewter moonlight dancing over the moored boats and the shifting tide was one view she'd never tire of.

"Sometimes, those bright city lights show up a whole cesspool you gotta learn to stay afloat in." The toe of his running shoe scuffed at a pile of sand blown onto the road. "You think you've learned to swim, when really you've just been keeping your head above the shit."

A vast emptiness hollowed his voice, a weariness she'd expect from a much older man. Del was three years her senior. Right now, the difference in their ages felt more like three decades.

"Was it hard deciding to leave LA and come here?"

"Yes and no."

One lazy wave after another hissed ashore. She swiveled toward him, but his features were a blank mask. "You want to expand on that a little?"

The white sliver of his teeth flashed. "Now that would mean having a heartfelt conversation. I didn't think you were interested in socializing with me outside of the kitchen."

"Hmmph."

Being with Del anywhere was like taking a supposedly harmless party pill—the buzz seemed innocent at first, then suddenly you were dancing naked on a table top, shaking your tail feather.

Shaye turned her back on the beach and leaned on the railing. She should go—return to her DVD collection and Kindle, and just forget about standing in the moonlight with Del Westlake.

Instead, she blurted, "Why was being your wedding date part of the bet?"

He huffed out a laugh. "It doesn't matter; you cleaned the floor with me. Lesson learned."

She shoved her hands deep into her coat pockets, ran her thumb around and around the grooved flashlight handle. "It matters. Saying something like that in front of my family and friends means they'll never forget it."

"Maybe I want you as my date."

She snorted. "You don't even like me."

"Not particularly. You're a bit of a princess."

Of all the—"I should roast your balls and feed them to West's dog. I'm not a princess."

"However, I like you much better when you talk dirty."

"God. You're such a...such a..." She reined in a long list of colorful phrases and settled for, "*Jerk.*"

"Guilty."

She gritted her teeth. "You asked me because we're both part of the wedding. It's sensible."

"I don't do things just because they're sensible."

"What's your reason?"

One second Del stood beside her all moody and mysterious, and the next, his hands gripped the railing on either side of her hips. He moved fast—fast enough that she made an embarrassing little eep-ish squawk. Nowhere to go unless she became flexible enough to do a flip over the wooden railing.

Shaye yanked her hands from her pockets and gave his chest a shove. "Back off."

Even after she added her sous chef *do it now or die* glare, he stayed, big and bad and way too close. He continued watching her with dark and unreadable eyes, his nostrils flaring slightly as he breathed.

Her hands didn't know what to do. She couldn't put them back on those two hard pecs, since every single nerve-ending had soaked up the heat burning through Del's shirt and transmitted swoony, oh yeah sighs into her brain.

Stupid nerve-endings. Stupid brain.

She wriggled her bottom, so she half sat on the railing, arching away from him. "What are you doing?"

"Showing you the reason."

The rough timbre of his voice stroked over her. Wickedly dark, decadently rich, scarily addictive. Like chocolate, the quality stuff made of eighty percent pure cacao.

He leaned forward, his face level with hers. "It's a compelling reason."

Shaye's hand shot out to grip his biceps—that or topple backward—but God, he felt amazing. All hard, sinewy muscle and why the hell couldn't she unhook her fingers?

Her breathing hitched, high and ragged. "My sister's a cop, and I know how to defend myself."

"So, show me your ninja moves."

"Daring a cornered woman to hurt you isn't very bright."

One of his hands rasped off the wooden railing and touched the end of her ponytail. He selected a strand and stroked it down her jaw. Shaye licked her lips, unable to suck her gaze from his mouth, which angled closer. Close enough that she could tell the flavor of the last handful of potato chips he'd eaten.

Salt and vinegar. Her favorite.

She strained upward to see if he tasted as good as he smelled...*Freaking hell—*

Shaye reared back a little, hair slipping from his fingers, her chin narrowly missing his. "Are you going to kiss me?"

Her heart gave a little bunny-hop at the thought and leaped around her ribs.

"Not unless you ask real nice."

"Ask you?" There was that damn smirk of his again. She should've guessed he was playing with her. "When pigs fly."

A muscle ticked in his jaw, but the smile didn't falter. "Now you'll have to say, 'Please, Del. With a cherry on top.'"

"I'd jam that cherry up your nose before I'd kiss you, Hollywood. Get outta my face."

His gaze dipped once to her mouth then flicked up. "I can't go anywhere while you're grabbing onto me."

"Fine."

She pried her hand off his arm, and he obligingly stepped back.

What was she supposed to say now? Her brain had disintegrated to mush and her knee joints appeared to have transformed into Jello.

Del stood, hands shoved in the pockets of his running shorts—calm, unruffled, unreadable. They could've been discussing the next day's menu or the weather forecast.

He'd been teasing. *So, get it together, girlfriend.* She blew out a slow breath and dredged up her most reasonable peace-making voice.

"I've given you the wrong impression. You've mistaken my friendliness for flirtation—"

"Friendly? You'd put a cleaver in my skull, given half a chance."

Don't give the cocky bastard the satisfaction. Just, don't, do, it.

Shaye straightened to her full five-foot-seven height. "I've been cordial and respectful to you in the kitchen; I don't owe you more than that."

Del folded his arms. "Hmm."

Which could mean any damn thing.

"You've never had to work with a man you're attracted to, have you?" He asked, quirking an eyebrow at her.

Blood sizzled under her skin. "No. And it doesn't apply in this situation."

"Bullshit. We've been ready to burn the moment we stepped in that kitchen together."

Shaye pushed away from the railing. "Not only are you a jerk, you're a delusional, self-inflated jerk."

"Ouch," he said as she stalked away, her heels clicking on the pavement. "Denial doesn't change the facts."

Shaye raised her bent arm, the middle finger popping into a vertical position. The low chuckle behind her signaled nothing was wrong with his night vision.

"Goodnight, princess."

A voice like melted dark chocolate, her butt. Shaye stomped around the corner of Due South and moved out of his sight.

The man was poison, pure and simple.

Chapter 6.

Lani swept into the kitchen, and Del glanced up. Friday night, the front of the house was slammed, all tables full, and they were headed into the weeds. Servers Lani, Charlie, and Helena were ordered to turn and burn the smaller tables, so the booked party of nine could be seated in thirty minutes.

"Need my soups, like yesterday. Table six is getting antsy," Lani said.

"On it," Shaye yelled.

Charlie, hot on Lani's heals, blew in with yet another ticket. "One firehouse pizza, one fish 'n chips hold the tartar sauce, and a ribeye that's kissed the fire."

"Add it to the stack." Del shot a glance over his shoulder at Vince, who stood stationed at the grill. "Where's table four's grilled vege? Pump it out, let's go."

As his gaze swung back, it hesitated at the shelf where his little camera recorded the chaos. Thank God they were putting on a good show. With all the mini-disasters the camera's indifferent eye had caught tonight, he'd have enough footage to get his audition clip ready to e-mail by tomorrow, at the latest.

Helena entered the kitchen at a run. "New bean and pasta for the salad bar, since some little shit just spit in both." Though Helena was a co-parent with her partner, Sara, Del learned fast the woman had no patience for fools and bratty children.

Goddammit, two ruined salads? He finished plating table two's mussel starters. "Eighty-six it—we haven't got time to make more before the party of nine—"

"Got seven vegetarians in that party, Chef. They need salad." Shaye swooped past him and grabbed a pot. "I'll get water on for the pasta. Won't take long to whip up a new batch."

"Hell. Do it."

She whirled around to the sink. Water splashed into the pot, and he smothered a grim smile. Helena's report of a kid spitting into the salad would be gold on his audition. Ethan Ward wanted to see a restaurant failing without his experienced input? Well, he'd get some bang for his buck at Due South.

He slid the two plates onto the pass. "Table two's entree, run it."

Charlie snatched them up on the other side. "Dude, I'm running."

Metal clanked behind him, and he whipped around to ask where the Wan Ton soups for table six were. He collided with someone, realizing who as Shaye screamed. His gaze shot to her hazel eyes, huge with pain and shock. Then down to the empty soup bowls. Her fingers flew open, and the bowls smashed to the floor.

"Oh, fuck. Sorry."

Scalding-hot chicken broth soaked her pants.

Del lunged for her. Grabbing Shaye under the arms, he lifted her off her feet and strode to the long counter beside the sinks. She panted in his ear, her nails digging through the heavy cotton into his arms as he carefully seated her on the countertop. He snatched up the pull-out spray head, and with the other hand he fumbled to lift her chef's jacket out of the way.

"Del! Please—"

A world of embarrassment filled those two words.

No time for modesty. He aimed the spray head straight at her crotch and toggled the switch. The cold water hit, and she squealed like a cat with its tail caught in a door. Squirming, she slapped at him, trying to get away. Water ran down her legs, most streaming into the sink basin but a lot pattering onto the floor.

He moved between her knees, pinning them open with his body, terrified of touching anywhere she'd been burned. "Dammit, Shaye—stop fighting! Where does it hurt? Your thighs?"

She nodded. Moaned. "Left thigh." Tears streamed from her eyes. "And hip."

Cold water soaked through his crotch, but he kept the spray on target. Reaching between their bodies, Del hooked a finger over the stretchy waistband of her pants. "I have to tug these down to get the spray directly on the scald."

Her gaze shot to his, her fingers scrabbling over his hand, trying to pull him away.

"No!" A harsh breath exploded out of her, then she rolled her lips in a moment, the pretty pinkness disappearing into a pale line. "The water—the water helps." She gasped again. "Don't need to take my pants off. Not that bad."

Feet scuffed on the floor, and murmurs of his staff's concern rose around them.

Without taking his gaze from Shaye, he shouted, "Lani—get out front—tell the customers there'll be a delay. Everyone else—get back to work, and keep your eyes to yourself."

He pulled on the right side of her pants, lowering the fabric to hip level. His balls contracted as cold water continued to snake down his pants and puddle on the floor.

"No," Shaye hissed and yanked the pants up again.

"Enough!" His voice came out a low snarl. "You want me to get Fraser and Vince to hold you down?"

He sounded like a monster, but the thought of her skin blistering and burned—and he the one who'd bumped her—well, he wanted to punch something.

She blinked up at him, and he felt even more of a shit.

"I'm sorry." He gentled his tone and released the thumb control so the water trickled instead of gushed. "It's just me, okay? The jerk who wants to take care of you. Let me help."

"All right." She pushed down with her palms and lifted her butt, giving him access. "Panties stay on."

"Deal." He dropped the sprayer into the sink, gingerly hooked his fingers over her waistband, and drew the soaked fabric down.

Down over the smooth skin of her stomach, down to the unexpected cupcake tattoo on her right hipbone, down to white boy-short panties. *Wet, white boy-short panties.*

He needed a smack upside the head for even daring to glance at them.

Del swallowed hard, finished wrestling her pants down to her knees, and forced his wayward brain to examine the red patches blooming on her otherwise pale skin. She had a small scald on her left hip, but the majority of the hot soup must've slopped onto her thigh. An angry rash spread across the front of her leg, but thank God, it hadn't blistered.

A glance around revealed Fraser hovering at the kitchen doors, trying not to sneak glances but failing, and Vince glowering at the grill, muttering to himself. Del popped the domes on his jacket and wrenched it off. He snatched up the sprayer again and draped his jacket over the top, so it hid Shaye's legs.

"Thank you, Del."

Her quiet gratitude punched into him. It was the first time she'd said his name without mockery or distain. Why his name on her lips should coil around him like warm silk, he didn't know.

"I'm going to keep the water running for at least ten minutes." He aimed the sprayer again.

She arched and clutched his shoulder, thrusting her breasts forward.

Dear God, he was going straight to hell.

"Most of the soup went onto the floor." She gritted between clenched teeth. "Bloody stings, but I don't think it's too serious."

As she spoke, she looked past his shoulder. Couldn't say he blamed her. The scalds must hurt like hell, considering she'd forgotten to take her hand off him.

He wasn't complaining.

"I'm sorry this happened to you, princess."

Shaye's fingers dug in then sprang wide open and she dropped her hand to the countertop. "Not your fault. Forgot to yell out when I brought the soup to the pass—and I'm not an effing princess."

"I'm sorry this happened to you...cupcake?"

She sucked in a breath, and her pretty hazel eyes clashed with his. "If my mother ever hears I have a tattoo, I will hunt you down like a feral dog. Are we clear?"

He grinned and shifted in his wet pants. Worth it to see her feeling okay. "Yes, Chef."

"Good." She laid her fingers over his. "I can do this now, thanks." She made a shooing motion at him with her other hand.

He froze at her touch. The last few minutes, she hadn't needed him holding the sprayer, let alone pressed up so close against her. "Ah, I'll get the first aid—"

"Del? Shaye?" West's voice came from the direction of the swinging doors, laden with pissiness and concern. "Lani said—holy fucking hell with all the saints in attendance."

Del swung around and backed up, blocking his brother's view of Shaye as best he could. If guilt hadn't mostly ruined the image of her naked thighs spread wide, heaven covered by her modest but surprisingly sexy panties, she would've taken the top spot of his fantasy list. He could only imagine what the scene looked like to his big brother.

Caught with his hands between the sous chef's thighs. Just awesome.

The hiss of water ceased, and the rustle of fabric being adjusted sounded from behind him.

"West, get outta here and go about your business," Shaye said.

"You are my business. Lani said you got burned." West scooted around the pass and gave Del a *what the hell did you do now* glare, tilting his neck for a better view.

Del angled his body sideways. Gave West a *don't be a dick* glare right in return.

"It's okay, I'm covered up."

Del stepped aside, leaned a hip against the counter, and studied Shaye from the corner of his eye. Her face was flushed a pretty rose, and at some point her cap had tumbled off her head, but otherwise, if you ignored his soaked jacket covering her lap, she looked good. Better than good. Embarrassed, defiant, hotter-than-hell.

He wrenched his gaze away and prayed the cold, clingy denim would discourage any reaction in that area.

Shaye huffed out a sigh. "It's just a scald, and I really, *really* don't need any more *assistance* from a Westlake male."

"Well, shit." West jammed his hands on his hips. "Sure you don't want me to take a look? A second opinion?"

"See, now, this is why I should talk Piper out of marrying you, you big pervert."

"She knows I'm a pervert," West said. "All men are perverts, given the opportunity."

"Hah." She tucked the jacket closer around her legs. "You want to help, get Denise to grab me a change of clothes from my room."

"Done." West turned to leave, but paused at the pass, giving them a loaded glance. "You sure you're okay, Shaye?"

"I'd be better than okay if you could guarantee everyone won't hear about this before the end of service."

West grinned. "Won't be from me, sweetheart."

She turned to Del as West hurried out. "Think there's some Aloe spray in the first aid kit. Top pantry shelf, remember?"

"Gotcha."

Del rummaged through cans and snatched up the first aid kit. He left the pantry, prying the lid off the container while he walked. Shaye sat rigid on the countertop, arms banded across her chest, her eyes focused on the high shelf opposite. Like a hound dog scenting.

He squelched through the puddles to her side.

Oh.

Shit.

"Why is there a tiny camera up on that shelf?" she asked.

Busted.

Shaye knew goddamned well who the camera belonged to, because Due South's kitchen was more familiar to her than her own room. The little black camera hadn't been there last week.

And the sideways shift of Del's eyes, the *oh, crap* pinched eyebrows, and slightly gaping mouth? Guilty.

"I can explain." He pitched his voice low and reasonable.

Didn't want anyone else to hear. Funny, that.

"Uh-huh. Better make it good."

"Hell." He raked a hand through his hair as the kitchen doors blew open, and Charlie and Lani bustled in. "It's nothing creepy or diabolical, I promise. I'll tell you everything after service. Will you trust me that long? Please?"

"You haven't earned my trust." Even though looking at him acting all sincere and not his usual cocky self, her resolve to pitch a fit until she heard a satisfactory explanation, wavered.

"No." A direct blue gaze, uncompromising and honest. "I haven't, and I probably don't deserve it. But I'm asking for it. Just until we get this hiking party served."

If he'd said he was trustworthy, she would've shot him down. But since he'd shown concern for Due South's reputation, she caved.

"All right. After dinner, you'll tell me everything."

"Deal." He handed her a clean dishtowel and the first aid kit. "Put the spray on. Denise should be here any minute with a change of clothes, and then you can head to your room to rest."

She snorted. "The party of nine's due, plus we've got tickets up the wazoo. I'll finish the shift."

"Shaye..."

The way he said her name...not as if he was about to go all alpha chef on her, but as if he cared about her wellbeing, made her insides go all warm and squishy.

Squishiness was unacceptable on the job. Mustering up some 'tude, she angled her chin. "You ask me to trust you, well, I'm asking for you to respect me. I know what I'm capable of, and I can work. This needs to get done."

He gave her a crooked smile. "R.E.S.P.E.C.T?"

"That's the one."

She flicked her fingers at him, because offering up another view of her pants shoved to her knees was also unacceptable. On her humiliation scale? An eight point five. At least she had on cute panties and not her desperate-for-washday ancient ones.

Small consolation.

But they coped. Much as it irritated her, most of the reason why they powered through the rest of service was due to Del. He'd gone out to the front of the house while she changed, apologizing to their customers and using that Westlake charm to smooth over any impatience.

Now, with the last ticket cleared, clean up began.

West swung through the doors at nine when the kitchen officially closed. "You're done, Shaye. Head upstairs."

She continued with her after-service routine and ignored him.

West pulled out his mobile. Tapped the screen a few times and then shoved the phone under her nose. "Glenna's number—I have my finger on the call button, see?"

"I've only got another twenty or thirty minutes to go."

She shot a glance over to Del, who stood on the other side of the kitchen, deep in conversation with Vince. No way would he get off the hook about that damn camera. She could've pointed the device out to West, but something held her tongue. Working with someone as closely as she'd worked with Del these last few days, and even if they were a giant pain in the behind—and they'd seen your underwear twice—you developed a sense of loyalty. Probably misplaced loyalty, but still...

"Glenna said to call if you got all belligerent and stubborn. Think this counts?"

"I'm not afraid of my mother, for goodness sake."

"No? Well, I am. And she'll make my life a living hell if I tell her you worked one minute after the last meal went out." West snatched the chef's cap from her head and dangled it out of her reach. "C'mon, Shaye-Shaye, do me a favor."

Shaye jabbed West in the stomach until he laughed and lowered her cap. She snatched it back. "For a guy, you are unbelievably scared of my mother."

"She's a force to be reckoned with."

She flicked a glance over her shoulder to Del, who was watching her and West. "All right. I'll go and read my Kindle; I'm not a bit sleepy." *Hint, hint.*

Del met her gaze as she walked past. *Later*, he mouthed.

With a curt nod, Shaye strode out of the kitchen and climbed the stairs, her leg and hip throbbing. Her eyes drifted shut while she rested briefly on the landing, conjuring up the image of Del's face as he'd eased her pants over her hips. Had she really seen desire shimmer through his gaze?

She shook her head, unlocking the last door at the end of the narrow corridor and stepping inside her room. Del wouldn't be finished downstairs for at least an hour, so after another shot of Aloe spray, she tugged on a flowing hippy skirt, which she could keep hiked up and off her skin until he arrived. Plumping up her pillows, she stretched out on her bed and switched on her Kindle.

At eleven, she gave up waiting and changed into her flannel pajama bottoms and a faded blue, gold, and maroon *Highlanders* jersey. Del was in for a rude awakening in the morning, the weasel. She eased under her duvet, thankful the scalds had transitioned from a hot throb to a light sting.

Her phone bleated to signal an incoming text. Muttering, she flung out a hand and snatched it up. An unfamiliar number appeared on the display, but she nailed the sender immediately by the message.

Can I come up?

Del was out there? Shaye carefully rolled off the bed, tiptoed to the window, and peeped through the drapes. Across the road, Del leaned against a fence post, the shine of his phone giving him a ghostly aura. In black jeans and a black tee, he blended in with the night, looking tough and big and ninja-ish enough to trip her heart into a quick-step.

She returned to her bed and picked up her phone. Whispered, "No, you can't, I haven't got a bra on."

She set the phone on the nightstand, where it promptly bleated again.

I know yr awake, cupcake. Yr drapes twitched.

Dammit, the man had eagle eyes. She wanted to know why Del put a camera in her kitchen, but she didn't want to deal with him tonight. Dealing with him meant getting dressed again—and *hell, no* to talking to him in her baggy sleep pants and her dad's old rugby shirt. Small mercies she couldn't see her reflection in the room's wall mirror. Her hair, after reclining on pillows for a few hours and out of its usual neat plait, would be horrific. Think electrified *Cousin Itt.*

Her phone stayed silent. She whooped out a sigh. He'd given up.

A soft knock sounded on her door. Ohmygawd—of course he hadn't given up. He was a damned Westlake male.

Her gaze skipped to the laundry sorter in the corner. Could she do a reverse Houdini trick and wriggle into her bra? The knock came again, this time louder and accompanied by Del's deep voice saying, "Shaye. I know you're awake."

Crapola!

Shaye hot-footed it across the floor, wincing as her sore leg rubbed against her pajama bottoms. No time to change unless she made him wait another five minutes—so she yanked open the door far enough to hiss, "Go away!"

"You need an explanation."

She caught a glimpse of tanned forearm braced on the frame, the dark and dangerous bulk of him blocking the light behind. Ah—*nope*—a horny woman who hadn't had sex in oh, *thirteen months* needed to keep that kind of temptation in the hallway.

Shaye got the door three quarters shut before a large hand shot out, forcing it to a halt. Keeping her crazy hair and unfettered boobs tucked out of sight, she swallowed a snarl. "It can wait until tomorrow. It's after eleven."

"Worried you'll turn into a pumpkin?"

She shoved the cool wood, but nothing budged. While the man might've lost some weight, he sure hadn't lost any muscle.

"Or am I keeping you from fantasizing about one of your book boyfriends?"

Hah! The only man she'd fantasized about in the last five days was him, and that wasn't something she cared to joke about.

A floorboard creaked from the room next door. Fudge. Short of causing a scene, she didn't have a choice.

"Five minutes. And the lights stay off."

The pressure from the other side abated, and she opened the door wide.

He slipped into her room like an inky shadow, accompanied by a low-pitched chuckle. "You do seem like a lights-off kind of girl."

"Oh, shut up." She stomped over and sat on the bed.

"Are you always this cranky when you're entertaining men in your bedroom?" He continued past her and yanked open the drapes.

The streetlight outside lit up her room, highlighting kitten-print flannel and wild-child hair. The look every woman aspired to when "entertaining a man". Although she *wasn't* entertaining Del.

"Four minutes, thirty seconds," she said.

With his back to the light, his expression was obscured, but she sensed he studied her every movement. Could he see her nipples hardening under her loose top? She crossed her arms, just in case.

Del slouched down, propping his butt on the narrow windowsill and crossing his ankles. "The camera is to record footage for a reality TV series audition."

An audition tape? As in, people would see her and Vince and—holy crap! "You are not using that footage of me from tonight!"

"No." A lot of humor in that one word. "Pinky swear." He held up a hand and wiggled his little finger.

"Why should I believe you?"

"You think I'm such a bastard I'd let that incident go public?"

She narrowed her eyes. "You recorded us without our knowledge."

His shoulders rolled forward. "If the staff knew a camera was recording, you'd all be delivering Oscar-worthy performances. I only needed a couple minutes footage of the kitchen in full swing."

"So what is this TV series?"

"*Ward on Fire*. It's Ethan Ward's baby."

"*The* Ethan Ward from *Ward's*?" The gorgeous celebrity chef owner of three Michelin starred restaurants.

"Yeah. Him."

Del's voice was as bland as boiled white rice, but something about the way he'd said Ethan's name nettled the hairs on her nape. "You're auditioning? Why?"

"The winner gets to work for six months in his London restaurant. After the trial period, if the winner makes the grade, he or she will become head chef of another *Ward's* restaurant scheduled to open in Chicago next year."

"That's an amazing opportunity."

"Yup."

"Does West know? Your father?"

Del's head lowered, and his fingers, down beside his hips on the windowsill, drummed a quick tattoo.

"No. I haven't told anyone else. Look—" He pushed away from the sill and sat on the bed with her.

The mattress dipped, forcing her to uncross her arms to steady herself. Without staff buzzing around and the buffer of work, she was once again uber-aware of him. And there she sat, next to a man who stirred her feverishly hot, naked apart from her pajamas and tee shirt.

Nake-ed.

She needed to stop acting like an awkward teenager who'd brought her first boyfriend home to an empty house. The fluttery feeling in her stomach was purely one-sided.

"Ethan's already started filming," Del said. "The producers agreed to let me send in a last-minute audition."

"You'd be a wildcard entrant."

"I might not even make it past the audition."

"But if you do?"

Del grinned at her. "Ethan and his crew will fly here later this month."

Ethan Ward, coming to Stewart Island? Working in her kitchen?

Excitement and pure nerves flooded her system. "This would bring in some amazing publicity for Due South—for Oban, too."

"Exactly. But I've no idea how West and Bill will react."

"Ah." She could almost guarantee West would be all for it. Bill, on the other hand, didn't like change.

From beneath the initial excitement, a dark thought rose. "What kind of reality series is *Ward On Fire*? A look at up-and-coming chefs in their fabulous restaurants, or...?"

Del's spine straightened and his hands, loosely relaxed on his thighs, turned to clenched fists.

"Or," he said simply. "The show's premise is so unoriginal it'd be laughed out of the studio if it wasn't Ethan's idea. It centers on head chefs of failing restaurants in interesting locations. The producers promise the owner they'll replace the contestant with one of Ethan's hand-picked chefs, should the contestant make it to the finals. Then, with Ethan's wisdom and British charisma, he saves the day and the restaurant."

"Due South's not failing."

"It's not doing well, either."

The slow but steady decline over the last year was undeniable.

"So, you want this guy in your face, telling you what to do?" She couldn't imagine Del taking orders from anyone, especially if he believed they were wrong.

He glanced over, his face unreadable. "I want a shot at landing the Chicago gig, so if that means biting my tongue and working with Ward, I'll do it."

Shaye pressed her lips together. "That's why you're really here, isn't it? Not to help your dad, not because you care about Due South, but to get on a TV show."

They stared at each other across the narrow but bottomless gap between them.

His throat worked then stilled. "Yeah."

"And if you don't make it through the audition, you'll be on the next flight." Her chest squeezed around her lungs like a boa constrictor.

"Maybe."

"To LA? Or have you burned all your bridges there, too?"

A flash of teeth in a grim smile. "Pretty much. There's nothing but trouble behind me in LA. I thought Chicago would be a fresh start."

Much as it galled, she said, "Why the hurry to leave? If TV stardom doesn't work out, and you can't go back to Hollywood, why not stay until—?"

God, she was thick sometimes! "The wedding! You'd miss your own brother's wedding?"

Del stood, stalking to the window again. "West'd be fine about it. It's not as if we're tight."

Shaye scrambled to her feet. "He absolutely would *not* be fine about it. You're his best man—his only brother. He *loves* you."

Del's shoulders hunched. "He loves the memory of a fourteen-year-old kid."

"Give him the chance to love the man the fourteen-year-old kid grew into, then. He's family."

"You're big on family, aren't you?"

He stepped toward her, and for some reason her knees wobbled.

Del stopped in front of the photograph on her dresser. The picture had been taken on one of their family-and-friends beach picnics. She'd been ten, posing cross-legged on the sand. Ben and Piper flanked her on either side, with West leaning an elbow on Ben's shoulder, making bunny ears behind Piper's head. Beside Ben knelt her parents—her mum laughing, her dad whispering something in his wife's ear. Missing from the photo, since he'd offered to take it, was Del.

"The perfect Harland family, always there for each other."

"We weren't perfect."

The churning in her gut over his dismissal of his relationship with West dissipated, because she remembered that day in great detail. It'd been one of the last picnics Del had gone on with the Harland family. They'd swam and dived for hours, played cricket in the sand, stretched out on beach towels and had competitions to see who could burp the loudest after drinking too much soda. Del had thrown himself into every activity with a hundred and ten percent effort, wrestling with his big brother with puppy-like affection. Almost as if he knew the summer was winding down, and nothing so wonderful could last forever.

So something must've happened to him in LA for him to change so much that he'd miss one of the most important days in West's life.

"We fought like cats and dogs." Shaye smoothed the folds of her shirt. "You were at our place often enough to hear it."

Del looked at her with a flat stare. "That's right. Never a quiet moment in the Harland house. Someone always shouting over someone else, everyone trying to be heard at the same time—and there you were, a bossy little girl in the thick of it, sorting out everyone's problems." Breaking eye contact, he chuffed out a soft laugh. "You're in the wrong job. You should've been a hostage negotiator."

"I often wondered why you and West wanted to hang with us so much."

He held the photo frame up to the light streaming over his shoulder. "I needed the noise and the chaos to make me forget. You guys had everything."

She smiled tightly. "And then we had nothing."

"I'm very sorry about your dad, Shaye."

His voice, so gentle when only a minute ago it'd scraped over her temper with sharp barbs, brought tears rushing to her eyes.

"Thank you." She swallowed the soggy lump in her throat and blinked rapidly. "He wasn't perfect, either. He made some bad decisions that cost him everything."

"I can identify with that." Del returned the frame to the dresser, touching the glass with a finger. "You're wearing his shirt."

Shaye wrapped her arms around her middle. "After Mum cleaned out his clothes, I took it. I couldn't bear to give it to the charity shop."

"Go *Highlanders*." He shoved his hands into the pockets of his jeans and angled his body toward the door.

Ohthankgoodness. He was planning to leave. The back of her knees nudged the mattress, giving him space to move past. The room shrank as he walked closer, stopping so they stood toe to toe. She struggled not to breathe in his warm, manly smell.

He reached out, tucking a flyaway strand of her hair behind her ear. "Your hair—"

"Is a disaster, I know." She squinted so she wouldn't catch a glimpse of it in the mirror.

"I was going to say pretty." His eyes crinkled in the corners and he finally let go of the strand, leaving her scalp to tingle. "It suits you, being a little loose and mussed up."

She felt loose and mussed up. His big body seemed to have sucked all the oxygen from the room. The only logical reason for why she found it so hard to keep breathing steadily.

"Oh."

She licked dry lips, and his gaze dropped to her mouth, which had the unfortunate side effect of waking up her happy-place. Telling her happy-place to go back to sleep when faced with such hotness was mission impossible. Her body swayed toward him.

"I should go." Before she touched him, Del shot to the door. "Will you let me tell Bill and West about the show, once I know whether I've made it or not?"

Right. Reality check. Her cheeks flared. What the hell had she been thinking? Standing there, begging the man with her eyes to kiss her? All Del wanted was a promise she wouldn't blow his cover.

"I won't say anything," she said. "For now."

"Thanks."

He opened the door, stepped out, and closed it softly behind him.

Shaye flung herself backward onto the bed with a groan. Such an idiot to want to put her mouth on that man.

Even more of an idiot to soften toward him when she knew—by what he'd left unsaid—that he only cared about himself.

Chapter 7.

Alone, at last.

Del surveyed Due South's kitchen. His kitchen. With lunch service over, the staff had dispersed for their break before dinner prep began, and Shaye had bolted the moment her duties were complete. Yet, they'd come to an uneasy truce during the weekend shifts, two days after talking in her bedroom.

Talking. The last thing he'd wanted to do after seeing her all mussed up and sex-kittenish-sexy. Even thinking about their late-night chat made him sweat. Made him hard. Shaye's nipples jutting against her shirt as they'd sat on her bed—close enough to smell the citrusy scent of her shampoo...

Whoa, buddy.

Del tore off his apron. Fifteen minutes of torture he'd better not dwell on if he wanted to work the rest of the day without a non-stop boner. Maybe he'd head outside, see if anyone else caught his eye.

Scrunching his face in distaste, he hung up his apron. Apparently, he only wanted to hook up with a snarky, cupcake-tattooed brunette.

The back door banged open, and his father lurched inside. Bill, once again, looked like a twice-reanimated zombie.

"What are you doing here?" The words popped out before Del could hold onto them.

Bill stabbed a finger at him. "Still my kitchen, Hollywood."

Frickin' great. Shaye's nickname had stuck. He'd told them 'til he ran out of air that *Cosset* was in Santa Monica, *not* Hollywood. Like anyone cared.

"Aren't you supposed to be resting?" he asked.

Snatching his apron off a hook, Bill grunted. "Can't rest. My house is full of bloody women."

"You've got a house full of women? And you left?"

Bill shot him a *you're yanking my chain* glare. "'Course I left. It's your mother's turn to host bridge club, and none of 'em can shut up longer than three seconds. Betsy Taylor decided I should learn to play—she's been on my case for years."

"Maybe you should give it a try?"

"Wash your mouth out." Bill finished tying the apron around his waist and made his way across the kitchen.

"Or take up some other hobby to keep you out of trouble. Like knitting."

A bark of laughter from his father who'd opened the fridge door. "You always were a little smartass."

Is that why you sent me away? The little voice in his head made him feel like a chunk of frozen steak had jammed in his throat. He brushed the question off with a roll of his shoulders. "You gonna start on some prep?"

"Yep." Bill dragged out butter and a small bunch of shallots. He shot a quick glance over his shoulder. "You staying?"

If he didn't know better Del'd think a hopeful tone had crept in Bill's voice. Del hesitated, torn between getting the hell away and wanting to keep an eye on Bill, to make sure the old man didn't collapse.

"Though I don't need a bloody nanny." Bill walked stiffly to the counter and put down the ingredients. "Been running this kitchen under my own steam for almost thirty years."

"Yeah, I remember."

All the times he and his mother and brother entertained themselves as Bill refused to leave Due South. How there'd been no Dad at Saturday morning rugby games—because Bill had lunch prep. No Dad taking him and West hiking and tramping and fishing in summer, because summer was prime tourist season, and Bill Westlake rarely had a day off work—in summer *or* winter.

Del grabbed his jacket. "I'm off for my break."

He strode out the back door without a glance and headed to the foreshore road.

Scuffing his feet and glancing around, Del paused. Where could he go to pass a couple of hours? Tourists opposite the hotel used the giant chess set by the kids' playground. A pre-schooler shrieked in delight, flying down the slide into his mother's arms. Del snuffed out a harsh laugh and shoved his fists into his jacket pockets. Yeah, no Mr. Popularity sash for him—unlike his welcome-anywhere brother.

He shook his head. West's place then—Del'd sneak in a power nap and maybe a quick run before service.

His phone buzzed as he hit the corner to West's road. He didn't recognize the number flashing across the screen, but his heart jolted at the US country code.

"Del Westlake speaking."

A pause and the faintest of hisses. "Del? Ethan Ward. Got a minute, mate?"

"Yeah. Sure." Del's fingers gripped the phone's cool edges. He'd never spoken to the man in his life, but something about the plummy accent mixed with commoner's slang—once described as a *slumming Mr. Darcy* accent—caused his hackles to rise.

"Brilliant. I won't faff around 'cause we're both busy men. We saw your tape, we want you on the show, and the crew and I'll be there near the end of October."

Del's feet stopped dead as did his heart. He stood blinking up at the blue sky.

He'd done it. He'd gotten through.

"That's great, *fucking* great. Thanks. I appreciate it."

"The camera's going to love you surrounded by all that nature rubbish, even if we do have to travel to the world's bumhole to get there." Laughter rolled down the line, a sneering, superior kind of laugh.

Hackles rose on Del's neck. Ethan had judged Stewart Island before even setting one polished Oxford here.

Prick.

Del caught himself and rolled his eyes. He'd pretty much called Stewart Island the same thing. Pot calling the kettle black.

"It's not so bad."

And why was he defending this place? Oban *was* the bumhole of the world, or close to it. He couldn't wait to leave. *But not for a month now, buddy.* Not without giving *Ward On Fire* his best shot.

"Well, we'll see, won't we?" Another disparaging chuckle. "Some underling will be in touch in the next few days to finalize details, sort out paperwork and all that. I'll be in touch later."

The line went dead.

Del shoved the phone into his pocket and walked up the hill to West's, his mind spinning. He'd made it over the first hurdle. Ethan Ward, coming to Due South. With a camera crew.

Holy shit, how would he convince Bill this was a stroke of good luck?

Del opened the door and stepped into the hallway. His eyes adjusted to the dimness inside, and he froze. West, bare-chested and jeans almost falling off his butt, had a wide-eyed Piper pinned against the wall, his hands tangled in her short hair. She appeared to be missing a few items of clothing.

"Fuck!" Del said as West moved to block his view of his fiancée's chest. "Sorry."

He took a large reverse step outside and closed the door. Halfway down the driveway, West called out Del's name.

Del whirled around. "Ever heard of a lock, asshole?"

At least West had buttoned his jeans, though the bastard only looked mildly embarrassed and actually kinda smug.

"Now where's the fun in that?" West folded his arms across his bare chest. "You don't usually come up to the house in the afternoons. Need anything?"

Other than some extra-strength brainwashing sessions? "Go back to your woman."

West's grin widened, so Del flipped him off and turned away.

Four more weeks here, like hell could he continue to stay in West's spare room. He needed his own place.

Del walked into town, pausing outside the Komekes' workshop.

Ford slouched on a bench, coverall-clad legs stretched out, a grease-stained mug in his hands. The same damn bench where he and West and Ben would wait for the twins to finish their afternoon chores. Back when he forgot the crap raining down on him at home by hanging with his mates—fishing, fixing up two crappy old trail-bikes the twins' dad had scored, and just running wild. Back when Ford Komeke had been his best mate. Not the cool-eyed stranger before him.

Stranger or not, Ford would know if anyone had a place Del could rent for a few weeks.

"Afternoon smoko?" he said by way of greeting and walked over, sat on the opposite end of the bench.

Ford gave him the upward eyebrow twitch of acknowledgment. Took a sip of his mug and crossed his work-booted ankles.

"Same every day."

Del leaned his head against the workshop wall, the tinny reggae music from the portable stereo inside drilling into his ears. "Your dad still playing his old Bob Marley CDs?"

"Same every day."

"Yeah. I bet." His peripheral vision caught the corner of Ford's mouth curling up.

They sat in silence. Bob Marley continued to wail, sea birds wheeled overhead, and people wandered past them on the way to Russell's next door.

"Saw you go past." Ford blew on his coffee. "Saw you come back again pretty damn quick."

Del massaged his fingers over his temples. "I walked in on Piper and West in their hallway. Jesus."

Ford snickered. "Thought I heard West's bike earlier."

"What's seen can't be unseen." He leaned forward, elbows on his knees. "Know of a place I can rent? I don't want to continue stumbling into my brother's afternoon quickies."

Ford rolled his head to the side, dark eyes unreadable. "You staying?"

"For a bit. At least until after the wedding." His stomach tensed, waiting for the inevitable barrage of questions.

But Ford looked straight out to the harbor, took a sip from his mug. "Wally's little fishing shack out on Shearwater Bay is empty. He might be open to a cash deal."

"Wally *Nolan*?" One of his dad's mates and the man who'd busted his ass once for vandalizing his garden. "You think he's forgotten about the roses incident?"

Ford barked out a laugh. "Nobody forgets anything in this damn place. But he's a nice old dude; he's probably forgiven you."

"I doubt it."

"Yeah, me too." Ford stood. "Good luck with that." He sauntered into his workshop and Bob Marley cranked up a notch.

Del stared after him then up through the bush-covered hill in the distance where Mr. Nolan lived. He could avoid the old man and continue to ask around. Except now Ford had mentioned Wally's place, Del wanted it. The idea of being away from Due South, away from playing third wheel to West and Piper, sounded damn good. With a sigh, Del stood.

Time to man up.

He found Wally in his front garden, tending to—what else—a rose bush.

A bee buzzed past Del's ear and the scent of roses transported him back in time, to age thirteen again, and he found himself re-living the wash of confused grief and rage he'd felt as he'd snuck into this garden after midnight. He remembered the panicked jolts of his heart when a flashlight beam pinned him to the spot, the heavy footsteps on the wooden deck, and the perfume of roses clogging his nostrils as his breathing rasped through aching lungs.

Earlier that day, Wally had brought his mother a few roses from his garden. Later, Del overheard her berating his father for never bringing her home flowers. They'd fought. Again. So, after midnight Del'd picked up some scissors, snuck out his bedroom window, and hacked off every bloom in Mr. Nolan's garden.

Wally hadn't hollered at him, just trained the flashlight on the ruin of petals at Del's feet. In fact, the only words he'd said were, "Feel better, son?"

Del had mutely shaken his head, and the light switched off. Seconds later came the soft click of the door closing. Far as he knew, the old man never told his parents about the incident.

West had guessed and blabbed it to their mates, earning Del few moments of peer approval, which instead of warming him had made him want to puke.

"Mr. Nolan?" He paused at the fence separating the garden from the road.

The bald head twitched up from the rose bush, steel grey eyes focusing on Del's face. Instant recognition.

"Ah, the youngest Westlake." He straightened, a gnarled hand pressed to the hip of khakis ironed with a military-sharp center crease.

So much for Mr. Nolan softening with age.

"Heard you were in town."

"Seems everybody has now, sir." Del startled at the knee-jerk term he'd once used when addressing his step-father. "I've come to ask about renting your place on Shearwater Bay, but before I do, I apologize for what I did to your roses all those years ago."

"You were a little hooligan, right enough." Mr. Nolan plucked his walking stick off the fence next to the rose bush and walked over.

Del kept his expression dialed to neutral. "Yes, sir."

"A little hooligan who had a lot of anger and resentment inside him."

"Yeah." He dipped his head in agreement. "Hopefully, I've outgrown my teenage ass-holism."

"Hopefully." Mr. Nolan fired off a toothy smile. "You going to vandalize my house if I rent it to you?"

He fended off a returning grin. "No, sir."

"Ah, well. Nothing much you could do to make it look any worse. South wall needs a coat of paint, but I'm too damn old to be climbing around on ladders, and the grandkids—pah." He thumped the walking stick on the ground. "They all go off fishing when they visit, no time for helping their grandpa."

"You rent it to me, I'll paint it." Where he'd find the time, hell if he knew. But the offer might be enough to sweeten the deal.

Mr. Nolan hacked out a laugh. "You'd better go see what you're up against 'fore you agree to that." He crooked his finger. "Come with me, and I'll get you the keys."

"Yes, sir." Del unlatched the gate and stepped onto the path.

"And stop with that 'sir' bollocks—I haven't been sir since my army days. It's Walter. Friends call me Wally." He shuffled toward the house, pausing to throw over his shoulder. "You can call me Walter 'til you've earned the right to Wally."

"Okay, Walter." The corner of Del's mouth tugged up as he followed *Walter* into his house.

The old man fished a keychain out of a small bowl on the hallway table and handed it over. “Here you go. Assume you know where it is?”

“Last beach house on Shearwater Bay Road.”

“Correct. Better ask your cohort, Ford, for a bike—if we can come to an agreement, it’s a long way to walk after a night’s work.”

“I’ll sort something out.” He’d hire a damn scooter if he had to.

“’Spect you will.” Walter gave him a shrewd glance. “You and your dad working together?”

Grist for the gossip mill, no doubt. Del’s fingers tightened around the keychain. “Bill’s not well enough to be in the kitchen. It’s why I’m here.”

“Bill, eh? Carrying some anger toward your old man, aren’t you?”

“I’m not the same little asshole who diced up your roses, Walter.”

“Maybe. Maybe not. But you’ve still got that same look in your eyes, like you’ve more holes inside than wholeness.” He shrugged. “I’ve known your dad a long time—knew him before he and your mum married. We’ve downed a few brews together over the years. You’d be surprised what you learn about a man over a beer or two.”

“I know all I need to about my father.”

“Maybe. Maybe not.” Walter scratched the side of his neck. “But a man will fill himself up with lots of stupid stuff if he’s got a heart like Swiss cheese. And a good-looking fella like you? You can’t fill yourself up with a woman, ‘cause she’ll slip right through all those holes. Need to plug ‘em up first.”

Hearts, Swiss cheese, and dating advice? Old Wally was a phone call away from the dementia ward.

Del retreated a few steps. “Right, thanks for that.” He jingled the keys in his hand before tucking them into his jacket pocket. “I’ll return these later this afternoon.”

“No hurry. I’ll be pottering in my garden.”

With a wave, Del walked out of the house and toward town.

Holes. What bullshit.

So, he'd moments when thinking about Bill sending him away pissed him off. Moments when he'd pause for a little self-reflection and wonder how come his relationships were puddle shallow and only lasted a couple of months. How the one serious relationship he'd had failed so spectacularly.

Why every time he saw Shaye, he wanted to kiss her senseless, just to...

Del growled another four-letter-word and glared over his shoulder at Walter's yard.

Just to fill myself up with her.

***

According to Holly, Shaye's online daily horoscope said: *An unexpected journey awaits if you're brave enough to take the first step.*

The only journey Shaye took after a quick coffee with Holly was up to Erin's counter to score another blackberry Danish. Now she'd need a journey—a walking journey—to work off the extra calories.

She and Holly were nearly at Russell's when the rev of a motorbike made them jump. From around the side of Komekes' workshop putted Ford's trail bike—minus Ford. Instead, Del sat astride, bad-ass in jeans and tee shirt, a black helmet on his head.

How did she know the man was Del, sitting there with the cords in his forearms flexing as he revved the throttle? Because unlike with Ford or any other guy around, she wanted to run her hands all over Del's body and squeeze his deliciously firm butt.

But she totally wouldn't.

He flicked up the face shield, and cool blue eyes examined her. "Ladies."

Holly, who'd already bowled up to Del earlier in the week and introduced herself, hissed out the side of her mouth. "Look at that *asssss*!"

Then louder, so her voice carried above the bike's rumble, she said, "Ford's letting you ride his Honda?"

"I'm borrowing it to check out Mr. Nolan's place."

"Privileged," Holly said. "He won't lend out his baby to just anyone."

"What's out at Wally's?" Shaye focused on the helmet's chin guard. Less intense than Del's eyes, less tempting than the span of his shoulders under the snug fit of his shirt.

The helmet tilted to one side for a couple of beats. "Why don't you come with me?" He patted the seat behind him. "Plenty of room."

Her stomach dipped as if she'd miscounted stairs and stepped down two by accident. "I don't think so."

"Got a phone call from the States this morning. I'll tell you about it after we get to Shearwater Bay."

A phone call? *The phone call?* Her heart beat a little faster. The blue eyes below the helmet edge gave nothing away. Hell. He'd tell her later—she'd make him—but the thought of being pressed up against that strong, masculine body? She stepped back, colliding with Holly, who stood positioned behind Shaye.

Holly's palms braced on Shaye's waist to stop her retreating farther. "Remember your horoscope this morning—an unexpected journey!"

Crinkles appeared around Del's eyes. "I'm not going to beg, Shaye." His rough voice issued both a challenge and a caress.

What would it be like to have him beg? She shivered, every cell in her body drawn to the temptation he offered.

Holly gave her another shove forward. "Go, you big Hobbit!"

"All right, all right. A quick ride," she agreed. "We're fully booked tonight."

The crinkles deepened before disappearing as he slapped the face shield down. "Come on, Bilbo. Let's blow this joint."

Shaye rolled her eyes and hustled into the garage to get another helmet.

A few minutes later, she swung onto the bike, keeping her touch on Del's shoulders light and impersonal. Kinda hard to stay impersonal when your thighs and boobs were bound to get snugged up against him. Ford's smaller Honda would be a different experience to the times she'd gone for a blast with West on his BMW. Something she should've considered before impulsively agreeing to this ride.

Del flicked up the kickstand, and the bike wobbled under her added weight.

"Er, when did you ride a bike last?"

"Been a while, I guess." He eased forward to give her more room.

Shaye felt like an octopus with too many arms—what was she supposed to hold onto? Him? "This is such a bad idea."

A warm hand snaked up to grab her wrist. Del tugged her closer, placing her hand on his hip. "Can't change your mind now, so you'd better trust me—and hang on."

The bike lurched forward, and they were off. Shaye fisted his tee, her knuckles brushing lean muscle. The hell with it—gravel rash wasn't an attractive option. She plastered herself to his big body as the bike picked up speed. Breasts smooshed against Del's broad back, thighs hugging his, she made like a limpet.

Due South and the primary school blasted past them in a blur.

"Okay?" he asked at a yell as they rounded the first corner.

Her hands moved from clenching his shirt to wrapping around his stomach.

"My life's flashing before my eyes, but yes," she hollered. "It's all good."

He laughed. A genuine, from the gut, *I'm glad to be alive* laugh. The first time she'd heard it. And oh, *myyyy...*

His laugh was like gooey caramel hidden in the center of a surprise muffin; you didn't know how good it was until you got a taste of buried sweetness. She clung tighter—one percent of the reason was the bike hurtling around another corner, the other ninety-nine because she loved the feel of his hardness and warmth.

All too soon, they reached Shearwater Bay. A few locals in their yards waved them past, and on a rocky outcrop beneath the low cover of trees, a small group of fishermen took advantage of the changing tide. Two kayakers cut through the dull emerald ocean, their paddles flicking up plumes of sparkling water.

Del eased back on the throttle, and Shaye regretfully untangled her arms from around him. They coasted by a few more properties right on the beach front, until the road abruptly ended—with Wally Nolan's shoe-box-shaped house.

Nestled against an impenetrable wall of variegated green bush and trees, the single-story house stood well apart from its nearest neighbors. Del rolled to a stop outside and killed the engine. Shaye clambered off the bike and removed her helmet, straightening her now wonky ponytail.

Del stood beside her, removing his helmet and holding his hand out for hers. "Hasn't changed much and he wasn't wrong about it needing a new coat of paint."

Even from the road, the beach house looked neglected, with paint flaking off the clapboard sides, and the dark blue window trim faded and chipped. Shaye crossed the soft sand to the deck. Two sets of glass sliding doors featured at the front of the house, reflecting the pewter clouds gathered over the distant Ulva Island.

She cupped a palm to the first door and peered inside. Circular dining table and chairs, a battered green couch, and a functional but sparse kitchenette. Two doors led off the main room, one to a bathroom, she assumed, the other—she moved sideways along the deck to where Del had arrived at the second doors—yep, a bedroom. Complete with a set of bunk beds.

Del turned toward her and tapped on the glass. "Dibs on the top bunk."

The corners of her mouth twitched up in an automatic smile. She got it. "Oh. You're going to rent Wally's place?"

Del edged past her and moved to the spot she'd vacated, looking in on the living area. "If we can come to an agreement."

"For how long? Wait—you said you heard from the States. Ethan Ward?"

He nodded, dug a hand into the pocket of his jeans, and pulled out a keyring. He slotted a key in the door and unlocked it. "Rang me about an hour ago. I'm in."

The grin he shot over his shoulder before he slid the door open stripped her defences bare.

"You got through? They're coming out to film?" She hurried inside after him, considered removing her shoes but after one look at the grimy, sand-speckled floor, she changed her mind.

Del poked through the kitchen, opening and closing doors. "Ethan and his crew are arriving later in the month. I haven't heard any more of the details. His people were going to call my people." He yanked open a cabinet and removed a cast iron skillet, holding it up to the tiny window over the sink for closer examination. "All very Hollywood, as you'd expect."

Running a fingertip over the dusty counter top, Shaye grimaced. "Now you've got to clear it with West and your dad?"

He placed the skillet back where he'd found it and shut the orange painted door, then straightened to pin her with a stare. "Can I count on your support?"

Shaye leaned a hip against the counter, folded her arms. "It's just going to be you and Ethan in the kitchen, right?"

He frowned, mirroring her posture at the counter's other end. "You know, I'm not a hundred percent sure. I'd assume most of the time it'd be me and Ethan. But the crew would want a glimpse of the restaurant in action."

"Ugh. Not cool. I hate the idea of being in front of a camera."

"Your mom was an actress; didn't you ever want to take to the stage or screen?"

"Mum says the camera adds ten pounds to skinny women, thirty to the rest of us." She twisted a strand of her ponytail. "I always thought it a miserable way to live, worrying what lumps and bumps the camera would show. So, no, I never wanted to be an actress." She let go of her hair and fiddled with the hem of her top. "But my little bit of vanity won't get in the way of Due South's need for good publicity."

"The camera'll love you, you're beautiful."

He moved closer, and her scalp prickled as a static charge zipped between them.

"And I happen to like your lumps and bumps. The camera mightn't see the real you, but I do."

She should've shoved him aside with sarcasm. A "Puh-lease" and an eye-roll. Del didn't see her as anything but a pain in his ass. Or, since her ego could use a boost, she conceded he was attracted to her—in an *I have boy bits, you've got the corresponding girl bits* kind of way. Guys like him called women beautiful the same as they labeled a sports car or a fine cut of sirloin.

She opened her mouth to say, "You don't see the real me at all," but he closed the remaining distance to zero. Words spun away as he touched his lips to her cheek. It wasn't quite a kiss—but definitely not a brotherly peck. Just a soft brush of his mouth, the last kind of touch she expected from the bad-ass Del Westlake.

And it stopped her heart for a second.

He pulled away far enough for her to see her dazed expression in the endless blue of his eyes.

"Tell me no."

Shaye blinked. "Huh?"

"Tell me not to kiss you."

She breathed him in. A hint of soap with a whiff of petrol he must've spilled while refueling the bike, but mostly sun-warmed male skin, throbbing with testosterone.

Her hand trembled, and she placed it on his chest, spreading her fingers wide over his shirt. Heat burned through the thin cotton fibers and the rapid thud of his heart throbbed against her palm, beating in time with her own.

"Please kiss me, Del." She slid her hand along his collarbone to his neck, skimming over the first prickles returning along his jawline, fingertips tingling. "Pretty please." She raised her other hand to cup his face. "With a damn cherry on top."

His eyes crinkled at the corners, and her heart flipped in a series of summersaults. God, that smile. Those eyes. *Him.*

Swaying forward on tip-toe, she tilted her chin. He misjudged the angle of her mouth and bumped her nose.

"Smooth move, Hollywood," she murmured.

The rumble from his throat could have been a laugh or a growl. Didn't have time to decipher it before his mouth descended on hers—hard, hot, and very, very smooth.

He kissed like a man starved, and she was a dessert bar. The flicker of his tongue against hers danced fire through her resistance. She melted, pouring herself into him. Her fingers thrust into his hair—keeping his lips locked in place. She opened to him, holding nothing back, offering him control to wield as he liked. And he took control, sealing their mouths together as if it would take a crowbar to part them.

Closer. More. Deeper.

He surrounded her with hard warmth, and she held on, the feel of her body—breast to thigh pressed tight to his—doing liquefying things to her bones.

Not just a kiss. Not even close.

Then she was sitting on the countertop, Del's big hands gripping her butt from where he'd lifted her. Her fingers clawed his shoulders, her legs hugging his hips, pulling him in, locking his lower body hard against her, and his mouth—*ohdearGod*—the man kissed like a demon and angel combined. To hell with *just a kiss*; she'd become a glutton wanting more.

She wrestled up the hem of his shirt, sliding her hands across miles of silky skin, tracing down the strong line of his spine. He pulled away, teeth catching her bottom lip in the softest of nips. Del repeated her name twice before her brain registered his mouth wasn't returning. Blue, blue eyes had turned a smoldering shade of thundercloud grey.

"Shaye. We can't."

The length of steely male trapped between her legs said *oh yes we can.*

She shifted her hips fractionally, rubbing against him. His ragged moan nearly compensated for the ache spiraling up from her core. His hands tightened on her and stroked down her thighs. Then he backed away.

"God."

Del's Adam's apple bobbed as he stood watching her. Watching her want him, panting for him like an inexperienced school girl who'd never been kissed before. *Hah.* The joke was on her—because she never *had* been kissed like that before.

Her cheeks burned as they continued to stare at each other.

"I shouldn't have done that," he said.

"Why?" Because she was inexperienced and waaay out of his league? Because while in her head that kiss would've registered off the Richter scale, for him it was more *meh* than earth-shattering?

Del must've caught the indignation in that one word, since his lips curved again in that damn sexy smile.

"Now I've had a taste of you, cupcake, I want more. Not only the frosting." He gestured down at himself, and like an obedient little hussy, she followed with her gaze.

Holy hell, the man packed some serious equipment in those jeans. Some seriously heavy-duty equipment. It took her at least five seconds to drag her gaze up to eye level.

She cleared her throat. "Maybe I want more than frosting, too."

Like the whole damn island's supply of frosting spread over his naked bod.

He rubbed his neck with a palm. "I can't offer you anything more than a—"

She hopped off the counter and jabbed a finger at his stomach, which hurt, dammit, because the man had some rock hard abs under his shirt. "I'm not asking for more than a..."

His eyes hooded and flared hot, and her voice stuttered to a halt.

"More than a quick fuck?" he said quietly. He grabbed her hand, cupping it loosely in his. "You're not the type of girl who should hook up with a guy like me."

"As I'll only be a quick, mindless fuck, right?"

He squeezed her fingers then, and let go. "Nothing like that. But tell me, how many years did you continue to send me letters when I left Oban?"

Oh, crap. He'd received the pages of handwritten letters she'd sent? She tilted her chin. "I forget."

"Up until you were fifteen. They stopped after your father died."

"You never answered a damn one."

"No." He shook his head, but his eyes never left hers. "I didn't know what the hell to say to you. We weren't buddies like West and Piper were. I couldn't understand why you kept sending them. Little tidbits of island gossip. What books you were reading. What the other kids did during the Christmas holidays. I finally figured it out."

"Did you?" Her voice flattened. She remembered now. The first Sunday of the month was *write to Del* day, the sad-eyed boy she'd hoped to make laugh again.

"You couldn't let me go."

"*Then*. I couldn't let you go *then*. I was a kid, and I guess I held on to you the same way I've held on to all my favorite childhood books and my Barbie doll collection. I won't be holding on to you this time." She forced her lips into a smile. "Sorry to pop your giant ego. Hell, when you leave after the wedding, I won't even send you an e-mail."

He chuckled. "Giant ego aside—sex complicates things. Especially for people who work together."

She arched a brow. "I haven't even decided if I *want* to sleep with you."

"Smart girl. You should slap my face now and walk away."

She tilted her head. "This, from a man who's probably slept with more than one employee in his life...Is there something else going on here? Is there—?" The thought blazed into her mind like napalm. "Is there *someone else*? In LA—"

Del flinched, closed his eyes for a moment. *Ohmygawd.* Of course the man had someone else. He wasn't a monk.

"Not exactly."

"What kind of answer is that?"

"I was seeing someone before I flew out here—it's complicated."

"Calling a relationship complicated is a cop-out. You're either in a relationship, or you're not."

"I'm not. Though I'm warning you, I'm a bad bet, so don't get attached."

His eyes clashed with hers, but there wasn't any deception in them, only finality. Topic shutdown initiated. He brushed past her and crossed the kitchen to the single bedroom, poking his head through the open doorway. "Haven't slept in a bunk since West and I used to fight over your brother's top one."

Shaye joined him. The bedroom contained one double bunk and a couple of battered dressers. Perfect for a little family get-away, interesting choice for a single man planning to rent the place. Her cheeks ignited, imagining the two of them rolling around on the bunk bed.

"I never saw you sleep in Ben's top bunk." She kept her gaze well away from his.

"West being two years older and Ben's mate, he scored that right whenever we stayed over. I got it once, though—they dared me to run naked along Honeymoon Bay beach late one Friday night."

"That was *you*?"

His gaze zipped to her, and she giggled.

"Kidding," she said.

Del grinned, and the power of this unexpected truce between them punched heat fast and low into her belly. Such dangerous territory. She retreated out the door and walked back toward the kitchen.

"Ah, cupcake?"

She glanced over her shoulder.

"You might want to..." He demonstrated by brushing his hands down his butt and giving her a pointed look. "That counter I nearly had you on needs a clean."

Her face grew even hotter. From a dusty bottom or from the truth of his words? If they hadn't needed to return to Due South for evening prep, likely he would've had her there on the counter. Dust or not.

She stalked outside, swiveling to face away from him while she swiped the dust off her pants.

"You could always volunteer to be a one-woman cleaning crew. Kind of like a house-warming gift." He stepped onto the deck with her and locked the door.

"Do your own cleaning, Hollywood."

He shrugged and jogged down the steps and across to the bike. She couldn't help but stare at the long line of his body moving so gracefully.

"Worth a try." He shot her another knees-to-Jello smile.

Shaye snorted but walked over and grabbed the helmet he offered. She jammed it on her head then climbed onto the bike, her teeth clenching as their bodies fitted snugly together.

Dammit.

She knew exactly what she wanted to give him for a housewarming gift. And it had nothing to do with cleaning and everything to do with his kitchen counter, the faded green couch, or even the double bunk.

Chapter 8.

Claire ambushed Del before he'd opened Due South's back door. He'd dropped Shaye off and returned the bike and key, and if his brain hadn't been fogged with the constant replay of their smoking-hot kiss, he might've spotted his mother sooner.

"Del? A word, honey?" she called out from the cottage gate.

He glanced down at West's dog, Donny, a one-eared Staffy cross, curled up in his basket.

"You could've given me a warning bark or something, buddy," he muttered. Donny tilted his head to one side and whined. "Too little too late."

He strode across the parking lot. Might as well get over whatever lecture she had in mind. Bill probably complained about Del running out earlier, instead of slaving alongside the old man.

"Bridge ladies still there, Mom?" he asked when he got within talking distance.

"They've all gone; it's safe." Claire smiled, tucking a strand of greying hair behind her ear. "Your father's napping in his room, but I wanted to catch you before dinner service."

"I need to get—"

Claire held up a palm. "I know, Del, and I won't take much of your time. But if I put off asking this anymore, I'll completely lose my nerve." She chewed on her bottom lip, something she hadn't done since Lionel got so sick.

His gut cramped, searing away all the feel-good fuzzies of finally getting his hands and mouth on Shaye.

"Just ask, Mom."

She sucked in a huge breath and gusted it out. "I want you to take a blood test to see if you're donor compatible."

The brain fog froze to ice crystals, and he stared numbly at her earnest expression as she continued talking.

"West and I have been tested, but we're not suitable matches. Bill's on the public donor system, but a family member's his best chance."

"You expect me to donate a kidney?" Sure, it wasn't a completely unforeseen request. Not with West and his mother's covert glances every time he and Bill were together.

"Honey, I don't expect you to do anything. I hoped you'd want to." She sighed. "I know you and Bill still have issues, but he's your father."

"Lionel was more my father than Bill Westlake." He could barely say the words.

She flinched then straightened her spine, planting her feet wide in her *now you've made me mad* stance. "And what do you think Lionel would say about this if he were still alive?"

"But he's not." His stepfather not being around remained a dull ache behind Del's breastbone.

"No, and my heart grieves for him every day. Here's the thing—Lionel called you son, and he meant it. I know you loved him, that you would've donated a kidney or any other body part to save his life."

He nodded, unable to put into words the measures he would've gladly gone through to save his stepfather's life. The ache transferred into a sharp, stabbing pain. "I'm sorry, Mom."

"Do you remember what he did to you the first time he heard you bad-mouthing your father to one of your buddies?"

He'd called Bill an ignorant asshole who didn't give a shit about anyone but himself. That'd been a few weeks before the end of his senior year, when he discovered his father wasn't flying out to see him graduate. "Got me up at 5:00 a.m. every day for a month to run five miles with him."

"The next time he caught you running your mouth about Bill, it was ten."

Del couldn't hold back a smile. "Lionel was one tough sonofabitch."

Claire just looked at him.

Del hooked his fingers into a belt loop. "Shit. I'll take the damn test." He glanced up at his mother's face. "But I'm not making any promises about handing him my kidney on a platter."

She squeezed his arm. "One step at a time. Remember what Lionel used to say, 'Don't go looking for trouble—'"

"Because trouble already has your name and number, kid. Yeah, yeah." Impulsively, he bent down and kissed her cheek. "Look, I need to talk to Bill and West about something tonight. Why don't you make that peach cobbler Bill loves, soften him up a little."

She rolled her eyes. "Funny, I remember cobbler being more your favorite when you were a boy.'"

"Maybe I haven't lost my taste for sweet things, after all. I'll stop in after service later."

He turned toward Due South, his mind circling around the memory of tasting Shaye's kisses—the sweetest things ever.

***

"Think you nailed it," said Shaye.

Del glanced at her as they crossed the parking lot to Due South.

"Nobody threw anything, swore at anyone, or threatened to cut off a body part," she added. "The Westlake family negotiation skills are improving."

He grunted. While Bill hadn't been ecstatic at the idea of Ethan Ward presenting Due South in a less-than-positive light, West, Claire, and even Shaye, had changed his opinion with very little drama. A scary indicator that his father had lost some of his iron-clad will to run things his way.

After a few minutes of swapping arguments, Bill had thrown up his hands. "If West thinks it's a good idea, we'll run with it."

If West thinks it's a good idea.

Del touched his tongue to the inside of his cheek, still raw from when he'd bitten down the urge to tell Bill his younger son's reasoning was as sound as his eldest's.

And God-fucking-dammit, give me some credit for not being a moron.

They walked into the kitchen, Del scanning to make sure everything was in order since they'd left Vince and Fraser completing the final clean up. He snuck another glance at Shaye, who still appeared fresh as a proverbial daisy in a pretty yellow tee shirt she'd worn under her chef's jacket. The shirt clung to all the right spots, and he dragged his gaze away before he got caught ogling his sous's rack. Again.

"Hey." He touched her elbow before she could disappear upstairs. "Buy you a wine? The pub's open for another hour, and Ford's playing. He's pretty good and music soothes the savage breast so they say..."

And now he was babbling, somewhat like a moron.

She paused by a counter and folded her arms. "I'm not much of a wine drinker."

"Beer?" He tried on his most charming smile. "Like your sister?"

She shook her head.

"Fancy cocktail? I hear Kip makes a good Slippery Nipple?" Aiming for a smile to replace the frown lines on her forehead.

Instead, one delicate eyebrow rose.

He was completely screwing this up, but he just needed to spend a little more time with her tonight.

"Ah." He edged closer. Fired off his patented *I'm a moron but still kinda appealing* smile. "Not a cocktail type. I bet you're a top shelf woman—Jack and Coke—am I right?"

Her eyes flared wide, and her lips pinched tightly together in a narrow white line.

What had he said? "No?"

Shaye shook her head and kept her eyes downcast, a pulse at the base of her throat working overtime. He rubbed his hands down her arms, along the goosepimples raised on her soft skin. She didn't pull away, but her muscles were tense as razor wire.

"What did I say?"

Her breath continued to snuffle in and out of her nose. Oh shit, had he made her cry?

"Help a guy out; at least let me know what I've said to piss you off."

She looked up with a small twisted grimace. "I'm not pissed off at you, Del. I'm just not much of a drinker. Not wine, or beer, or Slippery Nipples"—she gave a choked laugh at that—"and especially not Jack and Coke." She took another deep breath and met his gaze. "The other night, when I said my Dad made bad decisions? One of those decisions was getting drunk the night before he went diving with Piper."

"But your dad never drank alcohol because of his cholesterol medication—ah." Light bulb moment. "He had a reaction with his pills underwater. Shit, I'm sorry..."

Shaye shook her head, and his voice trailed off.

"He was never on any pills. Dad was an alcoholic—but sober for more than fifteen years. He used the medication excuse with his mates, so he could stick to non-alcoholic drinks Friday night at the pub."

Michael had been an alcoholic? An alcoholic who'd gone on a bender and paid the price. Like he'd paid a price the last time he'd gone on a bender with Jessica and ended up proposing. God, if Shaye knew about the last year of his life...

Del's heart tripped and righted itself into a full-out sprint. "So, your dad had been drinking that night?"

"Piper says the alcohol still in his system the morning he drowned would've affected his judgment. Diver error." She shrugged, a world of hurt in the movement. "Or he could've had a heart-attack, or a stroke, or any number of things might've gone wrong. We'll never find out what really happened."

"No one in your family knew about his problem?" He moved and leaned against the counter, his hip barely a few inches from hers.

"Mum knew," she said quietly. "And after his death we cleared out his office and found a half-empty bottle of whiskey stashed in a cupboard."

Fucking hell. "Jack Daniels, by any chance?"

She nodded, stared straight ahead as if the swinging doors contained the answers to all the questions she no doubt wanted to ask her father. "We never told anyone. Mum thought people should remember him as a good man. Not an alcoholic who ruined his life and the lives of his family."

Del winced. "Jesus."

Shaye would've been fifteen when all this happened. Kind of a dramatic warning about the dangers of excess alcohol.

"It's okay; I'm not a complete teetotaler. I like a glass of bubbly on special occasions." Her smile was fake and wide, almost embarrassed. "But I'm more a juice or soda girl, and I'm a cheap drunk. A couple of glasses of wine and I'm anyone's."

"Anyone's, huh?" He gently nudged her elbow.

"Even tipsy, I still have my standards." She stuck her nose in the air, but the sassy 'tude was missing.

"Good to hear. How about I buy you a virgin whiskey and Coke instead?"

Needy, much? When had he ever cajoled a woman into having a drink with him? Hell, when had he last cared if a drink offer got turned down?

Apparently, he cared now, because as Shaye moved away, his stomach clenched low and hard.

"I'll take a rain check, but thanks."

His mouth opened to say something charming enough to change her mind. Except she looked at him with those big hazel eyes—bloody *Bambi* eyes—filled with stirred-up grief and unbearable weariness, and he couldn't think of a damn thing.

She was so beautiful. And so sad.

Del inclined his head. "Goodnight, then."

Shaye left him in the echoing silence of Due South's kitchen. Alone with his thoughts. Alone with his guilt. Alone with a need for her he should immediately nip in the bud. Because the last person Shaye needed was a man who'd also let alcohol make wrong decisions for him.

***

The thing about spending the night in an unfamiliar house was waking up wondering where you were.

Raucous squawks, warbles, and tap-tap-tapping on the corrugated iron roof heralded Del's first morning of tenancy at Walter's beach house. He'd moved out of West's spare room after work the night before, and got him to drop Del and his bags off at Shearwater Bay.

"The hell?" He flung out a hand to grab his watch from the nightstand and smacked his knuckles against unyielding metal. "Fuck!"

Del whimpered since no one was around to hear his pathetic-ness and cradled his probably broken fingers. Goddamned ladder where the nightstand should be. He located his watch—on his wrist, dumbass—and squinted at the lit-up digits. Fifty-five minutes past five.

"Kidding me."

The sky outside was hazy with predawn, the low line of breakwater the only white in the landscape of grey. He could do with some blackout drapes. Shit outta luck there.

Another screech and flurry of wings. His feathered visitor strutted along the deck railing outside, paused, and cocked its head. Squawked.

An *I know you're in there* squawk.

As a kid, he'd wondered how the tourists could think the kakas were adorable with their rowdy antics—while he'd always thought they were the patched gang members of the parrot family.

And they sucked as reliable alarm clocks.

"Piss off, bird." He flipped onto his back and scissor-kicked inside the confines of his borrowed sleeping bag. Bending an elbow over his eyes, he tried to recapture the dream he'd been having about squeezing Shaye's lush breasts.

Squawk! Then tappity-tap against the window glass.

Del unzipped the sleeping bag and rolled off the mattress. After glaring at the sliding door for a few moments while the kaka shrieked and flapped, he got to his feet and staggered out to the kitchen.

Dust still coated every surface, including the old-fashioned kettle on the four-ring gas hob. He figured dust in his coffee would be the least of his problems. The place was a pigsty. But at least he was blissfully alone—he could walk around in his damn underwear if he wanted to. Del glanced at his bare stomach and low-riding plaid boxers. And he *did* want to.

Coffee made, he wandered over to the dining table and dragged out a chair. The feathery gang member continued to march up and down the railing.

Tough, bird brain. I'm not feeding ya.

The distant rumble of an engine rose over the gentle hiss of waves. Then headlights cut through the gloom and bounced off his windows, making him squint. *What the hell?* Car doors slammed—too close to be a neighbor's unexpected morning visitors.

Which meant they were his.

Del stalked to the glass door and slid it open, dull light from the single hanging bulb in the room spilling out over the deck.

"Bro." His brother stood on his front lawn with a power-tool of some kind in one hand and a bucket of cleaning supplies in the other. "Put your pants on. There are ladies present."

Sure enough, drawing up the rear were Piper and Shaye. Also the bulk of Ford and Ben, the latter of whom looked surlier than usual—which said a lot. The kaka screeched in happy greeting and flapped its wings. Del sipped his coffee, remaining rooted to the spot against the doorframe. Standing in his boxers before seven in the morning with a bat-shit crazy bird doing the Harlem Shake on his deck...frickin' awesome start to his half-day off.

"What are you all doing here?" he said.

"Cleaning crew," Shaye replied.

Her gaze seemed fixed somewhere off to his right, while Piper smirked at him, unrepentantly scanning him from head to toe.

"It was Shaye's idea," Piper said. "She promised to cook us a bang-up full breakfast if we came and gave you a hand."

"She did, huh?"

Ford rattled the plastic bottles in one of the buckets he carried. "Yep. More supplies are in the van. So stop parading your skinny white ass about, and let's go."

Skinny white...Del narrowed his eyes. Why were they really here? He switched his glare to Shaye. With one hand busy clutching a mop and broom, she stopped examining the kaka and looked over. He raised a querying eyebrow.

"Think of it as a barn-raising, like in the States," she said.

"There are no barn-raisings in Venice Beach."

And if there had been, no one would've bothered to show up to help him raise squat. With the exception of his stepsister, Carly. She would've had his back.

"You're not in LA anymore," growled Ben. "Around here, we help each other out."

West crossed the sand and climbed the steps to the deck. "Shaye told us what a mess Wally's place is in. It's too much for you to do alone. We'll help." When Del continued to glare, West leaned forward and murmured, "Delly, it's cold out. The underwear thing isn't doing you any favors and we're not going anywhere. Get some frickin' pants on."

"*Fine-but-don't-call-me-Delly.*" Realizing he sounded like the world's most ungrateful dickhead, he added, "I appreciate it, guys. The kettle's still hot if anyone wants coffee."

He spun around and stalked inside, deliberately keeping his eyes off Shaye but unable to stop wondering if she was checking out his ass.

And if she liked what she saw.

Two hours later, filthy with dust and grime but having made big inroads into creating a liveable house, Del left Ben, West, and Ford preparing the southern outside wall—Ben and Ford commandeering the two borrowed electric sanders, since he and West lost the coin toss. The guys ordered Del inside to be Piper and Shaye's cleaning bitch. He walked in the door and Piper's swearing cascaded out of the bathroom in a creative monologue. West wasn't the only one to lose a coin toss.

He poked his head into the bathroom. On her hands and knees, Piper scrubbed the ancient shower stall.

"Need a hand?"

She glanced up and swiped a pink rubber glove-covered wrist across her forehead. The glove left behind a streak of grime on her skin. Del pressed his lips together. If her aim was half as good as Shaye's, he'd end up with a scrubbing brush between the eyes.

Piper blew out a breath, ruffling the short strands of her bangs—except the one clump covered in grey goop. "Nah. Not enough room to swing a cat in here. Go help my little do-gooder sister."

Del grinned and backed out. He found Shaye quartering mushrooms in the tiny kitchen, along with the delicious smell of frying bacon. The kitchen counter gleamed, Piper and Shaye having elected to tackle it first. The sparkling countertop didn't have half the fascination for him as recalling the softness of her lips, the sweet taste of her mouth, and the lush curves beneath his hands. Red-hot memories. Nothing he should dwell on before he'd even had his second morning coffee.

"A working-man's breakfast." He sauntered around to the other side of the counter and rested his palms on the cool surface.

She focused on the wooden chopping board. "Get your dirty paws off my clean food-prep area."

Del raised his hands and turned sideways, leaning a hip against the counter instead. She scraped off the mushrooms into a waiting bowl, whirled around to the stove, and neatly flipped the bacon rashers over—in a twelve-inch cast aluminum fry pan.

"Where did that come from?"

Shaye speared a glance over her shoulder. "What?"

"The fry pan." He narrowed his eyes at the pot simmering on the back ring. "And the pot? And those?" He gestured to the set of stoneware bowls lined up and filled with chopped mushrooms and onion rings. "This stuff wasn't here last night."

She placed the tongs down on a white side plate—another item not part of his rental property's mismatched china and crappy pots and pans.

"I brought them with me this morning. You can use them while you're here."

"I can get by with the cast iron pan and a couple of pots."

"I threw them all out in the shed." She looked down her nose at him.

"What? Why?"

Actually, he'd planned to do the same thing. Petty of him to hate admitting she was right.

"Mouse poop." Her lip curled. "And you couldn't do squat with those awful, cheap pots."

"I won't be hosting a formal dinner party." He was still reeling over everyone showing up this morning. "They're yours?"

She opened the oven door, transferring the strips of bacon onto a waiting tray. "Yep."

"Taking the Good Samaritan act too far, aren't you?"

And why his mouth still spoke Assholish instead of saying thanks, he had no idea. He wasn't used to little kindnesses. Kinda creeped him out.

She straightened, shutting the oven door. "Gift horse, mouth, don't look. Mean anything to you?"

He grunted and shook his head. "You're not using them?"

"No, they've been in storage since I moved out of Kezia's spare room. I don't need them while I'm staying at Due South, so I thought you'd appreciate something decent for a few weeks."

"You were living with Kezia?"

"Until she and Ben got together. Before that, I shared a place with Holly after I'd come back from Invercargill. Before my course, I was at home with Mum."

"You've never lived by yourself?"

"What can I say? I'm an extrovert. I like being around people, and for a long time I needed to be around the house for Mum." She pressed her lips together, as if she'd said too much.

"After your dad died."

"Yeah. Somebody had to pick up the pieces." She smiled at him tightly, the shadows in her eyes making her appear far older than her years. "Mum couldn't cope with even the simplest of things for a long time, so I took over the cooking. It helped. Her—and me." She shot him a pointed look. "You'll need to cook while you're here, Del. You can't not cook. Trust me, I know."

An icy fist locked onto his spine. Couple of days without kitchen therapy and he'd go as crazy as that bird out there.

Del moved around the counter, careful not to encroach in her space. He hated it on the odd times he'd friends over for a meal and they insisted on hovering, staring as if he was a magician about to produce a bunny from a hat.

Cooking wasn't magic, it was part of him—it was his purpose, it was like fucking *breathing*. A magician could choose to stop performing tricks; Del couldn't imagine a life without a pan in one hand and a knife in the other. Some days, he wondered if cooking was the only thing keeping him from drowning in the bottom of a bottle.

He rolled his shoulders. *Lighten up, Delly.* He had that under control now.

"So your mum's doing okay?"

"Much better." She dumped the mushrooms into a six-inch pan. "She's got all three of her chicks on the island, and with Piper's and Ben's weddings to plan—she's in maternal-heaven."

"And you're bridesmaid for both."

Pretty hazel eyes rolled to the ceiling. "Oh, you're not starting with that dreadful cliché about bridesmaids, are you?"

"The last single Harland girl..." He grinned.

"Who is quite happy to wait for her Mr. Perfect, thanks." Shaye picked up a wooden spoon to stir the mushrooms.

Was she for real? *Mr. Perfect?* "You expecting him to show up any time soon?"

"I keep telling her to settle for a Mr. *Gotta-job-and-all-his-teeth*," Piper said from behind him. "But, you know, she's choosy."

Shaye arrowed a ball-shriveling stare over his shoulder. "You didn't pick that knuckle-cracking, trivia nerd Shane Martin at Police College, so why should I settle for less than Mr. Perfect?"

Piper nudged him in the ribs. "Tell her she should give Kip another chance. He's a nice guy. Dare I say a *perfect* guy?"

Kip *was* a nice guy. A friendly, *good-looking-in-a-non-gay-way* kinda guy. And still Del's gut twisted at the thought of Kip kissing Shaye. Or putting his suave, *I can mix you a Slippery Nipple* hands on her. Del braced his spine. He'd no right to even an ounce of possessiveness. Kip was a hell of a lot closer to perfect than Del'd ever be.

"Maybe he is," he said through lips that felt tighter than a crossbow. "I hope you find your Mr. Perfect, Shaye."

"Aw..." Piper draped her arm around his shoulder and leaned her head against his. "Aren't you the sweetest thing?"

Shaye's brow crinkled, and she scowled. "Will you stop trying to fix me up with Kip?"

Del couldn't help himself. "Doesn't he check some of your boxes? Handsome, house-trained, Mom-approved?" Bland as rice pudding...

"Actually, he does fit many requirements on my list." One eyebrow quirked up. "I'll take that under advisement."

"Hmm." Piper placed a finger on her lips. "Maybe you need a man with more of an edge. Find a bad-boy—but not too bad, since I'm an ex-cop, and I don't want to commit homicide on your behalf."

Shaye stabbed the wooden spoon toward them. "Enough. Both of you out of my hair! Piper, go and check how the men want their eggs. Del, Mum donated some spare drapes for the bedroom—they're in the van."

"Come on then, future bro. Let's leave before she decides to spit in the baked beans."

Piper slipped her arm through his and tugged him out of the kitchen, even though he would've loved to stay and find out exactly what was on Shaye's list.

Chapter 9.

Be a bridesmaid, they said. It'll be fun, they said.

Shaye glared at her reflection in the private dressing room of Invercargill's Next Stop, Vegas bridal boutique. She'd been the last dress fitted, and it'd looked fab-u-lous. Piper and Kezia had already finished getting into their street clothes and had retired to the shop's rear garden patio with the owner and Holly's cousin, MacKenna Jones—MacKenna luring them away with champagne and chocolate-dipped strawberries.

With The Police's Every Breath You Take being piped throughout the boutique, and her friends occupied with glasses of bubbly, calling out for help would be pointless.

And dammit—did she ever need help to get out of this ridiculous predicament.

If she could only untangle herself from this hellish, toddler-sized full slip, which had jammed above her boobs, leaving her arms waving helplessly in the air...

Shaye wriggled some more, but nope. Good and stuck. So getting her beige support panties in a twist about it wouldn't help the situation.

"Effing cinnamon sticks!"

Shaye sucked in a deep breath and prepared for the humiliation of contorting her body to pry open the dressing room door to yell for assistance.

A light knock sounded behind her. OhthankyouJesus—MacKenna or her sister had finally come to check on her. "Get in here now! I'm stuck!"

The reflected door swung open, and Del stepped into the dressing room.

Their gazes clashed in the mirror—hers flared wide in shock, his turning smoky and hooded.

"Need some help?"

Oh, this was perfect. Just freaking fantabulous.

"Bugger off, Del."

His handsome face splitting into a cheeky grin, he shut the door and leaned against it with folded arms. "Now, that's not nice."

Every inch of skin—and unfortunately, she was displaying a lot of bare skin—sizzled as if it'd been dipped in liquid toffee. Hot but sweet, boiling toffee. Embarrassed as hell, she couldn't deny her libido had awoken with a hello-bad-boy purr.

Her back still to him, Shaye once more attempted to free herself from the Spanx stranglehold. The flailing only resulted in her boobs wobbling all over the place—and based on Del's pointer-dog attention, he enjoyed the show.

"Where's MacKenna and her assistant?"

A nonchalant shrug. "Don't know. Got sent here on an errand, but there's no one in the shop. I was tracking female laughter when I heard someone in distress." His grin grew wider. "Then you ordered me in."

Shaye huffed out a sigh. "A gentleman would close his eyes, leave, and go find the assistant."

"A gentleman would."

The click of the dressing room's lock was loud in the small space. Del closed the short distance between them. The warmth of his big body brushed every hair follicle to attention, her nipples pebbling behind the plain beige bra.

"But cupcake, I'm no gentleman."

A finger traced down the knobs of her spine, bumping over the catch of her bra, stopping at the waistband of her panties.

She shivered and closed her eyes. "You shouldn't be in here."

The finger changed into a hand, which skimmed up her waist and stroked over her ribs. He moved closer, and his shirt brushed against her. Cedar wood and basil with a hint of sea brine tickled her nostrils. Her elbows folded weakly and rested on the top of her head.

"Tell me to go now and mean it," he said. "I'll leave."

"Del..."

Feather-light kisses on her knuckles made her shiver more. "This is crazy."

"Yeah, it is." He rescued her ponytail from the Spanx's evil clutches, winding the thick hank around his fist and gently tilting back her head. "It's fucking nuts. But I can't stop thinking about you, and God, the memory of you like this will keep me aching for you all night."

"I look ridiculous."

"You're the hottest thing I've ever seen." The hand resting on her ribcage circled around to her stomach, pressing her lower body gently into his.

He was hard. All over. As if he'd flicked a switch, her muscles lost all strength, and she sagged into him. The grip on her hips tightened, and she tried hard—really hard—not to grind her bottom against him. She only partially succeeded.

"Trust me; you're every red-blooded male's wet dream. Open your eyes."

"No."

His snicker was a soft puff on the curve of her neck. "C'mon, baby. I want you to see what I see."

She slitted her eyes at her reflection. Del cradled her from behind, his cheek resting against her hair, his body aligned with hers from chest to hip. Each deep inhale pushed her boobs into a dangerous spill-zone above the bra edge. Dropping her gaze, she saw his braced, denim-covered thighs flex as he supported more of her weight. The tan male hand contrasted with her insipid beige panties, his long fingers gripped possessively tight on her hip. His other hand snaked around to hover an inch from her right breast.

She swallowed past a throat clogged with lust and need. "Are you going to help me get this damn slip off?"

"Eventually. But why were you cramming your sexy body into this torture device?"

Torture device didn't do the beige horror justice. Right now, she'd happily burn it then set fire to its ashes. But while Piper was naturally tall and slender, and Kezia short, curvy and perfectly proportioned, Shaye had been cursed with never outgrowing her puppy-fat endowed boobs, hips, and ass. Spanx was both torture and blessed assurance that nothing would wobble under her bridesmaid's dress.

"The slip creates a smooth line under a clingy dress—and I thought men weren't interested in women's underwear unless they were trying to get them off?"

Del dropped his hand and splayed it high on her stomach, his thumb stroking delicious lines from the underwire of her bra down. Her mind blanked except for the repetitive mantra—little-bit-higher-little-bit-higher.

"I am trying to get them off."

In the mirror, his eyes crinkled and she caught a flash of a grin beyond her shoulder.

"I'd rather see you au-natural in a clingy dress. Screw the smooth lines; you're not a mannequin."

"Okay." Blame the single-syllable response on hormones exploding all over the place.

Okay? Okay, she wasn't a plastic mannequin? Okay, she'd go au-natural under her bridesmaid's dress? Or okay, he could strip off her underwear and take her hard and fast against the wall?

All of the above.

"Del..."

She tried again, but his fingers closed over her breast, gently rolling her nipple under her bra cup until she moaned, and her head dropped onto his shoulder.

Heat, raw and combustible, arrowed down from the sensitized peak to her core, and she squeezed her thighs together. A yank on the satiny fabric and cooler air rushed over her skin. Her nipple tightened to almost painful proportions.

Del hummed, a low and rough sound. "So pretty. A juicy little bud just waiting to be licked."

His fingers returned to the tip of her breast—teasing, tugging, driving her insane. She pushed into his erection, and he thrust his hips forward, grinding his thick length into the cleft of her bottom.

"Shhh, baby. That's all you get for now." His voice was a velvety whisper in her ear.

He returned the fabric of her bra cup over her breast, and before she objected, worked the stretchy slip over her head and tossed it across the room.

Shaye panted like a marathon runner, her heart pummeling the inside of her chest.

Del, still behind her, ran his hands up her arms. "You okay?"

Definitely.

Not.

Okay.

What had she done? Why had she allowed him to take her halfway to the edge of lustful madness, where she'd been about to beg him to do her and to hell with the consequences? Heat flared into her cheeks, and she dropped her gaze, which, dammit, didn't help one bit, since she discovered Del hadn't returned to "okay" either.

At least, the part of his anatomy filling out the front of his jeans hadn't.

Jittering-freaking-jalapeños.

She wasn't the town ho, but the men she'd fooled around with—and the select few she'd slept with—hadn't sexed her up on a kitchen counter or in a changing room. No, the men she'd been with were more tentative kisses and oh, look, a hand has crept under her shirt to fumble with her bra-catch type of men. The kind who asked earnest permission. The kind who turned on maybe two of her four burners, just enough to cook their own sausage as fast as possible.

She was waaay out of her depth with Del, since somehow, he managed to fire her up on all burners with a few kisses and caresses.

Dangerous stuff.

He cupped her chin and lifted it, forcing her to meet his gaze. Clear blue eyes bored into her. "I didn't mean to take advantage of you while you were helpless."

The corners of her lips quirked up. "Yeah, you did."

"Saw through me, huh?" His gaze flicked to her mouth. "You're right. And if I wasn't worried about Piper and Kezia crashing in here and sticking me with every one of those pins"—he gestured toward the loaded pin-cushion on a small corner table—"I'd have taken more advantage of you."

He dipped his head and kissed her, pulling away before she could wrap around him. But oh, how she wanted to.

Pressing his thumb to her lower lip, he stepped backward. "I'll see you at lunch then, cupcake."

And with a flash of a baby, you know you want me grin, he unlocked the dressing room door and slipped out.

Del yanked open the suit hire shop door, hoping he only looked the part of dutiful-best-man-back-from-the-groom's-errand—and not like a guy who'd had his hands on the bridesmaid's amazing breast and who'd nearly come in his boxers like a horny teenager.

Ben, slumped in one of the shop's chairs, pinned him with a speculative glance. "You get lost?"

"In a hurry to find the matching tie to your penguin suit, are you?" Del fished an envelope containing a fabric swatch out of his pocket and placed it on the shop counter.

He'd been lucky enough to exit the change room mere seconds before the shop assistant and Kezia came looking for Shaye. Luckier still, he'd managed to lose his raging hard-on by reciting his memorized Fahrenheit-to-Celsius oven conversions.

After the usual flurry of female excitement over the to-die-for color of the bridesmaids' dresses, Carolina Blue—which looked like plain old pale blue to him—MacKenna handed over an envelope and shooed him out the door.

Next time, he wouldn't trust Ben Harland with a coin toss. He wasn't complaining, all things considered. But Shaye's brother would tear him a new one if he found out what he'd done in the dressing room with his youngest sister.

"Fuck off," Ben said amicably. "It's bad enough having to wear a damn suit in the first place. Least you and me are finished. West's getting his inseam measured again"—he shuddered and crossed his ankles—"then it's lunch with my pretty lady."

Del sat in the chair beside Ben and gave him a shit-eating grin. "Maybe you should've bought the suit instead of hiring it."

Ben grunted. "Kezia says we'll have a low key wedding. No suit required."

Del said nothing, leaning his head on the wall behind them.

"Yeah. I'll be wearing a damn suit." Ben blew out a breath, and after a pause, chuckled. "She says low-key, but she deserves a fancy wedding like Pipe and West. So, that's what she'll get."

Del turned his head to the side. "Flowers and cake and fabric swatches and shit?"

Ben had a big, dopey-assed grin on his face. "Whatever she wants."

Jesus. Growing up, he'd been in awe of Ben. His brother's mate had no problem getting girls. During summer, Ben would go through the holiday-makers' teenage daughters like a kid in a candy store—pretty girls loved the whole brooding, Heathcliff thing. He hadn't been surprised over the years to hear Ben never settled down. But Ben with an eight-year-old daughter and taking on a widow and her little girl with gooey-eyed glee?

That was a kicker.

"She's a nice lady. Congrats, again."

West and the guys ribbed the hell out of Ben about his fiancée, but there were too many years spent away from his childhood friends for Del to do the same. The distance became acute whenever the conversation switched from easy subjects like fishing, rugby and poker, to topics like relationships. He was a brief interloper, gone a day or so after West's wedding. Not one of their inner circle of mates.

"You ever get married?"

Del shifted on the chair. "Nope. Not many women are willing to marry a man who works crazy late hours, six, sometimes seven days a week."

He'd come home more than once to find the woman who'd moved herself into his apartment had moved out again a few weeks later, leaving a shitty note stuck to his fridge—the only way to be sure he'd notice her absence.

"Never got close?"

Del slanted Ben a glance.

Ben raised his brows as if to say, "What?"

While he should've ignored the question, Del found himself answering. "I was engaged once."

A silent brain-snicker—look at him, male bonding with the groomsman.

"What happened? She figure out you were too high maintenance?"

"No, Dr. Phil. More a case of cold feet." Because he and Jessica had been toxic together—he just hadn't seen it at first.

Ben cracked his mouth open in a huge yawn. "Means you hadn't found your perfect match then."

A cold slick washed down Del's spine. What was it with the Harlands and their perfect? Something wrong with fucked-up-but-trying-to-be-a-better?

Del stood. "I'm going to check on West."

Ben slid his phone out of his pocket and stared at the screen. "Tell him to hurry up, I'm starving."

Thirty minutes later, Del found himself in an Italian bistro, surrounded by potted plants and a hideous mural of the Leaning Tower of Pisa. Why couldn't he sit next to the petite Kezia instead of being squashed between a wall and Ben? The big guy elbowed him in the ribs every time Del took a mouthful of mediocre zucchini tagliatelle.

He checked his last text message again.

Stumbling in on Shaye had almost made him forget the other purpose of this trip. A purpose he suspected would put him on West's shit-list for a while.

Del cleared his throat in a natural conversation lull. "Ah, West?"

West, on the opposite side of the booth, sandwiched between Shaye and Piper, looked up from his rigatoni.

"After lunch, I need to head out to the airport."

West chewed slowly. "Who've you got arriving? Someone from Ethan's crew scouting in advance?"

Del's fingers clenched around his knife and fork. "No, it's Carly. She's flying in from LA."

"Carly?" West said the name as if Del had announced a Vegas stripper wearing star-shaped pasties was on the flight.

"Our sister, remember?"

West straightened out of his relaxed slump. "Your sister, mate. Not mine."

Ben stiffened next to Del. Piper gave her fiancé a withering glance and shoulder-checked him.

"She wants to meet you, West. And Piper." Del's gut tightened, remembering the "Surprise! I'm in Auckland International Airport" phone call he'd received this morning.

While he and Carly used to be tight, Lionel dying had driven a wedge between them. She wanted to cling and talk, and he needed to work—and party to forget. He'd inadvertently hurt her more by pushing her away.

But for some weird reason, she loved him and wouldn't let him do that. Carly refused to give up their sibling bond, regularly showing up uninvited on his doorstep at 6:00 a.m. to drag him out of bed for a run, hangover or no hangover. Like hell would he turn her away now, when the catch in her voice over the phone told him she needed him.

"Aw," said Piper. "She's come all this way to meet the rest of her family."

West dropped his fork. "We're not related."

A point West made all those years ago when they'd hung out in LA. West refused to make the forty-minute drive with Del to Long Beach to visit their mother and Lionel. And Carly—who'd pretended she didn't give a shit, but was really crushed.

"She's got no one else," Del said. "With her dad gone and her grandparents dead, there's only a few scattered elderly relatives left."

West gave him a how is this is my problem look.

How long could his brother hold onto leftover bitterness? About as long as you can, good buddy, hissed a little voice in his ear. Tossing the thought into his fuck-it bucket, Del met West's gaze square on.

"Don't be a douche, darling." Piper slid her arm around West's waist and leaned her chin on his shoulder. "Carly had no say in what her dad and your mum did. Cut her a break."

West sighed and pressed a kiss onto Piper's short brown hair. "Where's she staying then?"

"Bunking down in Claire's room. Says she'll help out, so Mom doesn't get overwhelmed now Bill needs more care."

"Nice of her," West said stiffly.

"She's a nice person."

West grunted. "Piper and I have a few more wedding things to do around town before we head back to The Mollymawk. You take the car and pick her up."

Del kept his mouth shut. Hopefully, Piper would smooth out some of West's rougher edges before the trip to Oban. "Sure. Anyone else want to come for a ride?"

Kezia apologized and said she had school supplies to purchase, and Ben shrugged his beefy shoulders.

"I'll come," Shaye said. "She's about my age, isn't she?"

Del nodded.

"Another stray to add to your collection?" West said, stuffing a forkful of rigatoni in his mouth.

Shaye poked out her tongue. "Shut it, Westlake."

Conversation resumed, the awkward drama ending...for now. Even if she was stray collecting, a ribbon of warmth coiled through Del at Shaye's offer to accompany him to the airport. He swallowed a large gulp of water then crunched an ice cube between his teeth.

Don't get sappy now, the little voice in his ear warned.

Getting sappy over Shaye Harland came with a guarantee of disappointment and disaster.

Riding in cramped quarters with the guy who'd had a hand on your boob only hours ago was awkward, to say the least. Shaye ran through her entire repertoire of small talk during the short trip to Invercargill airport, terrified Del would raise the whole so, you're a D-cup gal topic. Fortunately, fiddling with dashboard knobs and buttons at every red light and stop sign kept him busy.

They found seats across from the arrival doors in the airport and sank into them. The moment they sat, Del's knee started bouncing.

"Aren't you happy about Carly flying in?" Shaye folded her arms to avoid the temptation to lay a soothing hand on his restless leg.

The bouncing immediately ceased.

"I am." He shot her a sideways glance. "I'm just hoping West won't continue the asshole ice treatment act after Carly gets here. He's hurt her before."

Ah. Piper had been on the receiving end of West's freeze-'em-out-behavior earlier in the year. Having worked with him for so long, Shaye knew the frosty outer shell he donned on occasion was his way of protecting himself.

"West'll come around. He's softened up a bit with your mum, hasn't he?"

Del blew out a breath. "I guess you're right."

Shaye reached over and squeezed his hand. "Get used to it, Hollywood. I'm always right."

A glimmer of affection flickered in his gaze, and he smiled, a panty-incinerating grin that flamed through her like Tabasco sauce, pooling low in her belly, firing her up. Again.

She so didn't need this moments before meeting Del's sister.

Shaye pulled her hand back and turned toward the now pinned-open arrival doors. People spilled through in haphazard dribs and drabs, and she scanned the female passengers for a feminine version of Del. She caught herself with a mental chuckle—Carly Gatlin wouldn't look anything like the Westlake brothers.

"There she is." Del stood, raising a hand in the air. "Carly!" he yelled.

Shaye followed the direction of his gaze to a woman dressed in khaki Capri pants and a slouchy, tie-dyed tee. Carly's face broke into a huge smile that almost touched the cascading waves of the prettiest auburn hair Shaye had ever seen.

Hoisting an enormous tote bag onto her shoulder, Carly crossed to them, her smile never shifting when she registered Del wasn't alone. She dumped her bag and wrapped her arms around him, balancing on her toes to give him a smacking kiss on the cheek.

Del pulled a face. "Jeez, Carly, quit it." But laughter tinged his voice, and he didn't struggle too hard to untangle himself. "Anyone would think we haven't seen each other in years."

"You love it." Carly peeled herself off Del and turned to Shaye. "My rude brother hasn't introduced us—"

Del threw up his hands. "I haven't had time."

"I'm Carly. Pleasedtomeetcha."

Shaye stuck out her hand. "I'm Shaye, Piper's younger sister."

Carly ignored her outstretched hand and enfolded Shaye in a spearmint, apple, and floral-perfume scented embrace.

"I'm a hugger, and now that my big brother West is marrying your sister, we're practically family."

Shaye hugged Carly in return, grinning at Del over her shoulder. "We practically are."

Del rolled his eyes and snagged the handles of Carly's giant bag. "If you're going to start singing We are Family, you can walk to Invercargill. We should collect your suitcase."

Carly let go of Shaye and stepped back. "Suitcase-es." She snatched her bag from Del. "Plural."

The three of them walked to the baggage claim. After Del pulled two big red suitcases and one smaller one off the conveyor belt, he said to Carly, "Why in God's name do you need three suitcases? Aside from the obvious fact you've no concept of the term pack light."

Carly turned away from him, her stunning, light brown eyes downcast. In the short time they'd been chatting while waiting for her bags, her smile had never slipped and her eyes hadn't stopped sparkling with excitement.

Carly extended the handle on the smaller suitcase and straightened her spine. "I'm going to stay a while."

"How long's a while?" said Del.

"I told you this morning, I've come to help Mom and your dad."

"Bill." Del yanked up the other two suitcase's handles. "And I still don't get why, when you don't even know the man." He shot his sister another glance. "Don't say because he's family."

Carly lifted a slim shoulder in reply.

"So, how long? A couple of weeks? Three?"

"Wanting to get rid of me already?" She turned her head to Shaye as they rolled the suitcases toward the exit. "My brother, so rude—but I guess you already know, since you're working with him."

Shaye made a non-committal noise.

"What about your job?" he said. "You can't just take off."

Carly stopped, dead center of the airport, ignoring the flow of people swirling around them. "I quit."

Del's eyes popped. "You fucking what?"

Now people gave their trio a wide berth. Shaye swallowed a grin. Kinda enjoyable, seeing Del thrown off balance by his little sister.

"Oh, stop with the drama queen act. It's not all about work, work, work, Del! I can get another job."

"You're twenty-five, not a teenager. Flight attendant jobs don't just drop into your lap."

Oh, crap. What did they say about redheads? Fireworks eminent...

"So, I'll do something else." Instead of smacking Del upside the head with her over-sized handbag, Carly cocked her hip and didn't even raise her voice. "I'll get a job where I don't get barfed on or verbally abused. A job where I don't have to miss my friends and family because of screwy schedules. And Mom's been in Oban for months, and now you're there, too." Her breathing hitched, and her eyes teared up. "I miss Dad and Mom and you so much. I'm freakin' sick of being alone."

Shaye's eyes stung in sympathy. Yeah, okay, sue her. She did have a thing for strays.

Del pinched the bridge of his nose and huffed out a sigh. "Shit, Carly." Then he let go of the suitcases and reeled her in for a bear hug.

Carly clung to him and sniffed, making Shaye's heart skip a little erratically at Del's unexpected tenderness buried beneath his outer layer of I don't do family jerktasticness.

After a few moments, Del patted Carly's shoulder and pulled away.

"I'm glad you're here," he said quietly. "But I didn't mean to give you the impression I was permanently moving to Oban. You shouldn't have quit your job. I'll be back in the US by mid-November."

Carly's brow crinkled. "Mom told me how sick your dad is. I thought you'd change your mind when you got here, you can't just leave—"

"We'll talk about this later." Del flicked a glance in Shaye's direction.

Could she feel any more like the third wheel? Definitely should've stayed with her sister.

"Don't mind me," Shaye said brightly. "I can wait over there."

Del grimaced. "Let's just go."

They walked outside into the crisp wind and crossed the parking lot to the car.

"Jeez, it's freezing." Carly hunched forward, tucking her handbag over her chest to block the wind. "I thought it was spring?"

"Welcome to the deep south," Del tossed over his shoulder as he popped the locks and hefted the first suitcase into the trunk.

The chill cut through Shaye's thin sweater, making her shiver uncontrollably. She should be happy Del was here for only a few more weeks—since it meant he'd be out of her hair for good.

So, why did the outlook for the rest of spring and into the summer seem bleak?

Chapter 10.

Frustration, stress, and horniness do not make a good sailor.

The Mollymawk pitched and rolled like a drunk navigating the trip from bed to toilet bowl at 3:00 a.m. Del was familiar enough with that analogy to smirk at his ironic humor.

Piper and West had disappeared into the boat's biggest stateroom once they'd headed into Foveaux Strait, Piper looking pale and sweaty, even though she wore her seasickness wristband.

West managed not to be too much of a dick, bestowing both a tight smile and a brief hug to Carly after they'd been introduced. Piper had obviously kicked his sorry ass since West didn't even flinch as his fiancée invited Carly to their wedding.

Kezia joined Ben in the wheelhouse for the return trip, and when Shaye noticed Carly starting to look queasy, she insisted Carly lie down in the other large stateroom.

Which left Del alone with Shaye.

Perfect time to apologize for dragging her to the airport and into his family drama. He should've expected Carly would pull this kind of stunt. He'd ignored the warning signs that she wasn't happy for months. Not just grieving over her dad's death, but unhappy and restless with life in general. Great big brother he'd been.

"You feeling okay?" Shaye asked him from across the galley.

He'd been staring into the Mollymawk's fridge for about thirty seconds. Del grabbed a bottle of water and shut the door.

Swallowing a couple of times, he grimaced. "God. It didn't look this bad when we left Bluff fifteen minutes ago."

He uncapped the bottle and sipped. The water went down easy, but his stomach still complained.

"It often doesn't." She curled into a bench seat, her skirt tucked around her knees. "Hate to tell you, but it won't get any better for the next hour."

"Hell." He drank more water.

"Go lie down in the bunkroom—sometimes it helps."

"And have West and Ben give me shit about wussing out? No thanks."

"I won't tell anyone, so you won't have to hand in your man card. Promise." She showed him her teeth. The smile missed her eyes though, and he didn't think it was because of her insincere promise.

No. His sous chef was scared and trying to hide it.

"Come keep me company?" he asked.

She raised an eyebrow.

"Please?"

"If you puke on my favorite skirt, I'll kill you." She untucked her long legs and stood.

"Zero puking, because like hell will I let you have that story hanging over me."

"It would screw up your growing reputation as the resident bad-boy chef."

"Bad boy? Who thinks that?"

A pretty flush spread to her cheeks, and she huffed, dodging around him to the narrow hallway leading to the staterooms. He didn't know whether to be offended, flattered, or intrigued, since the blush indicated she bought into his rep. *Bad boy?*

Del trailed after her, a hand held up ready to brace against the wall in case they hit a sudden trough. He didn't feel bad at the moment—

bad as in the *wouldn't-bring-him-home-to-mom-but-I'd-bang-him-silly* kind of a man who women seemed to lust over. But yeah—he was currently more the *you-look-green-so-back-away-slowly* kind of bad.

He walked into the small bunkroom after Shaye and flopped onto one of the narrow lower bunks with a groan. Squeezing his eyes shut, Del focused on regulating his breathing and stilling his churning stomach. Puking on the woman he desperately wanted wasn't an option.

A door squeaked, and moments later came the sound of running water. A short time after that, a damp washcloth draped over his eyes and forehead. Better, but not quite enough to distract him.

Without moving his head, he patted the mattress. "Lie down with me?"

A soft snort from across the room. "Not falling for that old trick, Hollywood."

"We can just talk."

"An original line that no man has used, ever. We can just talk with me safely over here."

With an arm that felt filled with lead, Del raised the washcloth edge and cracked open an eye, rolling his head toward her voice. She sat on the opposite bunk.

The corner of his mouth quirked. "Safely? You scared of me, cupcake?"

"Of course not."

He patted the mattress again, firing off a smile. "I'm incapacitated and helpless. I'll be at your mercy."

"Hmmph." But she smoothed down her skirt and stood.

Del dropped the washcloth over his face and wriggled closer to the wall. After a short pause, the mattress dipped under his spine.

"I guess this is tame, considering you've already seen me half naked." A thread of huskiness through her words betrayed her interest—and woke up his. "Thought I may as well put it out there instead of pretending it didn't happen."

Precisely the kind of distraction he needed.

"No taking that back," he said as warm, curvy woman settled next to him.

With a breathy sigh, she snuggled close—resting her head on his shoulder, the soft fullness of her breasts pressing into his ribcage. He resisted the urge to wrap his free arm around her and maneuver her even closer. Now that he had her near—and damn, it felt better than he'd imagined—he didn't want to scare her off.

He cleared his throat. "You doing okay?"

"I'm fine. I don't get seasick." A frown tinged her voice.

"That's not what I mean."

"I know."

A touch on his stomach then her hand settled, a light weight splaying over his heart.

"It's silly, really," she said. "After all the years I spent on boats as a child."

"You used to swim like a seal. All the Harlands could."

"Yeah. But I never liked scuba diving, not like Piper and Ben. And the free-diving..." A tremor rippled through her. "I can't stand the sensation of not being able to breathe."

Her father's death hovered in the spaces between them. Del covered her hand with his and squeezed her fingers.

The rhythmic grumble of the Mollymawk's engine and the slap and whoosh of her plowing through the waves filled the silence. A strangely comfortable silence. He couldn't remember the last time a woman had been in his arms and he'd just held her.

"How's the stomach?" She slipped her hand from beneath his and ran her fingers lightly over his abs, and then circled his belly button.

Del was tempted to lie and tell her he still felt awful. Only she'd guess it was a big, fat lie since his cock had woken up from the soft strokes of her fingers. Damned body. Seasickness was now the least of his problems.

"Getting better. Talking to you is a great distraction."

A quiet chuckle, which could mean any number of things. He thought about removing the washcloth from his face but discarded it. One glimpse of her beautiful face, one look at her amazing breasts in the stretchy top clinging to every curve, one glance of her hand, which continued to pet his torso, any would erode the last tenuous strands of self-control...the washcloth stayed.

"Talk to me some more," he said.

Like about flower arrangements, cookie recipes, Charlotte-fucking-Bronte—anything to stop him going out of his mind and flipping her under him, putting his hands all over her. From finding out what she wore under her flirty little skirt.

"Talk, huh?" Her fingers stilled.

OhthankChrist. Because now his hard-on threatened to poke a damn hole in his jeans.

"Talk's not distracting me enough," she said. "I need something more."

She shifted away from him, and he was about to complain when her breath ghosted against his lips, followed seconds later by the gentle pressure of her mouth.

Soft, so soft, she kissed him. The tip of her tongue brushed the seam of his lips, and he opened his mouth, his free arm curling around her, landing on the smooth slope of her back. Running his hand up to her nape, Del applied gentle pressure to angle her mouth closer, to deepen the kiss—but she pulled away with a hiss.

"You're incapacitated and helpless, remember?" She grabbed his hand and removed it from her nape, returning it to rest on the sheet. "At my mercy. So keep your hands to yourself."

Oh...he liked this more and more—though keeping his hands off her would be a challenge.

"And the washcloth stays on," she added.

"Yes, Chef."

Sharp teeth nipped his chin and then she soothed it with another kiss.

This time, when she kissed him, she parted her lips and slid her tongue into his mouth. Deep, drugging kisses cured him of any remaining queasiness, replacing it with burning hot need.

Fingers tangled in his hair, she broke the kiss. He arched his neck, the short strands tugging painfully as he tried to keep their connection.

"Hey!" he rumbled.

She shushed him with a finger on his lips. He could taste her, still—sweet, hot, better than any top-shelf drink he'd been craving. In fact, the craving seemed a distant itch in comparison to how much he wanted Shaye kissing him again.

She shoved up his shirt, exposing his stomach and chest. Cool air danced over his skin.

"Pretty." A wet tongue circled his right nipple. "A juicy little bud just waiting to be licked."

Del choked back laughter and the desire to reclaim control of the little witch—then her hand slithered down his body, and a fingertip traced the ridge of his cock from base to head. His hips jerked, the laughter dying in his throat. The finger vanished, replaced with the light weight of her palm. Through the denim, her touch ignited his blood to a fast boil.

Fuck. He was a goner.

Not even her cranberry and dark chocolate chip cookies tasted as good as Del's skin. She could've spent hours exploring the muscles spanning his chest, the ridge of his abs, and the narrow sprinkle of hair below his belly button—now he was at her mercy, and all.

She ran her fingers over him again, and his breathing became choppy. Something about the power of watching him while he couldn't see her removed her remaining inhibitions.

Propping herself up on her elbow, Shaye studied the rest of him. Nicely muscled thighs filled out his long legs; strong corded arms developed from lugging heavy kitchen equipment all day, and tanned skin that disappeared beneath his waistband.

Not to mention the package straining the front of his jeans.

Holy-freaking-guacamole-with-spicy-salsa.

She cupped him through the layer of buttery-soft denim. Thick, hard, he pulsed against her palm. Del made a small rough noise, his jaw bunching.

Perfect. Revenge.

Shaye slid her gaze along his golden skin to where the waistband of his jeans lifted off his flat stomach. She popped the button and eased the zipper half-way down. Another glance upward. Del's Adam's apple bobbed frantically.

With a last *ffzzzt*, she finished unzipping him and peeled the denim edges apart. The smiley face boxers didn't detract from what strained under the fabric. God, nothing was funny about this beautiful man's body or how much she wanted him, even though she shouldn't.

She slipped her hand under the tented waistband of his boxers, raking through crisp hair and hot skin—finally wrapping her fingers around his girth. Her fingertips couldn't quite meet around him.

Wow.

Her happy-place squeezed low and hard, and a fever flush travelled from hairline to tip-toes, threatening imminent combustion.

Loosening her grip, Shaye slid her palm down his length and up again. Something bumped against her, and she glanced over her shoulder. His hand, clenched into a fist, knotted around the sheet near her bottom.

Oh, he liked that, did he?

She liked it, too, so she did it again.

Del moaned a hoarse, gut-wrenching sound. She couldn't help tease, because dammit, she remembered how badly she'd wanted him in *Next Stop, Vegas...*

"Shhh, baby." She pressed a feathery kiss on the head of his penis. "That's all you get for now."

For a man supposedly drugged senseless with passion, Del moved freaking fast. One second she had her hand wrapped around him, and the next, the washcloth went flying, and he flipped her onto her back. Pressing her into the mattress, he kissed her, kissed her until she couldn't think any more deluded thoughts about being in control.

He pulled away, his eyes the blue fire of a gas flame, raking over her face as his breath came in harsh pants.

"You. Are. A big. Tease."

"You teased me first." She arched her hips, rubbing against him.

"Better finish what I started." He braced his weight on one arm, and his hand stroked down her body to bunch up her skirt.

Finish what he...? Wait—what?

His fingers trailed up her thigh, skimmed under the edges of her panties.

Oh...right!

Thank God she'd brought a spare pair of panties to change into after the dress fitting. "Del. Someone might..."

He parted her thighs and cupped her through embarrassingly damp lace.

Ohgodohgodohgod. They couldn't do it now—here! Could they? Damn. She very, very much wanted to.

"Yeah. Someone might." He ran a knuckle over her cleft, and even with the barrier of fabric, his touch electrified. "Which is why I'll let you keep your clothes on this time."

"This time." She licked Sahara-dry lips.

"Cupcake, this isn't gonna be the main course. This is a hors d'oeuvre. A bite-sized taste of the real thing."

"Bite-sized." Her turn to ache, to need, to lose her mind along with her ability to form complete, intelligent sentences.

"Lift your bottom."

She obeyed, and he eased her panties down her legs and flicked them over her bare feet, then stuffed them into the pocket of his jeans.

"Now, spread your legs."

Shaye sucked in a startled gasp, her thighs involuntarily squeezing shut.

"Don't make me go all bad-boy chef on you, baby." He bent to nuzzle and suck the soft skin of her exposed throat, one large hand spanning her knee but not forcing her in any way.

His fingers slipped off her knee and stroked higher, teasing through her soft curls. Her heart flittered and thrummed like a trapped bird.

Ohgodohgodohgod.

Her legs fell open without any further prompting.

Del tracked one finger down the crease of her thigh—not, quite, touching. Her happy-place wailed in disappointment, but he moved to fondle her nipples that were drilling their way out of her bra. He smiled down at her, rendering her a quivering mess. His hand drifted down to rest on her bare hip—covering the small cupcake tattoo.

Intimacy this intense was as unfamiliar to her as sky-diving—and almost as unwelcome. But she couldn't pull back. Withdrawing wasn't an option since every part of her screamed for his touch on a cellular level.

"Please. I need you." The whispered words pulled from her throat seemed to come from far away, from another time or from another woman who had far less inhibitions.

"I know."

Strong fingers slid between her folds, stroking down her slickness before plunging deep, filling her, twisting her from the inside out with pleasure so raw she would've cried out if Del hadn't kissed her again.

His thumb found her core and rubbed with sure, precise strokes. The man touched her with the same intensity and passion with which he cooked. No hesitation, no asking permission, just focused on making magic.

His tongue thrust into her mouth, mimicking the motion of his fingers—his magic fingers. Shaye writhed beneath him, bucking her hips in time with his strokes. Pressure built, and she wanted to claw him, rake her nails down his perfect butt and shred his clothes like a female version of *Wolverine*. She wanted to feel every inch of his hard body against her, inside her—but the orgasm came from nowhere and flung her wants into oblivion.

Shaye whimpered, clutching at one rock-solid biceps, which anchored her in place while the world went to kaleidoscopic pieces.

After her heart stopped needing a portable defibrillator, she let go of his arm. Del was propped on his side, a *cat who'd gotten the cream* look in his eyes, his smugness amplified by the action of leisurely licking his fingers.

Somehow, that was light-years more embarrassing than the fact she still lay spread-eagle under him, recovering from the most mind-blowing orgasm in...well...ever.

"Why are you looking mortified?" Del grinned down at her. "You taste as delicious as you look right now, all flushed and sated and sexy."

"God. Del..." She couldn't think of one thing to say, not with her blood still galloping around her body. Not with her brain reduced to total gooey mush.

"If we weren't short on time, I wouldn't be satisfied with just licking my fingers." He brushed a light kiss over her mouth, and she could taste herself on his lips. "But I'll keep savoring the anticipation."

Shaye wriggled out from beneath the leg he'd thrown over hers. She scuttled off the bunk bed, smoothing down her skirt and glancing at her watch, the two tiny hands a blur since she couldn't stop trembling.

"Someone'll come looking for us soon; we must be nearly to the harbor."

Any excuse to get away from Del, who lay there with his jeans undone and low on his hips, the evidence he still wanted her front and center. He wasn't the only one anticipating, and give her a few seconds, and she'd crawl onto the bed again. She darted a glance at him, and he grinned wickedly, as if he could read her mind.

He stretched, rolling onto his back and tucking his equipment—*Lord, he was so beautifully equipped!*— into his jeans.

"You go on now. I need to, ah, compose myself."

"Right. Okay, yeah," she mumbled, then bailed like the big chicken she was, slipping out of the bunkroom and shutting the door behind her.

"Hey!"

Her head jerked up at the voice across the hall. Carly peered out from the doorway of the other stateroom.

Oh, freaking crap.

"Hi. Feeling better?" She pasted on her most innocent no, *I haven't been fooling around with your brother* smile.

"Meh," Carly said. "Are we nearly there?"

Shaye checked her watch again, forcing her brain to make a quick calculation. "Yes, about another fifteen minutes and we should be on dry land."

"Amen-thank-you-Jesus."

A cool whisper of sea breeze swept along the walkway and swirled up Shaye's skirt. She froze, back against the wall, bare butt cheeks pressed to her cotton skirt.

Double freaking crap! Del had her panties!

Carly cocked her thumb to the right. "West and Piper still in there?"

Shaye nodded, surreptitiously holding her skirt to her side in case another wind gust blew past her legs.

The redhead's gaze narrowed. "Del's in there behind you, isn't he?"

No point lying, so time to call on whatever acting genes Shaye'd inherited from her mother. "Poor lamb is puking his guts up—he's not much of a sailor. I was just checking on him."

"Checking on him, huh?" Carly's pursed lips turned into a wide grin. "Is that a Kiwi-ism for kissing the turkey stuffing out of him?"

Clearly acting wasn't Shaye's strong suite.

"Absolutely not," she said.

Absolutely was—and she wanted to do it again. After she'd killed him for stashing her panties.

"Uh-huh." Carly mimed zipping her lips. "I got your back, almost-sister-in-law."

"It's not like that," Shaye said, and then at Carly's raised eyebrows added, "Well, maybe a little. It was a moment's insanity. A really crazy moment of insanity. Like certifiable." Somebody slap her so her mouth would stop moving. "I'm shutting up now."

"It's natural to feel a little crazy about the guy who put a hickey on your neck."

"What?" The word squawked out of her, and Shaye clapped a hand to her mouth. "He what?" She hissed in a lower tone.

Carly chuckled and curled a finger. "Come with me. I've got a scarf in my bag you can borrow. We'll kill two birds with one stone—no one'll know about my brother's vampire-like tendencies, and everyone'll think you've accepted me as your new best buddy since we've graduated to the clothes-swapping stage."

Shaye hurried into Carly's stateroom. "Far as I'm concerned, you *are* my new best buddy."

She touched a finger to the tingling spot on her neck, and although she wanted to be mad at Del for marking her, the feeling floating to the top of her emotional pool was a little more like pleasure.

Chapter 11.

Stewart Island lived up to its reputation for crazy-ass weather the next morning. Del hoped Ethan Ward and his crew enjoyed their turbulent, twenty-minute flight over from Invercargill. He and West had taken Due South's courtesy van to the airport to collect them and to help transport the crew's equipment.

"How many of these Hollywood nobs are we expecting again?" West said from beside Del as they lounged in a row of plastic chairs in Oban's tiny airport terminal.

"Terminal" being a generous term for a single-storied, shoebox of a building with an office desk and a single staff member who handled everything from bookings to luggage.

Del rubbed his hands down the legs of his jeans—again. Jesus, sweating like a pig. "We get the bare minimum. Nine crew plus *the talent's* personal make-up artist."

"The talent being Ethan. You don't like this dude, do you?"

"Never met him. And it doesn't matter whether I like him or not."

West grunted, slouched farther into the plastic seat. "Me and Pipe watched a couple of episodes of Ethan's last TV series. Is he for fucking real?"

"Nothing's real in Hollywood, West. Nothing and no one."

West laced his hands over his stomach. "You included?"

"Some days I'd say yes."

An empty plastic bag cartwheeled down the runway and disappeared into a thick grove of trees with branches waving like crazed football fans. Heavy droplets of rain pelted the airport windows and glass sliding doors.

"Then as your brother, I'm telling you to quit chasing Shaye. She is real, and she's got real feelings. She can't disguise them at the best of times—like when she's got a killer poker hand or somebody's getting on her last nerve—and she sure as shit can't hide her feelings about you. She's giving you the same sappy glances she gives to Donny when he whines."

Much as he hated being compared to a dog, Del realized West was right. Everything Shaye thought showed on her face—the woman was completely transparent.

Del shot a sideways glance at his brother. "I'm not chasing her, and there are no feelings, real or otherwise, involved."

West sat up straight, while Del's knee started bouncing like crazy. He felt like a thirteen year old again—like when West had threatened to punch Del's lights out if he continued making puppy eyes at one of the summer girls West lusted after. Even then, Del'd known West wouldn't have smacked him, so Del had shrugged off his brother's threats...especially as the girl in question had a laugh like a hyena on meth.

Shaye was a different matter—he didn't like West's implication that Shaye's feelings were directed at Del. Neither of them should have any sort of feelings for the other. Feelings were a big-assed red flag *for someone's gonna get hurt.*

"You douchebag. You've already slept with her, haven't you?" West punched Del in the biceps. "Fuck's sake, Del."

West kept his voice low, since the terminal's only employee, Robert, hovered at his desk, typing on his computer, presumably figuring out the best social media websites for posting candid photos of Ethan Ward.

Del continued to stare straight ahead, but blood thundered around his body. His brother was right. He was a total douchebag. He should never have touched Shaye.

"I haven't slept with her." Yet. But hell, he wanted to, needed to—needed her. "We're not discussing this now."

"Leave her alone, Del."

His heart wrenched again. "I tried, West. I *fucking* tried." He couldn't say he was still trying though, since he'd gone way past the point of walking away without having her first.

"You like her? Or are you messing around?"

"Thought we weren't discussing this?" At his brother's pointed stare, Del threw up his hands. "Okay. Fine. I like her."

West's shoulders slumped as he stretched out his legs again and lounged on the plastic seat. "Dad'll be pissed if you break his sous chef's heart. If he were well enough today to come with us, he'd be threatening to fry up your junk in his six-inch pan."

The mention of his father did nothing to stop the spikes pounding in Del's head. Invercargill hospital had called a couple of days earlier to let him know the blood results. He'd passed stage one. Which meant he now couldn't hide behind ignorance. He had to make a decision. Was he prepared to submit to the next, more invasive round of testing? And then—well...then he had to decide whether he'd allow surgeons to hack out a kidney and transplant it into a man who kissed him off thirteen years ago.

He wanted to hate the old man still. But Bill didn't seem anywhere near as cantankerous and cold as in Del's memory. The other day, when Bill helped with morning prep, Del found himself laughing at his father's dead-pan jokes.

Del folded his arms and stared out the window. "I don't want to break Shaye's heart or anyone else's."

Outside, a small plane, wings dipping erratically, zipped into view and landed on the runway. Del stood, walking to the sliding doors as the plane taxied to a crawl, and then drew to a halt opposite the terminal.

"She and I both know the score."

"That's the biggest bullshit cliché ever invented." West stood alongside him. "There's no scoring in Shaye's mind. Once she decides you're hers, she'll never let you go. You'll rip her to shreds when you leave."

"Who says I'm leaving?"

West inhaled sharply, and Del's teeth clicked together. *Where the fuck did that come from?*

He slanted his brother a quick look and found West staring as if Del'd sprouted a sparkling white unicorn horn.

"You're *staying?*"

Outside, the plane door opened, and a uniformed pilot hopped out. The man cranked the stairs down, and moments later, Ethan Ward, in jeans and a battered leather coat, came into view. Ethan...Del's ticket back to his real life in LA—or Chicago, since he'd burned his bridges on the West coast.

Would he consider staying here? The ass end of the world? Sure, he'd be the big fish in a small pond, as opposed to a tiny guppy in a shark's tank like he was in the States. But seriously? *Staying on Stewart Island?*

Del shook his head then scratched at his freshly-shaven jaw. "You know me—knee-jerk reaction is to argue with you."

He made light of it with an elbow to West's ribs, but West just held Del's gaze for three long beats.

"I don't think I know you at all," West said.

Before Del could react, shoes scraped on the floor behind them.

"'Scuse me, boys." Robert wiggled a finger at the sliding doors to indicate they were in the way. "Got to help unload the plane. The one with all their gear is due in another twenty minutes."

Robert slipped out, and on a blast of freezing air, Ethan Ward strode in. Even with his mussed blond hair and designer-stubbled jaw speckled with rain, the man looked as if he'd stepped from the pages of the gossip magazines Del's female staff at Cosset would pore over during their breaks.

Prick.

Del stuck out his hand. "Ethan—welcome to Stewart Island. I'm Del Westlake."

Ethan paused to emphasize whose balls wore the kingpin crown, then he squeezed Del's hand briefly and released.

"Recognized you from the audition tape." The wide smile Ethan switched on was hard enough to crush walnuts. "Bloody glad we made it in alive though; the weather's fucking barmy out there." His eyes flicked to Del's right. "And you must be Ryan, Due South's manager."

"I go by West—only my mother calls me Ryan."

"Mums are a bit like that, aren't they?" Ethan offered his hand, and West, being West, took his time about extending his, returning the slight.

No matter their differences, no matter West said he didn't know Del anymore, his big brother didn't hesitate to take his side.

"Well then, lads." Ethan turned toward the glass door. "Ah, here's the rest of the stragglers. I'll introduce you to my crew once they get in here." He transferred his walnut-crushing smile to Del and West. "Then we'll bugger off to the bumhole of the world, eh?"

Del forced out a chuckle, which to his ears sounded like a cat being throttled, but Ethan bought it and grinned even wider. West dug his hands into his jacket pockets, his elbow accidently on-purpose knocking into Del's ribs.

Yeah, thinking the same thing, bro. What an *arsehole.*

***

After ten minutes in Due South's kitchen enduring Ethan Ward slathering on the charm, Del's opinion of the man upgraded from arsehole to douchebag.

Shaye, who'd greeted Del with a curt nod upon entering the kitchen, looked at Ethan as if he were a rock god. The camera crew had dispersed to the B&Bs they were staying in, and the assistants remained at the airport to oversee the shipping of their precious cameras and shit from the second plane.

While Ethan examined their kitchen, Del's gaze fell on the polo neck top under Shaye's chef's jacket. She caught him staring and a pretty flush flared on her cheeks.

That's right, babe. Under your collar, you've got my mark on your pretty skin.

Her hazel eyes flicked to his and slitted into a warning glare, as if he'd spoken aloud. He wasn't at all sorry for sucking on her neck, only that he hadn't the opportunity to mark her in other areas. Other more *private* areas.

The back door creaked open, and Bill lumbered inside. His gaze zeroed in on Del.

"He here yet? Wasn't he meant to arrive before lunch service?"

"Mr. Westlake. So nice to meet the man who's the backbone of this whole establishment." Ethan stepped out of the pantry, where West had been yapping on about something while Del was distracted by Shaye's...everything.

Every single thing about Shaye distracted him.

Bill huffed his way over to the counter, and Del dragged over a stool.

"We're hardly an establishment." Bill lowered himself onto the stool with a sigh. "Just a humble pub and grub place."

Ethan's hearty laugh reeked of insincerity. "I've some ideas on how we can update your menu. Turn this pub and grub place of yours into something the tourists will come to for the food alone."

"You don't say?" One of Bill's eyebrows quirked up. "Well, the menu could probably use a do over."

Del's eyes popped, and he glanced at Shaye, who stared at him with a *who the hell is that man pretending to be your father* look.

Numerous times, he'd mentioned to Bill that Ethan would want a menu change, only to have Bill react with thunderous sighs and muttered curses.

"You'll sort it out with my son," Bill said. "He's head chef now."

Del's heart lurched in his chest. The undertone of resignation in his father's voice...

"Temporarily," Ethan said. "I have a feeling he'll be popular on my show."

"I'm not taking over for you permanently, Bill. You'll be head chef again soon," Del said.

Bill shrugged, leaned over, and patted Shaye's arm. "Del doesn't want our little pub and grub place, so it'll be yours and West's to run when I kick the bucket."

Shaye recoiled. "Don't say that!"

"I won't be around forever, girlie. I'm considering a move to Invercargill, so I'll be closer to the hospital for my damn dialysis appointments."

"Dad, no." West's face crumpled. "It'd kill you to leave Oban."

Del glanced at Shaye, who was busy running her fingers under her wet eyes and sending embarrassed sneak-peeks over at Ethan. Ethan—who appeared to be eating up this mini-drama like a teenage girl bingeing on ice-cream.

"It'll kill me to stay," Bill said gruffly. "I can't keep making the crossing, and it's not right me being a burden on Claire—and now young Carly."

"You're not a burden," West said.

Del cleared his throat, swallowing past a gullet-full of sharp rocks. "Mom and Carly want to be here."

Faded blue eyes clashed with Del's. "You think I'm gonna ask either of them to help change my incontinence pants if I get to that stage?"

Bill slipping into self-pity sent the sharp rocks tearing into his guts, and Del only knew of one way to snap him out of it.

He leaned forward, bracing his palms on the counter, meeting his father's gaze without blinking. "You can change your own fucking pants for a while yet, old man."

Bill's bushy eyebrows shot up, and Shaye and West choked in a gasp.

Then Bill smacked a palm on the counter and roared with laughter. "That's my boy." He eased up off the stool and stabbed a finger at West. "Get the sour-puss look off your face and go talk to your newest staff member. She's waiting out front."

West straightened. "Who've you been hiring?"

"Carly. She's gonna help Kip at the bar, so you don't freakin' kill yourself trying to do six damn jobs at once."

"I can handle it," West glowered.

Yep. West looked as if good ol' Dad had confiscated his favorite toy and given it to someone else.

"Like Shaye could handle the kitchen alone, eh?" Bill said. "You made me suck it up and let Del take over. Quit ya whining, and accept your sister's help."

West's eyes popped. "She's my *step*sister, not my sister—and you can't make her work; she just got here."

"This, from the man who made my sister a kitchen-hand the moment she arrived home," said Shaye.

West glared at her, and Shaye narrowed her eyes in return.

"I'm not making her do nothing," Bill said. "She offered."

"Excuse us, Ethan." West shot a glance over at the man smirking at the end of the counter. "There's not usually this much screwed-up drama at Due South."

Shaye snorted and stalked off to the cold storage room.

Del resisted the urge to laugh out loud at his brother's bald-faced lie.

"No problem, lads." Ethan Ward grinned his walnut-crushing grin, likely calculating his ratings shooting through the roof filming Del's fucked-up family. "No problem at all."

Chapter 12.

Sick owner, pain-in-the-ass manager, and a head-chef she wanted to bonk senseless—before she chopped him into tiny pieces, baked him in a pie, and fed him to the dogs, that is.

Damn those Westlake men!

Shaye adjusted the white scarf, craning her neck in the mirror to ensure the chiffon folds covered the faint mark. At least, with her vintage 1960s, floral silk dress, wearing a scarf a la Audrey Hepburn didn't stand out as an obvious, *oh, hai, I'm a big slut with a hickey on my neck.*

Lunch service that day, after their embarrassing first meeting with Ethan Ward earlier, had thankfully gone quickly. Slammed with guests hoping to catch a glimpse of the man himself, she barely had time to moon over her head chef. Yet she'd been unable to stop fixating on every minute, every second of the amazing cabin-fever incident.

Cabin fever. The heat generated between them could've flash-fried an elephant.

Shaye peeled back her lips and applied one last coat of lipstick—a bright crimson to draw attention away from her neck. She returned the tube to her makeup case. No one would be looking at her, anyway. Piper's bridal shower, put on by their mum and the church la-dies, was all about the bride. Not about Piper's sister hoping to disguise a hickey on her neck—something she hadn't had to do in a long, long time. How long had it been since she'd had a mark that made her fizzy and breathless every time she thought about the man who put it there? Ah...never?

Shaye hurried out of her room, heading down to the kitchen where she'd stashed the three dozen pastel-colored macaroons she'd baked the night before. A quick check at the bottom of the stairs revealed Ford sprawled in his mother's usual spot behind the reception desk.

He looked up at the sound of her heels and gave her the raised eyebrow salute then a gratifying double-take. "Hey. You look real nice."

From Ford, *you look real nice* was the verbal equivalent of a dozen roses, chocolates, and a hand-written ballad sung from below a balcony.

"Just for that, I'll save you some cake, especially since your mum's making you work the desk."

The grin he offered gave her the warm fuzzies but not a tingle more. So much easier if she could crush on sweet, dependable Ford.

"That's why you're my favorite Harland," he said.

"Like your mum hasn't promised you exactly the same thing. See-ya."

She breezed through the swinging doors, her peep-toe, six-inch heels clicking prettily—a much sexier sound than the usual hush of her work clogs. Crossing the kitchen floor, she swept her gaze over the stainless steel surfaces, checking everything had been left ship-shape and ready for dinner service that night.

Movement in the pantry caught her eye—Del.

Del jamming the lid back on her plastic container of macaroons.

Del with his eyes wide and cheeks bulging.

She stabbed a finger at him. "Thief!"

He showed her his palms but continued to chew as she stalked into the pantry.

"I can explain." The tip of his tongue flicked out and swiped a pale lilac crumb off his upper lip. His eyes gleamed, gaze slipping from her face down her body to the tips of her turquoise-painted toenails. "But let me pick my jaw up off the floor first—you looking fucking amazing."

"Uh-huh." She schooled her features into holding the *glare of death*, even though her pulse skyrocketed at the heat of his gaze. "I'd made an exact number of macaroons to fit on my mother's fanciest platter, and now you've screwed it up by eating one."

"I've a confession to make."

Del closed the distance and rubbed the ends of her scarf between his fingers, tugging it gently so it pulled against her neck. Reminding her again of what they'd done together. To each other. He bent down, and the scent of him—a hint of shampoo, warm male skin, and a trace of almonds from her stolen macaroons—wrapped around her. His hands closed on her bare up-per arms, and his lips brushed her ear.

"That was my second macaroon."

She gasped, more from the sizzle of contact than his admission. "You had two?"

Her heart pin-balled into her throat, making her voice come out a breathless squeak. As if she cared about the missing baked goods with his teeth closing gently on her lobe.

"Yeah. After I gave in to the temptation of trying the first one..."

His magnetic pull drew her hands to his chef's jack-et, where they fisted either side of his hips, anchoring her, since apparently her body had filled with helium bubbles and wanted to float to the ceiling.

Hot, damp kisses pressed along her jaw. The scrape of his soft bristles conducted a current straight to her happy-place via her nipples, which tightened unbearably against her bra. Her white demi-cup push-up bra that matched her bikini panties—since Slutty Bridesmaid liked being a little daring under her party clothes.

"I was hooked," he said. "One taste just wasn't enough..."

Shaye swayed into him, a small noise of pleasure vibrating in her throat. Breasts to pecs, belly to belly, thigh to thigh, her nerve endings lit up like fireworks. His arm slid around her waist and held her to him—like she had the strength to pull away. *As if.*

She licked suddenly dry lips. "I thought you didn't like sweet things."

The flash of his blue eyes scanning her face sent an-other bolt of feminine heat flushing through her system, weakening her knees.

"I lied," he said.

"Liar *and* thief—don't think I've forgotten you've still got my panties."

And didn't that weaken her knees even more?

He smiled his wicked smile, using his dimple to devastating effect. "Just living up to my bad-boy rep."

"Oh, you're bad, all right."

His talented mouth claimed her other earlobe, and her breath hissed out sharply.

Her hands released his jacket and slid over rumpled cotton to grasp his ass, pulling herself tighter against him. His tongue flickered out to trace a hot line along the curve of her ear. God, the man had an amazing—

"Excuse me?"

Del reared back, and their heads swiveled in unison to the pantry entrance. Holly leaned in the doorway with a hand on her hip and raised eyebrows.

Heat whoomphed into Shaye's cheeks like a gas flame had ignited inside her mouth. "*I-was-just-getting-the-macaroons.*"

Holly's lips peeled into a wide smile. "Oh? Has Del hidden them in the seat of his pants? Sneaky."

Shaye's gaze zipped down to her hands, which, yes, still clasped two firm and delicious male butt checks. *Crapola!*

Her fingers sprang open and she scrubbed her palms down the sides of her dress. Del's soft chuckle ruffled through the loose strands of her hair. He stepped away, arm slipping from around her waist.

"I ate two of her macaroons," he said. "Shaye was just exacting a little revenge."

Holly's sharp gaze switched from Shaye's face to Del's. "Her revenge was squeezing your bum and let-ting you put a tongue in her ear? Sounds like cruel and unnecessary punishment."

"She's got a mean streak even bigger than her sister."

Del's voice was warm with laughter, but Shaye concentrated on re-gathering her composure by pretending Slutty Bridesmaid—busted by her best friend—had turned into Virtuous Virgin, a sweet, innocent girl who wouldn't dream of groping a man in her place of employment.

Shaye popped the lid that Del hadn't properly re-placed back onto the container. "Since you're here, you can help me carry the macaroons over to the hall."

She held the container out toward Holly, exaggeratedly rolling her eyes to the side with an eye-brow wriggle, cueing her friend to *shut the hell up*.

Holly sauntered forward, the skirt of her fuchsia dress, which matched this week's dye streak in her hair, swirling around her knees.

"Sure," she said. "Wouldn't want you to get lost on the way over to the community hall and somehow *accidentally* end up in Del's bed."

"Holly!" Shaye hissed, shoving the macaroons into her friend's hands.

A masculine chuckle from behind contributed to an-other flare of heat across Shaye's face.

The thought of Del's bed tempted her more than a couple of hours playing Bridal Bingo and oohing over Mr. & Mrs. towel sets. And if she had a choice between Mrs. Taylor's honeymoon stories and Del Westlake kissing Shaye until she couldn't remember her own name?

Total. No. Brainer.

Shaye grabbed the second container, catching a peripheral glimpse of white chef jacket stretched tight over rounded biceps before she turned away. "We'd better get going before my mother sends out a search party."

"Have fun," Del said.

"We will." Shaye hurried after Holly, who'd already crossed to Due South's back door.

They stepped outside, and Shaye held up a warning finger at her friend's *I'm gonna burst if I don't talk* expression.

With her arm looped through Shaye's, Holly towed her along the path separating Due South and the low building at right angles to it, which housed an extra ten hotel units. They hurried around the corner onto the strip of concrete that served as a sidewalk leading to the community hall.

"Oh. My. God," Holly said, elbowing Shaye in the ribs. "You and freakin' Del Westlake?"

"Yeah." Shaye glanced over her shoulder in case any locals were close enough to catch a whiff of gossip. "But Hol, you can't tell anyone."

"Well, of course not." Holly's nose crinkled. "It's not my job to tell your friends and family the two of you are a couple."

Shaye stopped walking so fast her arms gave a half pinwheel. She choked out a strangled laugh. "We're not a couple. Gawd. Nothing like that."

"Oh, come on."

"Seriously. We don't even like each other. We just can't seem to stop, you know..."

Holly slapped an attitude-ridden hand on her hip. "Groping in the workplace?"

"Yeah. It's kind of a workmates with benefits thing."

"So Del doesn't check any of your anal *Shaye's Perfect Man* boxes?"

"Pffft." Shaye waved a hand. "Del is light-years be-hind any of my man requirements—which are sensible, not anal—so I'm surprised you'd even ask. Have you forgotten the list you sneakily read when we were thirteen."

"Never gonna let me forget, are you?"

"Nope."

Holly nailed her with a glance. "Since you punished me so severely for reading your precious list, I've memorized your top five requirements. Handsome, kind." She held up her thumb then forefinger. "Listens to you, dependable, and lastly, loves you more than anything."

"Like I said, *sensible*."

"Isn't it time you updated your list—you're twenty-five now, sweets, not thirteen."

Shaye's chest tightened, compressing her lungs into hard balls. She had updated her list—on her sixteenth birthday.

Piper had left for Wellington, and Ben and West flatted together in a small beach house. She remained at home, trying to cope with schoolwork plus endless household chores. When her birthday had passed with only a card from Piper, no acknowledgment from Ben, and a tearful *I'm so sorry baby I forgot* from her grieving mother, Shaye had curled up on her bed and rewrote her list.

Handsome. But didn't have to be in the same league as Christian Bale or Brad Pitt.

Kind. Kind to her, kind to animals, kind to little kids—he wouldn't freak if one of theirs flushed his mobile phone down the toilet.

Listens to me. Just once, it'd be nice for someone to listen to her thoughts and dreams.

Dependable. A man who'd always be there for her.

Loves me more than anything. Maybe it was selfish, but she wanted a man to love her more than his job, more than sports, more than his mates, or his beat-up truck.

The final thing she'd added, with tears snaking down her face, were three simple words.

Not an alcoholic.

Then he'd be the perfect man for her.

Shaye straightened her shoulders. "I'm a little more realistic now, thanks very much."

"Good. So you can't deny Del ticks a few of your boxes."

"He does not. He's not handsome—" She popped up her thumb.

"Not male-model handsome, but he's frickin' H. O. T."

Shaye ignored her friend's interruption, since, okay, Hol had a point. She raised her forefinger. "He's rude, not kind, and he looks bewildered whenever Jade or Zoe talk to him—"

"So did Ben at first; now both your niece and Zoe adore him."

Shaye held up her third finger. "Del doesn't listen to me—he sided with his dad when I told them about my ideas for a hot-meal delivery system for the oldies and a monthly catered meal at the community hall."

"Okay. Don't check that box then. But he's here helping Bill—that makes him kind of dependable."

"He'll be gone as soon as West and Piper come home from their honeymoon."

"He's not staying?" asked Holly.

"He hates it here."

"How can he hate it? He's a true blue Stewart Is-lander!"

"Trust me; he can't wait to get away from Oban." So you'd better not get any more attached, a little voice whispered in her ear. "So he's not dependable."

"Well, what about the last one?" Holly flicked up Shaye's pinkie finger. "You sure you're no more than workmates with benefits?"

Her heart had been knocking around her ribs for days, saying *Hello? Trying to tell you something here,* but she'd been too focused on feeling nothing to listen to it.

"He's leaving in a few weeks, so I'll just take a little stroll on the wild side"—She performed a neat avoidance of answering Holly's question—"and enjoy him. Since as you say, he's H. O. T."

"But you don't want anyone to know."

Shaye leaned into Holly and said, "That good-girl Shaye wants to do West's little brother? *Hell, no.* Ben and Piper—and probably West, too—would beat the crap outta him, then me."

"Sweets, they know you're not a virgin."

Shaye rolled her eyes. "Yeah, but they'd all worry I'll fall in lurv with Del and end up with a broken heart when he returns to LA."

"Uh-huh." Holly did the finger-shake-chastisement under her nose. "'Cause you won't, right?"

"Fall in love with Del? Another *hell, no.* Remember what you said after I told you he was an Aries?" She raised an eyebrow at Holly and answered her own question. "You said we're incompatible—like oil and water."

"He could still be your Mr. Perfect."

Shaye looped her arm through Holly's, and they continued toward the community hall.

"How about he's my Mr. Perfect-for-now?"

Holly snickered. "I bet he'll be your Mr. Perfect in bed."

After the tsunami-sized orgasm she'd had on The Mollymawk, Shaye didn't doubt it.

***

After Bridal Bingo, Bridal Pictionary, and Toilet Paper Wedding Dress, Shaye thought her face would crack from all the isn't this fun smiling.

Piper sat surrounded by church ladies who cooed while she opened her presents. Mrs. Randal, in her excitement, squealed out one of the party taboo words and had to sulkily give up her string of beads. Hilarity ensued. The bride-to-be looked as if she wanted to loop the beads still around Mrs. Randal's neck into a garrote to shut her up.

Shaye nibbled on a club sandwich and enjoyed her sister's torture. Yeah, she kinda did have a mean streak. But hell, it was fun witnessing Piper squirm at some of the raunchy comments coming from the Island's older constituency.

She glanced over her shoulder at the snack table. Carly still hovered there with a glass of champagne in one hand and a plate in the other. Piper had insisted Carly come, refusing to take no for an answer.

While their mum, Glenna, had welcomed her effusively when she'd arrived at the shower with West's mother Claire, the coolness from some of the older la-dies was palpable. Glenna's influence produced a grudging politeness from the locals when they were forced to socialize with Claire, but Stewart Island women had long memories. Claire had abandoned her man, and therefore, them. And although she'd begun to redeem herself with her return to care for Bill, her pretty, red-haired stepdaughter was an unknown.

Shaye slid out of her seat and crossed to the snack table.

"Don't touch Mrs. Brailsford's Anzac cookies," she murmured, standing at Carly's side. "They'll break your molars with one bite."

"Thanks for the warning. Maybe it's safer to stick to this." She tipped her plastic wine glass toward Shaye with a tight smile. "Or your macaroons. They look safe."

"They won't break your teeth, at least."

More crazed laughter and hoots from behind them.

"It was nice of your sister to invite me to her shower," Carly said.

"She wasn't being nice; she genuinely wants you here. So do Glenna and Kezia. And me." Shaye moved to the edge of the table and picked up a plastic glass of orange juice. "I want you here, too."

"West doesn't." Carly drained half her champagne. "You think I'll win him over?"

"Absolutely. Now you're working in Due South, you'll wear him down with a campaign of sisterly love."

Carly snorted. "He doesn't want a sister."

"But he needs one—he just doesn't know it yet." Shaye tipped her orange juice at Carly in a silent toast.

They moved to a row of seats against the wall and sat in silence, both sipping their drinks.

Carly turned slightly on her chair, crossing her legs and balancing the plate on her knee. "I'm glad Del's found you. I haven't seen him so happy in a long, long time."

"I don't think it's to do with me." She turned the plastic cup in her hands. "It's more about him scoring a spot on Ethan Ward's show." Keep the conversation in safe territory— that was the plan.

"The show's not why he's gained a little weight and is looking less zombie-like. Whatever is going on be-tween you two, you're obviously good for him—better for him than Jessica the party girl."

"Jessica?"

Carly's brow crinkled, her lips twisting. "His poor ex—"

Glenna waved frantically from the other side of the hall, yelling, "Shaye, Carly. Cake-cutting time!"

Shaye's hand trembled as she downed another gulp of juice, the plastic glass rattling against her teeth. "We'd better go."

Her scalp tingled, as if tiny fire ants marched across it. So Jessica was the *complicated relationship* Del mentioned at his place. Jessica, the ex-girlfriend. The party girl. The fun, wild, sophisticated girl. Everything Shaye wasn't. She pasted on a fat fake smile, deter-mined to ignore the tiny seed of jealousy sprouting in her belly.

Stupid, pointless, *ridiculous* seed.

She and Carly walked over to the proudly displayed wedding-dress-shaped cake made by Betsy Taylor. Shaye left Carly by her mother's side and went to collect a stack of paper plates, ready to do bridesmaid's duty of cake distribution with Kezia. Piper slid the knife through the buttercream icing, and everyone clapped.

"Don't forget, single ladies," said Mrs. Taylor, as Piper transferred the first slice to Kezia. "If you get the slice with the ring, it means you're next in line to marry your sweetheart!"

Shaye doled out plates of cake, napkins and forks, and the women moved away to sit in small clusters.

"That's your slice." Piper handed Shaye a plate. "Don't get all weepy if you don't find the ring. I'll help you practice your diving skills for the bouquet toss later."

Shaye snatched the plate from her sister. "I won't be diving for anything, and even if I did—"

"Holly's found it!" bugled Mrs. Taylor from across the hall. "Holly's found the ring! Who's the lucky man, dearie?"

Shaye turned away from her sister and waved at Holly, who'd gone crimson with the attention. Tears suddenly stung Shaye's eyes, and she blinked rapidly.

She'd nearly finished the thought out loud. *And even if I did...*what would be the point of finding a crappy ring-in-a-cake or catching a bouquet, since she didn't *even have* a sweetheart. No sweetheart, only a guy wanting to bang her senseless.

Pressing her lips together, she stabbed her fork into the cake. *Get a grip, woman.* Of course Del wasn't sweetheart material, but she could still enjoy hot, no-strings sex while he was around. But a small corner of her heart ached as she spotted Piper, a dreamy look on her face, smoothing plastic wrap over a slice of cake and a few other goodies on a paper plate.

To take home to West.

That same small corner of Shaye's heart wanted someone to go home to. Someone who'd smile, knowing she'd been thinking of him.

Chapter 13.

Del's feathered alarm clock woke him at 5:32 a.m. with a raucous squawk and a rata-tat-tat on the window pane.

Goddamned bird-brained kaka.

He flung off the covers and rolled to the bunk edge. Experience gained in the past twelve days had taught him the bird absolutely wouldn't quit until Del went out with his coffee and a handful of peanuts.

At least this kaka hadn't notified all his buddies about the sucker living in Walter's beach house, 'cause if he had, Del'd have a chain-gang waiting on his deck.

Del scrubbed his face and hauled on his jeans. With a morning off work, and Ethan's crew in meetings and who-knew-what-else until the planned Mollymawk trip tomorrow, waking early for some physical labor wasn't such a bad thing. Del hoped to have a coat of paint on the southern wall by lunchtime.

Rummaging through a drawer for an old shirt, Del spotted the flash of Shaye's lacy blue panties tucked in the back. Not even the bird's caterwauling could dial down the smile on his face from the sight of her sexy underwear. She'd called him a thief, but he fully intended to return them—after she'd spent a night in his bed.

For once, Stewart Island's unpredictable weather decided to play nice. After coffee on the deck—and yeah, the tiny waves curling ashore as dawn broke in gold and pink was maybe worth the brainless bird's wake-up call—Del fed his feathered blackmailer and then got to work.

By the time a car parked and cut the engine outside his place, he'd nearly finished the top coat of pale green Walter had selected. Del swiped a hand across his forehead as the car door slammed. *Damn.* He hoped the car's owner hadn't stopped to shoot the shit awhile. He continued to stroke the brush over the weatherboard, climbing another rung on the ladder.

It'd require Chinese water torture to force him to admit he enjoyed the hell out of painting Walter's house. Something about the bite of fresh sea air, the dull ache in his arms from stretching above his head, and the pungent smell of paint. Better way to spend his morning off than the way he usually wasted one in LA. That had often involved dragging his hung-over butt out of bed to laze around staring at his apartment walls, or, if he hadn't been totally trashed the night before, a punishing run.

"Looking good, boy."

His father appeared around the corner of the house with a faded legionnaire's cap on and a six-pack of beer in his hand.

"Hey." Del lowered the brush and stepped down a rung.

"No, no—don't stop on account of me." Bill walked over to a small wooden bench overlooking the beach. "I'll sit here and watch you work. Brought some beer for after you're done."

Del shrugged. "Thanks. Nice enough day for it."

See? He could be civil when his father decided to act like an actual human being.

Bill sat, placing the beers beside him. "Finish the wall, and I'll let you have one."

"Bit early for Happy Hour." Del carefully swiped excess paint off the brush, his gut knotting at the condensation pebbling the cans' sides. God. When he'd moved in, he'd sworn he wouldn't risk the temptation of bringing alcohol into the house.

"My age, you don't worry about waiting for Happy Hour." Bill chucked. "You enjoy a beer while you still can. I can't with these bloody kidneys."

"Right." Guess this conversation was long overdue.

"So...they ran some tests on me at Invercargill hospital." Del slapped the brush on the wall, his attempts to keep the paint evenly coated thwarted by his pulse throbbing through his body like a giant toothache. "Looks as if I'm potential donor material."

Loaded silence from behind him. He'd thrown the grenade into Bill's territory; would it explode? Or would he toss it back?

"Is this where you tell me I'm a terrible father and I don't deserve your forgiveness, let alone a body part?"

For once, no aggravation roughened his father's tone, or any hint of animosity. Just a weariness that had Del's fingers tightening on the paintbrush's handle.

"Do you even *want* my kidney?"

A derisive snort. "I sure don't want to spend the rest of my life on dialysis."

"A yes, then."

"Actually, my answer is more like *I don't bloody know*. It's a lot to ask, and we're not exactly...well. There's been more than the Pacific Ocean between us for a number of years."

"Thirteen, to be exact." Del loaded up the brush again, even though the hairs running down his spine had lifted.

"Yeah."

Bite the bullet, Del. Take the vicious bull by the horns and deal with this once and for all.

"Let's hear it, then." Del turned on the ladder. "The reasons why I should cut you a break for being a shitty father."

"Nothing good to say about me, then?" Bill crossed his skinny old-man ankles, looking completely unperturbed by the bitterness in Del's voice. "No grace because I didn't wale the crap outta you as a kid?"

"So you never beat us. Doesn't make you a shining example of fatherly concern."

Bill grunted, dug around in his pocket for a tissue, and blew his nose. The sun shone too brightly overhead for Del to identify the expression in his father's eyes.

"Far as West's concerned, you were a pretty good dad," said Del. "Then again, you didn't send him away to another continent when he was fourteen."

"You ever bother to ask why, as you got older?"

Considering he'd mostly refused to take Bill's calls, or the times he couldn't avoid the phone since it'd been Lionel who'd handed it to him, he'd answered Bill's questions in a monotone. No, he'd never been brave enough to hear why his father hadn't wanted him around.

"Seemed pretty obvious. We butted heads constantly, so it was easier when mom left to keep the son who didn't drive you nuts. You figured I'd be some other man's problem kid."

"And were you?"

"Yeah. But Lionel sorted me out. He was a good guy."

"I always said so. I trusted Lionel to shape you into the man you needed to be."

Del's hand froze, icicles creeping up through his fingers and tingling in his palm. The brush trembled, causing little eddies to swirl through the paint.

"You didn't know Lionel."

"No, not well. I only met him the one time, during the week we spent with your mother's family."

Del squinted behind his sunglasses. "I was ten, and we went to all the theme parks. You and I rode the coasters together because West and Mom said they'd puke."

"We screamed our lungs out and loved every damn second." Bill chuckled. "You remember meeting Lionel and his daughter?"

"Nah, we met too many different people—grandparents, cousins, distant aunts and uncles—"

"And some school friends of your mother's," Bill said. "Well, your future stepdad was Claire's old high school sweetheart. She broke it off after they graduated college, and he went into the Air Force. They both moved on with their lives. Me and Claire got married, and so did Lionel. Then nineteen years ago, Lionel's wife died in an accident and left him the sole parent of their six-year-old daughter."

Del stepped off the ladder and shifted it along to the edge of the house. Last corner, then he was done for the day. "I know about Lionel's wife."

"Course you do. You consider that sweet girl your sister, don't ya?"

Del nodded, picking up his paint bucket and scaling the metal rungs again.

"Lionel never got over Claire." Bill sighed. "When we came to LA for a visit, he couldn't resist coming to the family lunch at your grandparents' house. Lionel and I sized each other up, and he pulled me aside during the afternoon. He told me he'd loved your mother since they were in grade school, but he wished the two of us happiness. Told me to treasure her, as I'd never know when some drunk bastard could take her away."

"That sounds like Lionel. Guts of a Fly-Boy, heart of a romantic."

"I never thought badly of Claire when she told me she and Lionel were getting married," Bill said. "I figured she likely still had feelings for him, even if she wouldn't admit it out loud."

Del dunked his brush into the paint, slapped it against the remaining bare section of wall. "So you let her leave. You let her take me away from everyone and everything I loved."

"You remember what your mum was like the last few years before she left? Or was your head stuck too far up your pimply teenage ass to notice?"

"I remember."

His mom had been miserable. She'd wanted them to move to the States because of her parents' failing health. But Bill wouldn't leave Due South, so they'd fought all the time.

One night after dinner, Mom and Bill had sat him and West down. Del had known what was coming before either of them said a word. Any conversation taking place on their family room couch wasn't a happy one. Mom said she and Bill were getting a divorce, and she'd be returning home to Los Angeles. West had jumped up before she'd finished talking, yelling that he was sixteen and staying with his dad. Del, who'd thought the sun shone out of West's asshole, also leaped to his feet, saying he was staying with West. He'd expected his mom to protest—after all, she still called him "baby", even though she knew it pissed him off. Del had looked over at his dad's face, his stubborn-as-a-constipated-mule expression.

Bill shook his head and said, "You'll go with your mother. She needs you, so you're going."

He'd known with absolute teenage conviction then that his father didn't fucking want him. That day was the last time he'd called Bill *Dad*.

"I'll tell you what I remember about you as a boy." Bill folded his arms as Del climbed down the ladder and crossed to sit at the opposite end of the bench. "You liked to do things your way; you were never a team player. In sports, you chose athletics so you could compete solo. I seem to recall you didn't like being made to play cricket or rugby much."

"Much to your disappointment—though you never bothered to watch my games."

"Oh, cry me a river." Bill nailed him with a glacial stare. "No, I didn't watch your bloody rugby matches, which you hated, anyway, but I remember teaching you to cook and letting you sell your god-awful baking experiments to the unsuspecting public out in front of Due South every school holiday."

Del's cheeks flushed hot. "They were pretty bad, I guess."

"But you did what you always wanted to do, what I knew you were born to do. And after I agreed to let Claire take you to LA, I made her swear she'd send you to the College of Culinary Arts when you were old enough. I socked away money for years to make sure you went. I also told Claire if she ever married again, she'd better pick a decent bloke like Lionel Gatlin."

"Wait a second—Mom would never say where the money came from. It was from you?"

Bill said nothing, just stared with his watery old-man eyes.

Icy stones weighed down Del's stomach. "You paid for me to go to school, not Mom. And you wanted her to get back with Lionel?"

"I loved your mother too much, yet at the same time, not enough. She'd never be happy staying in Oban, and I couldn't live in LA. Claire would never leave you behind—the only way she'd move on with her life and be happy was to return to the States with you."

"You didn't want me around." Del's knee bounced a jig, and he slapped a hand on his thigh to keep it still. "I was always a pain in your ass."

"You were a pain in my ass because we're peas in a bloody pod."

"Bull. Shit."

Bill cackled. "What's the most important thing in the world to you? A woman?"

Del straightened.

"Or your work?" Bill continued, slanting him a wry glance. "Thought as much. The kitchen's your woman, isn't she? The demanding bitch has got you by the short and curlies, like she got holda me."

Bill twisted off a can and tossed it to Del. He caught it reflexively, the condensation gathered on the aluminum cooling his sweaty palm.

"Maybe." Del rolled the can around and around in his hands, his mind racing in a counter-clockwise whirl.

"Ambition blinds you, boy. Have you seen the article on the internet going around—the five regrets of the dying?"

"You're on the internet now?"

"Community hall runs a program every Wednesday morning, Social Media for Seniors. I'm top of the class."

"Good for you."

Bill grinned. "Conclusion of that article—nobody bitches about how they shoulda worked harder at their jobs on their deathbed." He stood and dusted off his butt. "It's all about the people you love. Best you figure out who they are and what's really important."

"I know what's important," Del said sourly.

Getting the hell away from these troubling revelations and his Stewart Island imprisonment. *Those* were important...at least, that's what Del told himself.

"Glad to hear it."

"Don't forget your beer." Del held out the remaining five cans, but Bill waved Del off.

"Put them in your fridge for later. Nothing like a cold beer after a hard day's work."

Amen. But somehow, the thought of drinking the remaining cans alone didn't have half the appeal of hanging out with Shaye and her siblings, who often wandered into the kitchen after it closed. Just shooting the shit and ragging on each other. They'd sometimes have a beer, but the drive for Del to have more seemed to have dissipated to a dull ache instead of a sharp burn.

Because for the first time in years, he didn't *feel* alone.

"Anyway, I'm off, and you'd better get on with it."

Del crossed to the ladder but paused at the foot. "Dad?" The word slipped past his mental blockage of *Bill, always call him Bill* and sounded foreign on his tongue.

His father turned back.

"Why did you come here this morning? To see if I'd give you a kidney?"

Bill tugged off his hat and swiped a wrist across his brow.

"No, son," he said. "I didn't come to ask for that sort of sacrifice. After thirteen years, I don't have any right to ask you diddley-squat."

"Then why?"

Bill offered a weary smile. "To try to shrink the bloody Pacific Ocean to a more manageable distance. I'm not much of a swimmer, boy."

"Huh."

He didn't know what to say. Since when had Bill Westlake started talking in analogies?

"By the way, you missed a spot." Bill pointed toward the wall, where, goddammit, Del had missed an area—right under the eaves.

How the hell hadn't he seen such a plain, in-his-face empty spot?

The snarky little voice in his head offered an opinion: *Maybe the same way you haven't noticed the big-ass empty gap in your life. Until now.*

Del waved off his father and then picked up the brush. God, he hated that little voice some days.

***

It'd been a last minute thing—or so Ethan Ward's director, Henry Fairburn, said. Ethan and Henry cornered Shaye while she was busy with morning prep.

"We need you," Henry gushed, as Shaye's knife rapid-fire chopped on her board. "And since Ethan's offered to help Vince with lunch service to get a feel for Due South, you're all set. *No worries*."

Shaye managed to keep her eye roll mental instead of outwardly mocking Henry. The five-foot-something ferret of a man, old enough to be Bill's peer yet dressed in skinny jeans and a rocker tee shirt, had decided the best way to win the locals' support was imitating their slang.

"We want footage of you and Del working together on the Mollymawk. It'll give Del's episode a bit of human interest. Whaddya *reckon*?" Henry twitched, eager to be off to the wharf, no doubt.

The whole time Henry talked, Ethan stood behind him, leaning a hip against the counter and watching her with olive-green eyes. Eyes that danced over Henry's narrow shoulder, as if she and Ethan shared some sort of private joke.

"Mmm." Her stomach twisted as it always did when boats were involved.

After seconds passed in a chop-chop-chopping blur and she still hadn't given Henry an answer, Ethan laid a hand on the shorter man's back and said, "Henry, Shaye and I'll have a chat while you get the crew sorted."

Henry threw up his arms in a jazz-hands display of resignation. "Fine. We're leaving in thirty."

He swished out of the kitchen.

"I'm sorry for the short notice, but I'd like you to go with them." Ethan didn't move from his spot at the counter end, but her scalp prickled as if he'd come to stand right beside her.

She'd seen within moments of meeting him why some women went nuts. Tall and blond, with an endearing flop of hair, a la Hugh Grant, and the plummy British accent to match—plus a healthy dollop of charisma that drew the average person's gaze like a magnet. Even if he hadn't been a TV celebrity, Ethan Ward would've caused a stir in Oban. He had *presence*, and, she couldn't deny, the man was some serious eye candy. Ethan's gorgeousness should've made her happy-place fire up as it did whenever Del walked into a room. Should've...but didn't.

"What I saw of you on Del's audition tape impressed me," he said. "It's important for a head chef to have a sous prepared to back him up, don't you agree?"

Or her, she added, but schooled her features in polite interest. "Yes, of course."

"So, you'll go? Might as well get used to Cruz and Ollie's cameras in your face now."

She laid down her knife. "I prepare the meals for the romance cruises; I don't serve them."

"Today you will, to support Del. Your future brother-in-law, isn't he?"

"Yes."

"Keeping it all in the family. Lovely." His smile exposed very straight, glowingly white teeth.

Great teeth, great smile. But a smile that didn't even blip on her sexometer—not like a glimpse of Del's slightly chipped incisor did when he flashed her his trademark wicked grin.

"I imagine the popularity of your brother's romance cruises will see a rise after the show airs. Be nice to support his business too."

Dammit. Somehow, the bastard had spotted her Achilles' heel, and she couldn't think of a viable excuse. Other than the truth of hating the endless fathoms of ocean below ready to swallow her every time she went out on a boat.

"All right, I'll go. I guess you want me like this?" She gestured at her chef's jacket then froze.

Oh, hell! That could've been misinterpreted. Her gaze flicked up, but there was no hint of a leering smirk on Ethan's mouth.

"That'll be fine, Shaye. Just head down to the wharf. Vince, Robbie, and I can take it from here."

Half an hour later, on-board the Mollymawk, Shaye wished she'd slipped up to her room to apply more antiperspirant. With Henry, two assistants, Annie the make-up lady, Joss the sound guy, and Cruz and Ollie the cameramen all buzzing around them—plus Kezia and Kip, who'd been roped into pretending to be a honeymooning couple—the boat felt overcrowded and stuffy, even though they were well below their passenger allowance.

"I didn't know they would ask you, Shaye," Del said, as she joined him in the galley. "I would've tried to nix the idea, but they sprang it on me only half an hour ago."

"It'll be fine. Preparing the meal with all these people getting underfoot will keep me distracted."

He reached down and squeezed her hand, then let go before anyone noticed. "Thinking about our trip back from Bluff is enough to keep me distracted."

His blue eyes crinkled in the corners, and blood sped in a fiery trail across her cheekbones. This time, the heat wasn't in dreaded embarrassment, but rather in a shared intimacy. Or crap, maybe she imagined it.

Ben piloted them out of the harbor, heading to a secluded bay where earlier in the year a pod of pilot whales had beached themselves. Henry got all excited at the idea of coming across another pod, but fortunately, the long strip of sandy beach edged with unending miles of native bush was deserted.

For an hour, she and Del created a three-course meal for the pretend honeymooning couple. Once the fake cooking shots had taken place, Henry sent one of his assistants to fetch Kezia and Kip for Annie the make-up girl to do her magic. The last sequence would be filmed on the outside stern deck.

Shaye found herself squeezed beside Del, crowded to one side of the deck with the crew positioned in front. Annie fussed with Kezia's dark curls, while Kip leaned against the bench seat and yawned. Make-up took longer than usual, the motion of the waves making applying anything other than powder difficult.

In a moment, Kip and Kezia would taste the food in front of them and provide much orgasmic praise—since this footage would run after Ethan Ward had saved Due South's reputation, taking Del and Shaye's cuisine from bland to brilliant.

Shaye narrowed her eyes at Henry, who flicked impatient fingers at Annie as she slid away from the table. She still resented being told to act like a puppet—there was even a script, for God's sake. So much for "reality" TV.

"Roll it," Henry said.

Kezia, on cue, slipped a forkful of roasted quail and Cumberland sauce into her mouth, squeezing her eyes shut with a moan worthy of Meg Ryan.

"Good, baby?" Kip slid an arm around Kezia's shoulders and kissed her cheek.

Shaye swallowed a snicker, knowing Ben, confined inside with the assistants, would be fuming if he could see Kip hamming it up for the cameras.

The Mollymawk heaved, angling down sharply into a trough. Shaye's stomach dropped with it. Joss the sound-guy stumbled backward, slamming into Del.

Joss fell, people cussed, flatware pinged, plates broke—a dull crack, splash, wetness on her cheek and—where was Del?

Shaye whipped around.

There—*oh, God.* Suspended eerily vertical in the water but sinking, Del floated with his arms floundering in lazy circles, a crimson stream of blood spiraling out from his temple.

Shaye's throat closed, her heart jammed into it so she couldn't breathe. Seconds seemed to turn into minutes. Her gaze zipped around. No one else had noticed Del; it was all on her. Shaye kicked off her chef shoes.

"Man overboard!" she yelled and dove off the boat.

The seawater closed over her in an icy grip, shocking her system to absolute clarity. Down, down into her nightmare of clear blue. Her eyes stung with the cold, with the salt, but she kept them open as she powered her muscles through watery resistance. Del hadn't gone far, since the initial crack to his stubborn male head hadn't knocked him unconscious, *thankyougod*, and he was trying to claw his way to the surface.

Their gazes connected, and her heart dipped and rolled like the hull above. No panic showed in his beautiful eyes, which were fixed on her face. No panic, just a slight wrinkling of his brow as if *he* were worried about *her*. She swam closer, grabbed fistfuls of his jacket and yanked, kicking her legs to propel them into the light.

Bubbles exploded nearby, clearing to reveal Ben and Kip surging toward them.

I got this, she wanted to say as Ben wrapped his arm around Del, and Kip appeared on her other side. *Hey, I got this*.

But she was grateful for their strength in the few seconds it took for their heads to break the surface. Shaye shrugged Kip's hand off her arm and trod water in a fast circle until she spotted Del and her brother, both sucking down huge gulps of air. Blood oozed down Del's cheek and jaw. An inflatable device splashed next to her. She flinched then grabbed hold, continuing to swim.

"Get. Out. Bleeding," Del wheezed when she reached his side. "Sharks."

"Please." She shoved the bright orange floatie at him. "Henry's more likely to attack you for stuffing up his filming than a great white."

Ben laughed. "No shark'll mess with a Harland. Not with her mad on."

Del's nose crinkled at the floatie, but he wrapped his arms around it. "Why's she mad?" He rubbed a hand on his forehead and glanced down, grimacing. "I'm the one...bleeding out...here."

"Man up. It's only a scratch." Ben nudged Del's shoulder but stayed at his side as they dog-paddled toward the Mollymawk.

Shaye stroked backward, watching Del for any sign of struggle. The surge and flow of the waves buffeted her, her cotton pants clinging to her legs. Nothing, strangely, that made her panic. Not even the blood seeping down from a shallow cut on his head, slowing now with the water temperature. Not while Del's gaze remained locked on hers.

"She's mad because she had to jump in and save your skinny ass." Ben grinned over at her, propelling Del and the floatie closer to the boat ladder. "Now her hair looks like ropes of seaweed. Right, sis?"

Shaye huffed out a sigh and issued an eye-roll. Seaweed? Super. *Thanks, big brother.*

Del winked at her and some of the tightness in her belly eased. Actually, mad was only one of many emotions tumbling through her body. Mad, relieved, wanting-to-hug-and-kiss-the-snot-out-of-Del. Wait, was that an emotion?

Shaye reached the bottom rail of the ladder. Kip climbed up before her and then stretched down a hand, helping her struggle up the rungs. Kezia wrapped a blanket and her arms around Shaye when she hit the deck. Shaye hugged her friend tightly, not wanting to admit the other emotion shredding her raw.

Fear. Not fear of the water, anymore. Fear of losing Del Westlake.

Kezia and Annie bustled Shaye into a stateroom, so she didn't see Del and Ben climb onto the Mollymawk. Piper and Ben kept a few spare clothes in a locker, so at least she had a *Coffee Before Talkie* tee shirt and a pair of yoga pants of Piper's to pull on after a hot shower.

Three sharp knocks sounded on her door while she towel-dried her hair. She opened to Del braced in the doorway, dressed only in Ben's old board shorts, which hung dangerously low on his hips. He smelled of seawater and antiseptic, with an adhesive bandage rakishly positioned on his forehead.

"Ouch. Nasty." She raised a hand to touch.

Del snagged her fingers and tugged them down, pressing his lips against them. Whether from shock or delayed reaction to the cold water, or even because the bare skin on display was mouth-wateringly gorgeous, butterflies the size of stingrays swooped around her stomach.

Shaye backed into the room, and he followed—not letting go of her hand and not breaking intense eye contact—as if they participated in some sort of ballroom dance.

When he was far enough inside, he flicked the door shut with a bare foot.

"Come here." He reeled her in.

Shaye wrapped her arms around his waist, resting her cheek on his chest and closing her eyes, the soft thud-thud-thud of his heartbeat pulsing through her skin. His hands skimmed up and down her spine then settled on her waist.

Del didn't speak, just held on.

"Thank you." His voice rumbled up from deep in his chest and vibrated along her lips, which had somehow pressed to his collarbone. "You saved me."

Her heart battered her ribs, once, twice, three times.

"I didn't save you, Hollywood." She couldn't explain why his words touched her so much. But the seriousness of his tone, the rawness shimmering through it, triggered a knee-jerk reaction of making light of the situation. "Ben was the one who hauled your butt to the surface."

A big hand moved to her head, smoothing damp strands of hair and then slipping down to rest on her nape. "You dived in after me without hesitation."

He swallowed hard, his breathing ragged.

"Even with your fear of boats after what happened to your dad," he said. "You went into the water."

"Oh." She hadn't had time to think of her father before diving in.

If it'd been a member of Ethan's crew, she didn't know if she'd have reacted the same. No heroics were involved—in fact, if Ben was next to her, she probably would've shoved him overboard to rescue Del.

But Ben hadn't been there, and so she'd jumped in without rationalizing all the reasons why she couldn't. The only reason that mattered, the only emotion pounding through her bloodstream, was the fear of letting Del Westlake go when she wasn't ready.

Not yet, goddammit. Soon...but not yet.

"You could've drowned." His breath whispered against her temples, stirring her hair.

"Rubbish. All Harlands are born with gills. I don't *like* to swim and dive, but it doesn't mean I can't kick ass in the water like Ben and Piper can."

His soft chuckle tickled her ear. "You kicked ass, all right. And Henry's as happy as a pig in shit, since Cruz managed to keep his camera rolling."

"God." Images of her floundering around with seaweed hair on international television floated through her mind. Ugh. "Really? They're going to use it?"

"All about the ratings, so Henry says."

Shaye sighed and wriggled out of Del's arms, avoiding the temptation to anchor herself to him and drop them both onto the room's queen-sized bed.

Bet Henry would love footage of *that* for his show.

"It'll bring more publicity for Ben, I guess—and more sympathy for you, being rescued by a *girl*."

A flash of his cocky Del smile. "Feeling sympathetic toward me too, cupcake?" He closed the gap between them. "Wanna kiss my boo-boos better?"

Shaye shoved at his chest with both hands, forcing him to walk backward to the door. He grinned down at her the whole time, making her tingle from happy-place to toes.

"Kiss your own boo-boos, Hollywood."

Del paused at the door, opening it but not stepping outside. He parted his mouth to say something then shut it again, shaking his head.

"What?" she asked.

He cupped her chin, mesmerizing her with his steady blue gaze. "I'll never forget the look on your face as you swam down to me. You were fearsome, like a mermaid warrior. Fierce and strong and beautiful. Your dad would've been proud of you today, Shaye."

Her chest compressed with unbearable pressure, her eyes stinging as if they'd been exposed to salt water again.

Del leaned forward and pressed a light kiss on her forehead. Then he left, pulling the door shut after him.

If Shaye didn't know better, she'd think the man had started to care about her, too. That maybe, he couldn't bear to let her go, either.

Chapter 14.

If Del had been a diabetic, he'd be in a sugar coma by now.

The staff had finally left for the night on Halloween Eve, so Del attacked Shaye's party food list with a vengeance. Maybe spun caramel garnishes and the perfect *crème brûlée* were more his style than chocolate-chip-fake-spider cookies, novelty cupcakes, and witches' poison toffee apples—but like hell would he renege on his end of the deal.

The swinging doors hissed open.

"Need a hand?" Shaye's voice echoed through the empty kitchen.

Up to his elbows in a huge bowl of cookie dough, Del was tempted to tell her he had it under control. Which would be a total lie, but at least he'd salvage his pride. She'd left with the rest of the guys at half past ten, with a smug grin and the laughing instruction to "have fun baking cookies."

He glanced over his shoulder. She wore her brown hair pulled high on her head, but damp strands had already escaped the messily tied bun. Not long from the shower, obviously—the tantalizing scent of flowery body wash drifted off skin barely covered by shorts and a tank top, which slid off one shoulder to expose a tantalizing red bra strap.

The woman was more dangerous to him than any poison apple.

"It's under control." The baking maybe, because he sure wasn't. What little control he had drifted through his fingers like powdered sugar as she sashayed over to lean against the counter next to him.

"Plus, you're not dressed for the kitchen," he added.

God, she was all big green-eyed innocence and girl-next-door freshness. Shaye crossed her arms, lush breasts pushed up and outward.

Ah, hell. Not so goddamned innocent.

Del swallowed with a papery mouth. "If you're only here to distract me, I'd rather you find someone else to annoy."

"I distract you?"

Since he refused to glance over to see if she was serious or teasing, Del scooped up another spoonful of cookie dough and rolled it into a ball. "It's a wonder I can function in this kitchen at all when you're around."

"Oh."

Definite smugness in her tone, and the scent of flowers wafted closer.

"Actually, I came to help," she said. "I'll take over the cookies while you do the frosting for the cupcakes."

Bossy wee thing...but since he didn't want to be baking kids' food until two in the morning, it seemed wiser to agree. "Great. I'll work over here."

He moved away before another glimpse of her perfect tits drove him half out of his mind and walked to an opposite workspace where he'd set out a block of butter to soften.

"You're welcome." Shaye's voice, dripping with sarcasm, came from behind him.

An easy silence developed, the quiet rhythm of two people doing what they loved. More so in Shaye's case, since he didn't particularly enjoy baking. But he *did* enjoy working close to her, even if she was hellishly distracting.

"So...I talked to Carly at the bridal shower the other day." Shaye slotted the next tray of cookies into the oven. "She mentioned Jessica."

Hairs rose on his nape, but he made a non-committal grumble in his throat and continued to beat the butter and powdered sugar.

"I'm not the type of girl you'd normally pick, Del, am I?"

"No." Cautious now. How many times had he put his foot in his mouth with a woman? Too many to count.

"Guess I'm pretty boring compared to the women you date."

Pointing out he rarely bothered to *date* women was probably not wise.

Muscles twitched along his shoulder blades. "Did you come here to pick a fight?"

"Not especially." Shaye turned to the cookie dough, displaying her cute short-shorts-covered butt. "Just making an observation that I'm not your type."

His hand slowed. "What type do you think I go after?"

Oh, yeah, she was spoiling for a fight. The temperature in the kitchen cranked up a few degrees. She wasn't the only one frustrated and horny.

"I couldn't say. But not someone like me." She raised an insolent shoulder. "I'm not a party girl. I don't drink or do drugs or sleep around, and I don't shop on Rodeo Drive."

His temper spiked. "Jessica sometimes drank too much, and she occasionally smoked weed. But she didn't screw around, and she didn't give a shit about Rodeo Drive. She was a nice girl—"

"Really? The kind of girl you'd have eventually married?"

He let the fork he whisked the buttercream with drop. "For your information, I nearly did marry her."

Her hands stilled in the mixing bowl, followed by three beats of deadly stillness. Another flare-up of foot-in-mouth-itus.

"This *complicated relationship* you mentioned the first time you kissed me," she said, her spine rigid. "You weren't only *seeing* Jessica, you were going to...marry her." She straightened her backbone farther, the fine bones of her shoulder blades shifting.

He sucked in a deep breath and then another, trying to see through Shaye's snark to the emotions beneath. Insecurity? Jealousy?

" *Were* is the key word here, and it's not as if Jessica's been on my mind every fucking day since I arrived in Oban." Shaye had commandeered his undivided attention in that area. "But in hindsight, yeah. Maybe I should've mentioned Jessica and I were more than just dating."

"Ya think?" Shaye's hands gripped either side of the bowl's rim. "Having an ex-fiancée is a not-so-small detail to keep from the boring chick you're messing around with."

Was that all she thought they'd done? Mess around? His fingers flexed open and shut over and over. "Will you stop saying you're boring? You're not bloody boring, you're simply caught up in some pastel-colored delusion where no one's ever screwed up and where the perfect man will one day waltz into your world."

Shaye spun to face him, her eyes blazing fire.

His blood fired hot in return, fed by every flaw he knew about himself. "Let me tell you something else, cupcake. I'm not perfect. I'm just a guy and a pretty ordinary one at that. I belch after a beer, hog the TV remote, and scratch my balls because I damn well can. I won't pretend to like Pride and Prejudice, I don't remember birthdays and anniversaries, and the day I get on my knees and grovel for a woman's affection will be the day I ask Dr. Joe to ring the psych department for a straitjacket." He stabbed a finger at her. "But I want you, and you want me—and it pisses you off because you can't bear getting messy with a man who'll never measure up to your unrealistic expectations."

"You are *such* a jerk."

"And you want a life-sized Ken doll, not a real man." He turned to his frosting. "Someone like that dickhead, Ward."

A soft missile hit him dead center of his skull, dropped to his shoulder, and slid to the floor with a plop.

"What the—?" He whirled back, his heel grinding cookie dough into the linoleum.

A second missile struck his forehead before he had time to raise an arm. Cookie or not, when thrown with enough force, chocolate-chip loaded dough stung.

Del swiped the mixture off his face, spotted Shaye's hand move, and lunged to the left. "Hey!"

"Asshole."

Another ball smacked into his ear. Man, she had a killer aim. He snatched a cupcake off the tray, and lobbed it across the room. It sailed straight past Shaye's shoulder and bounced off the swinging doors.

"You throw like a girl, Hollywood—not like a *real* man." She scooped up more ammunition and ducked around the edge of the counter.

"Oh, really?" He stalked after her.

Pop—dough ball to the shoulder.

"Yeah, really." She danced backward, keeping a safe distance between them.

Del rounded the counter—had her dead in his sights. She could go right and circle around to where they'd been working, or left, out of the kitchen doors.

No way would he let her leave now. Not when things were getting good.

Splat—dough ball to the chest.

The last of his temper vanished in a blaze of heat. Goddamn, but getting messy with Shaye Harland would be fun. His lips split into a wide grin, probably a risky target, but he'd walk on the wild side.

"You should quit that before I catch you," he said.

"Not scared of you, Hollywood."

Smack—dough ball nailed to his upper thigh. Too damn close to his junk for comfort—and considering what he planned to do after he caught her...

"Oh, you should be." His grin stretched wider at the flash of tanned leg as she slipped around the corner to their work area. "I'm gonna do real bad things to you once you finally break down and beg."

As planned, his words needled her into distraction. Shaye spun to heave another ball at him—but this time, he was ready. Del went in low and fast, knocking the last couple of missiles out of her hand and scooping her off her feet. He grabbed two sweet butt cheeks in his hands and backed her up to the counter. Soon as he'd wedged himself against her so she couldn't escape, he snatched up her right hand, which crept along to his neat rows of cupcakes.

"Nuh-uh."

She glared daggers at him.

"I might throw like a girl," he said. "But I'm still bigger and stronger and faster than you are."

Her knee jerked, and he thrust forward, grinding into the cradle of her hips. Her eyes widened. Yeah, the oven wasn't the only piece of hot equipment in this kitchen. Lush breasts rubbed against him as her breaths heaved in and out, her pebble-hard nipples stabbing into his chest.

He bent and nipped her bra strap between his teeth, tugging it sideways until it slid off her shoulder.

"Del." Her voice aimed for tart lemon, but sugar softened the sour, so he licked a strip of skin from shoulder bone to the pulse bumping in her throat.

Shaye wriggled, kneading him so sweetly he nearly swallowed his tongue. He was a man starved for her touch, and the wriggle signaled the buffet was about to open. Traversing the silky skin of her neck, he tasted a sliver of vanilla and sugar where she must've touched herself while forming the cookies.

Desire clogged up his lungs. Edible. She was so deliciously edible.

Lips closing on her earlobe, he rocked into her again, and a soft moan slipped from her throat. He sensed the moment her struggles changed from *desperate to get away* to *desperate to get closer*. She sagged, her fingers twisted into his shirt relaxed, splaying across his chest. He pulled her closer, and spacing hot kisses along her jaw, he reached out and yes...his fingers connected with the cool sides of his mixing bowl.

"You wanna get messy with me, baby?" He sucked on her lower lip, tugging it gently with his teeth, soothing the little sting with a flick of his tongue.

Hooded green eyes stared dreamily up at him. She nodded, so he swiped his fingers through the frosting and smeared it across her mouth.

Shaye's eyes flew wide open, and she smacked his chest. "You—"

He kissed her before she could say anything else—diving into the kiss, throwing the full weight of lust and frustration and need behind it. She tasted of sugar and slick heat, every inch of her mouth a new texture and sensation to explore. He sucked off frosting, rubbed his lips over the stickiness coating her chin.

Fingernails raked his shoulder then dropped, creating a spine-tingling trail down his biceps. He lost himself in the kiss; not even the bowl rattling on the countertop could deter him. Had he expected Shaye to capitulate without a fight? Not bloody likely; otherwise she wouldn't be the woman he wanted so desperately.

He pulled away to smile at her and got a face-full of frosting.

He swept his tongue around his lips, taking in more of the citrusy-orange flavor.

"Good?" She smiled up at him, batting her long lashes.

He scraped a hand down his face then smeared the leftover orange tinted cream over the enticing swell of cleavage exposed by her slipping bra.

"Admit it," he said. "I give good frosting."

Her eyes crinkled in the corners, green irises now missing the dangerous glitter of temper.

"Does this mean I'm forgiven for being an asshole?"

"It means I'll be mad at you later, so take off your shirt, Hollywood."

Del made short work of stripping off his tee. He tossed it on the floor and glanced back at her. She had another glob of frosting on her fingers.

"Are we going to get messy now?" he asked.

And please, God. Let her say yes.

"Very messy."

She slapped a hand on his chest, dragging her fingers over his pecs until her short nails gently scratched his nipple. With her free hand, she hooked him by his pants waistband and tugged him closer, bending forward to lap at his skin like a kitten.

A fucking *sex* kitten.

Her tongue circled the nipple that seconds ago she'd toyed with using her nails. Del's pulse exploded into a gallop. The wet heat of her mouth traced from one side of his chest to the other, her tongue flickering across his skin until she latched onto the other nipple, flicking the sensitive nub over and over. The pleasurable tug of it arrowed straight down to his balls. No innocent, this woman.

He ran his hands down her arms and caught the tank top's hem. "Your turn."

She released his nipple with one final rasp of her tongue. From the strength of her suction, he figured a red patch would form on his skin.

Lucky he was tough enough to handle a feminine hickey.

Her fingers dipped past his waistband and stroked the swollen head of his cock. *Holy shit.* Pity he wasn't tough enough to muffle a groan. Del mentally multiplied complex fractions in an effort not to humiliate himself like a thirteen-year-old boy who'd discovered his first dirty magazine.

She slipped her hand out of his pants and helped him tug off her top—since, apparently, one touch on his penis had rendered his fingers unworkable and his brain with limited muscle memory of how to unhook a bra. Shaye had that sussed too—thank Christ—and the scrap of red satin fell to the floor.

Del hauled her flush against him, her breasts smooshing into his chest and sticking slightly, thanks to the icing making his skin tacky. The playful idea of *I'll cover Shaye's amazing tits with frosting and slowly lick it off* evaporated the moment she kissed him again, her desperation matching his as she wound her arms around his neck.

No more games. No more teasing. There'd be time for slow, sexy discovery later. He was ready to burn, and from the thrust of her tongue in his mouth, so was she.

Hands kneading her sweet ass, Del lifted her, and she hooked her legs over his hips and ground against him. God, he'd go out of his mind before he'd a chance to taste her. No way. Del broke the kiss, bracing her shoulders and tipping her backward until his mouth found her breast. He swirled his tongue around the pebbled texture of her nipple, but the hint of citrus frosting didn't taste half as addictive as Shaye herself did.

She moaned, rubbing her cleft against his rolling-pin-sized erection. Things were getting serious fast. He needed to be balls deep inside her in the worst way.

The nipple he feasted on slipped from his mouth with a moist pop. "Condom."

Since he hadn't planned on ravishing Shaye amongst cookie dough and cupcakes, he wasn't carrying. Her legs tightened on his hips, and his cock jerked.

Yeah, lesson learned. Always be prepared.

She blinked up at him, her slightly swollen lips parting on a gasp. "Nightstand. My room."

"Let's go."

Shaye unhooked her legs from around him, and he helped her stand. Her legs wobbled as he bent down to pick up her tank top and bra, sending a rush of masculine pride through him.

"Stick your shirt on," he said. "We don't want a scandal."

The corner of her mouth quirked, but she tugged on the top. Rock-hard nipples jutted against the thin cotton, puckering the fabric as the wetness from his mouth made the shirt cling to her breasts.

Fuck, not a huge improvement—how would they make it to Shaye's room in time?

Del snatched up his shirt and wrangled it on, taking a full three seconds to discover he was trying to jam his head into the sleeve.

He had it bad for this woman, real bad.

Del took her hand, but she slipped away.

"Oven," she said, twisting the dial to zero. "Smoke alarms going off wouldn't be a good look."

He reeled her in for another mind-blowing kiss.

"Race you upstairs," he said, after they finally came up for air.

Shaye smiled, a smile that seared him down to his Converse soles, a smile he wanted to drown in. A smile he couldn't imagine not seeing every day at his side.

"Give a girl a head start?" she asked.

I'd give you anything, cupcake. The words hovered on the tip of his tongue. *Anything and everything.*

But he swallowed them back and used his cocky, bad-boy smile, instead—so she wouldn't guess his legs were just as weak, and this time he didn't think he'd catch her.

Shaye climbed the stairs to her room with her happy-place wailing for attention like an air-raid siren. Behind her, the steps creaked with Del's heavier weight, their shadows dancing across the wall.

In a few minutes, she'd be his. Completely his.

She could deny it out loud until someone pulled out the thumbscrews, but she couldn't deny it to herself. Casual sex wasn't listed on her menu. Neither would she give herself to a man with whom she didn't feel a strong connection. And the connection drawing her to Del grew stronger daily.

Dammit.

She unlocked her door, and Del pressed in close, his warm breath tickling her neck. Making love with him would mean far more to her than it would to him. But having his intense, blue-eyed focus on her was worth the risk. Besides, with the non-stick shield protecting her heart, she'd be fine.

The door swung open, and they stepped into her room. Del turned in the soft glow of the nightstand lamp and locked the door behind them. She wrapped her arms around her middle, conscious of her braless breasts shifting under her top.

She hitched her shoulder toward the tiny bathroom. "You could shower first, since we're all stick—"

Del covered the distance between them in two quick strides, lifting her up on tip-toe and fitting his mouth to hers.

Oh, God.

Hot, deep, wet, explosive kisses, tailor-made to flick all her erogenous zones to overdrive in one blast. She couldn't get enough.

Shaye swept her hand over the solid slab of muscle spanning his shoulders, burying her fingers in the silky hair at his nape. His lips still tasted of tangy orange; each dance of his tongue into her mouth spun her senses, weakened what little resistance she had left. She'd never make frosting again without being transported through time to this night.

He backed her up to the bed, Del breaking the kiss to haul the covers off the mattress. "Worried about your clean sheets?"

"No." Right now, she wouldn't care if they were both covered head to toe in frosting.

"Good. 'Cause we're about to mess them up big time." He wrenched off his shirt and let it drop to the floor.

God, he was beautifully made, a calendar man for "Sexy Chef" with his tanned pecs—though slightly orange-tinted—the ripped muscles of his arms, the dark smattering of hair below his flat stomach disappearing under black pants.

"Take off your top, Shaye. Let me see how beautiful you are."

Shaye swept off her shirt, unable to squash a tiny ripple of self-consciousness at having her breasts exposed.

"Now the shorts."

His words were rough with a hint of desperation, giving her a shot of confidence to unbutton and unzip her shorts, to wriggle them lower on her hips. She paused, drinking in the sight of him, hard as cast iron beneath his pants, his chest rising and falling with ragged breaths.

"You first, Hollywood. You used to like running around buck naked."

"Maybe I still do."

Del toed off his sneakers and hooked his fingers either side of his pants then yanked down both them and his boxers. His erection bobbed in front of him—thick, straining toward her, and at maximum arousal.

Some men had an inflated opinion of the attractiveness of their equipment—a fact she and her girlfriends had giggled about. Shaye had seen a few penises in her twenty-five years—none of which made her want to beg for a touch.

Until now.

Del's hand drifted down to fist around himself, his eyes never leaving her face. She swallowed, her happy-place squeezing deliciously with barely restrained anticipation. Del clothed caused her pulse to skip erratically. Del naked and stroking himself was enough to trigger a cardiac incident.

Shaye shucked off her remaining clothes, each inhale of Del's cologne mixed with citrus and the faint musky scent of their arousal amplifying her excitement. He crossed to her, and she reached for him, sliding her fingertips along his length.

Then he kissed her, lowering her to the bed. Feverish skin weighted with muscle bore her into the sheet, and her hips jerked up. There—oh God—she rubbed against him, a brief brush of her mound against his thigh. She wanted to hump his leg, and then him, until she couldn't remember her own name.

Down girl, down.

With his tongue continuing to explore her mouth, Del spread her legs farther apart, settling his larger body over hers. He dotted lazy kisses along her jawline, sliding down until his lips closed wet and hot over her breast. His hand slipped between their bodies, parting her folds to circle her sensitive bud with his thumb, two long fingers entering her almost simultaneously. Her gasp became a guttural moan, pleasure so intense snapping through her that she bucked helplessly against his palm.

"Please."

Please more? Please stop? Please now? She couldn't vocalize any request as his thumb settled on her, stroking, rubbing, driving her out of herself. She'd never been this close to the edge so quickly, so damn easily.

"Del!" The orgasm, with little warning other than a catastrophic increase of pressure, slammed into her.

Her muscles clamped around his fingers, and she writhed under his hands, sinking her teeth into the meat of his shoulder to keep from screaming out loud. After a moment, he leaned past her, dragged open the nightstand drawer, and removed a sealed box of condoms.

He pulled away from her to tear off the cellophane wrapping and remove a foil square.

She dropped her gaze to his chest. "It's been a while."

Nerves prickled along her skin as he sheathed himself. More than a while. So long that she'd bought supplies in Invercargill four days ago, figuring the last packet she owned had gone past its expiration date.

"I've probably lost the knack." The pleasurable ripples spreading through her faded, overwhelmed by a dull weight in her stomach.

So stupid to be insecure, but twice now he'd given her indescribable pleasure—what if she couldn't return the same? What if she'd forgotten how to do sex and sucked at it really, really bad?

Del rolled onto his back and dragged her to sit on top of him. He traced a finger in slow circles down her breastbone, around her nipple, past her bellybutton to feather at the soft curls covering her mound.

"Baby, you haven't lost a thing. Let me show you. Let me be inside you." Sucking her into the fierce vortex of his gaze, Del lifted her a few inches off his stomach.

She wriggled down, positioning the tip of him at her slick entrance. Her internal muscles clenched and released as she lowered herself onto his hard length. Inch by amazing inch, he stretched and filled her. Del held himself rigid, stroking her thighs, letting her adjust.

"I'm sorry," she said.

"Don't be. You're so fucking lovely." He squeezed her bottom, rotating his hips as she sank a little deeper.

She leaned forward onto him, hissing at her body's final acceptance. Her breasts brushed over his chest with the sweetest friction.

Del groaned against her throat as her internal muscles fisted him securely. Tilting her pelvis, he angled inside her deeper, the feeling of fullness, the sweet bliss of his body moving inside her overwhelming.

She whimpered his name again.

So. Damn. Good.

Del eased her upright, his thumb stroking down her slick folds, around where they were intimately joined, and then back to flick against her core.

"You set the pace, baby," he said. "For now..."

Bracing her hands on his pecs, Shaye rocked her hips, controlling each torturous stroke. Breath seething out between his bared teeth, he stroked his thumb faster. Her rhythm picked up from a lazy glide into a faster tempo, each movement an exquisite lesson in sensation.

So close...so close...

Del gripped her wrists and tugged her off balance, using his larger frame to flip her over. "My turn, cupcake."

He palmed her leg higher, angling her hips beneath him so every inch of him scraped along her sensitively charged walls. Too much. Their tongues dueled with the same frantic rhythm as his powerful thrusts. She couldn't think now, couldn't catch her breath as he took her faster, harder, higher. Each stroke fed the flames roaring within her, and she writhed under him, nails digging into the firm mounds of his butt.

"Come for me," Del rasped in her ear.

She opened her mouth to argue that she couldn't possibly come again and—a second orgasm, more powerful than the first, blasted rational thought into pretty colored lights that danced on her eyelids. Swept away, she surfaced long enough to hear Del's coarse groan muffled against her neck, his big body shuddering in release. She pressed her lips to the sticky, orange-scented strands of his hair.

She hadn't forgotten how to do amazing sex, after all.

Chapter 15.

If he'd known sex with Shaye Harland would be so soul consuming and adrenalin pumping and ball-drainingly incredible, he'd have taken advantage of his afternoon break to have a power nap.

Del lay spread-eagle and sweaty on the bed, with an equally sweaty and sticky woman sprawled across him. Shaye's arm rested on his chest, her bent knee limp on his thigh only a short distance from his cock—which was pretty damn sure it could go again in a few minutes.

But squinting at the glowing numbers of the digital clock on the nightstand, Del realized junior was outta luck. Nearly two in the morning and he still had work in the kitchen. He palmed the sweet curve of Shaye's ass, and she snuggled closer, exhaling a breathy sigh into his neck that caused him to start hardening again.

Goddammit.

He kissed her forehead. "I gotta go."

Shaye made a low noise of protest, fingers tightening on his biceps. He patted her butt then gently peeled her hand off his skin.

"You ruined my cookie dough, remember?"

She sighed and rolled over. "You deserved it."

Del swung his legs to the mattress edge and stood. "Your aim is uncanny, woman. Think you missed your calling as a bowler for the Black Caps."

He turned back to the bed. Shaye had pulled the sheet over herself, covering all her delicious flesh. The thought of not seeing it again caused a sharp gut twist. Raking a hand through his hair, he grimaced as his fingers caught in sticky snarls.

"I'll have a quick shower. You go to sleep; it's late."

Del walked into the bathroom before he caved to temptation and returned to her bed. Water temperature dialed to barely lukewarm, he stepped under the spray. He needed to wake up, clear his head of the dangerous thoughts about spending the rest of the night making love. He'd sated his craving for her, and now he'd move on.

Closing his eyes against the water, he let the spray pelt his face, tiny needles that stung and called him a liar. He wasn't fucking sated, and how he'd move on, he hadn't figured out yet. Everything about her—the small birthmark under her left breast, the whimpering cries as she climaxed—was now hard-wired into his very being.

The shower door squeaked open, and arms slithered around his waist, two soft mounds pressing slickly to his back.

"Holy crapola! Are you trying to flash freeze us? Turn the heat up," Shaye growled.

He angled his head out of the spray. "I told you to go to sleep."

But like an obedient little lamb, Del adjusted the mixer so a blast of hot water came through. A sigh, a hum of approval, and she jiggled closer.

"I don't take orders from you, Hollywood."

Fingers splayed across his abs; her thumb traced slow circles on his skin. His cock twitched to life. Well, how could it not when the sexiest woman he'd ever known was rubbing her wet, naked body against him?

To hell with cookie dough.

Del turned and wrapped her in his arms. She looked anything but sleepy with her green eyes smoldering, her cheeks prettily flushed with color.

He grinned. "You were pretty damn compliant when I ordered you to come."

She huffed out a laugh and slapped his butt. "Nobody likes a smartass."

"You do."

He bent and licked water droplets off her shoulder, flicking his tongue over the curve of her collar bone and up the slender column of her throat. One of her hands darted up and threaded through his hair, stopping him from reaching her lips.

"We have cookies to bake."

" *We* do?"

She brushed a kiss over his mouth, cotton candy light and gone before he could claim anything deeper.

"We're a team. A cookie-baking, cupcake-frosting team." She snatched up a bottle of yellow-colored liquid and squirted some into her hand.

His brain spun with the spreading warmth of her words. A team. The two of them working side by side during the day and at night, driving each other wild—

Then her fingers curled around his cock, and he lost that train of thought.

"Since it's a well-known fact men think with this, I'm electing myself as team-leader."

Her fingers glided slippery-smooth over his swollen length, tightening briefly on the head of his cock. Lust speared through him, and he braced a hand on the wall, muscles in his thighs flexing as he strained for control. Holy shit, she was amazing.

"Team leader?" He managed to find his voice as she continued to work magic with her yellow liquid.

If he didn't kill himself by crashing through the shower glass, he'd send the manufacturers an appreciative letter. *Best lubricating-shower-gel...ever.*

"But before I take charge of the kitchen, we need to get clean." Her hand slipped off his cock and trailed foam up his chest.

How had he ever thought Shaye Harland was innocent?

"And we will." *In his own sweet time.*

First he had other plans. Del backed Shaye up so her butt hit the shower wall then sank to his knees, pressing a hot kiss on her tattoo. "Soon as I get you all taken care of, cupcake."

***

Del walked past a duo of carved pumpkins and a hanging cardboard skeleton in the foyer of Oban's community center, the sheriff's hat slipping over his eyes for the fiftieth frickin' time.

The first of the kids had arrived, and excited squeals drifted out of the hall into the early evening air. He'd handed the kitchen reins to Bill fifteen minutes earlier—his father insisting he and Vince could handle a slow dinner service for one bloody night. Shaye had already taken off, telling Del with a shy smile she'd see him there.

Working close to her all day and not touching her had been torture. Leaving her at four in the morning so they'd both get some sleep had been worse.

"Are you meant to be a cop like Aunty Piper?"

Del jerked at the small, high-pitched voice. A sword-carrying ninja and a grey-faced zombie stood next to him, their brows raised. Right. He'd been standing, staring blankly at the center's noticeboard, instead of manning up and going into the hall.

"Hey, girls."

The black-garbed ninja with pigtails, Ben's daughter, Jade, scanned him up and down with a scornful expression straight from her father's repertoire. The curly haired zombie beamed at him and elbowed her friend and soon-to-be stepsister.

"He's Rick from *The Walking Dead.* He kills zombies." Zoe demonstrated a few arms limply out, shuffling zombie steps. She cut him a keen glance. "And I'm a zombie. So, c'mon, Rick, a clean head-shot, right?"

Del's lips tugged up in the corners. Zoe and Jade's antics never failed to make him laugh.

He whipped his toy pistol from the holster strapped to his hips and drawled, "You are one...dead...walker." The soft foam ball shot from his gun and nailed the nine-year-old zombie right in the forehead.

Zoe fake-staggered, groaned, and collapsed. Drummed her heels on the floor. Moaned some more. An Oscar-winning performance, if Del had ever seen one.

"Another shot to make sure she's dead?" he asked a giggling Jade.

Jade's pigtails bobbed. "Yep. Right in the kisser."

"Hey!" Zoe's head popped up.

Del shot her again.

Both girls collapsed in a tangle of giggles.

"Shooting innocent zombies? Shame on you, Del Westlake."

Del turned, and the sight of Shaye looking so damn fine in her black lace and red gown, whiplashed through his system. His finger squeezed the trigger, and another little foam ball shot out, bouncing off the soft mounds of her incredibly framed tits. Pretty sure drool leaked out his mouth, Del froze.

Shaye's eyes danced green fire. "Now you're shooting at me?"

Giggles erupted behind him and a small hand tugged on his pants.

"You can't kill a vampire with bullets," said Zoe.

His head swiveled back to Shaye, and he took in her long dress with the lacy stuff flaring out of the elbows, the black ribbons criss-crossing her stomach right up to the low bodice of her dress, and her—come-to-think-of-it— powdered, unnaturally pale face and blood-red mouth. Peeling open her lips, she exposed realistic-looking fangs and poked out the tip of her tongue between them. She wiggled it with an unmistakable glance at the crotch of his tan pants, no doubt counting on the fact his body blocked the girls' view of her actions.

Holyfuckingshit. Hot vampire chick does the sheriff then sucks him dry.

He swallowed—barely. "Oh. You're a vampire."

Jade tugged Zoe to her feet and towed her along to the double doors leading into the hall. "Aunty Shaye's a vampire *queen*. So watch out, or she'll bite you."

Please God. Yes. Over and over.

Somehow he managed to smile politely at the girls before they disappeared. Then his gaze immediately switched back to Shaye, as if she really did have supernatural hypnotic powers. Something of his intentions must've shown on his face, because he stepped toward her, and she planted a palm on his sheriff shirt.

"Hold on there, Sheriff Woody." Her eyes—covered in smoky grey and black stuff that made them look both huge and sultry—sparkled with humor.

"Sheriff Woody?" His brain blanked, too many neuron's firing off at the same time—likely caused by how fucking *amazing* she looked. Then his fake sheriff pants pulled snug across his crotch. "Ahhh..."

He stroked his thumb along the delicate bones of her hand. "We could lock ourselves in the janitor's supply room?"

She grinned, showing some fang. "Not when there are games to play with a bunch of sugar-hyped kids, and our friends expecting us to go in there any second."

"Right."

Okay, running into Shaye's brother with a residual hard-on while managing a Halloween party did dampen Del's lustful thoughts.

"So quit looking at me like I'm dessert," she said.

"Every single man in Oban will look at you like you're dessert in that outfit."

*Bloody hell...*part of him wanted to drag her into the supply room anyway, and the other part wanted to cover her with his shirt so no other man could look at her.

And where, exactly, had this possessive streak come from?

Shaye flicked the cascade of curls she'd done her hair in over her shoulder. "Puh-lease. I grew up with most of the single men in Oban."

The palm on his chest turned into a poking finger. "Don't even mention Kip."

"Your non-date for the wedding?"

Shaye's eyes narrowed. "He could be my date, if I wanted him to."

Del shot her a cocky grin. "Maybe you've got a better option now."

"Maybe I do." She fisted her hands on her hips and angled her chin. "But for this evening, you have a party to run."

Shaye swept away, the long skirt of her dress swirling up to reveal the black stockings covering her slender calves and a pair of come-fuck-me heels.

Del snatched off his hat and held the damn thing in front of his groin. He dredged up one of his most revolting experiences—his first part-time job as a high school senior. Working as a bubble-dancer, he'd taken out the trash, slipped in some slimy shit, and had fallen onto a stray cat's disemboweled rat-dinner.

Yeah. That worked. Del adjusted the front of his pants and strode into the hall. If he could handle rat guts, then entertaining kids for a couple of hours would be a piece of cake.

***

Two hours later, the kids weren't the only ones buzzing. Any event in the Island's social calendar was reason enough for a celebration, and the locals arrived en masse. Although the event included no alcohol, since minors were present—Del lost count of how many ghosts, witches, and cowboys were attending—the adults still found a way to have fun. And in some cases, a little too much fun. Mrs. Taylor ordering him to "Arrest me, Sheriff Hottie," by the enormous punchbowl of bright-red vampires' blood proved the perfect example.

But he'd enjoyed himself more than he'd expected. Playing games he hadn't played since he was a kid—and he killed it in the egg and spoon race—settled the rush of tension thrumming through him after a full day's filming.

Del edged around West and Piper and headed for the hall's kitchen facilities. Piper, dressed in a striped prisoner's costume, snatched the last two cupcakes off the tray Del carried and shoved one at West.

"God, these are amazing." She swiped a finger through the orange frosting and stuck it in her mouth.

Freshly made frosting, 'cause you know, he and Shaye had wrecked the old batch.

"Go home, and tell my sister to go home too," said Piper. "The rest of us can finish packing it away."

West studied Del with one unpatched eye, tucking a plastic cutlass under an arm in order to peel off the casing on the cupcake. "Got bags under your eyes, bro. Late night with Shaye?"

Del kept his gaze steady. He'd overheard Shaye telling Piper and West how she'd supervised Del's party catering so he didn't screw it up. "Try baking five dozen cupcakes, five dozen cookies, and a shitload of other sugary crap after a dinner service."

The eyebrow above West's patch twitched up. "Uh huh."

Shaye's flowery perfume alerted him to her presence nearby.

"Did I hear you mention we can leave?" Lace brushed his bare elbow. "*Ohthankgoodness*. My feet are killing me."

"Serves you right for wearing skanky heels to a kids' party." Piper jabbed a finger at her purple combat boots. "See these? They're the reason I got ten times as many lollies in the lolly scramble than you did."

"You trampled me to snatch up a Fruitie," Shaye huffed. "And you know I love the lime ones."

West wrapped his arm around Piper's striped waist. "Nobody gets in between my woman and a free-for-all battle for junk food."

Piper leaned her head on West's shoulder. "I think we should have a lolly scramble at our wedding."

West grinned. "Anything you want, baby."

"I'm out of here, then." Del hefted the tray and glanced at Shaye. "You coming?"

"Absolutely. You can give me a piggy-back ride to Due South."

Oh, he wouldn't touch that one with a ten foot pole, not with West's and Piper's gazes zipping from each other to stare at Del and Shaye with unnerving speculation.

Del stacked the empty trays in the kitchen and got the hell out. Shaye waited for him in the foyer, skanky heals dangling off her fingers.

"Really? That bad?" He held the door open.

"I haven't worn these for a long time. It's like having little knives stabbing into the balls of my feet."

She paused by the steps leading down to the sidewalk. Her hair gleamed in the light spilling out of the hall, a stark contrast to the shadows pooling around the concrete. A soft sea breeze whisked by, bringing with it the echoing shouts of the trick-or-treaters who'd left the party and now moved between houses.

Gripping the bannister with one hand, she slipped on her shoes with a wince.

"Why put them on again then?" *Women. So weird sometimes.*

She fired him an *are you thick* look and limped down the stairs. "Because I paid twenty bucks for these stockings, and I'm not going to wreck them walking to the hotel."

Del jogged after her and caught her by the wrist. She stopped, and he moved in front, crouching slightly, hands braced on knees.

"Hop on then, queenie."

"I was joking about the piggy-back ride."

"Figured," he said, keeping his gaze straight ahead. "But I'm not letting you hobble to Due South. Hop on."

The soles of her shoes scuffed over the concrete. A moment later, her warm weight descended on him. Del straightened, grappling to find purchase with the yards of silky fabric in the way. He got a grip on her under the knees and hoisted her higher. She squeaked, arms going from loose around his shoulders to clenched around his throat, her breasts squished deliciously into his back.

He grinned and walked down the path to the sidewalk. Piggy backing was more fun than he remembered, especially since Shaye's nipples had reacted to the cooler night air and jutted into him. Her chin rested on his shoulder, her breath puffing against his ear.

"Okay?"

She nodded, curls brushing against him and her hands loosening a little.

Finally alone with her, he experienced the burn of nerves in his gut. Her accusations the night before that he hadn't told her about his engagement to Jessica had been eating away at him. He'd wanted to tell her for a while, but every time he'd tried to figure out how to bring up the subject, she'd smile at him, or do something sweet like leave a plate of cookies by his evening paperwork.

Now was as good a time as any. Sweat popped out on his forehead, but he'd no way of swiping it off. "I wanted to explain about Jessica. About how we came to be engaged...and what happened later."

Her body tensed, and she returned to neck-strangling again. "Okay."

Del wished he'd gone with his first instinct to sweep her up in his arms, so he could judge her expression. To hell with what any onlookers might think. But he hadn't wanted rumors to affect her—after all, she had to continue living in this town with gossips like Mrs. Taylor.

"It's not a pretty story, but it's one I should've had the balls to tell you before we slept together," he said softly.

She blew a puff of air out her nose. "Better late than never."

Never would've been easier—never would've been preferable.

Before Shaye, he hadn't given much of a shit about what people thought of him while he continued working his way up the culinary ladder. It didn't matter if his line cooks tagged him as an asshole—so long as they, and management, respected his work. But sometime in the last three weeks, he'd started caring what Shaye thought of him, both professionally and personally.

Especially personally.

So, he needed to tell her about Jessica. But the idea of exposing his past to Shaye felt about as appealing as presenting a substandard three-course banquet to a food critic.

"On Jessica's twenty-fifth birthday, we celebrated a little too hard, and I was trashed by the time we left her surprise party. Total blank until I woke the next morning with a pounding head and Jessica saying she'd called everyone to tell them the wonderful news."

A mini princess and a taller accompanying ghost burst onto the sidewalk in front of them. Del jerked to a halt.

"Happy Halloween!" the children yelled, barreling past.

Shaye adjusted her grip on him and murmured in his ear. "You asked her to marry you?"

He continued down the gradually sloping road toward Due South. "Guess I must have. And since her daddy was *Cosset's* owner and my employer..."

"You didn't want to disillusion her."

"No, and I did like her, a lot. I thought maybe marriage wouldn't be so bad. She'd at least understand the dedication you needed to make head chef—the long hours, the drive to succeed in such a cut-throat business."

"What happened?"

He'd known he'd fucked up only months afterward. He started drinking more, sleeping less, and the pressure of maintaining normalcy with Jessica's dad breathing down his neck became too much. The full story about how badly he'd screwed everything up was something he still couldn't stand to share, so he'd stick with the bare bones.

At the front of Due South, he crossed the road to the empty playground, and Shaye wriggled off. While she peeled off her heels, Del slumped on the bench seat overlooking the harbor. Shaye sat next to him, her hand settling on his thigh with gentle pressure. He squeezed her fingers and pretended the difficulty catching his breath was due to the unpleasant memories and not from the surge of tenderness sweeping through him at her small show of solidarity.

"Jessica got caught up in the whole wedding-planning thing. Eventually she couldn't overlook my lack of enthusiasm about seating arrangements and notecards, and we ended up having massive fights. I broke it off a few weeks before...shit." He hunched forward.

God, he felt like the world's biggest asshole.

"A week before the wedding?" Shaye wriggled closer to him.

He shook his head. "No. A few weeks before she nearly drowned."

Shaye remained silent then leaned on him. "I'm so sorry, Del. It's a useless thing to say, but I am."

Del sighed. "Jessica erupted after I told her we were through, but I think she was more embarrassed about calling off the wedding than the fact we didn't love each other." He scratched fingers down his jaw. "I kept my head down and continued to work my ass off, expecting her father to fire me at any second."

"He didn't?"

"Not then. She didn't tell her parents we'd split, though some of her friends knew, and I suspect her mother did too. Maybe Jessica hoped we'd reconcile, I have no fucking idea. Anyway, about two weeks after we broke up, we arrived at the same party. Jessica came over to speak to me, and it was as if she'd turned the situation around in her head. As if she'd decided to end the relationship. 'Course I was happy with that if it meant no more histrionics. I saw her later, draped over a couple of guys." Del swallowed hard, staring at the line of white breakers hissing ashore.

The party in Santa Monica seemed light years away from the one he'd attended tonight. A few months ago, if asked which party he'd rather be at—one with booze and drugs, or one with cupcakes and giggling kids—he'd have picked the first. Now, with Shaye snuggled into his side, his head clear thanks to the sea breezes, and a belly comfortably filled with cupcakes and Mrs. T's punch, the world of schmoozing and boozing had zero appeal.

"I was about to leave, but once I saw Jessica with those guys, I couldn't go without talking to her. I'd only had one beer, so I offered to drive her home. She made a graphic suggestion of where I could stick my ride. Her two new boyfriends would take her home later...much later."

"She wouldn't listen to you?"

He cut her a wry glance. "Jessica wouldn't listen to anyone. She got what she wanted and did as she pleased. So I left, instead of making sure the boss' daughter arrived back at her apartment safely."

"You weren't a couple."

He'd been madder than hell and bent on getting back to his place to get righteously drunk. To make everything go away.

"Yeah." He rolled his shoulders, bumping her a little bit away from him.

He couldn't bear her sympathy for the worst bit of this sordid little tale. "So anyway, Wayne Tanner rang me at 5:00 a.m. looking for his daughter. You can imagine the shit flying after I told him I hadn't seen her since the party. Before I could even explain we weren't together anymore, he hung up. I went into work, and the head chef told me what he'd heard. Wayne finally tracked down Jessica. Nobody knew exactly what happened to her, only she'd likely gone skinny dipping since her clothes were found on the beach. She must've gotten into difficulty in the water. Whoever was with her got her to shore and called an ambulance, but they fucking left her naked in the sand for the paramedics to find."

"Oh, Del."

"She's alive—though she suffered some neurological damage. I went straight to the ICU that morning, but not being family, I couldn't see her. I talked to her parents in the waiting room. Of course, they blamed me for letting her go off at the party, and wouldn't listen as I explained how Jessica refused my offer of a ride." Del sucked in a lungful of salty air. It burned clear and cold, but not enough to quench the fire in his chest. "Under the circumstances, I don't blame them for thinking I was a misogynistic asshole or Warren telling me to pack up my stuff and never set foot in *Cosset* again."

"You did tell them you and Jessica weren't a couple anymore?"

Del shook his head. "In the face of their grief, it hardly seemed important."

"But you lost your job—that's so unfair." Shaye turned sideways and slid her arms around him. She hugged him, pressing her face into his throat. "It wasn't your fault."

Del stiffened under her touch, but she didn't pull away.

"Jessica could've died. If I'd never broken my own rule and gotten involved with her, things may've turned out differently." He gently peeled her off and rose to his feet.

"You're too smart to believe that bullshit."

"Yeah, maybe." He held out a hand. "C'mon then, cupcake. I'll carry you over to the hotel."

She shook her head and stood, smoothing down the billowy folds of her dress. "I can walk."

They crossed to the front entrance of Due South in silence.

At the bottom of the steps, she turned and brushed a soft kiss on his cheek.

"Guilt nearly destroyed my family and screwed up my sister's life for years. Don't feed that wolf anymore, baby, it'll *fuck you up*."

Then she disappeared inside.

The motorcycle he'd borrowed off Ford was parked out back, so Del walked around the outside of Due South, glancing up at the rear corner window. Shaye's light blinked on. His gut clenched low and hard. More than anything he wanted to climb those stairs and knock on her door.

But thinking about all this shit with Jessica churned through him like a bad dose of food poisoning. He was headed into the same dangerous waters with Shaye—more dangerous than the ones he'd dipped his toe in with Jessica.

Because this time, he wasn't messing around with an attractive woman who kept his demons at bay. This time he was messing with a woman he could fall for big time...and never recover.

Chapter 16.

"Cut—cut!"

Shaye looked up from plating her rib-eye to Henry's red-faced fury. *What now?* She tucked the cloth into her apron and slanted a glance at Ethan and Del, the latter who also glared at the little director.

Henry stomped over and threw up his hands. "The bleeding hell is wrong with you today?"

Shaye reared back as if he'd slapped her.

"Don't talk to my sous like that," Del snarled, leaving his post at the burners with Ethan to stalk across the room. "She hasn't done anything wrong."

"Exactly. She hasn't done *anything*. She's a doormat, all 'yes, chef, no chef, anything-you-fucking-say-chef.'" Henry bared his teeth like a terrier about to nip an ankle.

Shaye tilted her chin down to meet Henry's gaze. "I'm no one's bloody doormat."

Del didn't touch her, but the connection between them flared hot and bright. She'd tried everything this morning to disguise it in front of the cameras.

She'd focused her entire being on the lunch service rush—a fake rush, of course, since Henry had filled the front of house with pre-selected locals and tourists keen to be on the show. Fake. Everything about this production was faked except, she conceded, Ethan Ward's skill in the kitchen. The man was brilliant.

With the camera crew underfoot, and the scripted feel of the whole service—including directions given to their "guests" on what to say when their meals were delivered—she'd begun to loathe her part in this production. Her big-girl panties were pulled up high enough to continue for Due South's sake—for Del's sake. Didn't mean she'd allow the annoying little man to treat her like a cowering dog.

Henry sneered, leaning on the counter, getting in her face. "Viewers don't want to see you and Del acting as if you are an old married couple. They want the kind of conflict we saw on the audition tape. Your snark and witty one-liners."

Shaye narrowed her eyes, tempted to grab a roasting fork and stab his hand. A heavy palm landed on her shoulder, long fingers curling over enough to restrain her should she lunge.

"My sous has always behaved professionally while I've worked with her." Del's voice could've flash frozen a pot of boiling water.

"I think what Henry's trying to say"—Ethan strolled to stand on her other side—"is we need a little more disharmony between the two of you for today's shoot."

She pasted on a small, tight smile, which Holly had nicknamed her *I'm about to rip your face off* smile, and turned to Ethan. "I'm doing my job, and I'm doing it to the best of my abilities with a bunch of strangers in our kitchen."

"I understand. And no one"—Ethan glared at his director—"is suggesting you're not." He squeezed her arm. "You're doing great for a first timer in front of a camera."

Del's grip tightened a fraction. She needn't be a telepath to understand he didn't like Ethan touching her. Kind of flattering and irritating at the same time.

Shaye stepped to the side, pulling away from both men and walking around the counter to stand in front of Henry. Being a good two inches taller than him, she used her ram-rod spine to her advantage.

"What you saw in the audition tapes were teething difficulties and not my normal behavior. Del and I have sorted out our differences in the kitchen, and we work well together. We're a team." The words blurting out of her mouth were a revelation to her, as well.

The most truthful sentences she'd spoken all morning.

Once Del got past being an arrogant jerk, and she'd gone beyond trying to prove her balls were just as big as his, they actually *did* work well together. They *were* a team.

Henry's lip curled, but before he could speak, Ethan interrupted again. "That's wonderful, Shaye. Really." He spread his hands. "But for now, we need the viewers to see the tension and conflict between head and sous chef. Give them discord, so after I swoop in to help, it'll appear you've made enormous progression in your working relationship."

"Not to mention your personal one," said Henry drily.

Shaye's jaw sagged. *Oh, God.* Were they that obvious? Her gaze zipped to Del, who looked at Henry as if the man were something Del'd scraped off his shoe.

"Now you're a team, and all." The director switched on a blindingly insincere smile. "I can come up with a few bitchy lines for you, love, if you need."

Shaye stared icicles down her nose, hoping they'd stab him in the eye. "I know how to be a bitch without your lines."

Henry muttered, "Good, let's see it then," and went to instruct Joss and Cruz.

Ethan winked at her and turned back to the burners.

Shaye slapped her hand on the bell to summon Lani. "Run to table seven."

Del's shoes scuffed behind her. He ducked his head and breathed into her ear, the whiff of basil and cedar wood drifting into her nostrils. "Do your worst; I'm man enough to take it."

Only she could hear his next words over the rattle of pans, the chatter of Ethan's crew, and the hiss and sizzle of the grill. "And tonight, I'll make you pay for each and every bitchy word."

***

Okay. Maybe she shouldn't have had that second glass of bubbly on a nearly empty stomach. Shaye dumped the rest of her champagne down the sink and set the plastic flute on Kezia's kitchen counter, next to the empty plates and trays from Piper's hen party. The flute slid off and clattered to the floor. Dammit, why hadn't her brother fixed Kez's counter? It obviously wasn't level.

Shaye rubbed the toe of her strappy sandals in the few drops of golden liquid spilling out of the flute. They didn't magically evaporate. *Whoops*. She twisted around to look for a dish cloth.

The room tilted the teeniest bit.

Whoa, now.

She grabbed the top of a dining chair and glanced over at the women in Kezia's family room. Thankfully, nobody noticed. Hen party games over—her gift of handcuffs and crotch-less panties the subject of many good-natured barbs slung at her big sister—many of the guests had already left. Some, like Denise Komeke and Caroline Russell, to collect their men from West's bachelor night, held down the road at Due South.

Shaye and Piper had given West grief about having a bachelor night at the pub. Her future brother-in-law had rolled his eyes.

"Jeez, you two," he'd said. "Ben and Del aren't planning a girly night with pin-the-dick-on-the-fireman and party favors. We're going to get righteously smashed, and everyone'll congratulate me on what a hot babe I'm marrying this Saturday."

"Sounds like fun," Shaye had muttered and left them to make kissy faces.

And Piper's party had been fun. Being in the most fabulous, loosy-goosy mood after Del had rocked her world the night before—and not even another day's stressful filming could dull her glow—Shaye had let her guard down after the first round of *Pin the Dick on the Fireman* (yes, it had been her idea, and screw you, Ryan Westlake) and accepted a glass of champagne. Then, of course, she had to have another to do the toasting thing, plus another half, because let's not forget to toast the groom too. Well. She hadn't exaggerated when she'd said to Del that a couple of drinks and she was anyone's. She wasn't *anyone's*, but she sure wasn't thinking with icy clarity.

Actually...the only thing she could think about was missing Del. Would he be having fun with his brother and the guys? She hoped he'd let his guard down enough over the last few weeks to realize he'd been accepted into the empty spot missing from West, Ben, and Ford's little circle of mates.

Though none of them would ever admit such a thing.

Men.

Shaye snagged the wrap she'd worn over her cute, fifties style, rose-print tea dress and slung it across her shoulders.

"You off, sweets?" Holly said from beside her.

Shaye whipped around, wobbled in her heels, and righted herself. "Yep. Heading home to hit the sack."

Holly's brow crinkled. "You okay?"

"Just a little sleepy and light-headed—you know me. I shouldn't have had that last half a glass."

Holly bent down, taking off her bright yellow flip-flops with daisies on the straps. "Here, swapsies. I let you walk home in those heels and you sprain your ankle, Piper'll kill me."

Shaye shot a sideways glance at the women surrounding her sister. "I'm not drunk; just a little tipsy—and I won't fall on my ass walking back to the hotel."

Holly raised her eyebrows.

"Fine." Shaye toed off her heels.

Holly offered her arm, and Shaye grabbed it, sliding her feet into the flip-flops and picking up her small shoulder bag.

Holly squeezed her arm. "You want me to come too?"

Shaye shook her head. "I'll just sleep it off, 'kay?" She allowed Holly to tow her to Kezia's front door and flip-flopped out onto the deck and turned—slowly, because she'd learned her lesson about sudden moves—to her friend. "Night, Hol." Then she blew a kiss and carefully climbed down the steps to the garden path.

"Night, Shaye-Shaye. Be good."

Shaye rolled her eyes and headed down the road to Due South.

Getting real tired of being good, especially since Piper and West's wedding was in four days—ergo, the man she wanted to be bad with would leave town soon after.

Ergo, she didn't want to miss any opportunity to get up-close and naked with him.

Ergo—Shaye stopped opposite the bar windows and stared inside. Del—even at this distance the glimpse of his smile fired off all sorts of yearny-achy feelings down low in her belly.

Shaye pulled the wrap tighter around her shoulders.

Ergo, a night alone was ugh, unappealing. Maybe she'd send him a text and get him to come up once the boys' night was done. But biting her lip to stop from screaming Del's name and waking the guests next door wasn't the ideal way to spend one of their last night's together.

Huh. She blinked blearily at the windows. What to do...what to do?

A sous chef prided him or herself on solving problems that arose, allowing the head chef to focus on more important things. And she was a damn fine sous—if she did say so herself. She'd solve this little privacy problem by hiking her butt out to Del's place and climbing into his bed.

Thirty-minute walk? No problem. The fresh air would wake her up. Shaye flip-flopped past Due South toward Shearwater Bay.

***

Who knew he could make one beer last the whole evening and not give in to drinking a second? Who knew he'd not once feel as if he wanted a second beer, when he could only think about Shaye in her pretty flowery dress walking up the road to the hen party earlier.

Del checked his watch for the umpteenth time and caught a glimpse of the same flowery fabric outside the window. He glanced up to see the sway of Shaye's hips disappear out of sight along the foreshore road.

Where was she off to?

A coil of warmth spiraled through his chest. Guaranteed she'd snuck out of Kezia's place and was headed to his—and with any luck, into his bed. The warmth chilled as his brain registered two important things: pitch dark out and it appeared Shaye didn't have a flashlight.

"That my sister?" Ben's bulk leaned forward and peered out the window, blocking Del's line of sight.

Del put his empty beer bottle—which he'd had Kip refill a couple of times with soda water—down on a nearby table. "Yep. Looks like it."

"Where the hell is she off to at this time of night?" Ben's eyebrows twitched together.

Damn.

Del straightened his shoulders and braced himself. "She's looking for me."

"What?" Ben's voice contained a note of confusion as he twisted and rose up on his toes, trying to see beyond the outdoor umbrella one of the staff had forgotten to take down after dinner service earlier. "Why would she walk right past Due South looking for...?"

Ben jerked away from the window as if someone had shoved a cattle prod up his ass. Yep...he'd figured out the answer. Built like the proverbial shithouse wall, Ben Harland was the kind of guy you wanted on your side in a brawl. Not the kind of guy you wanted pissed at you for sleeping with his baby sister.

But he'd take whatever Ben decided to dish out. Long as he got it over with fast—Del didn't like the idea of Shaye wandering around in the dark alone.

"She's going to your place?" Ben glowered at him. "Aw, fuck no. Not you and Shaye."

He met Ben's gaze flatly. "Yeah, me and Shaye."

Ben shoved a hand through his hair, leaving it standing up in wild tangles. "You're gonna break her heart, aren't you?" He shook his head. "Shit. Then I'll have to rip your legs off, West's little brother or not. It's my duty, man. Sorry."

Something hot like an over-spiced meatball lodged in Del's throat and refused to budge. He didn't give a shit if Ben wanted to pound him, but why the hell did everyone assume he'd be the one to hurt her? The woman had a spine of steel—as a teenager she'd single-handedly helped her mum through her grief, she was a dedicated sous who'd gone above and beyond her duties to support his father, and he'd watched over the last month as she'd taken care of everyone else in Oban but herself.

She was the strong one.

She was the one who'd wave him off at the ferry terminal with a smile. She was the one who'd stand, while he fell to pieces walking away from her.

He folded his arms. "I'm not going to break her heart."

Ben narrowed his eyes and said nothing. Then he nodded, the corner of his mouth twitching. "You know what?" The twitch turned into a smirk. "I believe you. Because you're gone on her, aren't you?"

Del's jaw sagged, his mind going blank. "Uh. N-now, hang on a second."

Ben's smirk ratcheted up into a shark's grin. "Mate, you are really screwed." He moved around the table and yanked Del's jacket off the back of the chair. "So move your ass before she gets lost, eh?" He balled up the jacket and tossed it.

Del caught it, opened his mouth, closed it at Ben's raised eyebrows, and sighed. "Yeah. I'm moving my ass."

"Good. 'Cause I'm still tempted to lodge my size thirteen work-boot in it."

Del shot him a grimaced smile, and Ben cocked a finger in his direction. "I've been through this kind of drama once with your brother, so don't make me come after you."

"Remember, I've always been faster than you, Harland." Del shrugged on his jacket.

"You have. But one day, you're gonna have to stop running."

With a sour taste in his mouth he couldn't blame on beer, Del headed out of the bar and into the night. The breeze had picked up and clouds scudded across the sky, blocking what little light the moon spilled over Oban's quiet streets.

Shoving his hands in his pockets, he considered taking Ford's bike. Nah. The walk would clear his head from all these crazy thoughts swirling around in it. He hustled past the last streetlamp, his footfalls echoing. A moonbeam broke through the clouds and illuminated Shaye's silhouette about a hundred yards ahead. A silhouette definitely not walking in a straight line.

Prickles scurried down his spine, sucked into a gaping vortex left in his gut by the memory of seeing Jessica that last time. Del picked up the pace, easily gaining on Shaye, who appeared to be placing each foot on the road with studious care.

Suddenly, she whirled, something draped around her shoulders puddling to the ground. She tried to keep her balance, but her arms flailed. He sprinted the last couple of steps and grabbed her hand.

"Oh. Hey. It's you," she said. "My sexy chef with the very fine asssss."

Del reeled her in, and she poured onto him like sticky toffee, draping one arm over his shoulder, the other snaking down to squeeze his butt cheek. He jerked, not just from the ass-squeeze, but from the cold nose jammed into the crook of his neck.

"Shaye, you're freezing."

He ran his hand over her bare arms, goosepimples tickling his palms. Freezing, but thank Christ, safe.

"Cupcake. Call me cupcake." She snuggled closer, her limp weight knocking him back half a step. "I like it when you call me cupcake."

Del wrapped an arm around her waist to support her and peeled her hand off his ass, his heart still racing fit to burst. He held her close, sucking down the scent of her—floral perfume, a hint of chocolate and orange...and the unmistakable whiff of champagne.

"Let's get you home then, cupcake. You're drunk."

"I am not drunk." Some indignation got lost in transit, since her mouth remained mushed against his throat. She pulled away, smiling up at him. "I'm happy. Very, very happy. 'Cause we're going to your house, and we're gonna make each other very, very happy."

She wriggled against him, and his groin tightened. *God.* How much willpower was a man supposed to have? He swallowed and walked her around in a circle until they faced the opposite direction.

Then he kissed the tip of her freezing nose. "Rain check, huh?"

Her lower lip quivered. "You don't want me?"

The woman wasn't firing on all cylinders, considering he now sported a hard-on fit to pound nails, and how it was currently pressed into her stomach. He raised an eyebrow at her and waited. Took her a few seconds, but she got it.

"Oh. You do want me."

"Yeah. Very, very much."

Her fingers, still tangled in the hair at his nape, tightened. "Then let me come home with you. I don't want to be alone tonight."

Shit. He didn't want to be alone, either. Knowing before he'd suggested taking her home she'd refuse, and he wouldn't be strong enough to make her, Del closed his eyes. "Fine. But so you know, you'll pay for scaring the crap out of me this evening."

Her brow crinkled. "I scared you?"

He touched his lips to the cute wrinkles in her forehead. "Seeing you wobbling along the road in the dark—"

"I was not wob—"

Del cut her off with a kiss—a kiss that lasted long enough to set his heart pounding again.

"You taste like champagne and trouble." He brushed his thumb along her kiss-wet lower lip. "And you were wobbling, baby. All I could think about was something happening to you while you were on the way to my place."

"Something...? Oh. Like Jessica." Her mouth pinched shut, her eyelashes flickering down. "I'm so sorry I scared you."

She wrapped her arms around his waist and hugged him. The wave of tenderness flattened him in its path, turning the blaze of fear and lust fueling him only moments ago into a smoldering wreckage. He had to tell her the truth about the kind of man he really was and how *he* was so scared, knowing she'd want nothing more to do with him.

But not now, not tonight. She looked at him with adoration—he couldn't bear to see her opinion of him change, couldn't stand to disappoint her.

"Shaye?" He held her close.

"Yes, Hollywood?" came her voice, muffled against him.

"Think you can walk to my place?"

Her head twisted from side to side on his chest. "Nope."

Yeah, he didn't think so either.

With a sigh, he disentangled her arms and turned around, crouching down and gesturing with his hands. "Hop on."

Chapter 17.

Shaye's idea of the world's worst thing to wake up to? A cot and a row of vertical metal bars. The second? Finding herself in an unfamiliar bed, clad only in a tee shirt. With a headache throbbing like a radio with the bass turned up too high. A headache that pounded even harder, as a psychopathic bird began to screech.

Shaye cracked open an eyelid. Metal bars. Slammed the lid shut, got brave, and then looked again. Her brain finally ceased tossing thoughts of jail cells and handcuffs around. Ahhhh. Just the struts of a bunk bed.

Bunk bed?

Rustling noises came from beside her, followed by a muffled curse uttered in a rough tone. Basil and warm, sleepy-man smell crept into her nose.

She was in Del's bed.

Curled up, facing the wall and wearing...Shaye ran a hand over her stomach and up to her breasts, finding both covered in a loose, multi-laundered knit fabric.

Wearing Del's tee shirt.

Her hand skimmed down again and encountered high-cut lace, not the beige support panties she'd worn under her party dress. Oh, crap. But she'd arrived at Del's in her party dress. At least, she thought she'd been wearing a dress when Del poured her through his door and into his bedroom.

A big hand landed on her hip, and a hot, hard male snuggled up behind her.

"I can hear you thinking, Shaye. Oops—" Warm breath misted against her ear. "I mean...cupcake."

Shaye squeezed her eyes shut. *Cupcake*. She'd ordered him to call her cupcake and then...she groaned. She didn't remember anything after stripping off her dress.

"Oh. My. God." Her shoulders hunched forward. "Did I fall asleep on you?"

His lips, pressed against her shoulder blade, curved. "You did. And you snore. I believe it's a Harland thing or so Dad told me when he mentioned West's complaints about Piper when she has a cold."

"Ugh." Shaye exhaled through her nose, not wanting to be responsible for knocking Del unconscious with what must be truly awful morning-breath. "Sorry."

"Not a problem, cupcake."

She grunted and turned her face more into the pillow to breathe before she got dizzy and lost consciousness. "Why am I not wearing my underwear?"

"They *are* your underwear, just not the ugly things you had on under your dress. I had to strip you out of your clothes. Don't you remember?"

"I don't remember anything. My brain hurts." She lied, because, hello, it'd all come back in Technicolor gloriousness.

Del carrying her back to his place—and at some point she'd dozed off on his back. Del setting her down on his bed, slipping off her shoes, helping her into his tee shirt. Del tucking her under the sheets and stroking her hair as she dropped into unconsciousness, er, fell asleep.

Heat washed over her face at the memory. He'd been so sweet, so gentlemanly, and so...kind.

"Bird-Brain's early morning wakeup call probably isn't helping," he said.

"Bird-Brain?"

"Noisy feathered bastard on the deck who thinks this is his personal B&B." He tugged her earlobe and moved away. "Anyway, I'll go feed him and make coffee. Stay here, I'll bring you a cup."

The loss of his warm skin pressed to hers made her chest squeeze tight. Aside from a head the approximate size of an over-inflated beach ball, this was the best morning she'd had in...ever. It shocked any lingering drunkenness out of her system to admit how much she wanted to wake next to him every morning.

Del hauled on clothes and padded out of the room. She uncurled from the mattress edge and sat up, cupping a hand over her mouth and exhaling. She sniffed. Pulled an eww-nasty face. Thank God she'd been facing away from the poor man.

The family room sliding doors screeched open, and a short whistle and a low murmuring cut through the morning silence. Del talking to the kaka.

For some reason, this sent a flurry of warm fuzzies scurrying through her. The man she'd first met on the ferry a month ago would never have bought a supply of peanuts for an unwanted morning guest. The lonely guy, the prickly, proud man who couldn't stand to be in the same room as his father—well, she'd just heard him call Bill "Dad" for the first time.

Shaye slithered out of bed and shuffled to the bathroom. She glanced in the mirror and gripped the edge of the sink to prevent falling on her ass.

Holy-freaking-guacamole, she looked worse than little Zoe dressed up as a zombie. *Ugh.* She patted down her hair, which had started to frizz, and splashed cold water on her face. Contemplating Del's toothbrush, she crinkled her nose. Either get over the squick factor of using his toothbrush—considering how much their tongues had been in each other's mouths, it was ridiculous to be squicky at all—or breathe dragon breath on him.

After a lightning-fast brush, a gargle of mouthwash, and dry-swallowing two painkillers, Shaye tip-toed down the hall. She sneaked a glance to the left while she crossed the open area between bathroom and bedroom. Del was in the kitchen, his back turned, stirring two steaming mugs.

He twisted to drop a teaspoon into the sink, giving her a glimpse of the cut muscles jutting above the low-slung waistband of his jeans. The aroma of coffee was almost as good as sex.

Oookay. In a showdown between a cup of coffee and a cup of *smooshed up against Del's illegally hot, naked bod...*her gaze slipped to his denim-clad ass. He hunkered down to wipe something off the floor, and the tight mounds flexed. Good lord...what had she been comparing again?

Shaye hurried into the bedroom and crawled onto his bed, stomach quivering with anticipation. Now that her eyes worked with only tiny toothpicks stabbing into her skull instead of pickaxes, she appreciated the front view of him as he walked into the room carrying two mugs.

"You look more alive." He placed one of the mugs on a chest of drawers and handed her the other.

"Uh-huh."

She took the mug without looking down, her eyes apparently agreeing with her previous conclusion that a cup of Del beat a cup of wet, ground beans any day. They refused to stop staring at the hard ridges of his abdominal muscles and the sparse trail of dark hair disappearing under the halfway undone zipper of his jeans.

"Almost...perky, in fact."

He grinned his dimple-infested grin at her, she just knew it. But, nope, she had enough to deal with— *she could not quit staring at Del's crotch.*

"Uh-huh." Some willpower returned and she tore her gaze away.

He sat on the edge of the bed. "Drink your tea. It'll help with the head."

She glanced down at the insipid green liquid in the white mug. "Tea?" She sniffed it. "Green tea?"

"Good for hangovers." His smile slipped, and he looked down at his hands resting on his thighs. "I should know." A short pause while his fingers bunched into fists. "And so should you."

She sipped the bitter tea, the runaway urge to jump Del and see how gravity-defying his jeans were disappearing. What man over the age of eighteen didn't have a hangover story or two....or three? But something about the rawness of his tone sent warning prickles up and down her spine.

"Del? Join me?" She hated the slight quaver in her voice, but she couldn't seem to steady it.

She patted the mattress and held out the mug. Del placed her cup next to his on the dresser, and took a quick, fortifying sip of his coffee. Then he ducked under the top bunk and crawled onto the bed next to her. He lay on his side, his hand propped under his head, the lengthwise gap between their bodies like a canyon.

"I know this is a sore point, after what happened to your dad," he said. "But I need to tell you about the last year of my life. Before I came here, before I met you."

His Adam's apple bobbed in the strong column of his throat, his chest heaving as if he had to struggle on every inhale. As if he was about to say something he'd never, ever be able to take back.

Shaye didn't want to hear it. Not while he was looking at her with his beautiful storm-cloud eyes. Not now she'd started to believe Del could be her Mr. Perfect, right under her nose this whole time.

"You don't need to explain about your life a year ago." Though she couldn't meet his eyes in case he read her truth there—who he'd been in LA didn't matter so much as who she hoped he was now. "You're not the same man."

"No." The corner of his lip quirked up. "I'm trying to be a better man, but—"

Shaye pressed a finger to his lips and wriggled across the canyon-sized gap until she could slide her leg over his. "Forget buts, unless we're talking about your bare one. Just show me how much better you are, Hollywood."

She replaced the finger with her mouth, touching the tip of her tongue to the closed seam of his lips until he caved with a hoarse groan and returned her kiss. Del's tongue danced inside her mouth, transferring the rich taste of coffee to hers. The buzz bubbling through her veins couldn't solely be attributed to a second-hand shot of caffeine.

He gathered her closer and rolled, covering her with warm skin and denim. The weight of him, the sheer bliss of all his hardness bearing down against her softness...she wanted to absorb him into her very pores. Shaye wrapped her arms around his neck and hung on as if gravity might somehow reverse and tear them apart.

Their breaths mingled before his lips crushed hers with a soul-searching deep kiss. She hooked her legs over his and arched her hips, grinding against him.

"Sure about this?" he groaned into her mouth. "I don't want to make you feel worse."

With her throbbing happy-place sparking off all kinds of pleasurable sensations, she was light-years away from *worse*.

"Worse would be if I can't get your pants off in the next thirty seconds." She tried to grip his jeans between her toes to pull them down, but the damn things were too snug on his amazing ass. Oh, she could fill notebooks of cheesy poetry about Del's ass. "Help a girl out."

"Maybe you should finish your tea," he said, but he lifted his hips and reached behind to tug them down.

"Maybe you should shut up and help me get us both naked."

His grin could've started a kitchen fire. He dipped his head, caught the hardened nub of her nipple gently between his teeth, and tugged, his tongue making a wet patch through the cotton fabric.

"Helping?" He switched to her other breast.

"No. Not really."

Suckling at her nipple, Del caressed the breast he'd abandoned. Pretty sure her eyes were crossing, Shaye moaned and fisted his hair.

He shifted down her body and hiked up the tee shirt. She wriggled with him, helping to remove it. As soon as he'd flung it away, his mouth dropped to her breasts again, his tongue tracing circles on her skin. Hot, wet kisses trailed from her breasts to her stomach as he inched down the bed. His tongue flicked once in her belly button, and then his teeth grazed over her tattoo.

"Everything about you is sweet." He dragged his hand to her mound, the pressure from the heel of his palm against her core making her hips jerk up. "So sweet, I found out too late your sweetness is more like salt." Curling his fingers over the waistband of her panties, he tugged them down around her thighs.

She frowned, the fun and games of an early morning tumble turning serious again. "Salt?"

Del slipped her panties down her ankles and tossed them aside. He kissed his way up her legs, stopping to sink his teeth lightly into her inner thigh. "What's the one ingredient a chef would never be without in a kitchen, baby? Sugar or salt?"

Shaye couldn't breathe, her throat clogged with a wave of emotion. "Salt," she whispered after a moment. "No chef would give it up for sugar."

"Yeah."

He put his mouth at the juncture of her thighs and flicked his tongue over her core. Her hands fisted into the sheet.

"Cupcake, you're my salt and the taste of you fuels my deepest fantasies. I just can't seem to give you up."

You don't have to give me up, she wanted to say. *God knows, I don't want to give you up either.*

He lowered his head, and she squeezed her eyes shut in anticipation, his warm breath tickling her skin. Lips circling her core, Del coaxed her slippery flesh to tighten, sending pulses of hot pleasure flooding outward. He swept his tongue down her cleft and up again, torturing her with slow swipes, then faster, harder flickers. Back arching, Shaye felt her control slip farther into chaos.

Del played her with perfect timing, the same instinctive knack he possessed while focused on his work. He knew when to tease with soft, glancing brushes of his lips, when to speed up and drive her mindless with sensation, when to lock her tightly against his mouth and send her sobbing over the edge.

Before she could float down into herself, foil tore, and he drew her arms up over her head, guiding her hands to the metal bars of the bunk's low headboard.

"Hold on." He gripped her behind her knees, spreading her wide open to him.

One thrust filled her, took every preconceived notion of what her body could accept and spun it on its head. He stretched and demanded she take him deep inside her body, and so deep inside her heart she'd no hope of ever carving him out again.

Del quivered with tension as he held himself above, their only point of connection his hardness surrounded by her slick heat. He withdrew, the delicious friction making her cry out his name. Sliding between her folds, he rubbed against her then entered her again, taking his time, *every single inch* driving her out of her mind.

Something about the way he studied her in the pale slashes of dawn creeping through the cracks of his bedroom drapes caused her chest to squeeze off her air supply. Time stuttered to a halt, her heart beating a wild tattoo. "Del?"

He blinked, the intensity fading to a hot, raking stare. "Don't let go."

He moved inside her, long, sure strokes until his control fractured. His urgency and need triggered an insatiable response inside her. She drove him on with her body, with the cries she couldn't contain, as damp skin slapped against damp skin.

Hovering just above her lips, Del whispered again. "Don't let go."

Dark lashes slipped down over his eyes, masking the endless depths that had turned summer-sky blue.

"I won't." She drew a ragged gasp and then another.

He kissed her, mimicking the thrusts of his body. It took him over, this wild connection between them continually gaining strength. She felt it in the pounding of his heartbeat, the surge of his blood, the building pressure promising release for them both.

As he pulled his mouth from hers and buried his face in her neck with a hoarse cry, the orgasm slammed into her, spinning every last thought out of her head except one.

I'll never let go of you, Del Westlake. I can't.

***

A car door slammed as Del wrapped a towel around his hips and stepped out of the shower. He scrambled into a pair of board shorts and checked his reflection. For the first time in weeks, he didn't glance away from the man staring back. The man wasn't perfect, not by a long shot—look how he'd screwed up talking about stuff with Shaye yesterday morning when he'd had the chance—but the dude in the mirror seemed healthier, more relaxed, and most importantly, sober.

Three sharp knocks sounded on his sliding door, followed by a squawk and flap of wings. Bird-Brain deciding to try his luck with a second breakfast.

"It's open," he hollered and ran a hand over his hair, which jutted up in ten different directions.

Del had been up since before six and painting by seven. He'd ended up doing the whole damn house for Walter, instead of just the worst southern wall, but what the hell. Only the window trims left to finish and the house was done.

The sliding door shrieked in its runner—another thing he'd added to his to-do list—and he walked out of the bathroom. Henry stepped inside.

"Ah, your dad thought you'd still be here," he said by way of greeting, and perched on the couch arm. "I wanted to have a little chat with you before we started filming today."

A little chat with Henry required another coffee then a gargle with mouthwash. Dealing with Ethan's director always made Del feel as if he'd eaten something past its best-by date.

Del entered the kitchen and flicked on the gas element under the kettle. "Coffee?"

"Tea. Earl Grey, if you've got it." Henry rested one skate-shoe-covered ankle on his knee.

Skate shoes and fancy tea? Bloody hell. Del swallowed a smartass comment and said mildly, "Sorry. I've only got the ordinary stuff."

Henry winced. "I'll leave it."

Del shrugged and rinsed his mug, one printed with the phrase: *Never Trust a Skinny Cook.* Piper had picked it out for West to give Del as a best man gift—much to West's embarrassment at handing over the gift bag complete with girly bow.

"Why are you here, Henry?"

"Straight to the point. I like that about you."

Frankly, Del didn't give a shit whether Henry liked him or not. But on a professional level, he didn't want to screw with the little man's good will—and it made him feel as if he *had* swallowed something coated in mold.

"I prefer directness." Del leaned against the rear kitchen counter, keeping the server between them.

"Brilliant. I'll be direct then." Henry laced his hands around a skinny knee cap. "We had a team meeting last night, reviewing some of the footage shot over the past five days. Ethan says you're one of the most charismatic chefs he's worked with on camera. You're a natural. You get into the zone, and not even a bomb scare could break your focus." Henry beamed at him. The man's grin radiated so much fake warmth it could've turned milk sour. "But..."

Henry's smile toned down a notch, and Del's scalp began to prickle.

"The same can't be said about Shaye—"

Del propelled away from counter and slapped his palms on the server, a flash-fire igniting in his gut. "She's a solid sous—one of the best chefs I've worked with."

He'd take Shaye over Ethan-fucking-Ward any day—except Ethan could jumpstart Del's career and get his life back for him...in the US.

Henry held up a placating palm. "We're not talking about her skills, Del. Just her presence on camera." His eyes slitted, mouth drawing in tighter than a dog's ass. "Shaye is as dull as proverbial dishwater. She never looks natural, never gets in the zone, because she's always aware of the crew, and it shows."

"She's not an actress! Shaye didn't sign up for this shit; she's doing her job."

"I understand. But today, you're going to have a confrontation during lunch service, and you'll fire her."

"What?" Del froze, his blood icing when a moment ago it'd run red hot. He stalked out of the kitchen, his fists clenched, itching to plow them into the man's smug face. "The fuck I will."

Henry stood, staring him down. "You signed a contract."

"I don't give a shit about the contract." Del forced the words past a locked solid jaw. Henry could run his name into the mud, take him for every dollar in his bank account, but he wouldn't betray Shaye.

"Well, then. Do you care about Due South? We can pack up now and leave, but our legal team will take action against you, and your father and brother—both of them signed a contract with us."

His family? The little weasel was threatening Due South and his family? It'd kill his father and brother to lose the hotel in a drawn-out legal battle. Jesus.

Del pinched the bridge of his nose. "You're asking me to screw over the only person who keeps the place going."

And the woman he cared about far too much. Being a chef at Due South meant everything to Shaye. How could he take that away from her?

Henry rolled his eyes. "Don't be so melodramatic." He moved out of striking distance, scuttling to the sliding door. "Look—it's only for the show. Shaye will have a few days off before her sister gets hitched, and once we've finished filming, by all means, reinstate her. No harm, no foul."

"I doubt she'll see it that way, but I'll talk to her."

Henry held up a warning finger. "No. You won't talk to her about this—not before the shoot today. If you warn her of what's to happen, it'll show all over her pretty face. We want her honest reaction, not some farce where she pretends to be shocked and stunned."

They asked for Del to betray her, to use the trust she'd had in him to do the right thing for Due South against her.

"She'll be crushed. How can firing Shaye on international television do anything but make me look like a complete asshole?"

"As a *Ward On Fire* contestant, you're not aiming to be Mr. Nice-Guy." Henry waved his hand in dismissal. "The viewers need to see you're tough, to believe you can go from working in a tiny rural shithole, to working in Ethan's empire. A chef who puts his sous' tender feelings before business won't gain any sympathy from the masses. It's a wolf eat lamb world—show some teeth."

A month ago, Del would've agreed with Henry's description of his father's restaurant. But now...

Tying on his apron, the gut twist of apprehension Del felt the first time he'd walked through those kitchen doors had gone. He'd grown accustomed to his father's system of hand-writing everything down in ledgers, and the way Bill would show up to prep asking for Del's instructions, as if the man hadn't done it himself every day for thirty-plus years. He enjoyed swapping kitchen horror stories with Vince, and arguing the merits of rugby versus rugby league with Fraser. Even Shaye's damn swear jar made Del smile—and yeah, he often deliberately added to it, knowing the local kids needed the extra library books the funds provided.

And today, he'd shit all over what he'd been helping rebuild—not only Due South's reputation but his fragile relationship with his father and brother—by dismissing the person he believed was Due South's heart and soul.

But what choice did he have? Say no to Henry, and Del risked the only thing that kept his dad going and potentially removed his brother's only source of income. So, really, he had no choice. Easier to ask for forgiveness than gain permission. He'd do what Henry asked and make amends to Shaye afterward.

She'd understand. *She had to.*

"Okay. I'll do it your way."

"Good." Henry cocked his head, his dark eyes turning hawk-sharp. "Tell me, is it strictly business between you and Shaye?"

Del dropped his hand from his face, his heart a numb thing still racing far too fast. Like hell would he give the man any more ammunition to use. "Of course. But in two days' time, I've got to stand next to her at my brother's wedding. She'll fucking hate my guts."

Henry tsked. "Family dynamics, eh? Can understand why you moved halfway around the world to avoid them. Still, you'll be rid of the whole shambling affair in a few weeks. You're returning to the States, whether you make the finals or not, I take it?"

Was he? Would he just walk away from his dad, leave the old man alone to deal with his health problems? Abandon his mom and now his step-sister Carly—and his brother, who looked at Del as if West were proud they were related?

And Shaye. Who pelted him with cookie dough one moment then touched him with such tenderness that his throat clogged with emotion. The one person who believed in him, who thought him a better man than he was. Would he walk away from her, too?

"Yeah." The word felt like a grit-covered stone in his mouth. "I'll be returning to California in a few weeks."

He had to go. Any decision other than leaving was a stalling tactic. Time for a reality check. He didn't belong in Due South. He didn't belong on Stewart Island, period.

Chapter 18.

Something was going on with Del.

The man had a burr up his butt all morning, and she couldn't do a single thing right. If cameras hadn't been stuck in Shaye's face, she would've socked him in the shoulder and told him to stop being such a bloody asshole—and gladly paid the dollar to do it.

And okay, Del barking orders at her as if she were a first-year student on work experience hurt a teeny bit. This sudden return to *jerktasticness*, she told herself over and over, had nothing to do with the breath-stealing things they did with each other locked away from prying eyes. Maybe on afternoon break she'd sweet-talk him into taking her for a spin on Ford's bike then ride *him* like a bronco.

"Shaye!" Del yelled.

She startled, knocking a plated frittata off the counter. Oh, crap! She never dropped plates, and that was her second this morning.

"Goddamn it! What's the matter with you?"

Flustered, Shaye didn't know whether to reach for a cloth or kick him in the shins. She stammered an apology, and Fraser appeared at her side with a broom.

"I'll take care of it, Chef," he said.

Del snapped out more orders. Pressure, she decided, squeezing her lips shut. She slanted a glance at Ethan, who gave her a sympathetic smile. Why Del had to be such a dickhead when Ethan went out of his way to be polite and professional—she couldn't fathom. Admittedly, she wasn't at the top of her game. They were close to chaos, as today's lunch service was the first to experience Ethan's new menu. The rare beef and *foie gras*, crab frittata, roasted quail and other dishes all tasted divine—but how would they go over with the locals?

"Table three is getting antsy," called Charlie, fidgeting at the window. "Where's my frittatas?"

"Ask bloody Shaye," came Del's snarled response.

"Waiting on two beef, one pasta, one salmon for table six." This from Lani.

"Table nine is about to walk. Where the hell are my quails?" Helena chimed in.

Ethan and Del's orders flew around the kitchen like shotgun pellets.

"Fire the mussels for table two."

"Eighty-six the quail."

"Pump it out, Vince, c'mon."

"Table six, run it."

"Shaye!" Del appeared at her side. "What the fuck are you doing? You're meant to be expediting!"

She reared back, scalded by his tone. "I—"

"You're standing there like a fucking statue."

"Sorry, Chef." Her voice came out a choked squeak.

"Sorry's not good enough this time. Get out of my kitchen."

At first, she didn't understand what Del meant, the contours of the face she'd traced with her fingertips so contorted that he'd become unrecognizable. Then her gaze flickered to his finger, extended and pointing to the door.

"*What?*"

"Get. Out."

Cogs clicked and rotated in her brain. She had to close her eyes a moment to work out the significance of his words. "Wait—are you firing me?"

"Yep."

"You can't." Part of her—the bit not focused on her lover and the man she trusted ripping away the thing that mattered most—was proud of how she'd apparently learned to ignore Ethan's crew.

"I can. I have. You need to leave."

His eyes pierced her like cold steel, bereft of warmth or mercy. She saw the ruthlessness then, the determination that had transformed a heart-broken fourteen-year-old boy into a man who'd put ambition before anything else.

"But, Chef—Del...please." Everything she'd come to feel for him tore through her words, leaving them raw and bleeding at his feet.

The only reaction on Del's face was a slight muscle tic in his jaw.

Henry and his insatiable need for drama would be behind this—no doubt the little man, hunched evilly in the corner of the kitchen, was salivating with excitement. Perhaps the director even expected her to burst into tears and beg Del for her job? Hard luck. She was a Harland, daughter of a man who'd had the discipline to train and dive to depths unimaginable on one breath.

Shaye angled her chin. "You don't get to fire me, Westlake." She yanked on the ties of her apron. "I quit."

She balled up the apron and hurled it at Del's head—which hit a bullseye of course—and stalked to Due South's back door, where she whirled around to Cruz's camera and flipped it the bird. Childish? Hell, yeah. But boy, it felt *good.*

"Enough *friction* and *disharmony* for you, Henry?"

Then she walked out and slammed the door.

***

"You've got some nerve," Glenna Harland said after opening her door—the one reserved for friends and family at her B&B.

To say Shaye's mom looked at him like something clogging a bathroom drain was an understatement. The Oban grapevine was alive and thriving. Del resisted the urge to swipe his clammy palms down his legs and instead shoved his hands into his pants pockets.

"Been told that before, ma'am." Sticking with squeaky-clean politeness might work in his favor. "But I'd like to speak with Shaye, if she's here."

And please, let her be there...he'd looked everywhere else.

He'd texted, rung, and left messages while on bathroom breaks—the crew must've thought he'd had the bladder of an eighty year old—but nothing.

West shoved him into his office the moment lunch service and filming was over, demanding to know why Del had fired his soon-to-be sister-in-law. After he explained, West had shaken his head and sighed.

"I'm going to find her now and sort this out," Del said.

The best laid plans and all that shit.

After he'd banged on her door for five minutes, Denise had come upstairs and told him to quit it—Shaye wasn't there. So he'd tried her friends—Kezia, Holly, Erin from the Great Flat White Café. Figured women went to their female friends first when a guy acted like a horse's ass. The three women had stonewalled him with similar replies. *After hell freezes over, I'll tell you where Shaye is.*

He wasn't brave enough to ask Piper or Ben if they'd seen her.

Finally, Del returned to Due South and ran into Carly. His sister called him an asshat, and said, "Try her mom's place, but don't you dare mention you spoke to me."

So, he'd fronted up, asshat-extraordinaire, on Glenna's doorstep.

"You're the last person my daughter wants to see right now," Glenna said.

He swallowed past the thickness in his throat but didn't lower his gaze. "I think you're right, ma'am, even though I had good reasons for what I did." Time to play his trump card. "And I'd like to try to explain those reasons to Shaye before the wedding. I don't want any animosity between us to mar Piper and West's big day."

Glenna's rigid posture softened, and she huffed out a long sigh. "You'd better come in."

Del followed her into the hallway.

"She's in the kitchen," Glenna said quietly. "I'm sure you remember where it is?"

His stomach flipped in a sickening roll, though his childhood memories of the Harland's place were mostly good ones. He'd belonged here then, even if it were only as a tagalong. Glenna and Michael Harland had given him safe harbor and the messy noise of a family who loved each other to replace the vacuum of affection in his own home.

He nodded, reaching out for the door handle. Glenna's hand closed over his before he could turn it. When he glanced up at her, her hazel eyes were bright, intense.

"We never got over losing you, Del. None of us—me, Michael, the kids, and most of all, your father and Ryan."

His stomach dropped at the sudden topic change and the shot of emotion it fired through him. "Ah. I thought you were mad at me?"

"Oh, I am. Plenty mad." Glenna flashed a grim smile. "But I believe you when you say you had good reasons to do what you did. You'd never do anything to truly hurt her or your family. You're still one of my little tribe of hooligans."

Many times as a kid, he'd overheard Glenna refer to her children's circle of friends as her tribe, the words surrounding him in the warmth of inclusion and affection. Now it filled him with an aching loneliness. Maybe he'd left a hole here thirteen years ago, but it was too late for him to fit into it again. His shape had changed. He wasn't a kid whose biggest problem had been his parents' imminent divorce, but a man with jagged edges and a whole shit-load of baggage.

Yet, he was touched enough to kiss her cheek, the faint scent of her perfume—Chanel No. 5, he remembered—curling around him. "Thanks, Glenna."

"Go talk to her." She squeezed his hand then let go, moving out of his way. "I've seen the two of you together, I know you're..." A pregnant pause as Glenna dipped her head and looked up at him with a meaningful glance. "Good friends. So for goodness sake, don't make it worse."

Del nodded, because hell, what could he say to her? *Yep, I'm the kind of good friend who has boned your daughter every chance I got. Or, I'm the kind of good friend who'll continue to crave Shaye, even though we're almost at the bottom of this dead-end street.* Some friend.

"Right," he muttered and opened the door.

Good luck to him in not making everything *a lot* worse.

Shaye had her back to him in the massive kitchen, her right arm stirring something agitatedly in a big mixing bowl. Vanilla and caramelized sugar and chocolate drifted in the warm kitchen air, the sweet scents of a woman baking off her mad. Del pressed his lips together as her arm froze, and she turned her head.

She stared at him, her beautiful face for once devoid of emotion. He'd no idea what thoughts—homicidal or otherwise—flickered through her brain. Strands of her hair had slipped out of her mussed-up ponytail, and as he moved to sit on a breakfast bar stool, a few drips of batter splattered out of the bowl and dotted across her tight-fitting tank top. He'd spotted her chef's jacket dumped on a dining room chair when he first entered the kitchen.

Brushing her forearm over her brow, Shaye broke eye contact and continued to stir.

"You planning to dump cake batter on me, cupcake?"

Her head whipped around, the bland expression evaporating into a *now I'm gonna gut you with my paring knife* glare. She jabbed the wooden spoon handle in his direction. "You. Don't get to call me that again. *Ever.*"

Yeah, he'd figured after the nickname slipped from his lips that he'd just thrown gasoline over the situation. His bad. Del folded his arms and leaned on the counter. "I'm so sorry, baby, and I can explain—"

Shaye snorted. "Spare me your pathetic guy explanations for why you acted like such a butthead."

"I was told to act like a butthead."

"You had to act, you vain, lily-livered, half-witted pig's bladder of a man?" She dumped the bowl on the counter and spun around to grab a paper-lined cake pan off the opposite one.

His heart lurched, the corner of his mouth twitching in an effort not to smile. Good God, he was crazy about this woman—ass-over-teakettle, as his dad would say—and totally, royally screwed.

Del propped his chin on the heels of his palms. "Since you've ramped up the Harland temper, let me have it. I can take it."

She tipped the mixing bowl, the creamy golden batter pouring into the cake pan. Scraping out the last of the mixture with a spatula, she stared at him, her hazel eyes shooting fire. "No. You've taken enough from me." In contrast to her fiery gaze, her voice was corpse cold, freezing her temper into icy shards. "You took my trust and my reputation and fucked it over like a cheap hook-up. You think I'll yell at you for a bit then forgive you. You're counting on my tendency to mediate and smooth things over, so you don't have to feel bad."

Dammit, she'd nailed him by the balls. "Shaye. You haven't really been fired; it's just for the show."

"Henry's idea?"

"Yes! Of course it was Henry's idea. *Jesus.*" Thank God she understood. Yet the way she scraped out the bowl with stiff, jerky swipes..."You know I think you're a fucking brilliant chef." His voice softened at the sight of her pinched mouth and shiny eyes. "We're good together, Shaye, in the kitchen and out of it."

She placed the empty bowl in the sink. "Why did you throw me under the bus?"

It all sounded so sordid and selfish now. "Henry threatened to pull the plug on production here, to set his lawyers on me, Dad, and West if I didn't cooperate. They would've sued Due South for breach of contract."

Her eyes widened. "Holy crap."

"You've no idea what a pile of dog shit I felt like having to do that to you today. Yelling at you, goddamn firing you in front of everyone—fuck." The devastated look in Shaye's eyes when she'd called him chef...*totally did his head in.* "I just wanted to rip Henry's smug face off. I really am sorry, Shaye."

The murderous expression on her face softened to slightly homicidal. "That jacked up, scummy little bastard would've ruined your reputation and crushed Due South in one fell swoop if you'd refused."

"I couldn't risk him going after Dad and West. As to my reputation..."

His heart kicked into high gear, pounding so hard, colors suddenly seemed unnaturally bright. *Tell her now, you sonofabitch, while you've got the chance. Tell her how you're her worst nightmare of a man.* A guy tiptoeing along the razor blade edge between recreational binge drinker and alcoholic.

Wasn't as if she could be any less disappointed in him.

"Well, in LA, my reputation's already ruined, at least amongst the top restaurants." He stood up and edged around the counter as Shaye blasted water into the mixing bowl. One false move and she'd aim the nozzle in his direction.

She dropped the sprayer into the sink and turned to him. "Because of Jessica and her dad?"

"Yeah. Gossip travels fast in this industry." Del shook his head, bracing his spine, his stomach churning over and over.

He couldn't do it, just couldn't lay his heart bare. His goddamned pride at admitting how much he'd fallen apart jammed in his throat.

Then holy hell, Shaye wrapped her arms around him, hugging him so tightly his emotion-constricted lungs couldn't wheeze in another breath. Strands of her hair, flying loose from her ponytail, tickled his nose. Warm and soft and strong, she pressed her body to his, the feel of her in his arms both his deliverance and punishment. After her initial pity, which goddamn it, he didn't want, she'd pull away in disgust.

"Rock, hard-place, and you stuck in the middle." Her lips moved against his chest. "You couldn't let Henry go after Bill and Due South."

He froze, his hands, which had slid around her shoulders, gripping the thin straps of her top. "I'm not one of the good guys, Shaye. What I did to you today proves it."

She pulled away from him enough to meet his eyes. "You had a jerk relapse, and you are a good guy, you big dumb-ass. But you should've told me what was going on. I would've understood."

"Yeah. In hindsight, I should've—even though you know your acting sucks." He smoothed a hand over her hair.

She unwrapped her arms from his waist, her eyes narrowing. "I'm not that bad."

"You kinda are." Though damned if he knew why he was tempting her to get mad again. Somehow, her temper was easier to bear than Shaye defending him against himself. Easier if she kept her soft little heart out of his clumsy hands. He didn't want to hurt the one person who appeared to see the real him; but hell, after he stepped on the ferry one final time, he would.

"Look, Shaye, once the filming's done, things'll get back to normal. You'll return to work in Due South, and as head chef—which is what you've always wanted, right?"

Her chin lifted. "Right."

"I'll speak to West about advertising for another chef, and I'll help with the interview process when he comes home from his honeymoon."

"You'll still be here?"

"Henry says the finalists won't be notified for about three weeks. Plenty of time to set you up."

"And if you make it to the finals, you'll fly to London," she said dully. "To work with a man I know you don't like."

"It doesn't matter what I think of him personally. No chef would be stupid enough to turn down the opportunity to work in one of Ethan's restaurants."

"Because it's all about the adrenaline rush of working in a flashy kitchen."

The bitterness in her voice rankled.

"Don't bust my balls for wanting something more than Friday night pizza and Sunday roasts for the geriatrics. I like the buzz, the challenge of being driven to be the best, the never-ending opportunities to learn. You've never experienced the rush; your wings have been clipped by lack of ambition and your loyalty to this island."

Shaye backed away from him. "My loyalty has been to my family and to your father—they mean more to me than ambition. People are more important, Del, something I seemed to have learned on this goddamn island."

"It's not disloyal to put yourself first once in a while."

"But is it right to ignore someone's pain when you can help them?" She folded her arms and stared him down.

He cleared his throat. "Ah, yeah. About the whole kidney thing..."

She cocked her head. "You've made a decision?"

"I've been talking to the doctors. They can do the transplant laparoscopically, so I could be out of the hospital in two days and return to work between one to three weeks. I can fly from London to New Zealand and then be on a plane home within a week."

"Wow. Sounds as if you've got it all worked out." She gave him a tight smile, but her eyes remained cool. "Now, if you'll excuse me, I have baking to do." She snatched up the cake pan.

Hang on—didn't she hear him say he'd hack out a kidney for his father? "Are you dismissing me?"

She cranked open the oven, and a gust of super-heated air blasted out. She flicked him an icy glance over her shoulder. "I'm telling you to get the hell out of my kitchen."

Shaye Harland was the most frustrating, conflicting, irritating, baffling woman he'd ever met. Del threw up his hands and stalked to the door. He opened it and stepped into the hallway.

Then, through the doorway, he said, "Guess this means you won't be my date for the wedding?"

He managed to slam the door shut before the spatula hit the frame where his head had been moments before. That would be a no, then.

Chapter 19.

Shaye's mouth hurt. She blamed the fake "happy bridesmaid" smile. Her eyes stung. She blamed that on almost jabbing her eye out with a mascara wand. Her body hurt. Blame the Spanx, because screw it, she was gonna be the hottest wedding date Ethan Ward had ever had.

And the ache in her chest every time she glimpsed Piper looking so beautiful in her wedding dress? Totally indigestion from the cake and cookies she'd snarfed down instead of lunch. Nothing to do with the fact she hadn't spoken to Del *since he'd fired her.* Or that she'd sucked up the last of her pride and asked Ethan to be her plus one—because like hell would she show up alone now. Ethan had been a perfect gentleman and readily agreed.

So, even though Annie—who'd kindly offered to do the bridal party's makeup—had to apply concealer with a trowel to the shadows under Shaye's eyes, she looked good. Well, tolerably good, considering how much everything inside her hurt something fierce.

Holly fussed with the finishing touches to Piper's hair in Glenna's formal lounge, and in twenty minutes, they'd head off in Rob Komeke's '67 Chevy Impala to Kahurangi Bay. Where West would be waiting to declare his love forever in front of all their friends and family as the sun sank in a flaming ball over the horizon. Shaye'd stand on the beach with them, pretending everything was peachy perfect.

"Shaye?" Kezia touched her elbow. "You've gone all quiet."

Shaye bared her teeth in an *isn't this exciting* smile. Deliberately self-edited her reply so it wouldn't contain the phrase *I'm fine*, which any female knew translated to: *My life is falling apart, but see how brave I am?*

"Just thinking how gorgeous my big sister looks."

"Uh-huh." Kezia's chocolate-colored eyes narrowed to intimidating slits.

Short and curvy, with clouds of dark curls, Kezia might look like a sweet-natured angel, but she had the ability of a medieval witch hunter when it came to prying the truth from her friends. She'd been groomed by the best—the Harland sisters. Shaye'd only flown under Piper and Kezia's radar for this long because they'd been busy with their own men, and planning for Piper's big day.

"A lame explanation doesn't fool me for a second—concealer's not a miracle cure." Kezia squeezed her arm. "You're unhappy."

"I'm unemployed. Of course I'm unhappy."

"No, this isn't unemployment unhappy, this is man unhappy. I should know. Been there, done that, got the *maledetta* tee shirt."

Shaye sighed, wrapping her arms around her middle, rubbing the soft chiffon of the dress between her fingers, hoping the physical sensation would distract her from imagining Del in his best man suit.

"Del's gotten to you, hasn't he, *cara*?"

"No, not at all. I'm fine."

"No, you're bloody well not fine."

Shaye whipped around to a scowling Piper, who stood there with fists on white silk-covered hips.

Shaye reapplied her *isn't this exciting* smile. "Pipe—you don't need to worry about me. It's your *big day*! You're going to marry the man of your *dreams* in the most *perfect* wedding, ever." Any more ferociously upbeat and her head would explode.

Piper's glare didn't melt and return to the gooey expression she'd worn since early this morning. "Save your fake happy face for the beach."

"I am *fine*, dammit," Shaye said, and then contradicted herself by bursting into tears.

"Oh, fuck a duck," her sister muttered, patting her arm while Kezia raced to the coffee table for the tissue box.

Piper raised her voice above the sudden sympathetic female noise—her mother, Holly, and Annie all headed in Shaye's direction. "Hey! Everybody out of the room for five minutes. Annie—we'll need you back with your magic tool-kit afterward; this is gonna be messy."

After the lounge door shut, leaving them alone, Shaye curled into the couch corner and blotted her face with a handful of tissues. "It's not meant to be like this."

"What isn't?" Piper perched next to her. "You mean *love*?"

"I'm not in love with him. It's just one minute Del's the biggest pain-in-the-ass jerk I've ever met, and the next, I can't imagine how I'll get through a single day without him."

"Oh, Shaye-Shaye." Piper shook her head with a wry smile. "I'm sorry, but stick a fork in your chiffon-covered butt, because you're toast."

"It's *done*," Shaye muttered. "Stick a fork in you, you're done."

"Whatever. You're in love with Del Westlake. He's the one."

"He's *not* the one. He's nothing like what *the one* is supposed to be like. Remember the list, Pipe?"

Piper sighed. "How could I forget?"

"Well, I've already been through it with Holly, and Del doesn't check the boxes. He's *not* my perfect guy."

"One day, you'll figure out love doesn't give a flying squirrelly fuck about checking off boxes." Piper grabbed hold of Shaye's hand and squeezed. "Do you believe West and I can make a go of this?"

Shaye blinked at her. "Of course. You guys are amazing together."

"He's the only man I've ever loved, the only man I'll ever love." Piper's hazel eyes went soft and dreamy, then a second later switched to the flat gaze of the cop she'd once been. "Yet some days, I still consider whether my inside knowledge of police procedure would aid me in throttling him and burying the body in Raikura National Park."

Shaye laughed. "You do not!"

"Okay, slight exaggeration. But my point is, yes, neither one of us is perfect. Separately, we both have broken, fucked-up stuff inside us, but together, we somehow make a whole. A wonky, imperfect whole that'll require lots of work over the next fifty years to turn imperfection into something beautiful. But it'll be worth it. Because I love him, and he loves me."

"That's probably the most romantic thing I've ever heard you say. I just hope you left the *fucked up stuff* out of your wedding vows."

Piper grinned. "West made me. But back to you and Del."

"He's returning to the States as soon as he can find a replacement chef for Due South."

"He told you this?"

Shaye nodded. "I thought he'd changed. He and Bill are getting on better, and I thought maybe he'd let himself love his dad again."

Piper twisted her engagement rings—one West had given her when he proposed, the other he'd bought for her when Piper was still a teenager. "You don't think he'll donate the kidney?"

"Actually, I think he will. But in the way a good man with a conscience would donate blood or marrow to a stranger to save their life. He seems to be treating it like 'take out my kidney, shove it in the sick old dude, then I'm on the first flight back to my real life in the USA.'"

"Ah. You know, at one stage, I thought I'd rather gnaw off a limb than remain trapped on Stewart Island. Del's going through a lot of what I went through before I realized this would always be home."

"It's home for you, because West is here and you love him." Shaye uncurled from the couch and walked over to the picture windows, which opened up to a view of the Oban township and the sparkling water of Halfmoon Bay Harbor. She pressed her flushed forehead to the cool glass. "You'd live in a bloody slum in Rio or a high-rise apartment block in Hong Kong, as long as you were with West."

"True."

"Del doesn't love me." The words slipped from her mouth like heavy stones, but they didn't relieve the dull ache in her chest. He didn't love her. He wanted her, and at first, the thrill of that had been enough. A hot affair to burn off the attraction between them, then they'd go their separate ways.

Stupid woman.

Del warned her at the beginning not to get attached, not to make him one of her strays.

"Are you sure?" With a rustle of silk, Piper came to stand beside her, wrapping an arm across her shoulder.

"Well, I'm not you. I won't threaten to kick him in the nuts if he doesn't tell me," she huffed.

Piper chuckled. "I slept on your bedroom floor then hustled my ass back to Wellington, because I was too freaking terrified to ask my man if he loved me."

Shaye leaned her head against her sister, drinking in the warmth and solidarity that had returned between them after so long an absence. "I want love to be stress-less, uncomplicated, and sweet."

"I know, honey," Piper said. "But that's called the friendzone and believe me, you don't want a long-term thing with a guy who doesn't drive you crazy in bed and out. Besides, Del can be sweet."

Shaye snorted, even though, yeah, Del could be sweet. Sometimes. Like when she'd rolled over and watched him sleep in the faint moonlight slipping through her curtains. The harsh lines of the man had faded into boyish innocence as he lay in a starfish pose, the duvet shoved over her side because he'd kicked off the covers.

"One outta three ain't bad," Piper sang, which being her, was off-key and awful.

But enough to raise a genuine smile on Shaye's face and a roll of her eyes. "It's *two outta three.*"

"Whatever," her sister said. "Now let's fix your face before Mrs. Taylor decides I've done a runaway bride and forces West into becoming Mr. Taylor the second."

***

Del had worn suits before, dammit, so why did he want to crawl out of his skin and dive into the cool waters of Kahurangi Bay? Maybe it was Ethan Ward sitting two rows from the front, his arm braced over a chair back, flirting with Erin Donaldson—who wasn't his date. Nuh-uh. His date—Ben had taken great satisfaction in pointing out when the man rocked up at the beach—was Shaye.

Ethan laughed, a sound that probably made every female in his orbit quiver.

Douchebag.

Del shifted from foot to foot, and slipped a finger into the jacket's inner pocket to check he hadn't lost the ring in the past two minutes. *Still there. Thank Christ.*

He slanted a glance at Ben beside him. Got a *dead-man-walking* stare from the groomsman. *Ouch.* Big guy still hadn't forgiven Del for firing Shaye. Neither had the locals, judging by the occasional dirty looks aimed in his direction.

Del's gaze flicked right to his brother, expecting some outward display of nerves or jittering about-to-bolt signs. Ben, of course, would body-slam West face first into the sand before allowing him to ditch Piper at the altar. Or, specifically, the flower-covered arch thingy under a huge pohutukawa, which doubled as the altar. But West stared at the gap between the dunes where the bridal party would appear, grinning like a man about to receive a million dollar lottery check.

From the dunes, Ford waved a hand then jabbed a thumb over his shoulder. Murmurs of excitement spread through the guests, who were seated on folding chairs decorated with ribbons and more flowers, which matched the arch thingy. Periwinkles, West had said.

Dressed in matching dark blue dresses, Zoe and Jade crossed the beach together, earnestly scattering rose petals on the sand.

Shaye stepped out from the dunes. The blue floaty dress she wore hugged every curve and detonated every single brain cell in his head. Her long, nutmeg-colored hair cascaded down her back in soft curls, and her face...He was dazzled—blinded as if someone had whipped off his sunglasses as he'd been staring at the sun. And while spots of light danced in his vision, imagination transposed her short blue dress for a long white one. Changed her artfully arranged curls into her normal straight hair with a crown of flowers. Swapped the bouquet of roses for an armful of wildflowers.

Del blinked the vision away. Bloody hell; where had *that* come from? He reminded himself to breathe—and to remain upright.

Shaye passed by the first row of chairs, and Kezia, in a matching dress, followed close behind. Shaye smiled at the guests but kept her gaze away from Del, moving to stand on the other side of the arch.

Bill emerged from the dunes with his cane, joined moments later by Piper, who wore a white flowing dress. His father leaned over and kissed Piper's cheek, patting her hand resting in the crook of his suit-covered elbow. His sister-in-law looked radiant; her smile alone would've powered Oban's generators for a month.

The soft, haunting notes of a piano solo piped out of the speakers—*Autumn Leaves*—a piece he recognized West playing upstairs a few times on their mom's old piano. Piper and his dad walked across the sand, the bride hiking up her dress to reveal white combat boots.

Del smothered a grin, went to nudge his brother—stopped at the single tear tracking down West's cheek. As if a ghostly fist had ploughed into him, his stomach clenched. The raw emotion, the intensity in his brother's eyes as he watched Piper, crushed Del's ribs, made his heartbeat a hollow throb.

West had done it. West had found someone to love, someone who loved him in return. Someone who'd brought him to his knees and then helped him stand tall. A woman worth fighting for, a woman who'd fight for him.

The lucky, lucky bastard.

In that moment, as West extended his hand and their dad placed Piper's in it, Del had never been more envious of his older brother.

He risked a glance at Shaye. Her eyes were so green, they shone like polished emeralds. She'd been crying. That he knew this was another indication he was floundering way out of his depth.

The celebrant started the service, and Del had no idea what she said—her voice remained a background drone to the blood rushing around his body, pounding in his ears.

Could he be as lucky as West? His gaze traced down the line of Shaye's neck, the graceful flare of her waist and hips, her long legs and her pale-blue combat boots. Which made him smile, and ache, and his heart perform weird flip-flops.

All too soon, Piper handed her small bouquet of roses over to Shaye, and Ben jabbed Del in the ribs as a reminder to produce the ring. The rest of the ceremony passed in a blur of laughter, tears—not his, *thanksverymuch*—and promises of eternal love, *yadda-yadda-yadda*.

Yeah, sometime between the ring swap and the register signing, he'd got his cynical back on. He couldn't do it. No matter how much a part of him wanted to shout from the rooftops he'd found his sous for a lifetime, the bigger, hasher part of him knew Shaye Harland deserved better than a career-obsessed, selfish drunk like him.

Del lined up to follow the new Mr. and Mrs. Westlake down the makeshift aisle. Shaye offered him a brief, vanilla-mild smile as she slipped her arm through his, and then turned her real smile on at the guests.

With every step he took along the sand, the light touch on his forearm burned like a brand. He'd gone down for the third time trying to keep Shaye out of his heart, because none of his defenses were worth shit. Each attempt to keep her away, she attacked his walls from an unexpected angle and left him vulnerable.

Dammit. It was already too late for him to walk away unscathed.

***

After endless handshakes and obligatory posing for photographs, the wedding party and guests shifted from the beach to Due South.

Piper and West insisted no one would work at their reception, so the restaurant and bar remained closed to the public, and they used the kitchen for reheating the shared casseroles and salads guests provided for a "pot luck" buffet meal.

Del stood off to the side and avoided people. He smiled, and when he had to, he said all the right kinds of bullshit expected of a best man, and once left alone, he watched...

Bill sat in the corner while his mom tried to tempt him with something to eat. Kezia perched on Ben's knee, whispering in his ear. Carly sat sandwiched at a table between Kip, and Bree Findow, giggling at something Kip said.

He nursed his fourth beer—because, fuck it, a guy's big brother didn't get hitched every day—and watched Ethan at the buffet table. The man wore a slight sneer as he scanned the selection, some of which he damn well knew Shaye and her mother had spent hours making.

Local food not good enough, you snobbish prick?

He didn't know when his attitude had changed, but he found Ethan's obvious distaste for the food, insulting. The man hadn't even *tried* anything yet. And come to think of it, the idea of Due South continuing to serve roast beef with fucking *foie gras* after Ethan had gone made Del shudder. His dad's restaurant would never gain a

Michelin star rating. But they could provide tasty, quality meals to customers who wouldn't need a French dictionary to figure out what they'd ordered.

Maybe he felt differently now because in LA, he was only some anonymous drone, cooking his ass off behind the scenes. Here in Oban, he was a real person. One the locals stopped in the street to tell him they enjoyed his experimental Malaysian curry, or how they thought the seafood platter could be improved by adding a side of tangy apple coleslaw—and they'd be happy to pass on their Aunt Mary's secret recipe. The hell of it being, Aunt Mary's secret recipe was *pretty damn sublime.*

Due South was a good place, a solid place, and now he wanted to fill it with the kind of menu he and Shaye knew would appeal to both locals and tourists. But no, he'd had his head stuck up his own ass, thinking Ward's shitty TV show would fix something that actually wasn't broken. Yeah, the restaurant needed some upgrading tweaks, but not a whole teardown overhaul as he'd first thought.

Del was about to break for the bar when Shaye caught his eye. She came up beside Ethan, and he laid a light hand on her waist, guiding her away from a group of men intent on stacking a small mountain of food onto their dinner plates. Blood raced helter-skelter through Del's veins.

"Del?" Ford came up and nudged Del's arm. "Nearly time for the speeches according to Glenna's schedule."

Ethan bent down, his face turned into Shaye's ear.

Sonofa—

"Mate, don't go there." Ford's voice dropped to a low rumble, his hand clamping around Del's forearm.

Del grunted but allowed Ford to turn him aside.

"C'mon. Get the speech done without making a complete dick of yourself, and I'll buy you another beer."

"Booze is on the house, Ford." Del rolled his eyes then caught Ford's grin. "But you knew that. And thanks for the vote of confidence."

"West needs a good roasting, and you're the guy to do it." Ford slapped his back hard enough to make Del's beer slosh in the bottle.

The next ten minutes passed in a blur of speeches—starting with his thrown-together, *West's a lucky man* speech, and finishing with a toast to the new Mr. and Mrs. Westlake. The microphone then got passed around to anyone who felt duty-bound to recall both bride and groom's lives from birth onward.

Del managed to escape into the less crowded bar once the mic landed in the bejeweled hands of Mrs. Taylor. That'd give him an opportunity to grab another beer. Alcohol had done a bang-up job of smoothing the raw edge off seeing Shaye seated so close to Ethan.

He snagged a beer from the bar and headed to the picture windows on the far side of the room. The space around the windows was deserted, and the muscles across his back—which felt as if they'd been trussed up like a chicken—finally relaxed.

Outside, silhouettes moved back and forth on the beach, people stacking firewood on the bonfire, ready to be lit as part of the Guy Fawkes celebration. It was almost full dark, and soon, the wedding party and guests would move across the road to enjoy the bonfire and fireworks display. Trust West to want to get married with a bang.

Ethan drew alongside him, his hand shoved deep into his charcoal suit pants. "That old bitch, Mrs Taylor, still knows how to party."

Del's shoulders jerked, but he sipped his beer while the slow burn in his gut flickered into flames.

"She does," Del said. "She also knows how to treat kids dying of malaria, since she worked in third-world countries as a nurse for thirty-five years. So watch your mouth."

"Happiness and lovey-dovey vibes haven't rubbed off on you, have they, mate?"

Del turned his head.

Ethan returned his cool stare, eyes gleaming as he dropped his chin to indicate Del's beer. "Or did your monkey finally crawl out of its hole and climb on board again?"

His finger tapped out a rapid beat against the bottle's cool sides. "Don't know what you're talking about."

"Oh, I think you do, and now I understand the filthy looks you've been giving me all afternoon." Ethan took a sip from his wine glass and smirked at Del over the rim. "You've put down roots here again, haven't you? Maybe you even think your family and rag-tag bunch of islanders believe you're a local hero. Did you come clean with them, Del? Did you tell them how you'd show up at *Cosset* half-hammered and how you did a runner on the boss' daughter after she nearly drowned—class act, by the way...your old man would be so proud."

Every muscle in Del's body turned to granite, and saliva evaporated in his mouth, leaving it drier than the Sahara.

Ethan knew? He knew everything?

Ethan shook his head. "Oh, for Christ's sake. You really believed my people wouldn't ferret out the juicy gossip that you're a drunk? It's the main reason we wanted you on the show. The viewers are going to adore the bad-boy chef who's been given a chance to sober up and rebuild his dreams."

The revelation sank into his gut, a cold iron anchor weight. Ethan wanted Del because of the potential to milk his screw-ups for audience entertainment. His slot on *Ward On Fire* had little to do with his skill as a chef; instead, the producers had been attracted to the whiff of scandal surrounding him, like sharks scenting blood in the water. That they'd use him—and God forbid, drag Jessica and her family into it somehow—well, *fuck*.

Del wanted to punch the smug bastard's artificially whitened teeth out, but the two people laughing in the next room stopped him. He wouldn't ruin West and Piper's wedding by pummeling one of their guests.

So, he set his jaw and dipped the neck of his beer bottle at Ethan. "I guess I owe you." *A punch in the bloody nose.* "Working with you these last few days has opened my eyes." *To what a self-absorbed idiot I've been.* "And thanks for not mentioning my history to the staff." *Since I've managed to quite nicely screw things up without your help.*

Ethan huffed and then smiled benevolently. "There must be something about this place you see and I don't. But regardless of the lack of decent cuisine and the dreadful muck here you call coffee, Oban seems to produce some talented chefs. Like you." He raised his glass. "And my most excellent date, to whom I must return."

He turned away from the picture window and said, "And there she is."

Del spun around—*oh, shit.*

Shaye was a few feet behind them, a trembling hand clasped over her mouth and her cheeks flushed crimson. He didn't need to ask how much she'd overheard, the answer was in every terse angle of her body.

"Is it true, Del? What Ethan said?"

"You haven't told *her* about your little secrets, Del?" Ethan's finger ticked to and fro in a scolding metronome, and he clicked his tongue. "Oops. Kind of a no-no with the ladies."

Del resisted the urge to break Ethan's wagging finger off. "Piss off, Ethan." He set his beer bottle down on a table and stepped toward Shaye. "Can I talk to you privately—?"

"So you can *explain* some more?" Shaye moved closer to Ethan's side.

Ethan folded his arms. "I've no intention of leaving Shaye alone with you. Not while you're out of control."

"I'm not out of control," he snapped at Ethan—then turned to Shaye. "Look, I tried to tell you a couple of times, but we got distracted by—" He clamped his mouth shut in time. "Stuff got in the way. Please. Let's just go to West's office and—"

"No, I won't go anywhere with you while you're like...this." She flicked a hand at him, including the beer bottle in the gesture.

"Legless," Ethan supplied helpfully. "Your head chef is on the way to being completely shitfaced."

Del's fingers clenched into a fist at his side, but one glance at Shaye's shiny eyes and the fire in his belly dampened to hissing embers. Making a scene wouldn't solve anything. It'd only make this fucked-up situation worse.

Ignoring Ethan, Del lowered his voice and spoke directly to Shaye. "I'm not drunk, but you're right, I'm a little out of control, and I don't want to fight with you. For what it's worth, I'm sorry." He stared at her, desperate to identify any of the fleeting emotions crossing her face.

Getting zero reaction, zero feedback, Del sucked in a breath, his chest hitting an invisible barrier as if it'd been encased in concrete.

"I'll stay out of your way," he said. "Enjoy the rest of the party."

Then mentally apologizing to his brother who was still celebrating with his new wife, Del walked out of the bar and into the night.

Chapter 20.

Shaye loved Guy Fawkes night. The roaring bonfire, the fake Guy—made out of a collection of old clothes and stuffed with newspaper—which they threw on top of the blaze, the glee on kids' faces as they watched the fireworks.

Tonight, though...not so much. Tonight, she stood on Halfmoon Bay beach next to Ethan and the other wedding guests, forced a fat, false smile, and pretended Del hadn't diced her heart up with a cleaver.

He hadn't denied Ethan's accusations of being drunk on the job at Cosset—and how could he? The truth had been written all over his hang-dog expression. Caught out, busted, by Ethan confronting him. How could he have kept this from her the whole time? She'd bared her heart to him—telling him how her father had hid his alcoholism from his family with dire consequences. Would her father's life have been saved if he'd trusted his kids enough to accept his flaws? Did Del not trust her with his? Is that why he'd kept silent about his own issues?

She shook her head and shut her eyes, the bonfire flames flickering on her closed lids.

Sure, she'd shushed Del the morning after Piper's hen party—saying who he'd been wasn't as important as who he was now. And that was still true. She'd never seen him drunk or out of control. He *was* making himself a better man. But. A sob rose in her throat, but she forced it back, making her chest ache. She'd trusted him with her insecurities, with the circumstances of her father's death that still hurt her today, but *Del'd held back.*

Shaye sucked in a deep breath. *Keep it together, woman.*

"Not as impressive as the Fourth of July display over the East River, I guess," she said, as the silence between her and Ethan stretched into awkwardness.

He'd been very sweet after Del stormed out—gluing himself to her side, fetching her drinks, and fielding off curious locals who'd wanted to know where West's best man had vanished to. It'd been a relief when thirty minutes later the party had shifted to the beach.

"Have you seen it?" he asked.

"Only on video clips."

"Ah. So is New York on your bucket list?"

"Yes. It sounds like an amazing place."

A group of rockets screamed overhead, exploding into tiny stars and spangles. Red, white, and blue. So pretty, so fleeting.

"Come work for me at *Ward's New York.*"

She blinked up at the night sky, flashes of color still blinding her. Couldn't think of a single thing to say. Maybe he was joking.

"I'm serious," he said.

Shaye turned to look at him. "What?"

Ethan shrugged. "I can't offer you a high-level entry position like sous, but I'm willing to give you a trial run as a line cook."

Ethan Ward, the Ethan Ward, offering her a job? Then she got it. "I'm not sleeping with you, Ethan."

His eyes bugged wide, and he barked out a laugh.

Shaye's belly dropped into the chunky soles of her combat boots. Yet another humiliating outcome to a string of disasters today.

Ethan stopped laughing and patted her shoulder. "I'm sorry; you caught me off guard. Of course I'm not offering you a job in order to sleep with you—you're very pretty, but sadly, not my type."

"Oh," she said, her voice a mousy squeak.

"The offer is legit, no shagging me or anyone else required. You'd work with my team in New York, starting at the bottom, but with a drive to succeed, you wouldn't stay there long. New York's just one of my restaurants, and I'm always head-hunting talent."

"You think I have talent?"

"I think you've hidden your talent too long in this little town. Now's your chance to spread your wings and see how far you'll fly."

Another barrage of fireworks exploded, and Shaye tilted her head. Could she do it? Could she walk away from her family, from Due South, from...Del?

No chef would be stupid enough to turn down the opportunity to work in one of Ward's restaurants. You've let your wings be clipped by lack of ambition and your loyalty to this goddamned island. It's not disloyal to put yourself first once in a while.

Del's exact words.

Wasn't it her ego thinking Due South would fall apart without her? No one was irreplaceable, and after the publicity Oban got from *Ward On Fire*, chefs would be lining up to work there.

But her mother, her sister, her little nieces...She'd been the glue for so long. But again, would her family fall apart without her? Of course not—they'd be fine.

Del? A little voice inside her head whispered. *What about Del?*

A louder, more strident voice in her head piped up. *What about him? Are you still expecting to ride off into the sunset on his white frickin' steed? The only thing Dell'll ride off on is an Air New Zealand flight to London.*

Shaye curled her fingers, the French manicure digging crescents into her palms, holding back the tears that so desperately wanted to come. "Why would you offer me this chance, Ethan?"

"You want honesty?"

"After tonight, I don't want anything from men other than brutal honesty."

"Well, then. Reason number one is my show is to blame for getting you fired—temporarily fired, of course." His attempt to look sheepish failed epically. The man didn't do humble.

"Show business, right?"

He flashed a toothy smile. "Exactly, nothing personal. You don't hate me?"

Unlike another male she'd had to deal with tonight, she didn't let grudges fester. "Would I have asked you to be my plus one if I did?"

"I figured you hadn't kissed and made up with Del."

Shaye chose to ignore the dull ache that throbbed in her chest.

Stupid heart.

"What's the other reason?"

He cocked his head. "I'm the youngest of three brothers, all of them in the food industry. I was the overlooked baby for years. None of my siblings took me seriously, so I worked twice as hard as everyone else to be the best, to make them respect me. Maybe I see a little of myself in you." Ethan shoved his hands into his pants pockets. "Or maybe I'm hoping a good deed will get me off Santa's naughty list this year."

She sighed, tugging the light Pashmina shawl around her shoulders. "Can I think about it and give you an answer tomorrow?"

"Take your time," he said. "Long as the answer is yes."

Another explosion of sparks lit the sky above Due South. How could she possibly say no?

***

Shaye crept downstairs at 7:00 a.m. She did some funky ninja moves to avoid Charlie and Helena, there early to start the tidy up, and slunk through the front door. She couldn't bear to take a short-cut to Bill's place via the kitchen. In fact, she hadn't been back since Del fired her.

Hurrying along the sidewalk, she continued to check over her shoulder. It seemed everyone who'd been at West and Piper's wedding the night before still slept off the after-effects. Was Del, too, sleeping off the after-affects? Quicker than greased lightning, she slapped a pot-lid on *that* witch's brew.

Shaye cut across the parking lot and tapped on the cottage door.

Soft footsteps came from the other side then the door swung open to reveal Claire's smiling face. "Shaye, this is a nice surprise."

"I'm here to see Bill, if he's feeling okay this morning. I know he likes to get up early, catching the worm and all." Shaye nipped her mouth shut, stopping the stream of words desperate to babble forth.

God, she hadn't been this nervous about talking to Bill since she'd asked him for a job as a teenager.

"Come on in."

She followed Claire down the short hallway and into the open plan kitchen-dining room.

Bill glanced up from the table. "The hell you doing up already? You should be having a lie in after the wild party last night."

"I wanted to ask for your advice"—she shot a glance at Claire—"in private, if that's okay."

"Of course it is, honey," Claire said, patting Shaye's arm. "I'll hang out a load of laundry, it's going to be a beautiful day." Claire disappeared into a small room off the kitchen and shut the door.

Bill flicked a thumb toward the stove. "Kettle's hot if you want a cuppa."

Shaye shook her head and sat down opposite him. "No, thanks. I can't stay long."

"With all this wedding kerfuffle, I haven't seen you since Del fired you. He told me what the little director weasel made him do, and I'm bloody sorry my boy put you through that. Once the Hollywood lot clears out, you'll be back here—"

Shaye jerked in her seat and the words shot from her mouth like bullets. "Last night, Ethan Ward offered me a job. In New York."

Bill's bushy white eyebrows flicked up. "Well, now. That's not something you get dropped in your lap every day."

"No."

"And what did you tell him?"

"I said I'd think about his offer." Shaye couldn't drag her eyes from the folds of Bill's woolen jersey. The same jersey he'd worn for years—one Claire knitted for him before she left Stewart Island. Now, instead of fitting snugly around his stomach, it sagged loose, stretched to the shape of the man Bill was no longer.

He leaned forward, bracing his palms on the dining table. "Then you're a damn fool."

Must've been a trick of the light, but his faded eyes seemed to have sharpened into gas-flame blue.

"What—why?"

"This is your big break, girlie."

Hot tears stung her eyes. "It is."

"But you're holding back because of some misplaced sense of duty to me and Due South."

"Among other things."

"Your mum?"

She nodded.

"Not many daughters would do for their mother what you did for Glenna," he said. "She's strong again now, and she has your brother and sister here."

"After Dad died, I swore to his empty memorial I'd look after Mum."

Bill sighed. "And you have. You were always your daddy's girl—his princess. But Michael never treated you like one, did he?"

Shaye shook her head, kept her lips pressed tight together.

"He raised you to be strong, and smart, and to follow your dreams—whether it's a fairy princess like you wanted to be when you were six, or a chef as you got older. If your dad was alive, he'd tell you the same thing I'm telling you now. *Pack a damn bag and get on that plane.*"

"I don't want to leave you like this." She waved a hand at him, swiping tears off her face with the other. "I love Due South...and I love you."

"Ah, now, don't get like that." Bill slid the box of tissues over from the center of the table. "Don't make me go all mushy; you know how I feel about you, girlie. I never cut you any slack in the kitchen, and I won't cut you any now. This place'll keep running one way or another, don't you worry." He paused thoughtfully as Shaye snatched out a tissue. "The tears aren't just about work, or your mum, or stepping out of your wee comfort zone, are they?"

Shaye blew her nose, shaking her head at the same time.

"You and Del," he said.

"Yeah."

"Need me to give him a hiding?"

"No." But her lips tugged up in the corners.

"Good. 'Cause he's kinda grown on me again."

"You love him."

"He's my boy." Which in Bill-speak meant yes, he loved him. "Doesn't mean I won't kick his backside if he's hurt you." His eyes slitted and he took a sip of his tea. "Has he hurt you?"

Del had more than hurt her; he'd carved her up. Bill didn't need to know that, so she shrugged. "If I go to New York, it's a moot point."

Bill set his mug down. "Sometimes a man has to let a woman fly to the other side of the world before he realizes he's a fool."

"Like you and Claire?"

"Letting Claire and Del leave was both the hardest and best thing I ever did. A few times, I nearly sold up and went after her, but in the end, I chose my work. Like I said, a fool. When Claire rang out of the blue to say she and Lionel were together, and would I sign the divorce papers, well..." Bill shrugged. "For once in my life, I put her happiness first. I signed the papers and gave her my blessing."

"You did the right thing."

"Well, give Del a chance and likely he'll do the right thing, too."

What if Del's *right thing* didn't include her? Shaye's rose-colored glasses had been broken beyond repair last night. Maybe no happily ever after existed for her and Del.

She adopted a smile that'd likely fool no one, and stood. "I'm going to miss you." Shaye walked around the table and hugged him.

Bill patted her back. "Get away with ya. I know how to send an e-mail, and text on the fancy phone West bought me. Now go sort out your work visa and buy a ticket."

She blew him a kiss and walked down the hallway.

Bill was right; her dad raised her to be strong, and smart, and to follow her dreams. But was her dream working in one of the world's most vibrant cities? Or spending her life with a man who loved her?

Could she have both? But more importantly, was that man Del?

***

The one time Del could've used some brotherly advice, West was still snuggled up in bed with his new wife.

Del'd been desperate enough to hike to West's place to catch him before he and Piper left on their honeymoon. Except standing at West's front door with his fist raised, glancing at the closed drapes upstairs, he'd chickened out.

In LA, a pet therapist or a chakra cleansing or some such crap would be the norm. But he had veins filled with stoic, third-generation Stewart Island blood. He'd deal with the shitfest he'd created alone. Just as he always dealt with it.

He didn't need anyone's help.

Turning away, Del shoved his hands into the pockets of his wool coat and trudged down the driveway. A cool wind blew off the ocean, and puffy clouds scudded over the rolling hills behind them. It'd be a beautiful day, the last day of formal filming before Ethan and his crew left. He couldn't wait.

Once they were gone, he'd have an opportunity to sit down with Shaye and reason things out. She was, after all, a reasonable woman.

He sighed, scrubbing a hand over his unshaven face and continuing down the road toward Due South.

Shaye might listen, but how could he convince her *she* was perfect for him—even though he was very much a work in progress. Well, for starters, he'd sort shit out with his dad.

Five minutes later, he sat in the kitchen with his parents on one side of the dining table, him on the other—feeling like an eight-year-old, about to receive a bollocking for fighting with his older brother.

The way they kept exchanging glances...

He drummed his fingers on his knees and gulped a steadying breath. "I want you to have my kidney."

His dad's eyebrows popped up, and his mom squeezed Bill's hand.

"Dr. Joe said there are other tests to be done, but as long as we're a match, let's do it—let's keep you around for a few more years to bug the hell outta everyone."

"Including you?" Bill asked. "You want me around?"

Tempted to say something flippant, Del instead fisted his hand and said, "Yeah. I do. We've missed enough years together."

His mom started to make fluttery *I'm-gonna-cry* motions, so he rolled his eyes.

"Maybe there's still some stuff you could teach me," he added.

Bill's face creased into a slow grin. "Probably there is. Something you can show your cronies in LA."

"About that." Del folded his arms on the table. Once again, he'd have to eat a serving of humble pie, but Shaye was worth it. "I'd like to stay on as head chef." Saliva evaporated in his mouth, and he swallowed with a dry click. "At Due South. You know, while you're recovering."

Bill and his mom did the glance-swap thing again. Ah—he got it! Bill wanted Shaye to take over head chef!

His dad went to speak, and Del held up a palm. "No, it's okay. I mean, I know once the film crew's gone, you'll reinstate Shaye, and I'm happy to work as her sous." He shrugged. "Look, is there a place for me here? I'm done with the stress and pressure of LA or anywhere else in the States. I know you'll think it's fucking funny—sorry, Mom—but Oban is home now."

"Oh, Del." His mom pressed her trembling lips together and slanted yet another look at Bill.

His father lowered his eyes to the table and gusted out a sigh that sounded almost like a death rattle. "Due South is yours and West's now. I won't be working in the kitchen as chef anymore. You've more than proven you're capable of filling my shoes, and I'm bloody happy you consider Oban home again. But, son, I don't quite know how to say this, and hell, it isn't my place, but..." He released another drawn-out sigh. "Shaye stopped by this morning to tell me Ethan Ward offered her a job in New York."

Del's heart shot into his throat as if a cannon had blasted it there. He stood, his chair screeching on the linoleum, his fists balled so tightly his clipped nails dug into his palms.

"The bastard. The fucking—" Del's teeth clicked together at his mother's bugged-open eyes.

That Ward thought he could poach their sous from right under their noses didn't surprise him, not really. And he didn't believe the man had an interest in Shaye, other than a professional one—because she would've told him where to stick his job if she'd any inkling the offer came with ties of an unsavory nature.

"Did she say yes?" His lungs had apparently gone into shock and forgotten how to work. He couldn't catch his breath as he waited for his dad's answer.

"You'll have to ask her yourself," Bill said.

Del swore, pacing away from the table, his brain firing off machine-gun rapid questions but receiving no goddamned answers. He whirled back to his parents.

"You told her to take the job?"

Bill squirmed in his seat. "I told her she'd be a fool to turn it down."

"No chef would be stupid enough to turn down the opportunity to work in one of his restaurants," he muttered, stalking to the table. Bracing his palms on the smooth wood, Del hung his head. "You said the right thing, Dad. And a while ago I told her the same. Dammit."

"Even if you don't make it to the finals, you could still find work in New York to be near Shaye," said Bill. "West'll set up an ad for a new chef; you're not bloody indispensible, boy. Go."

And if he did go to New York? He'd have to work his ass off just to pay rent—if he could even find work—and when would he and Shaye ever get to spend time together? No poker with their buddies. No horsing around on the beach with his brother and new sister-in-law. No motorbike rides or impromptu picnics or hikes along the Rakiura track.

Things that now appealed to him more than any urge to blot out his problems with crazy long hours and excess alcohol. The desire for liquid oblivion had transformed into another kind of addiction. His brother. His dad. Friends. Plans for Due South. His little beach house. Community. Even bloody Bird-Brain. All the things he'd once tossed mindlessly aside in the wake of his own ambition, he now desperately wanted.

But most of all, Shaye.

He straightened and moved away from the table. "I have to find her and see what her decision is."

With a brief kiss to his mom's cheek—more of Shaye's influence rubbing off on him—Del met his dad's eyes. "Maybe I'm replaceable here, but she's not."

***

The window of opportunity was small—catch Del before the day's prep started and sort things out. She didn't want to wait hours and hours until dinner service ended or she'd lose her nerve.

Shaye's heart raced, and not in a good way, as she descended the steps. She'd been staring at the four walls of her room and at her laptop—open to a travel agent's website—dithering. *To go or not to go.* That was the million-dollar question. If she went, she only had to pack her clothes and a few odds and ends. Everything else was already stored in neatly labeled boxes in her mum's garage.

If only her life could be so neatly boxed and labeled.

With a wave to Denise, she headed into the kitchen to wait for Del.

Her kitchen was ghostly still, sunlight sifting through the high windows and sparkling off the stainless steel. Tiny motes spun in the air currents, stirred by the constant hum of the overhead fans. The fridge buzzed to life, and for a moment, she stood by her workstation with her head bowed. She couldn't claim Due South as hers any longer. Not when she was prepared to cut the apron strings.

The back door creaked open, and tiny hairs on her nape rose to attention.

Del had arrived. That her body still knew him, still craved his touch, still almost disobeyed her brain's order to *not* go running into his arms, emphasized how deeply she'd fallen.

Silly girl.

She turned to face him, her chin angled high. Kind of fitting this conversation would happen in the place where it all began.

Del filled the doorway, still clenching the doorknob, dressed in his black pants and chef's jacket, looking professional and ready for action. Good. Maybe if she could focus on being professional, she'd make the tingly, weak feeling spreading through her body disappear. A ray of sunlight drew out the golden tones in his brown hair, which was rumpled as if he'd run his fingers through it. The same way she had—over and over—when he'd kissed her to a melted puddle of goo.

So much for professionalism.

"Dad says you've been offered a job in New York," he said.

Shaye leaned a hip against the counter, the cool stainless steel seeping through her skirt's thin fabric and centering her. "Yes."

His eyebrows rose. "Have you accepted it?"

"Not yet. I'm still making a list of pros and cons."

A dimple appeared in his cheek, as if a smile lurked just out of sight. "Lists, huh? Should've guessed. What did your family say?"

She folded her arms. "I haven't spoken to them yet. I'm capable of making my own decisions, and I'm sure my family will accept whatever I think is right."

Wow. That sounded stiff and defensive. She made an effort to relax her muscles, but nope, tension continued to zip through her at Del's steady and unreadable gaze. Damn the man's poker face.

"Is the New York job what you want?"

Twenty minutes ago, while scrolling through the travel agent's website, she'd been ninety-nine percent positive she *did* want it. She'd flicked through some old e-mails from her graduating class—little snippets and photos of their lives in Auckland, Sydney, and a couple who now worked in London. Here she lingered, treading water in Oban, unemployed and hopelessly in love with a man who didn't love her. At least, love her enough to share with her the part of him that'd been broken and hurting.

Yet each second she stared into Del's clear blue eyes, her ninety-nine-percent-sureness scrolled downward like a stopwatch in reverse.

Make a decision, Shaye. Make a goddamn decision, see what he says.

"Yes. It's what I want."

A muscle twitched once in his jaw then stilled. He nodded, his gaze never leaving her face. "Then you're right. Your family will support you, but they'll miss you, too."

Er, wasn't Del supposed to say, *"Don't go baby, because I'll miss you?"*

Shaye frowned. "No more than your family will miss you when you return to LA."

Del crossed to the counter where she leaned and stood facing her. "I'm done with LA, I'm staying here. This is my home now."

Her pulse leaped from a dull thud to a jarring throb. *Hope. Ohmigawd.* "But you hate Stewart Island, ass end of the world, remember? And what about *Ward On Fire*, if you make it to the finals?"

He lifted a shoulder, his chef jacket clinging to the hard muscles beneath.

Don't think about what's under his jacket. Don't you dare remember how amazing he smells and the feel of his stubble-roughened skin when you kiss that spot under his ear.

"There's nothing in my contract saying I have to accept a place in the finals, so I won't."

Well, fuck a duck, as her big sis would say. Life sure had a narky sense of humor and ironic timing. She'd secretly hoped for weeks Del would change his mind and stay, and now he had. Just when she'd been offered a job of a lifetime.

But Del...staying at Due South?

No, she couldn't look at the world through rose-colored glasses anymore. Del had taken one issue—the issue of him returning to the States—out of the equation, but it didn't mean they'd removed the other, more important hurdle out of their path.

"Del," she said softly. "What Ethan said last night...about your drinking"—she sucked in a deep breath—"I'd like to hear what you have to say now."

"Do you really need to hear how fucked up I was?" His lips curved in a cool twist, which masqueraded as a smile. "How I was a mess for months after Lionel died—drinking almost every night, staggering into work the next day hung-over or still half pissed, hiding it from the head chef as long as I possibly could? Then how my life fucking imploded after Jessica nearly drowned?"

Two quick steps forward and he gripped her upper arms. "I was selfish, blindly ambitious, and yeah, a drunk. The kind of man you would've justifiably hated. Nothing mattered to me but getting wasted and getting laid. But I haven't had more than a couple of beers at a time since I've been back—West's wedding was the exception. I'm not that guy anymore. Do you believe me?" He dropped his hands from her arms and slid them around her waist, looking down at her with clear, guileless eyes.

"I believe you."

And she did believe him. In some ways, he was unrecognizable as the man she'd met on the ferry.

"What's between us is more than amazing sex—a lot more, and you know it," he said.

Shaye's eyelids stung, so she closed them—accomplishing nothing more than heightening her other senses. Her nose filled with his cologne, her ears with a thunderous heartbeat, and her fingertips tingled as she slid them over the crisp cotton of his jacket.

Hands cupped her bottom, pressing her intimately into him. She gasped, and he kissed her—a deep, wet kiss that unraveled her resolve. Unable to help herself, she rubbed against him like a cat.

Del groaned, a harsh sound vibrating through his chest. He pulled away, dropping hot kisses along her throat. "Baby, you're more addictive than anything on the top shelf."

Words the equivalent of an ice bath.

Shaye jerked, every muscle going rigid. She'd let him hypnotize her again, drag her under with his talented mouth, making her forget all the reasons why she and Del Westlake wouldn't work.

Shaye shoved his chest—hard. He stumbled back, eyes still hooded with leftover passion. As her breath heaved in and out, his gaze sharpened.

"Unfortunate choice of metaphor, huh?" He shoved a hand into his hair. "Shit. Look"—the laser beam of his intense stare sliced through her—"I'm not like your father. I won't cross the line into alcoholism; there are too many people here who'd kick my ass before letting that happen."

"You're saying you're accountable? To your father and brother? To Ben? Ford?"

"Sure." His eyes cut left then returned, but he didn't meet her gaze.

"You haven't told them how bad things were for you in LA, have you? Just like you didn't tell me—I had to overhear you telling Ethan. You didn't trust me enough to share that part of your life"—she sucked in a ragged breath at the guilt on his face—"and you knew, right back at the beginning, that your past would push my emotional buttons. But instead of being completely honest with me, you chose to keep me in the dark."

Tears stung her eyes but she blinked them away. "Do you really think so badly of me, Del? That I'm so judgmental, that I wouldn't feel any sympathy for what you've been through and how hard you've fought to change?"

"I don't think badly of you—you're making too big a deal about this." He took a step toward her.

Shaye backed up, slowly shaking her head. "It's a big deal to me, and I'm sorry you can't understand *why* it's a big deal. My father died because he was ashamed and hid his struggles from the world. When things got tough for you in LA, you didn't talk to anyone. You opted to turn to a bottle, and in your own words, *your life imploded.*"

She held up a hand to ward him off. "So, what if, God-forbid, your dad doesn't make it through a kidney transplant? How will you cope with the sort of shit life can throw at you if you won't let me or anyone else get close enough to you to share that load?" Her throat clogged, but she gamely swallowed. "Let the people who love you help you, Del."

He jammed his hands into his pants pockets and glared. "I don't need anyone's help or a fucking intervention, goddammit. I'm not one of your stray charity cases. I'm trying to figure out how to make us work."

"*You're not listening*. We won't work because you can't admit there will be times when your bad-ass self isn't enough to deal with shit alone." She arched her chin and looked him dead in the eye. "I love you, you big jerk, but how can I stay here when you shut me out?

When you won't let *me*, the woman who bloody *loves* you, stand with you when you need it?"

Del's jaw sagged, and his eyes widened. The only sounds in the kitchen were the hum of the refrigerator and the pounding in her ears.

Oh, cinnamon-freaking-sticks. She'd told him she loved him, and *ohgodohgodohgod,* he just stared and said nothing.

Del's mouth snapped shut, and his eyes turned flinty.

"Then go, cupcake." He swept a dramatic hand toward the door, a tight, sardonic smile on his lips. "Go to New York and take it by storm. Maybe you'll even find your Mr. Perfect there, since I can't possibly measure up."

A voice outside the kitchen grew louder, but Shaye's feet stayed glued to the checked linoleum. The swinging doors blasted open, and Fraser sauntered in, phone clamped to an ear.

"—And I was all, 'Yeah, whatever, dude'—oh." Fraser skidded to a halt, his gaze flicking between them. "Oops." He moved to scuttle back out.

"It's fine, Fraser. I'm leaving," she said.

As Shaye hurried around the counter, Del's Converse sneakers squeaked on the floor.

His clipped voice rang out from the far side of the kitchen. "Fraser, off the fucking phone. Ethan's due in fifteen minutes, and I want the floors mopped again."

The hope he'd prevent her leaving to tell her he loved her, and that they'd work their problems out together, died a fiery death. Shaye threw herself through the swinging doors.

Decision made, then. She'd ring Ethan to accept his offer. He'd promised to take care of everything, so she'd book a one-way flight to New York in three days' time.

Three days. Seventy-two long hours to figure out how to excise Del from the pieces of her broken heart, permanently.

Chapter 21.

Ten days later…

So…his life had come to this.

Del sat on his deck and fed Bird-Brain his daily peanut fix, staring at the ocean. All nine thousand miles of it, stretching between him and Shaye.

The waves hissed and tumbled, the kaka squawked and flapped his wings, and Del kept firing glances at the six-pack sitting on the step beside him. The same beer his father brought over nearly three weeks ago. The same beer that had sat untouched in his fridge, to prove to himself he didn't need it.

Didn't need anyone's help to remain stone-cold sober.

Del scrubbed a hand over his face. Closed his eyes. Felt his ribs contract as he pictured Shaye the last time he'd seen her at Due South. He hadn't attended her thrown-together going away party or shown up at the airport farewell to see off her and Ethan's crew.

Fucking coward that he was.

He'd copped an earful from West and Piper when they'd returned from their honeymoon. Didn't matter he'd almost bitten his tongue in half to prevent himself from begging Shaye to stay. Didn't matter that after hearing she wanted the job, he'd gotten the hell outta the way so she could follow her dreams. Did he get any credit for it? No. Just sad-eyes from Piper and a clip on the head from his brother. He'd walked away from the pair of them before he'd tackled West to the ground like they used to do as kids.

Yeah, pride had shoved a red-hot poker up his ass when Shaye nailed him about his inability to ask for help, and he'd reacted like a typical hothead male telling her to go. He groaned—and freaking suggesting she find her Mr. Perfect in New York? *Moron.*

But dammit...he'd still done the right thing.

Bird-Brain flapped his wings, dropped to the deck beside Del, and waddled over in the kaka's peculiar gait. The bird nudged Del's elbow, looking for more peanuts.

"Sorry, buddy."

The chink of beak on aluminum jerked him out of his daydream.

"Hey!"

Bird-Brain squawked and flew up to the railing. Del stared at the cans, the cool sides the right circumference to fit in a man's hand. The beer would be icy cold and just the thing to ease the raw burn in his throat. And hell, if six tinnies didn't do the trick, there was always the top shelf in Due South—since he would be, after all, part owner of the place soon.

Del lurched to his feet. Bird-Brain screeched and took off into the bush behind the house. He snatched up the beer and glared at the cans.

Was this the path he'd chosen?

With or without Shaye, was he *that* guy now? The one who kept promising to get his shit together—just a couple more beers first. The guy who stayed at home with Jack Daniels, lounging in the dark with the TV tuned to endless cooking shows, hurling vitriol because, hey, he used to be a goddamn *chef*, you know. Would he someday be the embarrassing uncle to his brother's kids, the one who arrived drunk to family events, until no one wanted him around?

Del popped all six tops off the cans and upended them over the sand at his feet. Then he tugged his phone out of his pocket and texted West.

Was he that guy?

Hell-fucking-no.

An hour later, Del sat at his dad's dining table with his mom, dad, brother and new sister-in-law surrounding him.

"This better be frickin' life or death," grumbled West. "It's not even half seven."

Piper nudged West's arm. "Haven't I taught you anything? You don't bitch at a family meeting."

"Now, now, lovebirds," said his mom, bringing over a tray of mugs. "Let Del explain."

Eight pairs of eyes lasered in on him. How the hell was he supposed to start?

Hello, my name is Del Westlake, and I'm trying bloody hard not to become an alcoholic?

His knee bounced, the vibration making his chair creak. Forcing his leg still, he took a breath, his lungs feeling like perished rubber sticking together.

"Here's the thing. I have a problem. With alcohol. I need..." His throat closed, and he swallowed twice before he could continue. "I need your help."

He looked from his father to his brother, expecting condemnation—to his mom and Piper, expecting disappointment.

Bill spoke first, reaching across the table to cover Del's hand. "Whatever you need, son. You'll get it."

West clapped him on the shoulder. "Anytime," he said quietly. "Night or day. I'll be there."

His mother, seated next to Bill, stretched over and squeezed Del's other hand. "What your dad said, honey."

Piper, on the other side of West, watched him with her Harland eyes, almost a carbon copy of her younger sister. She said nothing, her cop-face fixed on—the one she would've used in the city dealing with drunks and druggies on a regular basis. His sister-in-law was razor sharp, he'd give her that. She'd have immediately seen what had been the final nail in the coffin between him and Shaye.

Piper stood and gestured him to his feet. He got up—this would be where she kicked his ass in real time for letting Shaye go. Before his imagination ran wild any further, Piper covered the few steps to stand in front of him. Her cop-mask slipped, exposing the slight sheen of tears.

"This," she said, sliding her arms around his waist and hugging him so tightly it felt as if she cracked a rib, "is from me." She kissed his cheek. "And this is on behalf of my little sister, who I bet you loved enough to let her go to New York."

Of all the things that changed him since he'd returned to Stewart Island, falling in love with Shaye Harland had altered him down to his very DNA. He wasn't the same soulless, husk of a man who'd left LA all those weeks ago. Shaye brought the real Del back, layer by layer, her gentle touch like a master *pâtissière* creating tiramisu.

He wasn't the same, but Shaye was right. He needed to let her in—all the way in, and trust that their strength together could repair both their broken parts.

"No, I let her go because I'm an idiot. But I do love your sister. I love Shaye." The words spilled over the smile peeling back his lips, and he wrapped his arms around Piper and squeezed.

Piper beamed then leaned in closer to whisper in his ear, "Give her a reason to come home then, Hollywood."

***

3 weeks later...

She'd had visions of snowflakes falling between towering skyscrapers, of catching a Broadway show, and hailing a yellow cab with a whistle. Of plating meals on premium-grade china and being so busy she wouldn't miss Del Westlake. Not even for a single New York minute.

Hah!

Shaye avoided a clump of greying bubble-gum as she navigated the steps out of the Lexington/59th subway, crushed between a charcoal-suited businessman snarling into his phone and a teen grooving to the tinny music blasting from his headphones. Another day, another subway ride on the E train from her tiny apartment in Queens. Another freezing walk down slush-covered sidewalks. Another opportunity for touts to hassle her or shoppers and tourists gawking at *Bloomies'* window displays to get in her way.

A walk sign buzzed green, and Shaye crossed with the flow, a good little lemming. Now, of course, all the stores were decked out for the holiday season—each one more impressive than the next. The lights, and colors, and constant honking hurt her head.

Hurt her heart.

A little over two weeks until Christmas, and she missed her family and the green, *silent* hills of Oban so much her stomach remained in a permanent double knot. Great for the waistline though—hell, she could pass on some diet tips to Holly and the girls.

Never need Spanx again! Shaye smiled grimly as she skirted around a bell-ringing Santa. Just get your heart broken and move nine-thousand miles to chase a dream you no longer think you want, and voila! Pounds will melt away!

Seriously, she thought turning into the narrow alley that led to the staff entrance of *Ward's*. She should write a book.

Shaye rapped on the metal door with her *I'm so happy I work here and I don't care that I'm demoted to a fricken' commis-trainee chef* smile fixed solid. So much for being a line cook and Ethan Ward's protégé; she'd only clapped eyes on the man twice since she'd arrived.

The young dishwasher with spiked blond hair known only as Bub, short for Bubbles, opened the door.

"You back again, Kiwi?" His white teeth were a gleaming crescent in his chocolate brown skin.

Shaye returned his smile—a genuine one, this time. Bub was the only person who bothered to treat her as another human being. The girl from a teeny tiny island somewhere near Antarctica had never considered other staff members at *Ward's* would resent her presence. Or think she'd slept with Ethan to get there.

So that's what she'd endure for the rest of the shift—hours of non-stop orders and in-her-face blustering from the sous chef. Then freezing her ass off on the subway to her tiny place to spend the next few hours watching bad re-runs, and aching to feel Del's arms around her. Fun times.

"Yeah," she said, trudging inside.

Too dumb, too stubborn, too proud to quit, that was her. The door slamming behind her echoed like a cell-block lockdown.

***

"Whaddya want? Entrance is 'round front."

Del held his ground at the back door to *Ward's New York* and leveled a stare at the guy with punked-up hair. "I'm looking for Shaye Harland. She finished her shift yet?"

"Who's asking?" The man folded his arms over his solid chest. "You her brother?"

Judging by his food-stained apron and harried expression, Del figured he'd interrupted the dishwasher during his busiest time.

"A friend." He tried to crane a look into the kitchen, but the guy's bulk blocked him. "I've just flown in from New Zealand to see her. Twelve hours next to a screaming toddler, then another five cramped next to a fat guy in cattle class into JFK. So put me outta my fucking misery. She here?"

"Nope. She's done, man. Skipped out 'bout fifteen minutes ago."

Del swore and kicked the step. Knew he should've come straight from the airport instead of dumping his bags at a hotel. He glanced up at the man who watched him with cool, dark eyes.

"You're not going to tell me where she lives, I'm guessing?"

A bark of laughter. "Aw, hell no. Kiwi's a scary girl when she gets riled up."

"Yeah." Del shook his head, but a grin teased up the corner of his mouth. "She really is and then some."

The big guy showed him a flash of white teeth bared in what Del hoped was a smile. "Name's Bub, and Kiwi's more than your friend, isn't she? She's your girl."

"She was. I'm hoping to convince her to be again."

"Screwed up, huh?"

Del grimaced. "Big time."

"She know you coming?"

"Nope. Hoping to surprise her." And hoping she wouldn't tell him to piss off. Which was why he needed to speak to her face to face, and not try to convince her over the phone. "Shit. I'll have to come again tomorrow. What time is she on?"

Bub shook his head. "Brother, there's no use coming back tomorrow. I told you, she's done. She quit."

Del eyes popped wide. "Fuck. She what?"

Bub glanced over his shoulder and stepped down into the dirty alleyway. "You didn't hear from me, but they treated Shaye bad. Your girl stuck it out long past what any normal cook would. She's *stubborn*, that one."

Del bristled, his fists clenching. "And Ward? He around?"

Bub's nose crinkled as if he'd sniffed something rotten. "The man don't bother to show up 'round here less a camera crew's with him."

What the fuck was Ethan thinking, promising her a way into his world and then abandoning her like a new-born chick? His phone burned a hole in his pocket, an idea forming in his mind.

"I got this, Bub. Thanks for your help."

"You take care of my Kiwi girl," Bub said and went inside then he turned, the door half closed. "And you better do it quick. She probably stopped for a slice of that pizza she loves, but those E trains leave every five minutes—better hope she hasn't gone home already."

"Gotcha." Del nodded and dragged out his phone.

Standing in the now-deserted alleyway, Del scrolled through his contacts and hit send. While the call connected, he smoothed out the fury bubbling in his gut.

"Ethan," he said coolly, when the other man barked a hello down the line. "It's Del Westlake. We didn't part on the best of terms, but I'm asking you to do me a favor."

***

Graceful and not-so-graceful skaters circled the ice below, some wobbling, some spinning, others clinging to the handrail with white-knuckled grips. Shaye wrapped the knitted scarf her mother had made tighter around her neck, the merino-possum blend wool carrying a hint of Chanel No. 5. She closed her eyes to cast a wish at the Rockefeller Plaza's gigantic Christmas tree.

If you're listening, Santa, I want to go home. Even more, I want he-who-won't-be-named-because-I-can't-think-of-him-without-crying back. I think I screwed up big time.

Sucked to be an adult with little faith in Christmas wishes.

Stamping her cold, aching legs, she walked away from the rink and skirted the crowds to the 50th Street entrance of the Top of the Rock observation decks.

After telling *Ward's* sous to insert the job in his nearest available orifice, Shaye had stalked up Lexington to her favorite pizza joint. And to hell with it—she had stopped to eat, instead of returning to her cold, empty apartment. Alone. And unemployed. *Again.* Yeah, real happy thoughts she'd been entertaining when Ethan Ward rang. Bloody nark of a sous chef.

But Ethan still talked her in to meeting him on the sixty-seventh floor observation deck at ten tonight, promising an ear to her complaints.

"Why on earth would you want to meet there?" she'd asked.

"Didn't I promise to show you the world? You can see it from the Top of the Rock."

Trust a city slicker to think the world could only be seen from a skyscraper. Not *her* world. That was visible from the choppy waves of Foveaux Strait, or from the highest peak of Stewart Island, Mount Anglem.

New York wasn't her world and never would be.

Ethan probably thought by showing her Manhattan's lights she'd cave like wet cardboard and return to being Ward's dogs body.

Nuh-uh.

Shaye followed a group of tourists up the inside ramp, past the huge windows overlooking Radio City Music Hall's neon signs and into the elevator, which whisked her up to dizzying heights. She trailed after the tourists into the spacious lobby, funneled with them to the observation decks. Small clusters of people stood at the sheer glass walls. No Ethan, but then she'd arrived a little early, and Ethan was known for being late.

In the distance, the Empire State Building's red and green holiday lightshow dominated the nightscape. Shaye crossed the tiled deck and a beautiful mosaic compass with arrows pointed in four directions. North, uptown. East and the East River, West and the Hudson River. South... She tugged her scarf up higher, hot tears prickling her eyes. South, lay Due South and Stewart Island.

"I made it, Daddy." The protective glass walls were icy under her fingertips. Far below came the faint sounds of city traffic, and the expanse of lights shimmered. "All the way to New York City."

"He would've been proud," someone said behind her.

A rough, sweet, and familiar voice melted along her frazzled nerves. Boy, a woman could fry eggs on a voice that hot.

Del? Or had over-tiredness and stress caused her to hallucinate?

She turned slowly. But no, there was Del in his black pea-coat, jeans, and Converse sneakers, with at least forty-eight hours of stubble. He walked closer, his blue eyes brighter than any holiday lights.

Del's here! He's really here!

She sucked in a lungful of crisp winter air, the cogs in her brain spinning. "Ethan's not coming, is he? You set this up."

Del gave her a crooked smile. "Are you disappointed?"

Disappointed? She wanted to twine around his tall, hard body like gift-wrap and then kiss the turkey stuffing out of him. But until she knew why he'd come, she'd do her best to avoid a second humiliating experience this evening.

Shaye shoved her hands into her coat pockets, just in case they misbehaved and reached for him. "Not disappointed, just curious."

There. Her voice came out calm, smooth, and without a trace of *oh-my-gawd-kiss-me-already*.

He grabbed the strap of a small backpack on his shoulder. "I brought you something."

Del unzipped the bag and drew out a stack of what looked like cards, tied with a red ribbon.

"Love letters?" she said dryly, but her stomach gave a little pirouette.

"In a way, yes." He passed them over. "They're from all the people whose lives you've touched. Mr. Peterson. Mrs. Taylor. The Komekes. Jade and Zoe. Holly, Erin, Vince, Bill—and two dozen others. Even your brother wrote a card."

"That's..." Her voice caught. "That's very sweet. Thank you."

"They wanted you to know how much you mean to them. How much they miss you. How much they want you to come home."

"I have a job in New York now."

Ahh.

If Del had spoken to Ethan, he'd know her current employment status. "Okay, I had a job in New York. It turns out the big city is not for me."

"Turns out it's not for me, either—though I'm planning to stay here for as long as it takes to win you over."

"Oh?" Shaye folded her arms and cocked a hip. A girl needed some attitude to stop from melting into a gooey puddle. "You think you're going to win me over?"

"You forgot the 'you vain, lily-livered, half-witted pig's bladder of a man.' Alternatively, 'you big jerk' is also quite cutting." The dimple popped in his cheek.

So not fair.

"Hmmph," she managed.

Mellllllting...

"You were right." He took the stack of cards off her, returned them to his backpack, and dropped it on the ground. With another flash of dimples, he grabbed her hands. "The bad-boy chef from LA was scared he was just an unlovable jerk with baggage. You made me believe I was more than that—better than that. I didn't want to tell you about my past in the beginning because I was ashamed. Later I was fucking terrified, realizing I could lose you. Pride refused to let me say 'hey, guy drowning here.' Not anymore. I want to tell you about me and Rosalie."

Wait—wha—?

The man flies across the world to win her over by telling her about another woman? And the bastard had the gall to look all smokin' hot and edible while smiling at her. She gave an experimental yank of her right hand, but he tightened his grip, his grin spreading even wider. Blood surged up her face in a flash-pan of heat, a sharp contrast to the chill breeze oozing through the gaps in the glass walls.

Should've known this day could get worse.

"Screw you."

His eyes flew open, and he snorted out a laugh. "You're so cute when you're riled."

Shaye bared her teeth. Piper's desire to sometimes strangle her man now seemed rational, and her mother's scarf looked like a pretty damn convenient weapon.

"You really don't think I'd...?" Del rolled his eyes. "Rosalie is a counselor in Invercargill who specializes in helping people with addictions. I've been to see her twice, and I'll continue with monthly visits and weekly phone calls."

Shaye blinked at him. "You. Going to see a counselor?"

"Yeah. And my family knows too, so I'm accountable to someone—quite a lot of someones. I should hand in my man-card, but I have to admit, talking to Rosalie helps."

"Oh." Del going to a counselor was a huge step—a step she never thought he'd make. "Well, it's great you've found Rosalie—and I'm glad your family has your back."

He released her hands and cupped her jaw, stroking his thumbs over her numb cheeks. "The one person I truly need watching my back is you, Shaye. I'm letting you in. I'm trusting you to see all of me—even the ugly bits—and still love me. I'm such a sorry, stupid fool that I didn't trust you before. I didn't like who I'd become in LA, but I like the guy who emerged after falling in love with you."

If Shaye's heart pounded any faster she'd go into cardiac arrest on one of New York's landmarks. He loved her? He wouldn't keep her at a distance anymore? "Are you serious?"

"As serious as Mrs. Taylor cutting the red ribbon across the community hall's doors for the first Due South senior's dinner." He touched the tip of his cold nose to hers. "As serious as the hot-meal delivery system we're starting in January. And as serious as I am about you coming home as Due South's head chef, since it's your dream."

"Get out!" she blurted.

"I mean it." He grinned down at her. "I love when you go into bossy-chef mode. I love you."

She could hardly breathe.

"I'm not sure if head chef is my dream now," she said. "Working beside you at Due South before Ethan came is the happiest I've ever been. That's my dream now, to work with you."

"I thought you hated working with me." He waggled his eyebrows.

"I let you think that, because it kept your ego in check."

"My ego is well and truly checked. You fucking cut me off at the knees when you left. I know I'll never be your Mr. Perfect, but give me a chance and every day I'll be the man who loves you more than anything."

"You're not the only one cut off at the knees. I've had a lot of time to think stuck in my tiny apartment." Shaye placed her hands over his, stroking the faint raised scars on his fingers. "The whole time I was waiting for perfection, I had real and amazing under my nose. I love you, Del, the real, one-hundred-percent authentic you—even the ugly bits. I don't care if you hate Pride and Prejudice. I don't care if you belch, and scratch, and you'll never remember birthdays unless I set a reminder on your phone. And even though some days I'll want to bury your body in an unmarked grave—even then, I'll never find another man more perfect for me than you are."

He bent and kissed her, a kiss that made her blood sizzle and rocked her world's axis.

"Remember the fight we had when I said the day I got on my knees to grovel for a woman's affection would be the day Dr. Joe could cart me away in a straitjacket?"

"Will we have more of those kinds of fights?" she said, sounding a little dreamy. She so remembered getting naked and messy with Del soon after.

"Probably lots." His voice was a low, sexy rumble. "And with that in mind..." Del dropped to one knee and fumbled in his coat pocket.

"Dammit! Where's it gone?"

Shaye quit breathing. *Holy-freaking-guacamole with a side order of cinnamon sticks!* Was he...?

Del whipped out his hand with a red-plated I♥NY souvenir ring clasped between his thumb and first finger. Her heart did a crazy-happy-boogie in her chest. He was. He totally was.

"Del, get up." She laughed as the first tiny flakes of snow landed on his hair. "You don't need to do this!"

"Yeah, I do." He remained on his knees. "Because I'll only do this once, and if we one day have kids, I don't want you telling them their old man didn't know how to do it right. See? Lights, camera, action." He gestured to the sparkling lights all around and a couple of tourists who had their phones aimed at them. "I love you, Shaye Harland, and I'll love you with everything I've got for the rest of our lives. I didn't stop at Tiffany's to buy you a proper ring because I wanted us to choose one together if you say yes. So say yes. Say you'll marry me."

"You know I'll drive you crazy, right?"

"I'm counting on it."

"And although we'd never go hungry, I don't do ironing, and I loathe cleaning the bathroom," she said.

"We'll wear wrinkled clothes, and I'm good being on permanent john duty. Small price to pay." More snowflakes spiraled down, giving Del's rumpled brown hair a salt-and-pepper frost.

"I'm stubborn and opinionated. I jump to conclusions, and I have dreamy misconceptions about love and marriage."

"We've already established neither of us are saints." Del shrugged and reached for her hand again. "And not all your dreamy ideas are misconceptions. We'll define how our love and marriage should be."

His eyes blazed, but she couldn't quite form her lips around a one syllable answer.

"There's too much of you taking up space in my heart already," she said. "I couldn't bear letting you go again..."

He brushed his lips across her knuckles. "Baby, you won't have to. Get used to having me under your feet, because I'll continue to fill up your big, loyal heart for the next fifty years, and you'll fill mine. Don't you think we're worth the risk?"

She'd never have the easy, stress-free love she once thought she wanted. They'd need to trim, mold, sometimes even carve into their lives to make their two halves fit. They'd disagree and butt heads, and each would have to shoulder the burden of loving the other through tough times and painful decisions.

But the payoff...

Oh, the payoff of loving this incredible man and being loved by him. Of working together, laughing together, being the one he'd whisper to last thing at night, the one she'd wake to in the morning.

Del snapped his fingers. "Uh. Earth to Shaye? Please say yes, and let me put this crappy ring on your finger before my knee freezes to the tiles."

A laugh hiccupped out of her, and she shoved her left hand under his nose. "Yes, Hollywood. Yes, I'll wear your crappy ring and love you for the rest of my life."

"Oh, thank Christ." He slipped it on her finger and bounced to his feet.

The gathered crowd cheered, and New York's lights dimmed to a flicker as he kissed her again under the falling snow. Shaye wrapped her arms around Del's neck, holding tightly to her Mr. Perfect-for-me.

Epilogue.

One week later...

Del stood on the Mollymawk's stern deck with his arms around Shaye as the rolling hills of Stewart Island grew closer. Her long, brown hair blew in his face, and even when strands of it caught in his mouth, he couldn't bear to pull away.

"If I tell you I'm sea-sick again, will you come with me into the cabin and make me feel better?" he asked.

Even after twenty-four hours of traveling, his fiancée still smelled like sunshine—still smelled like *his*. Call him a Neanderthal, but he wanted to throw her over his shoulder and drag her into a cave.

Or a cabin, since that was closer.

"If my brother and Kez catch us sneaking off, they'll make you swim the rest of the way to Oban. They have spies."

Three little faces peeped out the window behind them—Zoe, Jade, and their little dog, Sparky.

"Can we bribe them? Maybe with the cookies you promised to bake this afternoon?"

Shaye's pretty brow crinkled. "I don't remember promising to bake cookies."

"Macaroons, I believe you said. Or maybe some chocolate chip cookies."

A slow smile spread across her mouth, and out of sight of the girls, she shoved her hands into his jean pockets and squeezed his butt. "Huh. Thought you said you didn't have a sweet tooth?"

"*I lied.* I'm completely addicted to your sweet face, your sweet smile..." He paused to nudge her stomach with his hip, cupping her sexy, no-ugly-panties-in-sight bottom. "Your sweet—"

Lips pressed against his mouth, muffling his last word. A short, lush kiss that warmed him from the inside out. Being so damn happy from just a kiss would take some getting used to. But now he had lots of time to get used to it—even if they had work tomorrow since Vince, Robbie, and her pal, Des, who'd come over temporarily from the mainland, were already bitching about the pre-Christmas rush.

Inside, Sparky yapped enthusiastically, egged on by peals of laughter.

"Don't underestimate the little spies," she said. "I'm pretty sure at least one of them can lip-read."

"Damn."

"I'll make it up to you tonight when we try out your new queen-sized bed."

"Assuming Ford and my brother have disassembled the old bunks and installed it."

"Oh, my mum organized a working bee once Wally agreed to rent you the place long term." She squeezed his ass again. "The bunks are gone, and my boxes are all stacked in the living room as you insisted. As soon as we unpack, we'll have a love-nest fit for two, baby."

"*We*? You mean I have to help unpack your twenty boxes of books, and make-up, and girly clothes?" he teased.

She stiffened in his arms, and he laughed, but this time instead of squeezing, she smacked his ass—hard.

"Ow—hey! You wanna deal with bruised goods later?"

"Just for that," she informed him, lips against the notch of his throat, "you don't get to unpack the bag I bought from Victoria's Secret on 5th Avenue."

Sunbeams sparkled on the waves, and the brine-filled breeze ruffled their hair. The Mollymawk chugged into the calmer waters of Halfmoon Bay Harbor, heading for the wharf and blasting the horn as they drew nearer. Sea birds whirled in the air currents high above the hills, some drifting down to rest on Due South's roof.

His brother stood at the wharf's end, his arm wrapped around Piper's waist. Next to them in a deck chair sat Bill, with Del's mom fussing on one side, and his future mother-in-law beaming on the other. Ford, Carly, Mrs. Taylor, Holly and Mr. Nolan—or Wally, as he'd ordered Del to call him now, encircled his dad's chair. In fact, it appeared as if half of Oban's locals waited on the wharf.

Del turned Shaye toward the crowd, who were waving like mad. Their families, their friends, their place, their future with people who'd walk beside them on this crazy, wonderful journey.

"Look, cupcake," he whispered in her ear. "We're home."

ABOUT THE AUTHOR

Tracey Alvarez lives in the Coolest Little Capital in the World (a.k.a Wellington, New Zealand). Married to a wonderfully supportive IT guy, she has two teens who would love to be surgically linked to their electronic devices.

Fuelled by copious amounts of coffee, she's the author of contemporary romantic fiction set predominantly in New Zealand. Small-towns, close communities, and families are a big part of the heart-warming stories she writes. Oh, and hot, down-to-earth heroes--Kiwi men, in other words.

When she's not writing, thinking about writing, or procrastinating about writing, Tracey can be found with her nose in her e-reader, nibbling on smuggled chocolate bars, or bribing her kids to take over the housework.

Follow Tracey on Twitter as @TraceyAlvrezNZ or Facebook as http://www.facebook.com/TraceyAlvarezAuthor
Her website is http://www.traceyalvarez.com and don't forget to sign up to her newsletter here: http://bit.ly/JR3Asu

What Readers & Reviewers are saying about Tracey's books:

"Out of the gate with her début at full throttle, Ms. Alvarez receives a blue ribbon!" ~InD'Tale Magazine.

"In Too Deep (Due South #1) is thrilling, raw and gritty giving the reader a real treat!" ~Amazon review.

"Tracey Alvarez has written an incredible story filled with amazing characters, strong conflict, interesting themes, and an amazing small coastal town setting." ~Amazon review.

"5 stars. Ms. Alvarez has done it again, with incredible, if not one-of-a-kind storytelling!" ~ InD'tale Magazine.

"The story was engaging, funny, heart-warming, sensual, passionate, and brought me back to people and a place I'm growing to love." ~Swept Away By Romance

"Their story is beautifully written, contains sexy and steamy scenes that heat up the bedroom...and the kitchen, and has moments that will break your heart and some that will make you laugh out loud. All this guarantees for an entertaining romance read." ~Amazon review.

OTHER BOOKS IN THE DUE SOUTH SERIES:

The Due South series focuses on family, community, and of course, each book contains a scorching hot romance.

In Too Deep (Book #1) Piper & West
Melting Into You (Book #2) Kezia & Ben
Ready To Burn (Book #3) Shaye & Del
Christmas With You (Book #4) Carly & Kip

Far North Series

Imagine an endless stretch of azure blue water and clean, unspoiled beaches.

Imagine a small town surrounded by ancient native forest.

Imagine neighbors who look after their own, who consider them *whānau* - family.

Imagine the secret lives, the hidden passions simmering under New Zealand's sultry, subtropical Far North.

Welcome to Bounty Bay, where the reward of true love is a price only some are willing to pay.

Book #1 *Hide Your Heart*
Book #2 *Know Your Heart*

Made in the USA
Coppell, TX
02 January 2020

14016399R00187